I0729544

THE
FIX
UP

BOOKS BY SHARON M. PETERSON

The Do-Over

The Fake Out

The Fast Lane

SHARON M. PETERSON

THE FIX UP

bookouture

Published by Bookouture in 2025

An imprint of Storyfire Ltd.
Carmelite House
50 Victoria Embankment
London EC4Y 0DZ

www.bookouture.com

The authorised representative in the EEA is Hachette Ireland
8 Castlecourt Centre
Dublin 15 D15 XTP3
Ireland
(email: info@hbgi.ie)

Copyright © Sharon M. Peterson, 2025

Sharon M. Peterson has asserted her right to be identified as the author of this work.

All rights reserved. No part of this publication may be reproduced, stored in any retrieval system, or transmitted, in any form or by any means, electronic, mechanical, photocopying, recording or otherwise, without the prior written permission of the publishers.

ISBN: 978-1-83525-016-7
eBook ISBN: 978-1-83525-015-0

This book is a work of fiction. Names, characters, businesses, organizations, places and events other than those clearly in the public domain, are either the product of the author's imagination or are used fictitiously. Any resemblance to actual persons, living or dead, events or locales is entirely coincidental.

To Gideon,
You are "fearfully and wonderfully made"
and I hope you know that.
Thank you for your giggles,
your squeezes, and whispered I-love-yous.
I love you even if your secret power
is pretending to not pay attention while
waiting for everyone else
to not pay attention so you can
get what you want.
For you, I'm gonna figure out a way to live forever.

ONE

Love is snuggling with my one-eyed rescue dog.

—AVIV K., AGE 16

My man picker was broken.

A truer truth had never been spoken. Everyone—my mom, my sisters, my brother, my six-year-old son, Oliver, the guy who worked the meat counter at the grocery store—knew it. It was an objective truth. The sky was blue, cheese made everything better, and my man picker was broken. At twenty-eight, I had receipts to prove it. My receipts had receipts at this point.

Receipt #1:

My first love ran away with me to Los Angeles the day after high school graduation. Three months later, he ran away again with our next-door neighbor—the model—and every cent we had, forcing me to move into a two-bedroom apartment with six other hopeful actors. I was the lucky one—I got a whole closet to myself.

Receipt #2:

My relationship with Oliver's father began after one date. He was a drummer (ugh, I know) in a struggling band, who was covered in tattoos including one on his face (yeah, yeah, *I know*). After taking me on a picnic in a park (in which I provided the food, the transportation, and the idea), he asked if he could sleep over. Because he was so tired from his gig the night before, you see. Oh, he slept over and never left. He also never got an actual job. Though it turns out, when I found out I was pregnant with Oliver, he suddenly found other faraway couches to sleep on.

Receipt #3:

I have been on thirty-two first dates, nine second dates, three third dates, and one fourth date over the last three years. Which also included:

Not one but two occasions on which my date brought his mother

That one guy who wondered aloud over hamburgers what human flesh might taste like

The seemingly sweet high school teacher who was excited to show me his collection of stuffed animals. An entire room dedicated to all manner of plushies—hundreds and hundreds of them. Big, small, oddly shaped, beady-eyed—which he'd named and slept with on rotation, so no one got jealous. I know, he showed me the sleeping schedule

The man who argued with the manager of the restaurant —to be fair, his steak was well-done when he asked for medium-rare and that was basically a capital offense in Texas —so loudly, he was escorted out of the place in handcuffs, and...

This guy.

Curtis Norfolk, aged thirty-five, an engineer from Nebraska who now resided in Houston. Never married. No kids. Nice smile. Maybe used a bit too much hair product but I could work with that. Owned his condo and liked to travel. Dog owner.

Oliver would love a dog.

The dating site I used had paired us because of our similar life goals: marriage, family, stability, fully funded IRAs.

I was on a mission to find a mate who was nothing like the other guys I'd dated. No drummers (or guitar players or lead singers, for that matter). In fact, no musicians. Or actors. Or anyone acting-adjacent. No jobless losers or professional couch surfers. No face tattoos. No motorcycle enthusiasts. No mooches or dudes with strange addictions.

I wanted normal. Maybe that sounded a little boring, but I'd already been through enough chaos. I *longed* for boring. I wanted an engineer who filed his taxes every year. I wanted Oliver to grow up in a good home where he felt safe and loved.

I wanted Curtis.

Probably.

If this idea of mine made my insides feel a little itchy, so be it. Sunny, my therapist, said that was because I needed to get used to the idea; the itchiness would pass.

I tried to give my all to each of these first dates. It had not been easy today, either. Since the appointment I'd had with the attorney mid-morning, my brain and emotions had been working double-time. But that's what happened when a person received life-altering news.

This morning, I woke up with not a whole lot to my name, besides my son, of course. Now, I was a proud house and business owner. Ollie had left me his house, the land it sat on, and the café. Ollie Holder, the grumpy old man who, three years ago, had given a job at the Sit-n-Eat Café to a tired single mom who was new in town. The same man who rented out rooms in his house for Oliver and me to have a place to live.

Ollie, who had treated me like the granddaughter he never had.

I could hardly catch my breath when I heard the news. A strange buzzing in my ears made it hard to hear anything else the lawyer said. Afterward, I'd sat in the car for forty-five minutes trying to process it all. The tears fell unchecked as memories of Ollie's perpetually grumpy exterior and the kind soul it hid circled in my head. His death had left a big hole in my heart. In Oliver's, too.

But I'd gone back to work until we closed at two and Oliver got home from school, and I had to feed him, then cry in the bathroom for fifteen minutes thinking of Ollie's last gift to us (but quietly because I didn't want to worry Oliver), then get ready for this date, and then finally hustle Oliver off to my brother's house for the evening.

Single mom life, amirite?

Frankly, I was exhausted and if I could have gotten out of this date, I would have. But I was committed to this whole idea of finding a nice guy and settling down, even if romantic luck was not on my side (like I said, broken man picker). I was so done with the guys in the shallow end I always seemed to attract. Like the guy I'd dated when Oliver was about a year and a half old. That ended after he'd gotten arrested for smuggling exotic animals. Sadly, he was not my first boyfriend with an arrest record.

So, I'd put on actual makeup, shaved my legs, tamed my long blonde hair into loose curls, plucked that one stubborn chin hair, and put on a pale-pink dress with fluttery cap sleeves and strappy sandals. It was a far cry from the jeans, t-shirts, and tennis shoes I wore six days a week at the café. I was kind of feeling myself.

I worked hard to feel good about my body these days. I came from a family of Amazons—big, strong, strapping Amazons. Amazons who were part milkmaids or Vikings or something.

My brother was six five, one of my sisters was pushing six feet. I was but five nine. But I used to be a willowy, waif-like five nine. The kind that could fit in sample sizes and ordered side salads at restaurants as a meal.

Then I'd gotten pregnant at twenty-one and I didn't quite lose all the weight. I started eating real food, and yes, even dessert. I was more a size twelve or fourteen these days than a size two. I was so much happier, even if it had taken me a while to get used to this new me. I appreciated it now. This body had grown a whole human child, and it could make the best muffins on this *and that* side of the Mississippi.

I strolled into my favorite restaurant, the Texican, only five minutes late. For me, that was practically early. Being on time had never been one of my strong points.

Unfortunately, I knew the second I saw Liliana's face the primping was all for nothing. Liliana and her husband owned and operated the Texican, a perfect blend of Mexico and Texas on a plate. Seeing as how it was halfway between Houston and Two Harts, the small town I lived in, it was where I tried to hold all my first dates. I'd probably paid for most of the mortgage on this place at this point.

Liliana eyed me over the top of her reading glasses. A picture might be worth a thousand words, but that look was easily in the seven figures.

"Is he here?" I asked.

"Yes, he is." Her voice practically dripped with displeasure. She was tiny, the top of her head barely hitting my shoulder, but she had a backbone made of steel and reinforced by hard work. Everyone knew Liliana was not one to mess with. Me included. "Ellie, *mija*, your man picker is broken."

"But he's an engineer," I whined, slumping against the counter, careful not to upset the bowl of complimentary *buñuelos*—fried pieces of tortilla covered in cinnamon and sugar and scarily addictive. I picked one up and took a bite.

Liliana harrumphed.

"He's a homeowner." I stuffed the rest of the *buñuelo* in my mouth and tried to keep the desperation from my voice. "He's never been married. He's a dog person."

She shook her head. "He is not the one."

"But—"

"No, not him." She patted me on the cheek. "I had to put him at the table by the bathrooms."

"The bathroom table? He's that bad?"

She leaned in and lowered her voice. "He is crying."

"He's what?" Maybe he was in touch with his feelings? Please be that. Please be th—

"He's crying and staring at photos of a woman on his phone."

So not that.

Curtis wasn't hard to find. I just followed the sniffling. Nor was it a challenge to get the story out of him. The woman on his phone? His ex-girlfriend. The crying? She'd texted him a picture of... her cat.

"That's Sugar-Bear." He pointed at a photo of an orange tabby with a supremely bored expression on its whiskered face.

"How long were you together?" I asked, determined to give this date the old college try.

"Three beautiful months." He sniffled again and glanced forlornly at the cloth napkin he'd already repurposed as a tissue.

Three months? I'd had rashes that lasted longer than three months. "How long ago did you break up?"

He swung his red-rimmed eyes in my direction. "Nine months ago."

A whole human person could be conceived, grown, and hatched in less time than he was taking to get over this woman. The saddest part? I was a little jealous. I doubted I'd been the cause of such heartbreak in a man.

"We were so happy." He held his phone out, pointing at a

new photo. "This is us in Galveston. We had such a good time. We went to the aquarium, and you would not believe what we saw."

He told me in minute detail what they'd seen while he flicked through photos on his phone, occasionally stopping to sob softly into his hand. I thought engineers were supposed to be stoic and unemotional.

I tried to get my brain to stay focused. Be in the present, my therapist Sunny liked to remind me. Bet Sunny had never been on a date with Curtis.

My eyes wandered to the wall mural of a mariachi band. Across the room, several sombreros in varying sizes hung from the wall. That warm terra-cotta color on the walls might be nice in the bathroom at home. We needed to get rid of the pink—

My phone vibrated, interrupting my thoughts. Curt kept on talking and sobbing as though he hadn't noticed. As discreetly as I could, I glanced at the screen to see it was the attorney I'd met with this morning. Maybe he'd forgotten to tell me something? I'd deal with it later. With a shrug, I sent the call to voicemail and flipped it over so I couldn't see the screen.

Pasting on what I hoped was a sympathetic expression, I took a sip of water, nodded, made encouraging noises, and tried very hard to focus on Curtis, but my mind kept replaying the moment the attorney had said, "It's all yours."

I hadn't expected it. It had been six months since Ollie's passing. With the attorney working out everything on the legal side, I'd been allowed to stay in the house and keep the café going. So, I had, the whole time wondering and worrying where Oliver and I would be in a few months' time.

Resisting the urge to fidget in my seat, I studied the room. Since I was an early riser (hello, 4 a.m.) and had a six-year-old to get into bed at a decent hour, I always asked to meet up at the very sexy and date-like hour of 5 p.m. On a Friday, this always made for an interesting mix of people out for dinner.

Four tables over, a man wrangled three kids into their seats. One of the kids, maybe two years old, was standing on his chair and waving a butter knife around like a sword. Divorced dad weekend, I'd bet.

At one of the booths, an older couple chatted quietly. They'd looked as though they'd been together so long, they were starting to resemble each other. Behind them sat a man and woman who looked barely legal making mooneyes over a plate of fajitas. He had that slightly dirty, messy-haired, tattooed look going on, a look that would have had me salivating ten years ago.

But it was the man sitting at the table closest to us I wondered about the most. He was alone, half of a burrito on a plate he'd pushed aside. Although he was facing me, his head of dark hair was bowed as he typed something on his phone. With his blue button-down and red tie, he looked like he'd just gotten off work. Maybe he was meeting someone. A girlfriend. A wife. An old college roommate. A mafia boss. The possibilities were endless.

Frowning, he leaned back and slid the phone across the table. I caught a glimpse of dark-rimmed glasses as he tilted his face up to the ceiling in an *Any time now, God* sort of way. A zing of awareness, a recognition of a kindred spirit traveled down my spine. I understood that feeling. A kind of hopelessness that settles in your bones when you aren't sure what to do next. I'd been there before.

I wondered what color his eyes were. Look over here. Pretty please.

And suddenly, he did. Our gazes caught and both of us froze for a beat, then two. He didn't smile or soften his face, but he tipped his head in acknowledgement. Maybe he could feel it too.

"...and then she said she was taking that job in Colorado and..." Curtis's sob brought me back to reality. A reality I would rather not have, if I was being honest.

I had no idea what he was going on about now. Something about the ex and a job in Colorado and how his world had ended. Maybe I should have cancelled. My heart wasn't in it and my brain was making plans and sticky notes at Ollie's house —er, *my house*—right now. Focus, Ellie.

I made an encouraging sound at the back of my throat and patted Curtis's arm.

Liliana came toward our table, probably to take our order. I met her eyes and shook my head. There was no way I was going to make it through an appetizer, let alone a whole meal, with this man. She nodded in such a way that communicated *I told you so* without saying a word. I hoped talent like that came with age.

With a wave of her fingers, she turned and headed to the table with the dad and kids. He'd managed to get two kids in their seat, but the "sword wielder" was now under the table eating a tortilla chip he'd found on the floor.

"Then she waved goodbye, and I watched her drive away." Curtis paused and wiped his nose on the sleeve of his shirt like a six-year-old.

Actually no. That was disrespectful to six-year-olds everywhere. Oliver was six. He would *never*... Although Oliver was really a forty-six-year-old accountant on the inside. There were a lot of things he wouldn't do that other kids his age would. I loved that kid and his ability to use a tissue. Loved that so much for both of us.

"Here." A handful of tissues was waved in Curt's general direction.

"Thank you." Curtis took the tissues without looking up and blew his nose. Loudly.

"Yes, thank you," I said. "That was so kind of you..."

But my voice trailed off when I looked up at the bearer of such good and practical gifts. It was him. The man from the next table. He met my eyes steadily. He had a serious sort of face, like it wasn't quite used to smiling. But it was a nice face, an interesting face. A strong jawline with the faintest dusting of dark hair, a dimple in his chin which seemed almost fanciful, the smallest touch of gray at his temples even though he didn't look much older than me.

And his eyes behind those glasses? They were dark and intense and yet, there was a kindness there.

I smiled slowly; he nodded once in acknowledgement. "No problem."

When he walked away, a wave of sadness hit me. I wanted to know his name and now I never would.

"Do you think that's a good plan?" My attention jerked back to Curtis. His eyes were still glassy with tears but there was excitement in his voice.

"Plan?"

"Yes. Do you think it's a good idea?"

I had no clue what he was talking about, but he was looking at me with such big puppy dog eyes full of expectation and hope. "Um... sure?"

"It is, isn't it? I'm going to do it." Curtis stood, mindless of the balled-up tissues that cascaded to the ground. He whipped out his wallet and threw a few bills on the table. "Dinner is still on me but if I leave now, I can catch the next flight to Denver."

"Denver?"

He grabbed my hand and shook it. "I'm going to go tell Shelly how I feel about her."

"Who's Shelly?"

"My ex. The love of my life." He leaned down and placed a loud, smacking kiss on my cheek. "It was nice to meet you. Thank you for being so understanding." That last part he said over his shoulder as he broke into a run toward the exit.

Several pairs of eyes swung my way. Even the dad who was now also under the table and trying with increasing desperation to get his kid to listen. I smiled weakly and waved. "He had an emergency."

Yeah. No one believed that.

Three minutes later, Liliana swept in and placed a heaping plate of *enchiladas verdes* in front of me. "I told you, *mija*, he was no good. *Un tonto.* A fool."

"You think?" My stomach rumbled. The real reason I liked my first dates to be at the Texican? When that date inevitably crashed and burned in spectacular fashion, at least I knew I'd get a good meal out of it.

Liliana dipped closer and lowered her voice. "The right man will be one who sees your value, who knows you are precious. He will see every part of you and love each part, even the things he doesn't like." She patted my shoulder. "This is a smart man."

My chest tightened. "Yeah, maybe."

And the thing was... I wanted that. I wanted a man who loved me for me. Someone unlike the guys I'd been with in the past. Oh, I'd loved them or thought I did, but they hadn't loved me. I'd made it all too easy for them. Falling hard and fast; the endings had been just as hard and fast.

We all wanted to believe there was someone out there for each of us, a lid for every pot and all that. But sometimes I couldn't shake the feeling that I was the odd one out. Three years of loneliness could do that to a woman.

But maybe that's just how it was meant to be.

TWO

I made it home by 6:30 p.m. with a full belly and mostly over my first date blues. Like with most things in life, I took the punch and kept moving. Otherwise, I'd be curled up in the fetal position somewhere. I'd just settled down on the couch with a fuzzy blanket, three scoops of chocolate peanut butter swirl, and the latest episode of one of those awful housewife reality shows I loved when I heard the crunch of tires.

As the only house down a long, winding driveway, it was unlikely to be a passing vehicle. Maybe my brother, Chris, had decided to bring Oliver home early. I set my ice cream down—it would probably be soup before I got to enjoy it now—and headed back to the kitchen to meet them at the side door.

But... nothing happened.

I waited a few beats before I pulled the door open and peered out. But Chris's monster-sized truck wasn't there.

"Weird." As I was stepping back into the kitchen, the doorbell warbled its way through the house. "Even weirder."

I didn't know we had a doorbell.

Besides that, *no one* used our front door. The mailwoman, the guy from UPS, the one dude who sold steak out of the trunk of his car—everyone used the side door. Until three years ago, the front door had been buried behind two bookcases full of gardening books. Which was ironic since Ollie hadn't seemed all that interested in lawncare. Although the bookcases had since been moved to the wall behind the door, I wasn't even sure the front door *opened*.

I hesitated. The doorbell sounded again. Maybe Chris and Oliver were playing a joke on me? I crept into the front "sitting room" and inched my way to the window by the door. Whoever it was had given up on the doorbell and was now knocking. Very slowly, I peeled back a tiny edge of the curtain and peeked outside.

But it wasn't the towering frame of my brother or Oliver's little face that I saw. What I saw was the shadowy figure of a man. Tall, lean, wide shoulders. I couldn't make any of his features out, but I didn't know any man who would just show up unannounced. Especially at night.

My heart climbed into my throat. THERE WAS A STRANGE MAN AT MY FRONT DOOR.

"Stay calm," I whispered.

The doorknob jiggled. A voice called out, "Hello? Is anyone here?"

My heartrate shifted into overdrive. As quietly as possible, I pulled out my phone from my pocket and dialed nine-one-one.

"What's your emergency?" a voice I recognized said.

"Cammie," I whispered. "It's Ellie Sterns. There's a strange man at my door."

"Do you recognize him?"

"Didn't you hear me? I said it was a strange man."

"Well, stranger and strange man are two different things," Cammie said. I swore I could hear her smacking her gum.

"I'm serious. There's a man on my front porch..." And then the unmistakable sound of a key sliding into a lock. "I think he has a key. How does he have a key?" The lock snicked open. "H-he unlocked it."

"Okay, okay, don't panic. I have someone on their way right now," she said, sounding much more serious. "Can you hide?"

I watched in horror as the doorknob turned.

"He's opening the door." I clicked over to speaker and set the phone on the edge of one of the bookcases. Frantically, I glanced around for something, anything, I could use as a weapon. My choices were limited so I grabbed the first heavy thing I could find—a gardening book titled *Say Aloe to My Little Friends*—and clutched it with both hands.

The door opened in slow motion; my whole body tensed.

"Ellie? Ellie, are you okay?" Cammie asked.

But there wasn't time to answer her. Instead, I screamed and swung that book with all my might.

The stranger yelped. "Oophf. What the hel— Ouch!"

I swung again and had a momentary flashback to playing softball as a kid. I'd never been any good—wildly swinging the bat had been my typical strategy—and I wasn't good now, but just like back then, I made up for it with enthusiasm.

With a grunt, he threw his hands over his head to protect it.

"I want you to know I've already called the police and... and... I have two, no, three, no, six rottweilers in the back-yard," I yelled. "They'll be in here any minute and see there's a stranger in this house and then when they attack, they're trained to go for where it counts. You..." *Swing.* "...get..." *Slam.* "...me..." *Smack.* "...mister!"

"Stop!" He ducked, covering his head with his arms.

"Plus, I'm a witch." *Swing. Miss.* Damn it. "Not the nice kind." *Swing. Hit.* "I'm cursing you in my head right this second." *Swing. Boom. Success.* "After this day, you'll have constant ringing in your ears except it won't be ringing, it will be that song 'Never Gonna Give You Up' playing forever and ever until you die."

"I'm not trying to—"

"The last guy I did that to ended up in a straitjacket. You're gonna wish you'd met the dogs instead." I stopped and heaved a breath. Turns out attacking an intruder with a book was kind of exhausting.

In the slight pause, he whipped around and yanked the book out of my hands.

I squeaked. "Give that back."

He tossed it on the floor. "No."

I held my hands out. "I wasn't kidding about the dogs."

"There aren't any dogs. Not a single bark." He rubbed his shoulder. Dark eyes glared at me from behind his glasses, hair disheveled, face red. He looked disgruntled, disbelieving, even offended. Like *he* had the right to be offended. "I am offended."

See? I stuck my hands on my hips. "You're offended? You broke into my house!"

Wait. He'd just broken into my house. Why? I took two small steps backwards until my back pressed against a bookshelf. "Is this... a home invasion?"

"Ellie?" Cammie's voice called from the phone. "Are you okay?"

"He's in the house," I said, a frantic edge to my voice. "I hope you're recording this for the very special episode of *Dateline* about my murder. Make sure to tell the producers how I lit up a room."

The man scowled. "I'm not here to murder you."

"That's exactly what a murderer would say," Cammie said.

"Where is that voice coming from?" the man asked in confusion.

I straightened. "I have emergency services on the phone. They can hear everything. The police are on their way."

He took a step back. "I'm not here to cause any trouble." He opened one of his hands and keys dangled from a finger. "I have a right to be here."

I stared at the keys. "How did you get those?"

"This is my house," he said slowly.

"No, it is not. This is *my* house." I grabbed another book from the bookshelf and waved it wildly. "Out. Get out."

"This is getting interesting," Cammie said. It almost sounded like she was eating popcorn.

"Alright. Alright. I'll go outside." With a hand held up, either to protect himself or ward me off, he shuffled backwards. "But this house is mine, or at least half of it is."

What? He was crazy. "Stop saying that. This is my house." I grabbed the door and started to close it.

"Wait. Listen." He paused, his face so serious it made me hesitate. In what felt like slow motion, his mouth opened. A tightness spread across my chest. Some part of me knew whatever he was about to say was important. It was the feeling I'd had just before I saw a positive on that pregnancy test I took seven years ago. Epically important. Life-changing.

"My name is Gilbert Dalton. Ollie Holder was my grandfather."

Cammie gasped. "Holy sh—"

The sound the door made when I slammed it shut was loud enough to drown out the rest of her sentence.

THREE

Deputy Frankie Ramos knocked on my door ten minutes later.

"Ellie, open up."

"Did you arrest him yet?" I asked even though I knew he hadn't. I'd been watching the whole scene from the window. Frankie had arrived and proceeded to hold an animated conversation with the stranger, which ended up in said stranger retrieving a file folder from his car, digging through it and presenting Frankie with paperwork which then ended in Frankie laughing and giving him a friendly slap on the back.

Like they were besties.

"Just open the door, Ellie," Cammie said from my bookshelf. "Do you really think Ollie has a grandson?"

I snatched up my phone. "I thought you were supposed to hang up when the police arrived."

"Eh. It's been a slow night, and I'm invested now."

Frankie knocked on the door again. "Ellie, open the door. We need to talk. There's been a... misunderstanding." He cleared his throat. "It appears he does own the house."

I ripped the door open and glared at Frankie. "He does not."

"Well, he has some paperwork here from a lawyer that says he does. Says he's Ollie's grandson." He held up a stack of papers. I glanced between it and the stranger, Ollie's so-called grandson, who stood a few feet away, looking much too smug.

"Ollie didn't have any children," I said. Everyone knew that. Nothing happened, or didn't happen, in this town without it being broadcast in every group text, phone tree, and most prayer chains. "So a grandson would be impossible."

There. Logic. Take that, Mr. Smug Smugface.

"Ollie did have a child. My mother," he said and somehow, impervious to all laws of nature, he looked even smugger.

Frankie took a step between us and directed his next comment to Gilbert Dalton. "Now, to be fair, no one knew Ollie had any family left. After his mother died, and that was when I was a kid, he was the last Holder in Two Harts."

"Thank you." Crossing my arms, I gave a curt nod. "So that's settled. Make him leave now."

"Except"—Frankie rubbed the back of his neck, looking slightly uncomfortable—"this paperwork here says otherwise."

"It's impossible. Ollie can't just have a whole grandson no one knew about." I snatched the papers out of Frankie's hand and glanced at the pile. I blinked at the words right there on the top page identifying this... this man as Ollie's grandson. "But how did this happen?"

"I really don't have the time to give you a lesson on the birds and the bees," Gilbert Dalton said.

I glared at him, wishing I had the power to slice and dice him with my gaze. Unaware of my violent thoughts, he snapped the ends of his sleeves straight. Adjusted his tie. Shoved his fingers through his hair. Dark hair with the smallest touch of gray. Glasses, too, and... Something in the back of my head niggled as I stared at him. Some weird sense that I knew him.

Narrowing my eyes, I pushed the paperwork into Frankie's chest and stomped over to him, stopping within a couple of feet. It only took a second for it to click. "It's you."

"Who?"

"No. I mean, you're... you!"

"Yes, I'm me," he said and if a voice could sound like an eye roll looked, it was his at that moment. "And you are you. I'm glad we have that covered."

"But you're *here*."

One dark eyebrow raised. "Right again. Is there another adult here we could talk to? Maybe a mature child? We seem to be having trouble."

I huffed in frustration. "I mean, we met... or kind of met... at the restaurant earlier tonight." A new realization dawned on me, and I turned to Frankie. "He's stalking me."

"Lady, what are you talking about?" The guy rubbed his forehead with the tips of his fingers as though a headache was coming on. It was a gesture I'd seen from my father a million times growing up. "I'm not stalking you."

To be honest, I was a little annoyed he didn't recognize me. I mean, I'd noticed *him*. Then again, I guess maybe the squirrel slippers and sweats were throwing him off.

"Earlier at the Texican, you were there, and I was there with a date, and you brought him tissues because he was..."

Recognition swept across his face. "You were with the crier."

"His name is Curtis," I said.

"Curtis the crier." He smirked. "Makes sense."

"Aw, another dud, El?" Cammie said from the phone I still had clutched in my hand. "Your man picker is definitely broken."

I ignored her. "At least he didn't follow me home and break into my house."

He frowned. "He called you."

"Who?"

"The attorney, Doug Carmichael."

"He did not call..." But then I remembered getting that call at the restaurant. There had been a voicemail but who checked voicemails anymore? "How do you know that?"

"Because I was standing in front of him when he did it. I talked to him later and he said he left you messages." With a curse, he put his hands on the top of his head and began to pace. Three steps, turn, three steps, turn. Repeat. "He gave me a copy of the key. He said it wouldn't be a problem if I showed up, that you'd get the voicemail, and it would be fine." He muttered more to himself than to me.

"Who said what?"

He pointed a finger at me. "You are definitely a problem."

"I'm a problem? I was minding my own business. I wasn't bothering anyone. You"—I poked him in the chest—"burst in my house and became the problem."

"I rang the doorbell. I knocked. I called out. No one answered."

"I am definitely here."

"I needed to get back home to Austin. It's a long drive. Like I said, I rang the doorbell, I knocked." He paused in front of me. "No one answered."

"Okay, now." Frankie appeared at our side. "I think we need to take a deep breath."

"He came into my house uninvited. He could be a serial killer. Even now, he might be working on his recipe for pickled people feet or something. He could be figuring out the proper way to cut me up and—"

"I am not going to eat your feet," he said. "I'm more of a rib guy anyway."

"Hilarious," I said.

"He really is Ollie's grandson, isn't he?" Cammie said from the phone, sounding incredulous. "Is he single? Is he hot? He sounds hot."

"Seriously?" I glared at the phone. "Why are you still on the line?"

"I don't know. You haven't hung up yet. I thought you wanted me here," Cammie said.

"Well, I'm hanging up now."

"Fine. But maybe take a photo of him and text it to me." She hung up before I could reply.

Gilbert Dalton held his hands out like he was trying to calm me and maybe himself at the same time. "Look, I didn't mean to scare you. I did ring the doorbell and knock. I thought it would be okay to come in. I just wanted to see the inside. In hindsight, that might not have been my smartest idea."

"I could have been naked," I blurted.

Silence. Then, "I said I was sorry. The lawyer called you. He contacted me later to say he'd called you two times and left messages. Said you weren't great at returning calls right away, but you always got his messages. Check your voicemail. Please."

"I'm not doing any such thing." But it's exactly what I did. Because the lawyer wasn't exactly wrong; I wasn't great at remembering to call people back. I pulled up my voicemail, stabbing at the phone with more force than necessary. There were actually three voicemails from the attorney. I played the last one I'd received today at fifteen minutes after five o'clock.

"Hello, Ms. Sterns, this is Doug Carmichael, Ollie Holder's estate attorney. I've been trying to reach you. Didn't really want to do this over a voicemail, but... Mr. Holder's grandson, Gilbert Dalton, appeared today right after you left. I'd been trying to reach him for months, but he never responded so I assumed he wasn't interested. But, well, he is. You'll remember we talked briefly about him also being named an heir and..."

The message kept going but I was no longer listening. I dropped my arm, the phone dangling in my hand, the tinny sound of Doug Carmichael's voice still ringing out. Vaguely, I remember hearing something about the attorney trying to contact a possible relative, but he hadn't seemed all that concerned, so I hadn't been either. And to be totally honest, I'd barely heard anything after the first bit of news he'd given me.

All I could do now was stare at the man in front of me. He looked nothing like Ollie. For instance, he was a good eight inches taller with all that thick dark hair and distinctly non-caterpillar-like eyebrows over dark-blue eyes. I took in the square jaw, the five o'clock shadow, the sharp cheekbones.

Except... the pinched, mulish set of his mouth sparked recognition. There, that expression. *That* was Ollie.

My heart pounded. I wiped a sweaty palm on my pajama pants and shivered, even though it wasn't at all chilly. When I spoke, my voice was more of a croak. "You're Ollie's grandson."

"Now she's getting it." He crossed his arms. "I'm not here to cause trouble, but it was a three-hour drive to get to the attorney's office in Houston and I figured since I was only forty-five minutes away from Two Harts, I should stop by. From what the attorney explained, we have some decisions to make."

My stomach clenched. "What decisions? We are not making any decisions. We will talk to the attorney and straighten this out. That's what we're going to do." I channeled my inner beauty queen. Shoulders back, head high, I marched back to the front door. Once there, I twisted around. "You can leave now."

"Excuse me?" He stomped toward me. Frankie flanked his side, having to practically skip to keep up with Gilbert's long strides.

"You're not coming in my house."

"My house."

"I think it technically belongs to both of you," Frankie said.

We both ignored him.

"Have you lived here for the last three years? Was it you who pulled up the pink carpet from the bathroom floor? Did you spend hours of your life painting or convincing Ollie that getting Wi-Fi wasn't going to mess with his brain waves or that having a copy of every single electric bill since nineteen sixty-nine wasn't really necessary?" I leaned toward him, my voice rising with each word. "This isn't just my house; it's my home."

He glared; his jaw ticked. The heated silence between us was one tiny spark away from a full-on inferno. "Fine. I'll leave."

"Fine."

"Good."

"Great."

"But Monday, we talk to the lawyer."

I stuck my hands on my hips. "Sure."

"Then you won't be able to stop me from coming in."

"We'll see about that," I said.

"We sure will."

I couldn't help but notice it sounded more like a threat than a promise.

FOUR

[Love is]... I don't know how to explain that, so I won't.

—ALESSIO G., AGE 6

From the group text of the Stern Sisters:

AGGIE: *Paging Eleanor Anne Sterns. How'd the date go?*

MILLIE: *The engineer, right? Sounds boring.*

AGGIE: *It's always the quiet ones, Mills.*

BETSY: *I had a date, too.*

AGGIE: *And?*

BETSY: *He had red hair.*

AGGIE: *???*

BETSY: *It made him look... squirrelly.*

MILLIE: *Flying or ground?*

AGGIE: *What?*

MILLIE: *Flying squirrel or ground squirrel?*

AGGIE: *How are you related to me?*

BETSY: *He had beady eyes too.*

AGGIE: *So, you're just judging them on appearance now? That's so...*

BETSY: *Unevolved? Yes, ma'am. Call me a cavewoman. He also told me he wasn't feeling it between us about ten minutes into the date. At least he paid for my dinner before he left.*

MILLIE: *Aw, Bets, I'm so sorry. I hope he chokes on a nut.*

BETSY: *Thank you for your loyalty.*

AGGIE: *Ellie! How'd it go?*

BETSY: *Maybe not answering is a good sign?*

An hour and a half later, I plopped the tray of (slightly) burnt brownies in the middle of the kitchen table. Stress baking was a time-honored tradition. When my grandma died, I spent hours making dozens and dozens of her favorite cookies. The first time I got stood up for a date, I baked an apple pie. The day I found out I was pregnant with Oliver—twenty-one, unmarried with a boyfriend who didn't know what the word *job* meant, and sharing an apartment with four other roommates—I made a German chocolate cake.

Sunny said it was a coping mechanism. I thought it was a way to take all those big, scary feelings and make them a little sweet. It can't be all bad if I can eat cake, right? Whatever it was, it usually managed to take my mind off the problem in front of me. Most of the time, anyway.

Gilbert Dalton was going to be a real big problem.

So, by the time Chris brought Oliver home, it was no surprise to anyone I was making brownies... or that Chris had already heard about Gilbert Dalton's arrival. I'm sure Cammie had broken a nail sending that text out.

I'd begun whipping up the brownies about five minutes after Gilbert Dalton left the premises, promising to be back on Monday.

I frowned down at the pan. These were my special triple-chocolate brownies made with milk, semi-sweet, and white chocolate chips. I could make them with my eyes shut. Yet they still got burned because my mind was not calmed, it was not coping; it was worried.

Thanks, Gilbert Dalton. You ruined my brownies.

A tug on my sleeve shifted my attention. Oliver stood in front of me, his hands on his hips. His face was scrunched in concern. My heart squeezed, as it did every time I looked at my son. I'd made a lot of mistakes in my life, but Oliver was not one of them. "You look mad, Mommy."

I plopped on a chair at the kitchen table. "I'm okay, honey."

He shook his head slowly. "Nah-ah. I know 'cause it's bedtime and you made brownies, and you look mad like the time I woked up early and made myself breakfast."

Ah, yes, I remember that well. When I'd gotten up with the alarm, I'd found five-year-old Oliver standing on a chair he'd dragged to the counter and mixing an entire five-pound bag of flour—or rather the one pound that made it in the bowl, the other four were all over him and the floor—and a dozen eggs, shells included. Oliver, his face and hair decorated with flour, had explained he'd wanted to make muffins as a surprise for me. Oh, he'd surprised me alright.

Huffing a laugh, I pulled him onto my lap and breathed in all the yumminess that was a freshly bathed little boy. "Okay, maybe I'm a little... unhappy."

He pressed a hand to my cheek and stared into my eyes. "You should be more happy then."

If only it were that easy. "You're right, kiddo. How'd you get so smart?"

"Uncle Chris says it's 'cause he's my uncle and I have his genes."

Sounded like my brother. "Of course he did."

"'Cept I don't have any of his jeans. They'd be way too big for me."

Laughing, I hugged him. "I love you."

He grinned and not-so-subtlely eyed the pan of brownies. "Could I have a brownie, please?"

"Since you asked so nicely."

He climbed on a chair as I cut him a square. "Mommy, who was that man you and Uncle Chris were talking about?"

"You heard that?" I maybe had given Chris an earful the second he'd arrived with Oliver. "He's Ollie's grandson."

And a home invader. And a possible stalker. And a brownie burner.

He blinked up at me, his expression serious. Oliver came in two modes: serious and slightly less serious.

Also, too smart for his own good.

"Why was he here?"

To make my life difficult. And burn my brownies. Have I mentioned that? "He came because part of our house is his house, too."

His brow furrowed. "It is?"

I knew that look. It preceded five hundred and thirty-six rapid-fire questions. Time to change the subject. "You know what? How about you take this brownie into the living room, and you can watch TV before bed?"

His eyes lit up. "For one hour?"

"Twenty minutes."

"Forty-five."

Hiding a smile, I sighed. "You drive a hard bargain. Thirty minutes. Final offer."

He held out his hand and I shook on it. "Done."

My brother came around the corner and held out his fist. "Give me one, O-Man."

Without breaking his stride, Oliver bumped his little one on my brother's massive one. Oliver would grow up one day and be big and tall, I was sure of it. His dad had been over six feet and I was no slouch, but for now, he looked tiny next to my brother and still the perfect size to cuddle with.

"I'll take one of those." Chris sat down at the table and started to cut himself a brownie roughly the size of New Jersey. Then again, Chris was roughly the size of the state of Texas.

Of the five Sterns children, he was the only son and the only one older than me, by five years. He'd recently announced his retirement from the NFL and had taken to a life of leisure. He planned to head to medical school in a year or so—nothing like being an overachiever. First, he wanted to enjoy married life, and I didn't blame him. For all his quick smiles and golden retriever energy, he'd worked non-stop since high school, even before that. Football was hard on a body. More than once, I'd caught him wincing when he moved a certain way.

I smacked his hand away. "You do not get half the pan. Let me cut them."

Mae, Chris's wife, rounded the corner into the kitchen, returning from her ninety-seventh bathroom break in the hour since they'd arrived. "Brownies," she breathed in awe. "You made these just for me, right?"

She grabbed the knife from me and cut an even bigger piece than Chris had. With her hand on her very pregnant stomach, she practically inhaled half of it in one bite. "So good," she half moaned. "So, so good."

Chris scowled. "Hey, how come you get a big piece, and I don't?"

"Maybe because she's going to give birth to your nineteen-pound baby in a couple of months and she needs all the sustenance she can get." I patted Mae's stomach. Which wasn't something I thought Mae would ever allow. Soft wasn't her personality, exactly. She was a natural-born Mama Bear and kind of intimidating, at least to me. As the head librarian at the Two Harts Public Library, she put all that energy to work.

But she'd definitely become a bit of a softie in her third trimester. She would never admit to it, but I saw her tear up over an article about the plight of pink dolphins in the Amazon a couple of weeks ago and she'd become obsessed with videos of unlikely animal friends. Which she texted to us several times a day.

"I need to keep my strength up," Mae said around a mouthful of brownies.

Chris hooked an arm around Mae and gently pulled her to perch on his lap, a dopey, besotted grin in place.

"So," Mae said once she'd settled and inhaled the rest of her brownie, "Ollie has a grandson. Who would have thought?"

I plopped down at an empty seat. "Yeah, Gilbert freaking Dalton."

Chris shrugged. "Frankie said he seemed like a decent guy."

I glared. "It's been less than two hours, how have you already talked to Frankie?"

A phone buzzed on the table. Mae held it up. "It's Ali. Should I answer it?"

"Yes," I said. "If you don't, who knows what she'll do."

Ali Goodnight had been Mae's best friend since elementary school and, as of two years ago, she was also the mayor of Two Harts. It had surprised us all how well she'd fit into the role. Ali was known for her... *strong* sense of justice that usually presented itself through an array of revenge pranks. Since I'd moved here, Mae and Ali and I had become close. They were the kind of friends I imagine would help me bury the body. If the situation ever arose. It hadn't.

Yet.

"You're on speaker," Mae said.

"Ollie has a grandson? That can't be. The man never stepped foot out of Two Harts unless he was forced to. You should demand a blood test, or something," Ali said as a way of greeting.

"He has a lot of Ollie's grumpy energy," I muttered.

"Well, we don't know this guy," Ali said. "We need to check him out."

Chris groaned. "Please, no. Because when you say check him out, you mean dressing like a ninja, doing some light stalking, and maybe digging through his garbage, too."

"Oh, I hadn't thought about digging through his trash," Ali said, sounding excited. "That's a great idea. I'll call down to the motel and see if they can save it for me."

"Please don't," I said.

"No undercover missions," Mae said, going for a second brownie.

I dropped my forehead to the table. "Ollie, what the heck were you thinking?"

Three years ago, when I moved to Two Harts, a small Texas town west of Houston, I hadn't had much to my name except for a three-year-old, a twenty-year-old car, a thousand-dollar loan from Chris, and about five hundred bad decisions weighing me down.

I'd been on my way to my parents' home in Oklahoma when I'd made the decision to stop off in Two Harts to meet the girl who'd stolen my brother's heart. Except instead of leaving, I got a job at Sit-n-Eat, the café in town owned by a curmudgeonly man with wild eyebrows named Oleander "Ollie" Holder who, like the café, was small, rough around the edges, and completely set in his ways.

My interview had gone something like this:

Ollie: *You been a waitress before?*

Me: *Sure.*

Ollie: *You start tomorrow.*

It took months for Ollie to say more than five words to me in one go. But he'd given me a job without batting an eye, even though I'd brought my preschooler to the interview. He hadn't said a word when Oliver trailed along with me to work every day for two weeks because I didn't have the money for daycare and didn't know a soul who could watch him.

Oliver latched onto Ollie almost immediately, first delighted they almost had the same name, and then fascinated with the man himself. It felt like a sign. Somehow, someway, Oliver and I were meant to be in Two Harts.

Ollie had offered me two rooms to rent in his house, one for me and one for Oliver. The rent was dirt cheap, so pathetically low I knew he wasn't doing it for money. I tried to thank him, but that was only received with a harassed, "I don't know what you're talking about. It's not a favor. I need the extra cash."

But I knew. There'd been something about Ollie that drove me to make him proud and I found myself working harder than I ever had. It had felt... good and right.

For the first time, maybe in my entire life, I'd found my place.

Then six months ago, I found Ollie slumped over in a booth at the Sit-n-Eat.

It was a Monday morning and like always, he'd arrived

before me. As was his custom, he'd sat down with the first cup of coffee of the day and a newspaper before the café officially opened at 6 a.m. A heart attack, I'd been told. It had been quick; he hadn't suffered. But my heart ached with sadness because he'd been all alone at the end.

We buried him four days later.

I'd stayed on at the house, paying rent to the estate and taking over the utilities until the attorney had worked everything out. I was grateful for that. Besides the grief of losing Ollie, the constant anxiety of not knowing what the future held hung over my head constantly. Ollie had been the source of both my job and home. So, I kept going. I opened and closed the café each day. Under Ollie's sink-or-swim tutelage, I'd learned to keep the books and pay the bills and order supplies and everything else. I did that, too, even though I hated the business-y side of things. But I loved the café and this town and these people, and I wanted Oliver to grow up here. Ollie's house was the only home he remembered.

For the first twenty-two years of my life, my dream had been to be an actress. I hadn't been a great student. If I was interested in the subject matter, I learned everything I could. But if I wasn't interested, I spent a lot of time woolgathering, as Grandy called it. After I had Oliver, my dreams changed and, looking back, giving up the fanciful dream of a teenager and replacing it with a son I adored and a job I loved was the best decision I could have made.

Moving into Ollie's house hadn't been smooth sailing at first for any of us. Ollie had lived alone for most of his life and getting used to a woman and a child all at once hadn't been easy for him, or me. But sometimes things work out in the most unlikely of ways. Ollie helped us out and I think in a lot of ways, we helped Ollie out. Not just with cleaning and fixing the things we could and making the house more livable. But in even more important ways like companionship and the feeling of knowing someone was looking out for you.

I'd be the first to admit that Ollie's house was a hundred years old, and it showed. The hot water didn't work sometimes. The wooden floor was warped and a little soft in some places. Something had fallen on the roof—Ollie had never told me what —and it had been boarded up with plywood. I lived in fear it would fall down and fatally wound me during a storm.

But this house could be something, I could see it. It just needed a little TLC and elbow grease and duct tape and prayers and money to get it into shape. I had so many ideas, things I wanted to do and paint and change.

All I wanted was to make a home for Oliver, keep the café going, maybe one day fix my broken man picker. I wanted simple. I wanted contentment. I wanted peace. That was the dream now.

Gilbert Dalton was threatening that dream.

Chris patted my shoulder. "It's gonna work out."

I lifted my head. "No, it has to work out."

FIVE

[Love is]... a relationship, I guess. I don't know.

—ABBY L., AGE 12

Douglas Carmichael, the estate attorney, was a tall, spindly kind of man with gangly arms and legs and enormous hands. With his long face and rather oversized nose, he reminded me of a horse.

"I don't know what you put in these muffins, Ellie, but they're something else." After brushing away the crumbs from his first muffin, he took another from the plate in the middle of the table.

A horse who liked baked goods. Unlike Gilbert Dalton. He hadn't touched a single muffin. Hadn't wanted the lemonade I offered either. Water, that's it. Maybe he was allergic to things that tasted good. Or into some weird form of self-deprivation.

He was dressed in another long-sleeve button-down with dark-wash jeans, every hair on his head in place, looking cool and unruffled. My hand itched to reach across the table and... and do something. Muss his hair, steal his glasses, smack him.

After a weekend of thinking of every worst-case scenario imaginable (a special talent of mine), followed by a brief dance with self-awareness in which I wondered if I was overthinking this whole situation and should give this Gilbert Dalton a chance, I wasn't any closer to feeling calm or collected.

Yet at night when I lay down to sleep, my mind produced one awful scenario after another. Like the one where Gilbert Dalton poisons me so he can claim all the property for himself. Or the one where Gilbert Dalton smothers me in my sleep so he can claim all the property for himself. Or the one where Gilbert Dalton... well, you get it.

I could already hear Sunny telling me I was jumping to conclusions, and she'd ask me if I thought he'd really hurt me. She would say that my subconscious was worried about how him showing up would affect everything I'd worked on for the last three years.

I really hated when Sunny was right.

As you might imagine, I baked. A lot. Those muffins the lawyer was partaking in right now? There were three dozen more in the deep freezer at the house. This morning when I woke up at 4 a.m., I'd been determined to make the best of the situation. All through the busyness of Monday at the café, I tried to stay positive. Honest, I did. Until I sat down with the attorney and across from Gilbert Dalton.

All that to say, I was an exhausted, sweaty mess wrapped in an anxiety burrito.

Doug thumbed through the stack of papers on the table in front of him. He'd agreed to drive over to Two Harts for this meeting and so we sat in the quiet of the café after closing time. "I'm glad to have both of you together finally. You're a hard man to get ahold of, Mr. Dalton." He smiled at us—he even had big teeth like a horse—and rested his folded hands on the table. "So, what are your questions?"

"How did this happen?" I nodded at Gilbert. "Where did he come from?"

"You remember me telling you there was a possibility of a relative?" Doug said. He had a crumb on his upper lip. It was hard not to stare at it.

"I think you mentioned it once, months ago, before I even knew Ollie had left anything to me," I said.

Douglas frowned at me. "And on Friday when I met with you. When I told you Ollie had left the house and the café to you, but that Mr. Dalton would have a year to come forward if he was interested in claiming the half Ollie had also left to him." He shot Gilbert a stern look. "Although he'd ignored all the phone calls, voice messages, texts, and certified letters. I was surprised when he showed up in my office."

Well... crap. I definitely had not been listening to every word that came out his mouth that day, apparently.

I cleared my throat, trying not to look too blindsided. "So just like that, he owns half of everything now?" My leg jiggled under the table, so hard the water in Gilbert's glass rippled.

"Well, not exactly. Neither of you owns anything yet. For your claim on the property to be valid, you must live on the premises for six months."

My hand shot up in the air.

Gil's gaze landed on me, one dark eyebrow raised. "Are you raising your hand like a fourth grader?"

I looked down my nose at him. "I didn't want to interrupt, thank you very much."

"And look how well that worked."

"Look, you big je—"

"What was your question, Ms. Sterns?" Doug's eyes zipped between Gilbert and me with a hint of concern.

"When you say 'live on the premises,' what exactly does

that mean?" *Please don't mean what I think it means. Please don't mean what I think it means.*

"Both you and Mr. Dalton need to live on the property"—he glanced down at the paperwork—"on Garden Valley Road for the next six months."

Ollie's house was the only house on Garden Valley Road. Panic fluttered in my stomach. I swallowed hard. "But you don't mean *live* live on the property. Maybe around the property. Within twenty miles? Or something."

"No, the will says in order for your claim to be valid, your primary residence must be the property on Garden Valley Road. If that is completed, your portion of the property will be deeded over. After that, you're free to decide what to do with it —keep it, sell it, that's up to you. But you can't do either if you don't live there for six months first."

"Six months." Gilbert crossed his arms, his button-down straining at his shoulders. Not that I was looking.

"Indeed." Doug sounded almost cheerful.

"And if we don't?" I looked back and forth between Gilbert and the attorney. "What if he decides he doesn't want to live on the property? Then what?"

"Then he'd be forfeiting his right to his half. Simple as that."

"Six months would give us some time," Gilbert said, looking thoughtful. "We'd want to get everything fixed up in order to sell."

"I suppose so. I would thin—"

I interrupted. "Wait, what? We aren't selling."

"Why wouldn't we?" Gilbert asked, looking genuinely confused.

"I don't want to, for one," I said, attempting to keep my voice calm despite the panic building in my chest. "I've spent three years helping to fix it up. I have sweat equity in that house. I love that house and this town. This is my home."

"That's not my problem," he said slowly.

My mouth dropped open. "Not your problem?"

He shrugged. "Buy me out at the end of the six months."

Was he joking? I had a twenty-plus-year-old car, a job at a small-town café, and that was about it. I could ask Chris for the money, but even the thought made my stomach squeeze uncomfortably. While it would solve all my problems, there was a stubborn part of me that wouldn't allow it. Chris had done so much for me already; besides, he had his own family now to take care of. He didn't need to take care of me, too.

I glared across the table. The desire to punch him was strong. Instead, I drew in a long, slow breath and smiled. Because I'd found it was easier to get people on your side if you were polite and nice and friendly. Which punching was not.

"I don't have the money to buy you out," I said between clenched teeth. Okay, maybe that wasn't exactly friendly.

Doug, having lost interest, picked up yet another muffin. "These are heavenly, Ellie. I don't know what you put in them."

"Love," I snapped, my eyes never leaving Gilbert. "They're made with love."

And about a pound of pure sugar.

"If you're planning to sell, you'll want to fix it up some." A bit of muffin crumble clung to Doug's upper lip. "Maybe a new coat of paint, freshening up, that sort of thing."

The need to laugh manically bubbled up in me. Fix it up some? That was like calling a puddle a lake. Only if you're a worm. "It needs a lot more than a coat of paint."

In all honesty, it should probably be bulldozed, but I didn't want to do that. It was a hundred years old. More than that, it had provided shelter and protection for decades and generations of Ollie's family. It was a treasure. And the café? Well, that was both my livelihood and my new dream. It would need a complete and total remodel someday. But I could do a little at a time. I'd already started over the last three years. I wasn't afraid of hard work.

One thing at a time, as Sunny would say. Deal with what's right in front of you first. Thusly, I glowered at Gilbert.

"I'm no real estate expert." Doug shuffled through his paperwork yet again and pulled one out. "But I checked around and found out some developers have been looking to invest in some land here in Two Harts, and as you know, the property comes with quite a bit of land. There was some mention of a new high school football stadium, too. A Peter Stone from right here in Two Harts."

I made a disapproving sound from the back of my throat.

Peter Stone was the former mayor of Two Harts. He'd been sniffing around for a while now since Ollie's passing, asking if I knew what was happening with the property. Oh, no way was he getting his hands on Ollie's land. It would be strip malls and big box stores and planned communities for the city folks. Two Harts would cease to be Two Harts. Ollie would come back from the grave to haunt him *and me* if I let that happen.

"Mr. Holder left behind a good chunk of prime real estate. It could make you a lot of money without having to fix up the house at all. Might end up in a bidding war." Doug raised his muffin like it was a glass to be toasted.

"But we still have to wait a whole six months before we need to make a decision," I said, more to remind myself than anyone else.

Gilbert nodded silently, but his mind was busy behind his eyes. Don't know exactly how I knew but I did know, with certainty, he was thinking.

Danger, danger, my brain said. Don't let him think too long.

I needed a Plan. Capital P. Because I was not leaving Two Harts. Or that house. Or this café. Period.

"I'll need the rest of the week to get some things taken care of. I can move in on Saturday," Gilbert said.

I could show him the friendly folks of Two Harts, the Easter parade, the Founder's Festival, the muffins I could make...

Wait.

"What?"

He leaned forward and an unholy light began to glimmer in his eyes. Alarmingly, my pulse began to thrum, and not from anger. "I have to live there for the next six months, don't I?"

Something in my stomach swooped. I frowned. Silence grew between us. I fidgeted, gnawing on my bottom lip. He sat still as a cat right before it pounced. Prey meet predator. Except he didn't look like a predator; he looked like an accountant.

"But you're a stranger," I said. "And I have a son."

Gilbert leaned back in his seat slowly. "A son?"

"Oh, Ollie had me do background checks on both of you," Doug said. "You'll be happy to know neither one of you has been in any trouble with the law."

"That just means he hasn't been caught." I whipped my phone out. "I'm googling him."

"Maybe I'm the one who should be afraid," Gilbert said. He held his phone up and began typing.

The first page of results was for a politician named Gilbert Dalton who lived in Wisconsin. Then a few entries about a guy who owned a cattle ranch in California in the eighteen eighties. But when I loaded the second page, I found him.

I bit back a smile of anticipation. Please be something good. Oh, maybe he'd been involved in a pyramid scheme, or he'd been writing *Fifty Shades* fanfic.

"Miss Tomato Harvest?" Gilbert turned his phone around. "Look, there's even a picture."

I grabbed his hand to hold the phone steady. A zing snaked up my arm at the contact. I ignored it. In the photo, sixteen-year-old me had just been crowned Miss Tomato Harvest, as the wide white sash I was wearing announced. I remembered searching high and low for the tomato-red dress I had worn. Not everyone could pull off wearing a tiara with a large sparkling tomato on top of it like I could.

"Let me guess, you got free tomatoes for a year." He wasn't wrong but I wasn't going to admit that. With a knowing smirk, Gilbert pulled his hand away. "Your parents must have been so proud."

"Yes, they were," I said. "It was a great honor."

Back on my phone, I redoubled my efforts to find something sketchy about Gilbert. Ah-ha, a newspaper article with his name in it. I clicked on it and greedily read the title, "Two Local Teachers Nominated to be Named Texas Teacher of the Year." I scanned the article, my heart sinking as I went. There was his name—as a nominee.

"You're a teacher."

Gilbert didn't lift his eyes from his phone. "Was. I left to work as a youth counselor at a community center." He glanced up, an eyebrow raised. "After I got my master's degree."

"Good for you," I mumbled.

"Look at this, you have a page on the movie database. You do some acting, Eleanor?"

No, he couldn't find *that* info. I glanced across the table and gave serious thought to lunging across it and tackling him for the phone.

"*Kangaroo'd Three*," Gilbert said. "Three? They made three of these movies?"

Actually, five of them. With a groan, I dropped my face into my hands.

"A woman is kidnapped by a giant kangaroo that has been genetically modified in a lab," he read aloud. "To escape, she must survive on her wits while living inside the kangaroo's pouch... if she doesn't fall for her captor first." He smirked. "Wow. How have I never heard of this? Surely it was nominated for awards."

I'd been offered the role of the kidnappee three months after moving to Los Angeles. The script had been terrible. The plot, terrible. The director, terrible... and weird. But my boyfriend was convinced this would be my breakout role and it was my first paid acting job (a whopping five hundred dollars). Up until then, I'd gone on about five million auditions. Just me and every other tall blonde in a fifty-mile radius for a bit part in a cable TV show.

It had become clear even then that making a living acting was going to be much harder than I expected. No one cared about my success in high school and community theater back in Oklahoma. Aside from a starring role in a short movie for a film student, mostly to get something for my acting reel, I hadn't had any luck.

Also, living in LA was expensive. So, I took the role. Spent a lot of time in a human-size wool pouch. When I wasn't popping out to make moon eyes at my kidnapper.

"Do male kangaroos even have pouches?" Gilbert wondered aloud. I jerked my head up and glared at him.

"I don't think so, now that you mention it," Doug said.

"Okay, yes. I was in the movie. I'm not embarrassed."

Yes, I was. My face had to be five shades redder than a fire truck. I quickly went back to my phone. There was another mention of Gilbert Dalton in an Austin paper. It announced the winners of the National Merit Scholarship in the area. And, yes, Gilbert's name was on that list, too.

"Chris Sterns is your brother?" Gilbert asked. "*The* Chris Sterns? From the Oklahoma Stars?"

I heaved a sigh. Sometimes—scratch that, most of the time—guys got weird when they found out this bit of information. One of those men made it to the fourth date before I discovered he was a huge fan. The creepy kind. The kind who had all of Chris's stats memorized and wore his jersey to bed at night and tried to break into my phone to steal his number.

More than that, I'd lived under the shadow of Chris's fame for years. Even before he went pro, he was the perfect son, the perfect student, the perfect football player, the perfect everything. He was even a freaking Eagle Scout. I loved him; he'd rescued me at one of the worst moments of my life. But, gah, the pressure to live up to the legend?

"Yes, he's my brother," I said wearily. "So what?"

Gil's head tilted to the side. He set his phone down and stared at me with something like curiosity. He gestured toward me. "What did you find out?"

"I'm still looking." But every link I clicked that mentioned him, only made him look better. In high school, he'd rescued a dog from a hot car by breaking the window and had been given a hero's award by the local animal rescue. In college, he started a community peer support program between college students and disabled adults. Last year, he'd been featured in a local magazine for his work with underprivileged youths.

Whatever. Who cared what he looked like online. I didn't know the guy in real life, and he was not moving into the house. I had Oliver to think about.

"You can't just uproot your whole life and move here. Don't you have a job, or something? A girlfriend? A goldfish?" I asked.

"I'm between jobs. We broke up two months ago. And no."

"How are you going to afford to live then? Electricity, gas, food?"

His eyes darted to the left. "I have some money saved."

"Don't you have a lease or a mortgage or something?"

He shrugged. "I have it covered."

I turned to Doug who was eating what had to be his seventh muffin. "He just has to live on the property, right? It doesn't have to be in the actual house?"

"I suppose not," he said slowly.

"What about a tent or a trailer or a sleeping bag on the lawn?" From the corner of my eye, I saw Gil straighten. His eyes drilled into the side of my head.

"As long as it was on the property, I suppose that would work."

"Good." I turned back to Gilbert. "You can stay in the back-yard." He opened his mouth, probably to argue with me but I cut him off. "I'm not letting a stranger move into my house."

I stared at him, willed him to argue. But he just stared back, his big, dumb, National Merit brain working overtime. Finally, his face softened. Just a little. His eyes seemed a touch kinder or at least not as hard and indifferent as they had been. "Fine. I'll stay in the backyard."

"Really?"

"I've been camping before. I'll survive." He shrugged like it was no big deal, but it was kind of a huge deal. He grabbed a backpack he'd brought with him and pushed his chair back.

"I... I..." I tamped down the panic again. Was this really happening? How would Oliver handle a strange man living in a tent in our backyard? Oh, who was I kidding? Oliver would take it in stride. I was the one who would freak out. I didn't know this guy. I wasn't even sure I liked him.

Even worse, I didn't think he much liked me.

Here's a little bit I've learned about myself in therapy—I like to be liked. When I wasn't liked, I tried harder to get liked. I felt guilty and apologized for things that weren't my fault. In fact, I felt like it was my responsibility to make things right. Looking back, I understood now it had all led to some pretty question-able choices and relationships where I was the one who did all the work to fix things. In the end, all that came out of it was disaster.

Sunny said my official diagnosis was Grade A, certified People Pleaser.

It had been two long years of learning how not to take on the burden and responsibility of other people. And it was still there. It didn't matter how much "self-awareness" I obtained. It would always be a struggle.

"Sounds like a plan to me." Doug shuffled more papers around and held out two envelopes, one to each of us. "Here's what was left over from the estate after funeral expenses. It's not much."

Gilbert tucked the envelope in his backpack without opening it. "I'll move in on Saturday."

Holy forks, what had just happened?

SIX

Love is something you see and you're like, "Ooh, I LOVE that."

—LIBERTY B., AGE 6

"The guy at the counter wants oatmeal." Iris, one of my two employees, gestured over her shoulder.

"Do we even have oatmeal?" I turned away from the oven where I'd just pulled out two dozen blueberry sour cream muffins. The smell wrapped around me and I smiled. Props to the baker; they looked amazing.

"I don't know. No one's ever asked for it before." She tucked a lock of blonde hair streaked with hot pink behind her ear. "Unless it was in cookie form."

I wiped my hands on my apron. It was bright yellow with Sit-n-Eat written boldly across the front and a tiny muffin dotting the i. I'd gotten them last month after deciding we needed to jazz things up around this place. "Get him oatmeal then."

"Oh, Jorge," Iris said in a sing-song voice. "You got some oatmeal laying around?"

Jorge Benitez was my other employee, and he manned the kitchen. He grumbled something about *boring gringos* and started rustling around on a shelf. Ten seconds later, he slapped a box of instant oatmeal packets on the counter. "Found it."

"Thank you, sunshine." Iris blew Jorge a kiss just to annoy him. As was her way.

He shot her the least sunshine-y look ever, playing along. Iris laughed; Jorge grinned.

"He want eggs or anything else?" Jorge asked.

Iris pulled down a bowl and dumped the contents of the packet in. "He says he just wants oatmeal. Plain."

I made a face. "Who likes plain oatmeal? It's like eating mushy cornflakes."

"Obviously no one told him that."

Curious, I peeked over the top of the swinging door separating the dining area from the kitchen. "Who is it?"

"All the way at the end, dark hair, glasses, big shoulders, square jaw." After mixing in a cup of water, she stuck the bowl in the microwave. "Very big hands. You see him?"

Normally, I would have commenced with objectifying the man right along with her (don't judge, I have to have my fun where I can get it), but I was too busy gawking. There, scrolling through his phone like he didn't have a problem in the world, was Gilbert Dalton.

A streak of something hot shot through me. Clearly annoyance.

"He's not all that," I muttered.

"Seriously?" Iris gave a low chuckle. "He has hot accountant/history professor/but knows his way around a toolbox energy."

"Is that even a thing?"

Iris arched an eyebrow. "It's totally a thing." She peeked over the door at Gilbert and fanned her face with a hand. "It's definitely my thing."

"Whatever would your boyfriend say?"

"Have you met Aidan? He's got accountant/history professor/but knows his way around a toolbox in training energy."

I laughed. She was not wrong.

With a wink, she pushed open the door with her hip. "Told you I had a type."

When I'd moved to Two Harts, Iris had been a sullen, sarcastic seventeen-year-old with a potty mouth and aspirations of becoming a card-carrying member of the Emo Girls Club. She'd sported dyed-black hair, black lipstick, alt rock t-shirts, and Dr. Martens. She was also Mae's little sister, so practically family. It was strange how two people could be so alike and so very different all at the same time.

Neither sister was one you wanted to get in a verbal battle with. Unless you enjoyed getting cut into teeny-tiny pieces by the perfect blend of word choice and attitude. Then go for it; it's your funeral.

Iris had started working at the café over a year ago when I'd finally convinced Ollie we should open for breakfast. The Sit-n-Eat was a town staple, having been around for decades. And for decades, it had only been open four hours a day, five days a week, to serve lunch. Lunch was whatever Ollie said was for lunch that day. No substitutions. If a patron disagreed, it was no skin off Ollie's back. He wouldn't argue; he would ignore you.

The first time I suggested opening for breakfast, he didn't talk to me for three days straight. Don't get me wrong. I talked to him. Constantly. Wore him down finally. And now, despite Ollie's less than compromising attitude, the café was always busy when it was open.

A bell dinged behind me, pulling me from yet another woolgathering session. I bet I had enough wool at this point to make blankets for half of the state of Texas. A bowl of oatmeal appeared in the pass-thru window. "Order up," Jorge yelled.

"I got it," I said when Iris turned away from the group of

grumpy old men she was cracking (dirty) jokes with. That girl knew how to get her tips.

Carefully, I picked up the bowl and reminded myself to stay calm and friendly. As I lay in bed last night, I'd thought of a plan. If he moved in next Saturday, his time would be up at the beginning of August. I had to change his mind about selling by then. Which meant he needed to fall in love with Two Harts and see the roots he had here. His family had lived in Two Harts for over a hundred years. Two Harts was a great town. Number two hundred and eighty-seven of the three hundred best small towns in America... even if that had been in nineteen eighty-seven.

I slid the bowl of oatmeal in front of Gilbert. "Thought you'd have left after the meeting yesterday."

Setting his phone aside, he leaned back in his seat. "I was too excited to watch *Kangaroo'ed Three* to make the drive back."

My face heated. "You didn't."

"My favorite line of yours: 'You've hopped right into my heart.' Really loved the play on words. Hopped... kangaroo. Powerful stuff." His eyes sparkled with amusement.

Maybe calm and friendly were going to be harder than I thought.

I pointed at the bowl of mush. "Can I get you some sugar for that?"

He shook his head. This morning, he wasn't so formally dressed, still neat, still with perfectly parted hair. I think his dark-orange henley had been ironed.

"Syrup?"

"No, thank you." He crossed his arms, his eyes steady on my face. They weren't brown like I'd thought, but a dark navy-blue. And judge-y. Very judge-y.

I resisted the urge to fuss with my apron or straighten my hair. "Fruit, then. I have some nice blueberries."

"I'm good." He was openly inspecting me now, from the top

of my head to as far down as he could go before the counter got in the way.

I mimicked his position, crossing my arms and staring right back. I tried not to look at his hands. But now that Iris had brought it up, I wanted to see what the fuss was. They were big, with long fingers. Not elegant, like a piano player, but strong, useful. They were clean, too, tipped with trimmed nails. His left pointer finger had a black spot on the nailbed, a bruise from hitting it with something heavy, like a hammer.

As the daughter of a contractor, I'd seen that injury more than once.

Expression unreadable, his head cocked to the side. I squirmed. It reminded me of dress code checks in school when I was a kid. He did give off strong principal energy. The hint of gray in his hair, the stern expression. Except younger and kind of... hot?

Did I think he was hot? No, of course not. This was Ollie's grandson, and he held my future in his admittedly very nice hands.

I straightened, refusing to wilt under his inspection. "How about some walnuts?"

"Can I just get a spoon?"

"Sure thing." I hustled over to the silverware tray to grab him one.

He was *not* hot; he ate plain oatmeal. There was clearly something wrong with him. Tragic disease that took away all his taste buds?

"Very smooth there, boss," Iris said.

I snagged a spoon. "Do you know who that is?"

"I'm kinda hoping he's the new male model for my art and the human form class. I would ace that assignment, for sure."

"First, gross. Second, that's Ollie's grandson."

"No way," she breathed, turning to face him. He was back to messing around with his phone.

I elbowed her. "Don't stare."

"I'm not staring. I'm reevaluating everything I know about genetics."

"Go away." I pointed the spoon at her. "Far, far away."

Iris grinned and headed to the other side of the café. I hurried back and set the spoon on a napkin beside Gilbert's bowl.

"Thank you." He unfolded his napkin, placed it on his lap, and took a bite of his breakfast, seemingly uninterested in me.

I should walk away. There was plenty to do but I was curious about him. The two of us were strangers and yet our lives were entwined in ways neither of us had expected. Like that red string of fate people talked about. Although in our case, the silver duct tape of destiny might be more appropriate.

"How can you possibly enjoy eating oatmeal like that?" I blurted.

He shrugged. "It's oatmeal."

I pressed my palms onto the edge of the counter. "I think it's one of the signs of being a psychopath. You know, right after lacking empathy, or something."

Spoon inches from his mouth, he paused. "It's just how I eat it."

"Fascinating," I said. "So, do you go by Gil?"

"No."

"Really?"

"Yes."

"Not even when you were a kid?"

He sighed. "No."

"You look like a Gil." Whatever that meant. He didn't look much older than me, even though he gave off much older energy. He probably owned a grandpa sweater somewhere. And not ironically. "Can I call you Gil?"

"No."

I decided then and there to always call him Gil. "How old are you?"

His spoon clinked against the side of his bowl when he set it down and crossed his arms, glaring at me like a ticked-off teacher. Which, I'm not going to lie, was a look I saw often in my younger years. "Thirty-one. Why?"

I shrugged. "I don't know. I guess it seemed like something people who own a house together should know about each other."

"We aren't going to know each other for long," he said.

I held my hands out and took a step back. "I guess I can put 'sensitive about his name' on the list after psychopath."

"What list?"

"The list of things I know about you."

His head tilted. "Are you really keeping a list?"

"Yes. Though it's a very short list right now." And for the record, there was a list. Because I liked lists. And sticky notes. I just lost the lists. A lot.

With a shake of his head, he picked his spoon back up. "Any more questions?"

Yes, about a million. "I'll let you get back to eating, Gil."

He scowled. "Gilbert."

"Sure thing." I gave him a syrup-y sweet smile and walked away. But I could feel his eyes following me the entire way back to the kitchen.

The rest of the morning sped by. By the time we flipped the sign to CLOSED, I was wiped out and I still needed to get a head start on the baking for tomorrow.

But first, it was Tuesday, and I was expecting a visitor.

After Jorge and Iris left and before I had to get Oliver from the bus stop, I gathered up all the leftovers and day-old goods and a few extras I collected during the last week—canned tuna fish, peanut butter crackers, cheese sticks. I packed it all together in a box with a few bottles of water and this week, a new toothbrush and toothpaste I'd picked up from the store a couple of days ago. The knock on the back door came around three.

"Howdy, Ellie," Teddy Cane said when I opened the door. He smiled at me with a gap-toothed grin and rheumy blue eyes. As always, he carried with him the faint smell of alcohol. He was too thin for his height and lately, he seemed to be losing weight.

Teddy was about twelve hundred years old. That is if you went by the creases and wrinkles in his face. His gray hair was too long and stringy at the ends, but he was always careful to come with it freshly washed and combed.

He tried. But he lived in a little ramshackle house not too far off the main street. His whole life was a cautionary tale about the evils of alcohol. He'd tried to quit more times than he could count. Most recently, a couple of months ago, but his body hadn't had any idea how to function without it.

Ollie had been his best friend, or so Teddy said the first time he showed up at the café after Ollie passed, knocking on the back door one day after we closed. I'd never seen him before and wasn't sure I believed him. But I felt a little sorry for him; he seemed lonely. After asking Ali and Mae if they knew him (turns out, everyone did), I invited him in for a meal. In return, he told me stories of growing up with Ollie and the trouble they got into. I found myself laughing at their antics and liking Teddy.

The more he kept coming around, the more I saw his threadbare clothes or scruffy, unkempt beard and the more he sort of wormed his way into my heart. I understood the power alcohol could have over a person if you let it. So, every Tuesday and Saturday, Teddy showed up and I fed him, and I fussed over him while he pretended not to like it.

I ushered him inside. "Where did you get that cut on your cheek?"

"Oh, it's nothing." He put a hand to his face. "Just took a little spill the other day."

I frowned. "Have you been taking care of it?"

"It's fine. It's fine." After waving off my concern, he rooted around in the box. He held up a container, grinning widely. "Ah, you made lemon bars. They're my favorite."

"Come sit down and I'll find you a band-aid."

He scoffed. "I don't need a band-aid."

"I need you to have a band-aid. How's that?"

"Bossy, aren't you?" With a chuckle, he settled at the counter and began nursing a glass of iced tea I set before him. "You remind me of my sister. Have I told you that?"

"A time or two." Or a million. He liked to talk about the past, Teddy did. His sister was a favorite topic.

"She was always trying to boss me around even though she was younger than me." I returned as he was laying a paper napkin across his lap. "Liked to gripe I needed someone to take care of me."

"Sounds like a smart woman." I set a plate of food in front of him.

There was a touch of sadness in his eyes. "I miss her griping at me."

"How long since you've seen her?"

"Oh, she's been gone a long, long time now." He shook his head like he was trying to physically shake the memories away and grinned. "Don't worry none about the ramblings of an old man."

"I like your ramblings. Now eat. I'm going to find that first-aid kit."

"See? Bossy." But he dug into his meal with relish. He raised his voice so I could hear him while I rummaged around in the back. "Hey now, what's this I hear about Ollie's grandson showing up?"

"It hasn't even been a week yet. Does the whole town receive text alerts when new gossip hits?"

"And emails, too."

"Well, then you already know the answer." I returned, setting the first-aid kit on the counter. "Why don't you look surprised about it?"

Teddy shrugged. "I was Ollie's best friend."

"But no one knew..."

"I can keep a secret and that's how Ollie wanted it." He pointed at me with his fork. "You don't seem so happy about him showing up."

"It's complicated." I inspected the cut on his cheek. The edges were a little red and angry. "You need to take care of yourself."

"I've been doing it for years actually."

I snorted and applied some antibacterial gel to the wound. "And look how well that's going."

"I'm still alive and kicking." His grin cracked his face open, creating more wrinkles and creases.

Gently, I placed a band-aid on his cheek. "A true miracle."

"So, the grandson, what's he like?"

"He's... okay?"

He nodded, looking more troubled than anything else. "He's not a bad sort, right?"

Gilbert Dalton's scowling, stern face flashed in my mind. "The jury is still out on that."

"Well, I'll keep my eye on him." Teddy stood, pulling his pants up. I made a mental note to find him some suspenders and maybe a new pair of pants. "Ollie would have wanted me to."

"You do that, Teddy." I handed him the box of things. "Come see me Saturday, okay?"

He winked, or tried to, and left out the back door. I watched him amble down the alley until he disappeared around the corner.

SEVEN

[Love is...] Being kind. Giving people hugs. That's all I know about it.

—JEFFERSON, AGE 7

"Mommy?" Oliver asked, his big blue eyes sleepy. "Can you read two chapters tonight?"

I ruffled his hair and snuggled him closer to my side. This was my favorite moment of every day. If there was one slice of time I could cut and save to relive years from now, it would be one of these moments—Oliver, sleepy and freshly washed and curled into my side. It never failed to remind me that although I'd made a lot of mistakes in my life, Oliver was the good thing that came out of it. I might struggle with my previous decisions —Sunny said I needed to give myself more grace—but I could never regret how all those things had given me my son.

The day I found out I was pregnant, I'd been terrified. I was a twenty-one-year-old wannabe actress with four dollars in the bank and a loser boyfriend whose idea of a job was playing with the band for tips on open mic night. I wasn't in any place to have a kid.

But when I heard his heartbeat at my first doctor's appointment, I was a goner. Ironically, the baby daddy was also a goner. As in gone, far, far away. It had been Oliver and me, just the two of us, from the beginning.

"I think we can do that, but we need to talk first," I said.

Oliver sat up, his little face serious as he looked down at me. "Is this a cookie talk or an ice cream talk?"

This was code. An ice cream talk was a celebration, but a cookie talk...

"Cookie. Definitely cookie." I patted his arm. "Why don't you go grab a couple?"

"Cookies in the bed?" His eyes widened. "But we aren't supposed to eat in bed."

"I won't tell if you don't."

Without another word, he scrambled off the bed and darted out of the room. I stared up at the ceiling. With the lights still on, the glow-in-the-dark dinosaur footprints were just faint green blobs but it had taken a whole day to get them arranged the way Oliver had wanted them. I smiled thinking of how he had bossed Chris around until they were placed perfectly.

"Here's one for you." He held out a cookie and climbed on the bed after I took it. "What do you need to talk about?"

"Yeah, that." I picked at the dust jacket of the book resting on my stomach. "Do you remember when I told you about Ollie's grandson when Uncle Chris brought you home last Friday?"

"I 'member."

"Good. Good. Well..."

"Will I get to see him?"

I knew Oliver would handle this better than me. "Actually, yes. You'll be seeing him a lot. He's going to be living in a tent in the backyard."

His little face screwed up in confusion. "Like camping? Why?"

"Because..." My voice drifted off as I figured out a way to explain. "Well, that's just how it is, okay? He'll be living in the backyard."

"When is he coming?"

"On Saturday." In less than forty-eight hours. I bit back a groan. Not for the first time, I wondered what Ollie had been thinking.

Oliver's eyes sparked with excitement. "Is he your boyfriend now?"

I sat up slowly and faced him. "That would be a no."

"Oh." His shoulders slumped. While he knew his dad was a guy somewhere in the world who sent a birthday card (always a week late) and called on the holidays (sometimes), he'd never expressed much concern about not having a father. And he sure hadn't asked about me getting a boyfriend.

"Do you want me to have a boyfriend?"

"I want for you to have someone who loves you. Mrs. Sullivan said everyone needs to love someone and someone to love them. We talked about it for Balentine's Day."

Ah, yes, the most annoying of all the made-up holidays. "I see."

"She said there are lots of different kinds of loves like how I love you and you love me or when we help a stranger it's like love, too."

"That's all true."

"But then she said grown-ups love each other too, like so much they be boyfriend and girlfriend and then get married and she said being married is like having your best friend with you all the time and I thought about how you don't have a boyfriend and then how will you ever get married?"

Mrs. Sullivan had been Miss Everett last year before getting married over the summer. Clearly, the honeymoon was far from over.

"Do you want me to get married?"

"Yes." He climbed onto my lap and put his hands on my cheeks, turning my face so our foreheads touched. "You need someone who loves you the best. Like me, but a boyfriend."

My nose stung from the tears welling up. Gah, this boy was all the good things in the world. I covered his hands with mine. "I love you, kid."

"I know," he said and climbed off my lap. After he'd snuggled into his blankets, he smiled up at me sleepily. "You promised two chapters."

I laughed softly and opened the book.

EIGHT

Love is something cheerful. Actually, love is the answer.

—ISAAC J., AGE 16

Saturday showed up overcast and gloomy. Which seemed fair as it was the day Gil would be moving onto Ollie's property. I got up at five as usual. Oliver and I headed over to the café where we'd be busy from the moment I flipped the lock on the door until we closed.

Opening on Saturdays was one of the few changes I'd made since Ollie's passing. We started about three months ago and it had been an instant hit. Ollie never, and I mean never, worked weekends. He wasn't real big on anything that messed with his routine.

I think that's why the entire town was surprised when Ollie had taken to Oliver and me so quickly. Especially Oliver. The two of them had been inseparable some days—going fishing, watching old cartoons, taking long walks on the twenty acres behind the house. Someone had nicknamed them the Double

Os, which delighted Oliver. I even had matching t-shirts made for them and, shockingly, Ollie wore it.

It should have been weird, I guess, a single mom and her son living with the grumpy old man who bordered on antisocial. Maybe others thought that. But Ollie had given me something I had desperately needed—a reason to keep going, a space to learn and grow, a new dream I hadn't realized. Sure, he hadn't been eloquent with his words, and he was set in his ways, but he had a heart bigger than anyone realized.

But, boy, oh, boy would he have hated Saturday brunch.

A month ago, the Houston newspaper had started a series about small towns in the area. Ali had campaigned hard to get Two Harts a spot, but she'd made it happen. After the paper had done a review of the Sit-n-Eat (and my chocolate zucchini muffins), business had picked up more than we expected. I was even considering hiring another server.

When we got to the café, Main Street was quiet and still, the dusky-purple early February sky hinting at daybreak. Most of the shops wouldn't open until later in the morning. I let us in the back door and Oliver took off to turn on all the lights—a task he did every single morning. The clink of the chairs being taken from the tables and set on the floor came next, another of his chores.

After putting on an apron, I pulled out the ingredients to make the pancake and waffle mix in bulk. We'd go through a lot of it today. The kitchen was small and outdated. Not enough counterspace, as Jorge was quick to point out, but it had a small island, a finicky walk-in fridge, a large griddle, and double ovens. Would I like to give it a makeover? One day. But for now, it worked.

The dining room, on the other hand, needed a major overhaul. The once bright-yellow walls were faded and chipped; most of the seven tables wobbled. The booths along the walls were solid but the red vinyl that covered them had seen better days—about forty years ago. The floor was basic linoleum in a muddy (and unappetizing) brown. Tarnished metal stools were tucked under the counter for more seating. It was clean and tidy though, and people didn't seem to notice the imperfections here. Instead, they found good food and better company.

As one of the two oldest continuous businesses in Two Harts, this place held a whole town's worth of history. One wall was covered in senior class photos from the high school. It was tradition that every year on Senior Skip Day, the kids would end up at the Sit-n-Eat for lunch. That day, they'd present Ollie with a class photo, which he hung up on the wall next to all the others, going back decades.

Sadness pinged my heart; Ollie wouldn't be here to do that this year. He'd always complained about having to deal with all the teenagers but every now and then, I'd catch him looking at those class photos with a mix of nostalgia and pride. On the other walls were Holder family photos through the years, newspaper clippings that mentioned the Sit-n-Eat, or any Two Harts' residents for that matter.

I pushed through the half-door and into the dining room.

Oliver skidded to a halt in front of me. "Mommy, I turned on all the lights, set the chairs up, put the con-a-ments—"

"Condiments."

"Yeah, that. I put those on the tables. Can I help put the money in the register?"

"Sure." I figured by the time he was ten, he'd be running the place on his own and I could relax a little.

Ten minutes later, Oliver was sitting at the counter eating an orange spice muffin and chattering away. "Is today when Mr. Dalton comes?"

My shoulders tensed. "Yes."

"I'm going to draw him a picture so I can give it to him."

"Why?"

"'Cause we're gonna be friends."

Sighing, I leaned next to him at the counter. "We talked about this. He's a stranger. You need to keep your distance."

"But he's Ollie's grandson." Oliver's lips pulled to the side. "Ollie said he was a good guy."

I froze. "Ollie said what?"

Oliver's eyes darted from my face to his muffin. "Um, he said—"

The back door burst open, and Jorge yelled, "Morning."

"Jorge's here." Oliver popped up and ran to the kitchen, I suspected more in a hurry to get out of answering that question than saying hello to Jorge. We would be revisiting that later.

Jorge got to work with any prep he needed with a surprisingly chipper attitude. Then again, the guy had six kids at home. Sometimes I thought he viewed work as a vacation. After sending Oliver into the office to watch cartoons, I settled down with a cup of coffee and an egg-and-sausage breakfast muffin. Had to eat before we opened. There wouldn't be time again until we closed.

Iris dragged herself in fifteen minutes before we opened, looking a little rough around the edges. Her blonde and pink hair was wound messily atop her head, and she didn't have a drop of makeup on. After hightailing it to the coffee, she sighed deeply with the first sip and leaned against the counter.

"Rough night?" I asked.

"Being in love sucks."

Iris and her boyfriend Aidan had been together for three years. The first two years, they attended the nearby community college, but this year, Aidan had moved to Lubbock after getting a scholarship to Texas Tech.

"Ouch. Do you want to talk about it?"

"He brought up marriage again." Absently, she fiddled with the slim gold band, the small round diamond catching the light, on her left ring finger. Aidan had given her the promise ring at Christmas.

"And?'

"And I don't know." She slipped on her apron and patted the pocket for her order pad. "I'm not even sure I want to get married, like, ever."

"I don't have much advice on the subject of marriage." Never married, and all that. "But I don't think you should rush into anything if you don't feel right about it."

"Yeah." She stared over my shoulder. "I guess it seems like I should feel right about it though. I love him. My mom loves him, Mae loves him. But maybe tha—"

Someone rapped on the front door impatiently, interrupting whatever she might have said. When I saw who it was, I groaned. "Why is he here?"

He was Peter Stone, former mayor of Two Harts, former jackass boyfriend to Mae, and Two Harts' newest real estate "developer," the same one who'd apparently contacted Ollie's estate attorney about buying the property.

"I got it." Iris sauntered over to the door. She made a big deal of checking the imaginary watch on her wrist.

Peter thumped the glass door with all the impatience of a three-year-old. "Open up, already."

Iris cupped an ear. "I'm sorry. Did you say something? You know we open at seven on Saturdays and it's six fifty-eight."

"Come on, I'm in a hurry."

"Ellie," she said, "do you think we could open a couple minutes early?"

I tapped a finger on my chin, playing along. I had to take joy where I could find it, ya know? "No, I don't think so. How would that be fair to the other customers?"

"That's what I thought." She shook her head, her expression both sad and gleeful all at once. "So sorry. You'll have to wait."

Peter banged against the door once more before turning around and pacing the sidewalk. Two minutes later, he thumped again on the door and pressed his phone against the window. "Seven o'clock on the dot."

"Oh, look, he can tell time," Iris said. "Before we know it, he'll be able to add and subtract. Our little boy is growing up."

The look Peter gave her could have set her on fire. If eyes could do that. Which seemed like a waste of a superpower if you asked me. What if you accidentally set someone on fire when you sneezed, or something?

The snick of the door lock turning was followed by Peter's voice directed toward Iris. "You are ridiculous."

Iris arched an eyebrow. "Is that so?"

"Yes," he said, adjusting his shirt. "You and your sister, both ridiculous."

An achingly sweet smile spread across her face. With the blonde hair and blue eyes, Iris looked like the girl next door. All apple-cheeked and sturdy, tall frame. Like she would gladly bake you a pie right after she milked the family cow. "Can I get you anything? A cup of coffee, orange juice? Something easy to spit in?"

"You wouldn't."

She twirled around and strolled toward the counter. "Sure."

"Iris, there is no spitting in anyone's coffee," I said without any heat.

"Even if they have stupid soul patches?"

"Not even if the devil walked in and asked for a frittata and a cup of tea." With a quick pat to Iris's arm, I marched over to the front window and flipped the CLOSED sign to OPEN. "Very bad for business."

"You never let me have any fun." Pouting, Iris traipsed into the kitchen and asked Jorge loudly, "If I found a roach, would you be able to hide it in someone's order? Asking for a friend, of course."

I bit back a laugh. "So, Pete, what can I get for you this early on a Saturday?"

He hated being called Pete. I knew that; he knew that I knew that. Still, he flashed his best "trust me" smile. "Just here to say hello and get me one of those amazing blueberry muffins."

Yeah, sure. "Let me get that for you then."

With a smile, I placed a blueberry muffin in a to-go bag and handed it over to Peter. He paid and leaned across the counter. "Heard you came into a little bit of property. Twenty acres of prime Two Harts real estate, to be exact. Have you thought about what your plans are?"

"I am not interested in selling."

"Don't be hasty. Think about it." He snapped his fingers. "I heard Ollie has a grandson."

"Yes," I said warily.

"And that he also inherited Ollie's property."

"And?"

"I heard he'll be around for the next six months. Gonna have to introduce myself to him."

"We are not selling," I said firmly, ignoring the sick feeling in my stomach. "You can stop asking. It's not happening."

Peter smiled. It was not a nice smile. "We'll see."

Whistling, he grabbed his muffin and sailed past Iris to the door.

She shivered. "Did anyone else feel that chill? It was like a sheet of ice passed right in front of me. Mama says that's what it feels like when a demon passes by."

"Shut up, Iris," he growled.

"Oh, Peter. I didn't see you there." She smiled sweetly.

He muttered something about evil waitresses before the door shut behind him.

The morning melted away quickly. The café filled up, a few people passing through from Houston. The group of old men from town who practically made their home at the Sit-n-Eat huddled around two tables where they'd nurse a cup of coffee for two hours. Sometimes they brought out a chess board to keep them busy. They took up space for other paying customers, but they also liked to give Iris a hard time and that was worth it.

It was eleven o'clock before the anxiety started to kick in. Anytime now, Gilbert Dalton would be here. In Two Harts. For the next six months.

"Miss Ellie, Miss Ellie," a voice called about three seconds before a pair of strong arms wrapped around my waist. "I missed you."

"Girl, I missed you, too." I smiled down at Annie Littlefoot. Annie was in her thirties. Short and stout with bright-red hair and the biggest smile around, she'd never met a stranger. She also had Down syndrome.

Her face split into a wide, devilish grin. "I have a boyfriend now."

"Annie, he's not your boyfriend," her father, Malcolm, said, coming up behind her. Once upon a time, Malcolm had been a writing professor before retiring to Two Harts where he'd grown up. Before that, Annie had lived at home but when her mother passed away, she'd moved to a group home.

It had been a hard transition from what I could tell. Annie had changed homes three times over the last two years but seemed to have settled into the one she was at now. Still, she was over two hours away. Although he had turned eighty last year, Malcolm made that trek every week so Annie could come home for the weekend.

"Hi, Ellie," Malcom said.

Annie crossed her arms and glared at her father. "Yes, he is. He took me on a date. We went bowling."

"Honey, he works there. It's his job to take you bowling."

"Whatever, Dad." Annie plopped into the booth at their regular table.

"I'm too old for this," Malcolm said quietly so only I could hear. "She needs her mother for this."

I patted his shoulder. "You're doing great."

"Sure wish she were closer," he said. "That drive through Houston is enough to give me a heart attack."

I took their order, got a smile out of Annie, and did a round with the coffee pot. Just as their order was ready, my phone vibrated with a message. I pulled it from my back pocket and stared down at the notification from a number I didn't recognize.

"You okay?" Malcolm asked when I set his chorizo and cheese breakfast burritos in front of him.

"Totally okay. The okay-iest of okays."

Malcolm hummed. "If you say so."

"I do. Of course I do. Why wouldn't I be okay?"

My phone vibrated again. I marched back to the kitchen and opened my messages.

UNKNOWN NUMBER: *Hello.*

ME: *Who is this?*

UNKNOWN NUMBER: *This is Gilbert Dalton. I got your number from the attorney.*

ME: *Right. Gil.*

GILBERT: *Gilbert.*

ME: *That's what I said.*

GILBERT: *No, you said Gil. My name is Gilbert.*

My mouth twitched. For some reason, I could picture him

frowning, all stern-faced and laser-eyed and school principal-like, annoyed at me for daring to call him something other than his full name.

ME: *So I've heard.*

I swore I could hear his sigh of exasperation via text.

GILBERT: *I'll be in town around 2 p.m. Don't worry; I have a tent.*

ME: *Roger that, Gil.*

He did not respond back. I saved him in my phone as PRINCIPAL GIL.

NINE

Love is when you like something really much.

—MERIC, AGE 9

By the time I closed up the café, prepped as much as I could for Monday, ran a couple of errands, and made it back home, it was after two. Gil was already there.

I had a feeling Gil was never late for anything.

If his car in the driveway wasn't enough of a clue, when I went to change into something that didn't smell like maple syrup and bacon, I saw the tent. In fact, it was hard to miss seeing as he'd erected it to the right of the broken-down trailer, about twenty yards from the house, and directly in front of my bedroom window.

The tent was neon-highlighter yellow, so bright it probably glowed in the dark. It was smaller than I expected, big enough for perhaps two adults with a little neon-yellow awning over the entrance. Beside it, he'd placed a camping chair (blue, not yellow) with what looked to be a portable firepit in front of it.

It was early February. In Texas, that could mean anything

from twenty degrees to eighty. Thankfully for Gil, it had been a mild winter, and the temp hovered around sixty-five. Perfectly acceptable tent weather. Even if it was supposed to dip into the forties tonight, he'd be fine.

Probably.

Oliver had his face pressed against the large window that faced the backyard when I made it back to the kitchen lugging a basket of clothes to throw in the wash. "That's a cool tent, Mommy. Look!"

"I saw it."

"Can we go say hi, please?" He bounced over to me. "Pretty please?"

I guess it would have to happen sooner than later. With a sigh, I set the basket of clothes on the kitchen counter and ushered Oliver to the side door. But when I opened it, Gil was in front of it, a hand raised to knock.

I startled and then got annoyed I'd been startled. "What do you want?"

"Thank you for such a warm welcome," he said dryly. "I was hoping I could see the kitchen and bathroom since I'll need to use them. My tent didn't come with plumbing."

"Right. Come on." I stepped aside and let him into the kitchen. I may want him to sleep outside for Oliver's safety, but I'd already come to terms with the fact that he would need to use the bathroom and kitchen. I didn't have to be happy about it, though.

Oliver pressed against my side. I put a hand on his head. "This is Oliver. Oliver, this is Mr. Dalton."

Gil crouched down to Oliver's level. "It's nice to meet you."

"You, too. I like your tent. It's the same color as a banana. Is yellow your favorite color? My favorite color is red or sometimes blue," Oliver said. "When I grow up and go be a pale-tologist and study dinosaurs, I'm going to live in a tent. Maybe just like yours."

"You like dinosaurs?" Gil asked.

Oliver was obsessed with dinosaurs. Everyone told me he'd get over it and move on to something else. But he seemed to double down. He'd had three straight years of dinosaur-themed birthday parties. His favorite book was a giant encyclopedia of dinosaurs. All his pajamas had dinosaurs on them at his insistence.

Oliver nodded. "I love dinosaurs. I'm gonna go get my favorite dinosaur toy and show you."

Before anyone could say another word, he took off, his feet pounding through the house.

"No running," I yelled.

"'Kay." The pounding stopped and then started up again, a little less loudly.

Gil stood up slowly and faced me. "Cute kid."

"Yeah, he is. And he's sweet and wants to be everyone's friend," I said, giving him a pointed look.

He held up a hand. "I get it."

"Good."

"Great." Our eyes met and I got a wobbly sort of feeling in my stomach. Frowning, I looked away and crossed my arms; he rubbed the back of his neck.

"I guess I should give you the tour." I'd spent time after Oliver went to bed last night tidying up as best I could, but I knew the house was... unique. I waved a hand around the room. "This is the kitchen."

It was my favorite room in the house. Right out of a nineteen sixties design magazine, with lime-green Formica countertops, oak cabinets, and dark-green linoleum floors. You'd think since I spent so much time baking for the café, I'd be tired of kitchens by the time I got home, but all the best things happened in kitchens.

Families congregated, food was cooked and enjoyed, people talked and laughed, milestones were celebrated. At least that's how it had always been at my house growing up. In the kitchen, I'd felt one step ahead of the rest of my siblings. My brother could brag about winning a football game, my sisters about an art project or basketball game or grades, but me? I could brag about two things: drama club and baking.

I turned to ask Gil if he planned to cook a lot and found him standing in front of the wall above the little round kitchen table, arms crossed as he studied the wall.

"What is this?"

"Oh, that." I moved next to him. "It's something to keep me organized."

It had been Sunny who suggested I might have ADHD and encouraged me to seek a diagnosis. That had been a huge step for me. And, let's face it, it explained a lot. But a diagnosis was just that... it wasn't a cure. So, Sunny helped me find ways to calm myself when the overwhelm overtook me. She helped me set up systems. Some of those failed spectacularly and some of them I'd adopted as part of my life.

This one had worked.

I'd used painter's tape to create three connected boxes. One labeled TODAY, another said SOON and yet another said FUTURE. Each box held brightly colored sticky notes.

One task per note. The TODAY box was only allowed to have three notes at any given time. But the other two boxes were crowded with sticky notes upon sticky notes, hastily scribbled tasks I needed to complete. Things like all my hopeful house projects, a reminder to pay a bill or make a dentist appointment. But it was only the TODAY box I had to worry about. Three little notes I could do right now. When I cleared one off, I found another to replace it.

Today's three notes:

- Make two pies for church potluck tomorrow

- Grocery list
- Two loads of laundry

The visual helped.

So did medication.

It wasn't a secret I had ADHD, and it was nothing I was embarrassed about. Which made the curl of discomfort in my stomach all the more surprising. Why did I care what Gilbert Dalton thought of me? He glanced at me, his eyes more curious than anything, and I opened my mouth, ready to defend myself.

"It's smart. Good idea."

That took the wind out of my sails. "Oh, thanks."

I snatched the note about the grocery list from the wall and crumpled it up. It always felt satisfying to throw one of these away. A mini hit of dopamine, I guess.

I scanned the SOON box, passed over GET OIL CHANGE and HAIRCUT and FINISH MOM'S SLIPPER. Reaching across Gil, I pulled off the note that said GET V DAY CARDS FOR O'S CLASS and stuck it in the TODAY box.

Gil turned toward the kitchen. "Am I allowed to store food in here?"

I marched to the cabinet on the right of the stove, a cabinet I didn't use much because the middle shelf was missing one of those pegs that kept it level. If the items weren't balanced just so, they'd all fall out when the cabinet opened. He could have that one.

"Only because I don't want to attract the coyotes with food outside."

He froze at the word coyote. "Thanks."

I quickly pulled out the paper goods I had stored in it. "Is that enough room or do you require half the cabinets?"

"That's fine."

"Great." I grabbed a sticky notepad—I kept them everywhere to make sure I could write things down as I remembered them—and wrote GIL. I stuck it on the cabinet.

He scowled. "Gilbert."

"Close enough." I popped the lid back on the pen. "Let's go see the rest of the house."

As we passed the window looking out on to his tent, Gil asked, "There aren't really coyotes out there, are there?"

"Oh, no. I mean, probably not." I bustled out of the kitchen without looking back. That way he couldn't seem my fiendish grin.

We trooped through the living room and to the hallway where the bedrooms were.

"Is this a sliding glass door in the middle of the house?" Gil asked.

"What? You don't have one of these in your house?" I patted the door, which we always kept open.

A hundred years ago, this house had only two rooms. Over the years, each generation had added onto it without any real concern for aesthetics. This was a house built for practical purposes.

"The dining room and this formal living room were added on in a renovation in the sixties. They never bothered to take out the sliding glass door when they did it."

"Huh."

"Gives it character, don't you think?"

I liked to think of it as a Franken-house, parts pieced together with screws and nails. Not pretty, but it did the job. There was a certain charm in it, quirky though it might be. Some part of me felt a little like this house. I often felt like a Franken-woman, pieced together from all my dumb life choices.

Sunny said I needed to give myself grace. I bet Sunny's man picker was working just fine, though.

"There are four bedrooms. Oliver has the smallest one,

there. Mine is next to his." I paused and slid him a sideways glance. "It has a very sturdy lock on it, too."

"Don't lock it on my account," he muttered.

"The one at the end is Ollie's room. I haven't been in there since, you know. It didn't feel right." Pushing aside a wave of sadness at the thought of Ollie, I patted the door across from mine. "This is a spare bedroom. For guests."

He pressed his lips together but didn't say a word. He wanted to though, I could see it in his eyes, the way they fairly glistened with sarcasm.

I opened the next door. "And this is the only bathroom. At least for now. I think there might be one in Ollie's room, though."

The bathroom was very... pink. Pink tile, pink bathtub, pink sink, pink flowered wallpaper, pink curtain. It was a lot of pink. Maybe he wouldn't notice.

"This is very... pink."

"Oliver and I call it the pink palace. It even has a throne." I pointed at the toilet and snickered.

Unamused, Gil stood in the middle of the bathroom and turned in a slow circle.

"It used to have pink carpet. That was one of the first things I removed when I could."

He stared at the tub. "Where's the handle for the faucet?"

I picked up a pair of pliers I kept on the lip of the bathtub. "It broke off, but this works well enough."

I hedged around him, brushing his shoulder, and showed him how easy it was. Except it took me four tries and one hard yank before the water sputtered out. Gil's look said he wasn't impressed.

"Is there something wrong with the floor?" He pressed the tip of his shoe into the cheap linoleum that had been under the carpet. I was sure there was a lot of water damage under that. Probably mold. Maybe a large family of armadillos.

"That's nothing. You should see the living room floor." Whoops.

"What?"

"These old houses. So many quirks. That's what makes them special."

His hands went to his hips and his frown deepened. "Right."

"Lots of potential, don't you think?" I led him out of the bathroom as Oliver barreled out of his room, waving a plastic figure in his hand. "Mr. Dalton, this is my favorite dinosaur."

"Velociraptor, right?" Gil said.

"If you want, you could come play with me later. I'm doing Dinosaur Extincting."

"No," I said firmly to Oliver. "Mr. Dalton isn't here to play. He lives outside. We live inside. We can be polite, but we aren't... friends."

Oliver's forehead wrinkled. "But why not?"

How to answer that one? I pulled out the trusted answer parents had used for generations. "Because I said so. Go on back to your room." I patted him on the head. "I'll come play with you in a few minutes, okay?"

His shoulders drooped. "Yes, ma'am." He walked, albeit slowly, down the hall and disappeared into his room.

Gil stopped in front of the only door I hadn't addressed, his hand going to the doorknob. "What's in here?"

Without thinking, I threw myself in between him and the door and wrapped my fingers around his wrist. He froze. We stared at each other for a long beat.

He smelled good, like the expensive laundry detergent I only splurged on when the budget allowed, and I had a fleeting thought of leaning in and taking a bigger whiff. The urge was so strong, I pressed my back against the door to put more space between us. No smelling the enemy. I needed to remember he wanted to sell my house.

"This is nothing. Just a little closet. Let's go see the living room."

"But I want to see what's in this closet."

"No, you don't. It's just... stuff."

"What kind of stuff?"

My secret shame. Every single craft project I'd ever started... and never finished. So many skeins of yarn. So many. An embroidery machine. Two dozen plates I had been excited to hand-paint... for about a week. That was just the beginning. "Stuff?"

"Are you asking me?"

"No. It's just some stuff I collect." With a wobbly smile, I put a hand on his chest and patted reassuringly.

The corner of his mouth twitched and if I didn't know better, I would say he was almost amused. "You aren't collecting human skulls, right? Roadkill? The skin of your former roommates."

I scowled. "If I were going to collect anything like that, it would be jewelry made from human hair. I saw this video about it. It used to be popular in the eighteen hundreds. After someone died, they'd collect some hair and make brooches and necklaces and rings. You would never guess it was made of hair. Pretty amazing stuff. I'll send you a link to the video."

He didn't make a sound, just stared at me like I'd grown a third eye. Just as well. He should probably know now I could be... eccentric at times. His chest expanded with a breath, and I realized my hand still rested there, against the warm, solid wall of his chest.

Objectively, he was handsome if you liked uptight, principal types with hints of gray in their hair and dark-rimmed glasses and nice hands. Some people might even say he was a ten. But he was also here to take my dream away from me. Minus eight points. Plus, he ate plain oatmeal *on purpose*. Take away another three points. Which makes him a negative one. So there.

I snatched my hand back like I'd touched a hot oven. "Let's finish this up, okay? I have things to do." I slid out from between him and the door and hustled down the hallway and back to the kitchen. "Oliver and I moved in about three years ago. Honestly, I think Ollie might have been a bit of a hoarder, but we'd been making real progress getting everything sorted. Still have more work ahead of us, but that's okay. I don't mind the hard work. This house is worth it."

"Is it?" He leaned back against a kitchen counter. "This place is a dump. Everything needs to be updated. It would be better to sell it as-is and move on."

My hands balled into fists. I forced myself to take a deep breath. "This house is over a hundred years old. Generations of *your* family have lived here."

"My family?" he scoffed. "You need to get something straight right now. I'm not going to agree to keep this house or the café or anything else."

"You aren't the only one who gets to make the decision," I said, trying to keep the outrage out of my voice. "I own half of it."

And I can't afford to buy him out for the other half.

A mulish expression settled on his face, the one that reminded me of Ollie, and I had a flash of a dark-haired little boy who'd been told his favorite sweater vest was dirty and he couldn't wear it to school. "So do I."

"I know that." I took a step forward, poking him in the chest. "And you know what, it's not fair. You didn't even know Ollie. You are—were—his grandson. How can you just take one look at this house, this legacy he left to you, and decide you don't want it? This is part of your heritage. Aren't you even a little curious?"

"I'm curious about the money I'll make when we sell it."

"I am not selli—"

"And I sure as hell don't want to keep a house I can't even sleep in."

I let out a frustrated growl. He was right. It was unfair of me. He wouldn't get anything out of keeping the house. I hated that he was right.

"Fine. I know you probably think I'm some selfish brat and you know, maybe I am right now. But I loved Ollie." My voice caught when I said his name. "You didn't even know him, and he still wanted to give you this. Give it a chance, at least."

"A chance to what? Get to know a man who abandoned my grandmother and my mom? Doesn't sound like the kind of guy I want to know."

"Ollie didn't abandon them," I said fiercely. But truly, I had no idea what Ollie's story had been. No one did, but the Ollie I knew wouldn't have done that.

"You don't know that." He took a step back, his dark-blue eyes like lasers burning into my skull. "And you don't know me."

With a jerk, he opened the door. I jumped when it slammed shut.

TEN

Love is when my parents stay in my room with me at night because they know I'm afraid.

—DAELYN G., AGE 12

I fumed while I folded the clothes. I fumed while I made dinner. I fumed when Oliver got water all over the floor during his shower. I was one big fuming... fum-er.

Sunny would say I should just go talk to the guy. But you know what? Sunny hadn't known Ollie, hadn't worked with him and lived with him and loved him like my own grandfather. Sunny couldn't expect me to accept Gilbert Dalton with open arms.

She would expect that. Because, she'd say, it was the mature, adult thing to do. "Communication is the key to any relationship," she liked to remind me.

Why did I have to be the adult? It wasn't like Gil had come back with his tail between his legs and apologized for storming out. Oh, no. He'd gone and started a fire, roasted some hot dogs, and last I looked, he was settled in that camping chair, reading a book with the aid of a lantern and book light. Not that I was checking on him. Because obviously I was not. He just happened to be in my line of sight. Or whatever.

Ugh. I guess I'd have to be the adult.

After Oliver was tucked in around seven-thirty, I pulled on a hoodie and slunk outside to the backyard. Gil was still reading. I crept closer; he didn't look up. I cleared my throat; he held up a finger in the universal sign for 'one moment.'

With a sigh, I crossed my arms and waited. The temperature had dipped to the low fifties. I shivered and stared out in the backyard and the twenty acres beyond. Aside from the campfire, Gil's lantern, and the glow from the house windows, it was inky black, but I knew what was out there. It was rare to find a piece of property this big so close to town nowadays, but it had been in Ollie's family for over a century. Out there was an old, decrepit barn, a couple of rusted cars, an old trailer, and acres and acres of all the overgrown grass, weeds, and bushes a snake in Texas could ever want.

But if I looked beyond the junk where the grass waved in the breeze and old-growth oak and magnolia trees stood tall and wildflowers popped up unexpectedly, there was a beauty to it. Having grown up in the suburbs, I loved the idea of Oliver having space to run and explore and play and be excited about a new rock or hiding place he found.

Ollie had given that to him. My heart twisted with both grief and gratitude. Even from Heaven, Ollie was looking out for Oliver. And me, too.

Finally, Gil stuck a bookmark—a real bookmark, he didn't even dog-ear the pages like I did because I was forever losing the bookmark—in the book and snapped it shut.

"Did you need something?" he asked, his voice polite and detached.

"I have a list." I pulled said list from my pocket.

He raised a dark eyebrow. "Of what?"

"Rules," I said firmly and handed it over.

Gil opened it, snapping the paper taut. "Number one: the house doors are locked at nine each night."

"I think that's fair. We're an early-to-bed, early-to-rise family."

"What if I need to use the bathroom in the middle of the night?"

I waved a hand around. "There's twenty acres out there. Pick a tree."

"Classy." He read again from the paper. "Number two: the house will be unlocked by five in the morning."

"Probably a little earlier. I usually leave around a quarter to. The café opens at six."

Gil nodded. "Number three. Please shower during the day when the house is empty."

"There's only one bathroom," I said. "So that would make things easier." And we wouldn't have any awkward "oh, I didn't know you were here and I'm standing in just a towel" moments.

"Number four: I am not your mama." He looked up. "That's not a rule."

"It means I am not doing your laundry, cleaning up after you, or making your meals. I already have a kid."

He handed the paper back. "Anything else?"

I took it and stuffed it back in my pocket. "Not at the moment but I reserve the right to add more rules at a later date."

His head tilted to the side. "What about me? Do I get to add rules?"

"I'll think about it." I took a step back. "I'll let you get back to whatever you were doing."

With an awkward wave, I turned on my heels and headed back to the house. A brisk wind rustled my hair and brought goosebumps to my legs. It had cooled down a lot since the sun had gone down. I shivered at the thought of sleeping outside, even in a tent. Having been raised in the South, if it wasn't exactly seventy-three degrees, I was too hot or too cold.

I slowed my steps and peeked over my shoulder. Gil had his face buried in his book again. Would he be warm enough?

No, that was not my problem.

But also, I was trying to be an adult about the whole situation. Being an adult was so... annoying. With a sigh, I turned around. "Are you warm enough? Do you need any blankets?"

Gil looked my way. "Now you're worried about me?"

"No, I'm not worried about you. But I don't have time to deal with a dead body in my backyard. Took forever to bury the last one."

"Funny," he said and if I squinted, I thought he might be smiling. "I'm fine. Don't worry about me. I have plenty to keep me warm."

"Okay." I took a step backwards. "Well, good."

I could still leave a couple blankets out on the back porch. Just in case.

"Night, Eleanor."

I scowled at the use of my full name. Only my mom called me that and it usually involved yelling at me until next Tuesday. "Night, Gil."

ELEVEN

Love is a feeling. That's all.

—JOSEPHINE, AGE 12

From the sticky note correspondence of Gilbert Dalton and Ellie Sterns:

Eleanor—

What's the Wi-Fi password?

—Gilbert

P.S. Thanks for the extra blankets.

Gil—

Glad you asked. I just changed it.

Password: YouNeedToPayForHalfOfThis

(Caps sensitive)

—Ellie

P.S. I left them outside for the feral cats that come around. But I guess it's okay if you use them.

"So, what's he like?" Ali asked. She was sprawled on the oversized sectional couch in Chris and Mae's living room. A room that had been stripped to its bones as soon as Chris bought the place.

The previous owners had been into Hunter Chic, which I didn't even know was a thing until I saw the house for the first time. Let's just say there were a whole lot of stuffed animals. The dead, glassy-eyed kind. All of them found new homes except for Chuck, the nine-foot moose that lived in their over-sized living room with the vaulted ceiling and huge stone fireplace. Mae claimed some kind of sentimental feelings toward it; Chris said he had no idea how the moose got into the house and even less of an idea of how to get it out.

They decorated Chuck for the holidays. Twinkle lights at Christmas, an Uncle Sam hat for Fourth of July, that sort of thing. Right this minute, paper hearts hung off his antlers in honor of upcoming Valentine's Day.

He was staring at me right now. His mournful dark eyes seemed to say, *How did my life turn out this way?* Chuck and I —we were kindred spirits, I think.

I fisted the throw pillow on my lap. "He's a jerk."

Mae paused in her total demolition of a plate of loaded nachos which she'd rested on the top of her pregnant stomach like it was a shelf. "Iris said he's hot."

"Iris says a lot of things," I muttered. "He's very... uptight."

"Oh? Uptight how?"

I shrugged. "I don't know. Doesn't seem overly friendly, stern. He probably irons his underwear and socks. That kind of uptight."

"Frankie said he seemed pretty decent," Ali said. Frankie, the deputy who'd come to the house that night, was also Ali's brother. Everyone was related to everyone in this town if you dug deep enough.

"Oh, you mean when he broke into my house?"

"Technically, his house too," Ali said.

I glowered at her. "I don't like him. And he didn't seem to like me much either."

"Oh, please." Ali reached over, rather bravely I might add, to steal a nacho from Mae's plate. "Everyone likes you."

Mae slapped her hand. "Mine. Get your own, lady."

"Wow." Ali leaned back. Probably in fear. "Is this the pregnancy talking?"

Mae hunched over her plate like a pit bull on yard duty. "I don't know what you're talking about."

"I'm talking about the crazed look in your eye right now. That kid is sucking all the nice out of you."

"Then what's your excuse?" She dug out a chip and shoved it in her mouth.

"Okay, now," Ali said. "We have been friends, *best friends*, forever, but don't think I won't fill the library with balloons one night to annoy you."

"That's the best you got?"

"No," Ali said, all wide-eyed innocence. "That would be the beginning."

Mae sneered. "I dare you."

Ali crossed her arms and glared at her best friend. Mae was usually the voice of reason around here. She was cool-headed, calm. As the town librarian, she'd had to deal with budget cuts and the last mayor, Peter Stone, who'd also been her ex, on top of her mother's stroke, a deadbeat dad and, well, Iris. She could handle anything with poise.

But in the last couple of weeks, she'd gotten a little... emotional. Not just the crying, but the feral-ness of a woman who was so done being pregnant. I understood. I remembered that feeling of never being comfortable, always tired and hungry, and not sure if I needed a good cry or to kick someone's ass.

"Did I tell you about my last date?" I said, hoping to change the topic before it came to blows.

Mae shook her head and went back to her nachos. "How was it?"

"Terrible." I picked at the fringe on the throw pillow. "He left in the middle of it to fly across the country and profess his love to his ex-girlfriend."

The nacho fell out of Mae's hand as she stared at me. "That's bad."

"Cammie said he cried," Ali said. Being the mayor, she got all the good gossip practically hand-delivered to her.

"That's because my man picker is broken." I fell sideways, my head landing on the arm of the couch. "Maybe I'm broken. Maybe that's it."

"Ah, don't say that." Ali tugged on my foot. "You've just had a run of bad luck."

"That's lasted three years? Yeah, that must be it." I sat up slowly. "I've been thinking maybe I should take a break from dating. I've got Oliver and the café and now this whole house mess to sort out. I'm starting to think there aren't any more good guys left."

"They're still out there," Ali said. "Just last year you met that nice postman. What was his name?"

"Ah, Kyle." I sighed. "Turns out his wife had a problem with us dating."

"Oh, now I remember." Ali slumped in her seat. "You can't just give up."

"Yes, I can. I can just not go on dates anymore. It's that easy." Saying it out loud was almost a relief. Dating was exhausting, grueling work. I could work three weeks straight at the café and not be as tired as I was after a horrible date. "Maybe I'm not meant to have someone."

Mae placed a hand on my arm. "Why would you think that? You're wonderful. Any guy would be lucky if you chose him."

"I don't know if that's true." Because the truth was that I was kind of a mess, even on a good day.

"I know it's true." Mae turned to Ali. "We need a plan."

Ali tapped her mouth with a finger. "Yes, we do."

"Something to get her on the right track."

"I've got it." Ali grinned and shouted, "Hey Chris, where does Mae keep all the romance novels she pretends she doesn't read?"

"In the cabinets under the built-ins," Chris shouted back from the next room where he and Oliver were playing video games. "All of them. Full of romance novels."

"Excuse me." Mae sniffed. "I don't know what you're talking about."

Chris appeared in the doorway with a huge cat-that-ate-the-canary grin. "Aw, Sprinkles, you know exactly what I'm talking about."

He waltzed over to her, leaned down and whispered something in her ear that had her cheeks almost matching the red of her hair. With a gasp, she shoved his shoulder; he chuckled low, dropped a kiss on her forehead and stole a chip from her plate.

"You should check out the pirate ones by Alicia Night. They're Mae's favorite." Mae chucked a throw pillow at his head as he ambled away.

Ali skipped to the cabinets and came back with an armload of books. She dumped them on the couch next to Mae. "All the Alicia Night books."

I picked one up and stared at the pirate on the front cover, his shirt unbuttoned and billowing in the breeze. In his arms, a woman with long dark hair and one long leg peeking out from her dress. To be honest, I'd never been much of a reader unless it was a true crime novel.

"O-kay." I stared down at the pile. "So, ah, which one should I read first?"

"*The Pirate's Booty*," Mae and Ali said in unison.

"You've read it?" Mae asked, her eyes wide.

"Yeah." Ali's eyes darted to the left. "You know, in my spare time. Alicia Night is a pretty amazing writer. Really knows how to tell a story."

Mae's eyes narrowed. "Huh."

"What does that mean?" Ali asked.

"Nothing. Just huh." She shoved a chip in her mouth and smiled around it.

"So, *The Pirate's Booty* then." I plopped on the couch and stared at the book. "I'll give it a try. Although I've never been one for romances. People don't fall in love like that. Not in real life. Honestly, these things should be classified as fantasies."

Mae and Ali shared *a look*, the kind that communicated things only best friends could understand.

"I mean, sure," Mae said. "Love isn't exactly like the romance novels tell us it's going to be."

"No kidding." I set the book on the coffee table. "I, for one, have never been the recipient of a grand gesture."

Ali perched next to me on the couch. "Real love, truly loving and being loved by someone, it's better than anything in a romance novel. It's hard to put it into words what that feels like." She shook her head, a small, secret grin on her face. "It's magical."

I slumped back into the couch. "You're going to have to forgive me if I am leery of the magic of it all. You two seemed to have done that but I don't think it's in the cards for me. No one has ever been close to putting a ring on this finger, no pining or secret kisses. Definitely no meet-cutes. The last guy I met in the wild that seemed interested in me ended up trying to sell me cryptocurrency."

Ali winced.

"You should have all those things—the grand gesture, the proposal, the meet-cute," Mae said quietly. "The right man will want to do those things for you. It might not look exactly how you expect it to but he's out there."

Ali nodded. "Maybe you haven't been looking in the right places."

Mae set her plate aside. "Exactly."

"But how?" Ali murmured.

The two of them stared into the middle distance for what felt like an eternity. Then Mae snapped her fingers. "We should take over her love life."

"Of course." With a gasp, Ali jumped to her feet. "We could be matchmakers."

"Um, no. I told you, I'm giving up on dating."

They both ignored me.

"I love this idea," Mae said.

"We know the kind of guy she needs," Ali said, her eyes twinkling. "Kind and thoughtful and good with kids and loves her for just being her."

Mae nodded. "Not just loves her. She needs a man who is crazy in love with her. Who makes her smile and laugh and knows how to take care of her." Her eyes took on a dreamy haze and I knew she was thinking of my brother. To which I say, gross.

"Oh, yes." Ali sighed happily and clasped a hand over her heart. "A man who doesn't try to change her or fix her or anything like that."

Annnd now Ali was thinking of her husband, Theo. It was kind of annoying to have two of my closest friends be so terribly, horribly, irrevocably in love.

"We should make a list of potential men." Mae pulled out a

small notebook and a pen from her purse.

"Good idea." Ali paced the floor before she paused and snapped her fingers. "The new city planner in Brookshire is single. I met him last week at a countywide meeting and he wasn't bad. Put him on the list."

I groaned. Who wouldn't want to go out with a guy described as *wasn't bad?*

"You know, I bet Chris knows some single guys from the team who would make—"

I waved a hand. "Do I get a say in this?"

Like a weird, synchronized friendship bot, the two turned to me.

Mae blinked slowly and frowned. "I guess?"

"We should ask her questions, at least," Ali said. "For research purposes."

"Fine." Mae picked up the pen and scribbled something at the top of a new page. "What are you looking for?"

"Someone with a good job, likes children. It would be great if he already had a well-funded retirement plan and owned his own home. Someone responsible and reliable and loyal."

Ali's forehead wrinkled. "You're looking for a man, not a golden retriever, right?"

"Ha. Ha. Yes, a man. I'm not interested in anyone who drives a muscle car or a motorcycle. Definitely no one in a band. In fact, no musicians at all. Tattoos are not a plus. Drinkers, smokers, and wrestling fans need not apply."

"Chris likes wrestling," Mae said, rubbing the top of her stomach.

"What about hot?" Ali asked.

"Hot is nice but not necessary. Decent-looking is fine. No horns growing out of his head or whatever."

"Huh. That's a big no-go list." Ali frowned. "I feel like we're missing something."

Mae nodded. "We are."

With a sigh, I leaned back in my seat. "Look, y'all don't get it. It seems to me you both have made solid decisions when it comes to your love lives. But me? I know it's a joke, all these horrible dates I've gone on, but I can't seem to help it. I attract the wrong kind of men."

"That's not true." Mae placed a hand on my shoulder.

"Oh, but it is. If there were thirty good men in a room and one jerk, guess which one sees me and thinks, 'That's the one?' The jerk, and I follow right along because he picked me. For a little while, everything is good, and I feel like I'm special and loved. But then little things start creeping in, the little things that show I'm not really anything to them except for ways that are good for them. I'll let them borrow money or give them a good time and it blows up in my face every time. That's why, when I moved here to Two Harts, I promised myself I wouldn't put myself in that situation again. I want a good one this time and if that means I have to wait for it, I will."

Boy, o-boy, Sunny and I were going to have an epic session later this week.

"I'm so tired of the jerks." I stared at my hands clenched together in my lap. "I want a non-jerk. That's all. That's the only requirement."

The silence grew but I was afraid to look up and see pity in their eyes. Because that was surely what I would find there.

Ali's hand thumped on the table. "Ellie, I promise you we will find you the perfect non-jerk. He'll be the non-jerk of your dreams."

Warily, I lifted my head. "I don't know if this is a good idea."

"This is a great idea," Ali crowed. "Give us ten dates."

"Ten?" I shuddered. "No way. One."

"Eight." That was Mae, her game face set.

"One."

"Oh, come on," Ali said. "Okay. Six."

"One."

"Three," Mae said in her no-nonsense librarian voice. It was effective. "Final offer."

They glared at me, daring me to argue. I knew when I was beat. "Fine. Three dates. And that's it."

"Excellent." Ali rubbed her hands together in a way that strongly resembled an evil scientist.

"Why do I feel like I've just signed my life away or something?"

Ali smiled. With a lot of teeth. "I have no idea what you're talking about. You just made the best decision of your life."

TWELVE

Love is nice things, like giving people a hug.

—AUSTIN W., AGE 5

From the text conversation of Ellie Sterns and her mother:

MOM: *Good morning.*

ELLIE: *Hi mom.*

MOM: *I started my spring cleaning early. Do you know what I came across? That beautiful slipper you made for me a couple of years ago for Mother's Day?*

ELLIE: *Yes, I remember.*

MOM: *Do you think you'll be able to finish the matching slipper soon? It's okay if you can't. I know you're busy and that's why you could only finish one of them...*

ELLIE: *I promise I'll get it finished soon. I promise.*

MOM: *How soon is soon?*

Gil and I did a fantastic job of avoiding each other the first few days. He stayed out of my way; I stayed out of his.

Oh, don't get me wrong. I still noticed the ten-foot canopy he added next to the tent under which he placed a cooler, a small barbecue, and a folding table. He strung up fairy lights around the canopy and stretched an extension cord from an outside plug on the house to his camp where he could charge his phone, a laptop, and one of those fancy coffeemakers that made one cup at a time.

He'd made himself right at home out there.

But there were signs he'd been in the house when we weren't home—almond milk in the fridge, protein powder and oatmeal packets in his cupboard. (Yes, I peeked.) Sticky notes with questions were placed on the fridge so I was sure to see them. In fact, it was the only way we'd communicated with each other in three whole days. I approved.

On day three of his first week in the backyard, I drove home from work in a haze. Work had kicked my butt. Jorge had an existential crisis because we ran out of butter. Iris left an hour early for class. And me? Well, everything from my feet to my hair was exhausted. And let me tell you, exhausted hair is a sight to see.

Unfortunately, Oliver didn't get the memo about the day I'd had. He was practically vibrating in his car seat. I think it was the class birthday party at the end of the school day; there had been cupcakes.

"Mommy. Mom. Mommy. Mooom. Mommy."

"Yes, Oliver?" I said, trying to sound like the patient, calm mother I was most definitely not.

"Today Teacher read us a book about a family that goes to

the ocean, and they see all kinds of stuff like seashells and crabs and fishes and they made sandcastles and I asked Teacher if it was called sand because it's halfway between the sea and the land and she told me she didn't know but to ask you."

Thank you, Mrs. Sullivan. I'd have to get her a very special gift for Teacher Appreciation Week.

"Is that why it's called sand, Mommy?"

I knew he would keep asking until I gave him an answer. So, I did what most parents had been doing for generations when they were exhausted, and their feet hurt, and their kid was bouncing off the walls; I lied. "Yep. That's exactly why sand is called sand."

"I knew it." He shot a fist in the air in victory and settled into a moment of quiet. It didn't last. "Mom. Mom. Mommy."

"You know, you only have to say it once, kid. I hear you."

"Can we go to the ocean?"

"Sure. That would be fun." I turned down the private gravel road to the house.

"Soon?"

"Soon." Please. No more questi—

"Can I have a baby brother?"

I slammed on the brakes and used the rearview mirror to peer back at him. "What?"

Oliver's face was set in a serious expression. "I want a little brother. Uncle Chris says he and Aunt Mae are going to have a baby soon and I could borrow it sometimes, but I would like a baby brother of my own. Then I don't have to share."

A vein in my head began to pulse. That couldn't be good. After putting the car in park, I unbuckled and turned to see him better. "No, you can't have a baby brother right now."

He frowned but was blessedly silent for the twenty seconds it took to pull in under the carport and turn the car off.

Oliver hopped out of the car. Right before closing the door, he leaned in and said, "If it's too hard to get a baby brother, I guess a baby sister would do."

He skittered away before I could reply. I let out a tired laugh. "This kid."

When I got out of the car, he was waiting for me. "Mommy, what is that?"

At first, I wasn't sure what he was talking about. The carport was attached to the house on the side of the kitchen. It was big enough for two cars to park side by side. The right side, closest to the kitchen door, had always been my spot. Gil's car was parked on the left where Ollie used to park his ancient pickup. I followed Oliver to the other side of Gil's car.

"That, Mommy. Where did that come from?"

That was a shiny red and chrome motorcycle. I didn't know much about motorcycles but even I could tell this one was very nice. Past Ellie would have freshened up her lipstick and hunted down the owner of that motorcycle. Past Ellie would have been lulled by the siren call of a man who rode a motorcycle once.

Oliver's father rode a bike with blue flames on the side. The first time we went out, I'd picked the spot and packed the picnic, but he'd driven us there. That feeling of the wind whipping past mixed with that edge of danger? It has been like catnip for me.

Good thing I wasn't Past Ellie anymore.

"Is it Mr. Dalton's?" Oliver asked.

"I guess so?" The only thing more ridiculous than Past Ellie's mistakes was the thought of Gilbert Dalton riding a motorcycle. Did they make khaki-colored leather pants?

Oliver touched the seat. "I like it."

"No, you don't. Motorcycles are dangerous." And so are the men who ride them. "Come on, let's go figure out dinner."

. . .

Once again, I waited until Oliver was tucked in before making my way out to Gil's camp. Another camping chair had been added. Gil was standing with his hands on his hips, head tipped back to take in the dazzling display of stars.

"Whose motorcycle is in the carport?" I asked in way of greeting.

"Nice evening, isn't it?" he said. "So many stars. You don't see this many in the city."

"Rule number five: no motorcycles. I don't want Oliver around them."

He gave me a sharp look, made a little ghoulish in the flickering light from the campfire. Over his long-sleeved, navy t-shirt, he had a fleece vest. Practical, sturdy hiking books and jeans rounded out the outfit. He looked like the cover model for a magazine probably called *Camping Attire Monthly*.

"What's wrong with a motorcycle?"

"They're dangerous."

He scoffed. "They're perfectly safe."

"Is that thing even yours? There's no way you ride a motorcycle."

"Yes, it's mine and what does that mean?" He sounded more than a little annoyed.

"You don't seem like the type."

"What type am I, then?" He sat in a camping chair, stretched his legs out and crossed his ankles.

"The kind who remembers to change the batteries on your fire alarms every year whether they need it or not. I bet you get your car oil changed every three months to the day. You never remove the tags from your pillows."

"Yes, yes, and sometimes I do, if I'm feeling rebellious."

"You know what I mean," I said.

"I wear a helmet when I ride and follow all the traffic rules." He pointed at the empty camping chair. "You can sit."

I looked down my nose at him. "No, thank you. I didn't

come for a visit. I just wanted to know if I'm going to get a call they had to scrape you off the highway one day soon."

"Should I be concerned how many ways you've imagined my death?" he said and rested his folded hands across his stomach. "I know how to ride. Survived every time I've done it."

"Oh, okay." I rolled my eyes. "That makes it totally safe then."

His head tilted to the side. "Why do I feel like you're not going to be satisfied with any answer I give you?"

"I don't know. A moment of self-awareness. A realization that your heart might not be as dead as you think it is?"

"Who said my heart was dead? My heart is fine."

I crossed my arms. "Sure."

Both of us went silent. In the quiet of the moment, punctuated only by the sound of the crackling campfire, our eyes met. My skin prickled, and not from the cold. I resisted the urge to fidget. For one suspended moment, I wanted to know everything going on behind those eyes. What was he thinking about?

"The motorcycle is—was—my stepdad's," Gill said, quiet and low, breaking the silence. "A friend had a trailer and dropped it off for me. I'm selling it."

"Oh." I blinked, losing some of my bluster. "Was? Did your stepdad...?"

"He passed in November."

That was just three months ago. "I'm so sorry. Were you close?"

Gil's smile was small and sad. It slid into my heart like a warm knife in butter. "Yeah, we were close."

His gaze fixed on the flickering fire in front of us, staring off into memories I couldn't see. For a minute, I think he forgot where he was completely. Or that I was right next to him.

It gave me time to study him in the firelight. The dark hair not quite as neat and tidy at the end of the day, the merest hint of a five o'clock shadow, the way his mouth naturally turned down in the corners and gave him a resting frown face.

"Well, um, I'll leave you to it." I took a couple of steps backwards. "Night, Gil."

"Night, Eleanor."

After I closed up the house for the night and got into my room, I moved to close the curtains. But I couldn't resist looking outside once more. Gil was as I'd left him, sprawled in the chair, legs stretched out, and staring into the fire. Even through the window, I could feel his sadness.

THIRTEEN

Love is a feeling that you feel and it says that you like someone or something.

—SAVANNAH W., AGE 8

From the sticky note correspondence of Gilbert Dalton and Ellie Sterns:

Eleanor—

I'll be leaving this Friday afternoon and returning Sunday afternoon. Please refrain from holding a rave in my tent.

—Gilbert

Gil—

Just so I'm clear. No parties at your place?

—Ellie

P.S. Where are you going?

Eleanor—

No parties. PLEASE.

—Gilbert

P.S. Austin. I'll be going every weekend.

Gil, Gil, Gil—

Are you sure? I was going to make people pay a cover charge. I promise to follow a strict no-glitter policy.

—Ellie

P.S. What's in Austin?

Eleanor—

Hilarious.

—Gilbert

P.S. The state capitol building.

Gil had returned from his weekend trip with a free-standing hammock he set up in his compound.

And he got very busy while Oliver and I were away during the day.

On Monday, the kitchen faucet stopped drip-drip-dripping.

On Tuesday, the door to the clothes dryer no longer required duct tape to keep it closed.

On Wednesday, the overgrown bushes in the front yard had been neatly trimmed.

On Thursday, I went to see Sunny.

Sunny's office was twenty minutes down I-10 east in a little unassuming house that had been converted into an office building she shared with four other counselors. The waiting room was small but cozy. I checked in at the front desk. Only two minutes late today—that's what we called progress—and took a seat in the middle of a long row of chairs lined up against one wall. Generic prints dotted the beige walls. Four of them in total. The second to last picture was just a tiny bit crooked.

Four other people sat scattered down the row. A guy in a beanie with a jiggling leg stuck to his phone screen. A middle-aged couple who sat ramrod straight without touching. And a woman who looked in her forties and was in a sweater that would win an ugly Valentine's sweater contest. She also had on matching earrings. And a headband.

It was deathly quiet. People did not make small talk in the waiting room at a therapist's office. It wasn't like a dentist's office:

"What are you here for?"

"Just a cleaning."

No, the small talk at a therapist's office would go something like:

"What brings you in?"

"Oh, you know. Daddy issues with a strong side of social anxiety, negative self-talk, and an inability to hold meaningful relationships. You?"

I snorted and the couple's eyes swung my way. With a little wave, I settled back in my seat and clutched my purse to my chest. Before a therapy appointment, I was always nervous. Patience had never especially been a strong trait with me. But in this waiting room, it was worse for some reason. A million questions raced through my head.

What if I didn't have anything to talk about? What if Sunny didn't care about what I did have to talk about? What if Sunny didn't really like me and was only counting down the minutes until she could kick me out? What if I was so messed up, Sunny couldn't help me? What if this was all a waste of time? What if Sunny went home every night after my appointment and over two huge glasses of wine, she told Mr. Sunny all about her most messed-up patient?

It's weird I'm in therapy, right?

Intrusive thoughts aside, I'd been seeing Sunny for over two years. I'd learned a lot about myself—some things I liked, other things not so much.

"A huge part of therapy is gaining self-awareness," Sunny often pointed out. Sometimes self-awareness sucked.

One of the other therapists stuck her head into the waiting room. "Dolores?"

The woman in the ugly Valentine's sweater pushed to her feet and hurried across the room but she paused at the crooked picture. Quickly, she straightened it, sighing happily with her work, and continued to her session.

Sunny called me back a couple of minutes later. I plopped onto the oversized love seat and grabbed one of about a dozen throw pillows to hold on my lap. The office was small and cozy with soft colors and lighting. "A cocoon for feelings" Sunny had once described it.

Sunny settled into a matching chair across from me and picked up the notebook she scribbled in when we talked.

"How are you?" she said, arranging her skirt as she settled back into her chair. She liked broomstick skirts in bright colors and layers. Loose, linen shirts, and she especially loved a good crochet vest. She always smelled faintly of patchouli and sandalwood. My therapist was kind of a hippie.

"Okay." I played with the fringe on the pillow.

She waited me out. I had never been able to pinpoint her age, but it was somewhere between thirty-five and fifty-five. She had one of those smooth, unlined faces with big dark eyes and long flowing dark hair.

"There's a man living in a tent in my backyard."

She froze and slowly set her notebook on the coffee table. "Why?"

"You remember the appointment with the lawyer?" It was wild that appointment had been only two weeks ago. "Ollie had a grandson. No one knew about him. Ollie never said a word to anyone. But he knew about him. He left the café, the house, the property, everything to him and me. Fifty-fifty if we live on the property for six months."

Sunny leaned back in her chair. "And now Ollie's grandson is living in a tent in your backyard."

"Yes." I nodded firmly. "He's a total stranger. I didn't want a stranger living in the house with Oliver."

"What's his name?"

"Gil."

"What's he like?"

"He's quiet, kind of stern, keeps to himself. Doesn't smile much. But he's not awful, or anything. I don't think I like him."

Sunny hummed. "Really? That's surprising."

"Why?"

"You tend to like everyone. Why not him?"

I leaned my head on the back of the love seat and stared up at the ceiling. "He has no interest in keeping the house or the café. At the end of the six months, he wants to sell. It's been in his family for years and he doesn't seem to care at all."

"Has he told you why?"

"He said Ollie abandoned his grandmother and mother and he doesn't want anything to do with him." I bit the inside of my cheek. "I can't see Ollie being like that though. Wouldn't a normal person be at least curious to learn more about his family history, about this town and the café and Ollie? But nope, he's set on selling."

Sunny frowned. "But why would he want to keep it?"

"Because..." My mouth snapped shut. She had a point. I hated it when she had a point. He didn't have any emotional attachment to Ollie or the house or Two Harts. I sighed and hugged the pillow closer. "I guess when I say it out loud, it doesn't make much sense."

"How does that make you feel?"

The dreaded feelings question. "Horrible. Angry. Sad. Frustrated. That's the only home Oliver knows. We've been so happy there the last three years. Gil doesn't get that. He missed out on knowing Ollie." But there's another feeling, too. I was almost embarrassed to say it out loud. "A little selfish, too."

Sunny hummed. "Why's that?"

"I guess all I've been thinking about is how my life is changed by all this." But Gil had to be feeling some kind of way about gaining a grandfather and a chunk of property in the middle of Texas. He'd picked up his whole life and plunked it down in small-town Texas. In a tent. "I haven't thought about how this is all new to him."

Sunny arched one elegant, dark eyebrow. "That's good work, Ellie."

"Thanks," I muttered.

"What does Gil think about living in the backyard?"

"He... actually, he hasn't really complained at all." Thinking back, he'd agreed without much of an argument. "Why do you think that is?"

Sunny picked up her notebook. "Why do *you* think that is?"

"I hate it when you make me answer my own questions."

She grinned.

"I don't know. Maybe because of Oliver?"

"How so?"

"When he found out I had a kid, he agreed to the arrangement without even an argument."

Sunny wrote something else on her notepad. I liked to think

it was a grocery shopping list and not one more thing wrong with me. "That's rather respectful of him, isn't it?"

"Yeah, it is. He fixed the bathtub faucet, too."

"That's good, right?" Sunny asked.

"Sure, yes, of course. It needed to be fixed." I'd discovered it last night when Oliver was about to take a bath. That shiny new handle turned so easily. I hadn't realized how not-fun it was to wrestle with the pliers every day.

Sunny's gaze moved from her notepad to my face. Another moment of waiting me out. Ugh.

"The thing is... I think he hates me," I blurted out.

"Why do you think that?"

"Because." I shrugged. "He does. I can tell."

Sunny leaned forward, her dark shiny hair falling around her shoulders like a curtain. How does hair move like that? Mine took a hot iron and a lot of patience to wrangle into something mostly smooth and straight.

"I've known you for two years now, Ellie, and you are a hard person to not like."

"Stop. I'm blushing."

She smiled. "He does not hate you. You're getting to know each other and you both have a lot of big decisions to make. Together." Tapping her pen against her mouth, she sat back. "You know, maybe he's scared."

I snorted. "Of me?"

"Maybe not you exactly but that you are a big part of what his future is going to look like."

"But it's the same for me. I don't know what I'm going to do if he sticks to this plan to sell."

"I think you need to get to know each other. It's the only way this is going to work."

I frowned. "So how do I do that?"

"Ellie, my dear, it's easy. You rely on your strengths."

FOURTEEN

[Love is]... something single people think is foolish and even you think it's stupid, but you still want it.

—PATIENCE, AGE 16

From the sticky note correspondence of Gilbert Dalton and Ellie Sterns:

Eleanor—

Could you please move your clothing from the washing machine to the dryer? The same load has been in there for three days now.

—Gilbert

P.S. When do you have time to start cleaning out Ollie's room?

Gil—

Whoops. Sorry about that. Moved, dried, kind of folded
and put away.

—Ellie

P.S. Soon. Probably.

Eleanor—

What does "kind of folded" even mean?

—Gilbert

P.S. How soon?

Gil—

It means they're now in the clean pile, okay?

—Ellie

P.S. Soon is... soon.

"Mommy, do you think it's gonna snow?" Oliver blinked up at me from this bed, hope shining in his eyes.

"I doubt it, sweets."

Not snow, but the weather had turned chilly for the first time this winter. Yesterday had been a balmy seventy-one degrees with puffy, white clouds dotting a blue sky. After church, Oliver and I had gone to Legacy Park with a picnic basket and stayed for three hours. But as the saying goes, if you don't like the weather in Texas, wait thirty minutes, especially in early February. Sometime during the day, a fierce wind brought with it a biting chill. It would drop to freezing temps tonight.

Oliver's face fell. "I wanna see snow."

The dream of every kid in Texas.

"One of these days, you will. But not today. It is going to be cold though. We'll have to find your hat and gloves in the morning." I brushed his hair from his forehead and dropped a kiss. "Get some sleep. Love you."

He yawned and curled on his side, his eyes already drooping in the time it took for me to turn off the light in his room. "Mommy?"

"Yeah, buddy?"

"Do you think Mr. Dalton will be too cold tonight?"

"He'll be fine." He'd been living in that tent in the backyard for two weeks now and had not once complained about being cold. Or that he could only take showers during the day. Or that I locked the door to the house at night. Begrudgingly, I had to admit, it hadn't been so awful having him in the backyard, especially with the free handyman services that were included.

"Are you sure?" he asked sleepily.

To be honest, I'd had a fleeting thought or two about Gil and his tent. We lived in Texas, we weren't built for this kind of weather and I doubted that tent was insulated. "I'll check on him. Will that make you feel better?"

When he didn't reply, I realized he'd fallen asleep. I couldn't resist one last look, at the softly curling dark hair, or the freckles I called mini chocolate chips that dusted his face, the way his hands were tucked under his cheek.

The day I'd found out I was pregnant with him had been awful. I'd gotten into a fight with my idiot boyfriend, arrived late for my shift as a cocktail waitress because of traffic which resulted in a talking-to by the manager, got a lousy tip from a party of twelve, and ended up wrapped around a toilet puking my guts up after getting a whiff of an order of fish and chips.

I loved fish and chips.

The niggling thought I might be pregnant had dogged me all week, but I'd been too afraid to test. Avoidance by procrasti-

nation was an art form I excelled at. By the time I got home
from work, it was close to three in the morning. I'd tried to go
right to bed but I'd laid there for hours, knowing I had to take
the test. Blurry-eyed with exhaustion, I'd sat on the bathroom
floor, leaning against the bathtub, waiting for the results.

Two pink lines.

Oliver turned over on his back, kicking off his dinosaur
comforter in the process. I covered him up and tiptoed out of his
room.

Even though I had been terrified, I'd never thought for a
moment about not having the baby. He was mine from the
beginning. The best thing I've ever done.

I'd done it on my own, too. Oliver's father heard the words
"I'm pregnant" as a sign to disappear. My parents had been
supportive, but they lived across the country. Chris offered me
money; I only took what I absolutely needed, and I always paid
him back. But the nitty-gritty, every day of life? The waking up
four times a night. The feelings of inadequacy. Juggling two
jobs, babysitters, bills I couldn't quite pay, and always being one
flat tire away from total financial disaster. That I did all on
my own.

All worth it for Oliver. For that kid, I'd do about anything. I
tiptoed back across the room and was pulling the door shut
when I heard a tiny voice, "Don't forget to check on Mr.
Dalton."

FIFTEEN

Love is hugs.

—THEODORE D., AGE 4

Gil wasn't sitting out in his camping chair. Which was wise given it's not only cold but also starting to drizzle. I shivered and wished I had taken the time to put on a coat instead of a thin cardigan. A light shone from inside the tent, and it allowed me to make out the shape of Gil, sitting up. He was talking softly. Shamelessly, I crept closer.

"...sure you wear your big coat, okay?" he said. After a pause, he laughed softly. Must be on a phone call. "I'm doing great. The new house is nice, and I like my room a lot."

His room? Is that what he was calling his tent? Who was he talking to? His voice was gentle and measured; it reminded me of someone speaking to a child.

"Sure, I'll send you pictures of it." Another chuckle and then I heard my name. "Well, Eleanor has long blonde hair and blue eyes and a big smile." Pause. "You know, she does kind of look like a princess. You'd like her, I think."

I found myself biting back laughter. A princess, huh?

"Okay, yes. Love you, too. Sleep tight. Don't let the bed bugs bite."

The tent went silent. I waited a couple of beats before clearing my throat. "Gil?"

The tent flap unzipped, and Gil peeked his head out. He was wearing a hat with triangle ears and curly, white fur.

"What is that on your head?"

With a grunt, Gil snatched the hat from his head and climbed out of the tent. He had a lantern in one hand and the balled-up hat clenched in the other. "It's nothing."

"No, that was definitely something." I pointed at his hand. "I want to see."

"No."

"Please?"

"No."

I batted my eyelashes. "How can you say no to a princess?"

His eyes narrowed. "Were you eavesdropping?"

"I wouldn't call it that."

After setting the lantern next to the camping chair, he crossed his arms. The red and yellow flannel shirt he wore tightened across his shoulders. "I would."

Hadn't Sunny said I should get to know him better? Maybe this was my chance. I crept closer. "Who were you talking to?"

"None of your business."

"You realize you know way more about me than I know about you? You practically live with me."

He snorted. "Actually no, I don't. I live in a tent in the backyard."

"Come on."

With a shake of his head, he walked around me and headed for the carport and his car. I followed.

"Please?"

"You aren't going to stop asking, are you?"

I pretended to think about it. "Chances are slim."

"I was talking to my brother."

"Your brother?" I asked in surprise. A much younger brother from how Gil was talking to him.

"Yes, my brother." Abruptly, he stopped; I didn't.

With a surprised yelp, I smacked into his back and sort of bounced, my feet coming out from under me. I squeezed my eyes shut and braced for the fall, but it never came. The next second I slammed into yet another immovable object. When I opened my eyes, it wasn't the ground, it was Gil. Somehow, he'd spun around fast enough to grab my waist with his arm and prevent a fall.

Both of us froze.

We were chest to chest. I could now confirm he was as big and solid as he looked. The air around us seemed to crackle. I wondered if he felt that.

I lifted my eyes to his face. It was much too dark, but somehow, I knew he was looking right at me. My breaths came out in rapid puffs visible in the chilly air. I heard him swallow and he loosened his grip on my waist. Getting my feet under me, I pushed my hands against his chest to stand.

"Sorry about that," I said quickly, shuffling back a few feet. "Wasn't paying attention."

"Wasn't all your fault," he said in a way that sounded like he thought it was indeed all my fault. He stomped the rest of the way to his car and set the crumpled hat on top of it. "Did you need something?"

The sky began spitting rain. I ducked under the carport and leaned against my car. "Oliver was worried about you. I told him I'd check on you."

"I'm fine."

"Good." I stared down at my shoes. "It's pretty cold out."

"Yeah, it is."

I peeked up at him. "Can I ask you a question?"

"Will it make you go away sooner if I say yes?"

"Why haven't you asked to move into the house?" Since Sunny had mentioned it, I couldn't stop thinking about why he would do it. Why wouldn't he insist on using what was his?

"What?"

"I mean, half the house is yours. But you agreed to living out here without even arguing."

His head tilted to the side—I'd noticed he did that when he was thinking. "Because you have a kid."

"Sure, but a lot of people would never have agreed, even with a kid involved."

He shrugged. "It's not that big of a deal."

"Yeah, it is," I said quietly.

His chest rose and fell with a deep breath. "I was raised by a single mom until my stepdad came along. Guess I understand where you're coming from." He opened a car door. "And I work with kids. You did the right thing, putting Oliver first. I respect that."

"Oh. Thank you," I said. "That's kind of you."

"Not kind. Just the minimum needed to be a decent human." From the car, he pulled out a heavy winter jacket. The kind of jacket almost no one in our area of Texas bothered owning because the cold days were so few and far between. He slipped it on and zippered it. The tag dangled from the sleeve; he didn't tear it off.

"Then thank you for being a decent human." I wrapped my cardigan around me tighter.

"If we're done here, I'm going to bed." He ducked back in the car and pulled out a new pack of socks, the thick, heavy kind.

A twinge of guilt tickled my brain as I shivered against the cold. The cold Gil was going to be sleeping in. It had been over two weeks and well, he hadn't murdered us yet. I chewed on the inside of my cheek.

The slam of the car door brought me back to the present. Gil marched over to the tent. He'd left the hat on his car, so I snagged it and unfurled it. With a giggle, I put it on.

"A sheep hat, huh?"

Gil turned. "My brother likes sheep."

"Baa." But honestly, the thing was doing a good job of warming me up.

He unzipped the tent. "Goodnight, Eleanor."

"Night." I walked slowly back to the house, tugging on the flaps of the hat I'd taken with me. That twinge of guilt was quickly becoming an insistent pang. Could I ignore it? I could try...

With a groan, I turned back and stormed over to the tent.

"Oh, fine. You can sleep inside. But you get the clown room."

SIXTEEN

Love is friendship on steroids.

—OLIVER M., AGE 11

"This is the clown room." I opened the door to the bedroom across from my room and flipped on the light.

Gil set the backpack and pillow he'd brought with him from the tent and surveyed the room. There was a lot to take in. The usual—a full-size bed, a small nightstand and chest of drawers—but it was the other things that were less... usual.

"Are those dress mannequins?" He stared at the thirteen forms lined up against the wall like a headless army.

"Someone in Ollie's family..." I paused "...*your* family was a seamstress and owned their own shop. Or so I've heard. I guess this is where everything ended up when it closed. I wasn't sure where else to put them."

"And the walls?"

"There's a lot of wallpaper in this house." Although the wallpaper in this room was borderline terrifying. It was white with brightly colored circles intermixed with the faces of laughing clowns. Their eyes followed you around the room. I cleared my throat. "The clowns aren't so bad."

They were; they were so, so bad.

He slowly unzipped his coat and peeled it off, eyes still darting around the room, not sure where to land. Fair.

Not only were there clowns on the wallpaper, they were also on the curtains, the decorative pillows—and the entire wall of floating shelves was filled with more. There was even a handful behind a fancy display case. Dolls, figurines, a few masks. Some smiling, some with tears, most with a maniacal look in their eyes. I shivered, more than a little relieved I wouldn't be sleeping in this room.

I waved a hand toward the collection. "I tried to talk Ollie into getting rid of them, but he refused. Kept saying his mother had collected them and they might be worth something one day. Personally, I think we might have to pay someone to take them."

His gaze swung back to me, looking a bit ragged, to be honest. His hair was tousled, a piece in the back sticking up in rebellion. "Great. Yeah, great. I guess I can't see them when the lights are off."

"That's the spirit." I wouldn't mention the glow-in-the-dark ones right now. "You can move the rest of your stuff in tomorrow, I guess."

His gaze swung once more to the wall of horror. He scratched the back of his neck, shifting the collar on his shirt. For a nanosecond, I swore I saw the smallest bit of a dark swirling line, like a tattoo. I blinked and it was gone. Must be seeing things. If I'd ever met a person least likely to have a tattoo, it was this guy.

"Yeah, I'll do that." He tucked his hands in his pockets and met my eyes with sincerity. "Thanks for the room."

"No big deal. Thanks for sleeping outside." My smile was very small. "For understanding."

We both stood suspended in an awkward silence. Finally, I couldn't take the weird tension and hustled to the door.

"If you need anything tonight, I'm across the hall." I paused in the doorway and took the hat off. "Here. Your hat. Don't want you to lose that."

Gil strode to the door and took the hat from me, his fingers brushing mine. Only a foot of space stretched between us. I frowned as again I felt that crackling air around us. Slowly, he lifted a hand and brushed a piece of hair from my face. "Night, Eleanor."

Then he closed the door softly in my face.

SEVENTEEN

Love is where you can basically show how you feel like if you like somebody.

—GABRIEL E., AGE 9

From the text correspondence of Mae, Ali, and Ellie:

ALI: *Ellie, there's a rumor.*

ELLIE: *What now?*

ALI: *That you have a man living in your house.*

ELLIE: *I mean, Oliver is only six so I'm not sure I'd say man.*

MAE: *You're stalling. Just spill it.*

ELLIE: *Gil moved into the spare room. It's not a big deal.*

ALI: *Are you kidding? This is the biggest deal since the Warrens' cows got out and managed to make it all the way to town last month.*

MAE: *How's it working out?*

ELLIE: *So far, he hasn't dismembered me and hidden my body in the freezer.*

ALI: *That doesn't seem like his style. Poisoning though? Yeah.*

MAE: *It is too early in the morning for this.*

"You, young lady, have a date." Ali pointed at me across the counter.

"I do?" I set a plate of the heart-shaped pancakes Jorge always made specially the week of Valentine's Day in front of her.

"Yes, indeed. This is officially one of your three blind dates so you can't back out."

I groaned. "I totally forgot about that. Do I have to go?"

The last date I'd been on had been the day Gil showed up at the front door. Frankly, life had been hectic enough without dealing with my broken man picker.

"You are going. It's next month so you even have time to get excited about it." Ali pointed a finger at me. "Give him a chance. He's my choice, but Mae approved. Fully employed with a very nice benefits package. He has an accent, the cutest dimple, and oh, the dreamiest eyes."

"I'm sitting right here," Theo, Ali's husband, said. "You know that, right?"

Ali's face split into a grin. "Nobody's as dreamy as you."

"That's better." Theo winked. Ali leaned in and whispered something in his ear that I couldn't make out, but I swore I heard something about going on a "treasure hunt" and "x marks the spot." Whatever that meant made Theo blush. And then they were kissing. Right there at the counter at the Sit-n-Eat. That was my cue to walk away.

Iris passed behind me. "Ugh, they're insufferable."

"I think you mean inseparable," I said.

"Yeah, that too," she said over her shoulder. "Love sucks."

I made a mental note to ask Mae what exactly was going on between Iris and Aidan. Whatever it was sure wasn't improving Iris's attitude. She'd been a dark cloud the last couple of weeks, more than usual at least, and we'd had three customer complaints (which I filed in the garbage can). Iris played the tough girl but deep inside, she was all gooey marshmallow.

She'd slice me into a million pieces if she knew I even thought that about her.

A lull between breakfast and lunch hit around ten. I was working on refilling condiments, a job I detested for its tediousness, and Iris was handling the one table of customers, when Gil walked in. Instead of acknowledging me, he looked around the place, his gaze stopping briefly on a small grouping of photos that hung to the right of the cash register. After a moment of hesitation, he walked over and inspected them.

The photos featured the previous owners of the Sit-n-Eat, all from the Holder family. It had started in the nineteen thirties with Ollie's grandfather, then it was passed to his son, Ollie's father, and on to Ollie. Ollie was the last Holder anyone knew of. But there stood Ollie's grandson, staring at those photos with an unholy focus, like he was trying to will the people in those pictures to come to life. I wondered what he'd ask them if he could. I suspected there would be yelling and angry words.

But Ollie, what would Ollie say?

I walked to stand beside him and pointed to one of the photos. "That's Ollie in his twenties with his dad, Simon, and his mom, Margaret." The man next to a young Ollie was about

Ollie's height with a big, wide smile and an arm around the shoulders of a tiny woman with wispy dark hair. "And that"—I pointed to the next photo—"is Sinclair Holder. He started the Sit-n-Eat back in the day."

The photo of Sinclair was black and white, but he looked to be in his seventies and a carbon copy of Ollie around the same age. My gaze drifted from the photos to Gil. "You must take after your mom's side of the family."

He laughed without humor. "Yeah, maybe."

"Except the eyebrows. That is unfortunate." The heat from his glare smacked me in the face; I grinned. "So, what brings you here?"

"I own half of this place. I should do half the work, right?"

I gave his creased khakis and blue button-down a once-over and smirked. "Alright, then. I know you don't cook."

"I know how to make oatmeal."

"Nobody wants that." I tapped my chin with a finger. "What about taking orders? Ever been on a waitstaff?"

"I've never done it before, but I'm sure I can handle it," he said smugly.

With a snort, I shook my head. Why did people think being a server was easy? It was not. Not even close. I'd waitressed a lot in LA. Cheap bars, fancy restaurants, diners, cocktail bars. It was not easy. "It's not that simple, you know. How are your soft skills? Cleaning up spilled milk? Topping off coffee cups? Do you feel the customer is always right?"

His eyes drifted to the side, and he shifted on his feet. "I'm not exactly a people person."

"No biggie." Iris strolled by with a plate piled high with the hungry man special. "I'm not a people person either."

We watched as she practically slammed the plate in front of Griffin Jones. "There. Eat, old man."

Griffin snatched his fork from the table and glared at her. "You'll not get a tip from me with that attitude."

Iris rolled her eyes. "Well, since you still tip like it's nineteen sixty-two, I guess I'll have to earn those ten cents from someone else."

"Mouthy brat."

"Senile goat."

Suddenly, Griffin grinned and pushed his coffee cup toward the edge of the table. "Top off my coffee for me, would you?"

Iris sighed with feeling. "I guess." But she winked at him as she strolled away to grab the coffee.

Griffin's grin widened, showing off the dentures he'd gotten last month. "I do like the feisty ones."

Gil frowned. "Maybe not customer service."

"Right. Come on. Let me introduce you to Jorge and then you can learn how to top off the ketchup bottles. It's fun, I swear."

EIGHTEEN

Love is a thing that we use to make relationships, we wouldn't have Valentine's Day without it.

—JORDAN C., AGE 9

From the group text of Ellie and her sisters:

BETSY: *I hate Valentine's Day.*

AGGIE: *Aw, come on. All the chocolate…*

BETSY: *I didn't say I hated Valentine's candy. That's what February 15th is for. I love Discount Candy Day.*

MILLIE: *Caleb sent me roses.*

BETSY: *Of course he did.*

MILLIE: *We're going to dinner tomorrow. He's driving up* *from Dallas and he made reservations at a fancy restaurant and everything.*

ELLIE: *Why did I even bother to check what you all were talking about? Millie, read the room. No one wants to hear about your perfect boyfriend and your perfect relationship.*

AGGIE: *How are you really feeling there, El?*

ELLIE: *It's fine. I'm fine. Everything is fine.*

Oliver threw himself down, making the entire bed shake. Two little hands pushed against my shoulder. "It's Balentine's Day, Mommy. Time to get up."

I groaned and cracked one eye to find him grinning down at me. He'd lost four front teeth within weeks of each other and seeing that gap-toothed smile always brightened my day. Except when it was before my 4 a.m. alarm.

"Sir. We have talked about waking Mommy up before the alarm goes off."

He stuck out his bottom lip. "But it's a holiday."

"It's not Christmas." I pulled my phone from the nightstand. Three fifty-two. There was something wrong about waking up minutes before the alarm went off. Like I'd been robbed of the best eight minutes of sleep in my life. "There are no presents under a tree."

"You neber know," he said with a sly little smile. "There could be presents."

Not for me, kiddo. I had one Valentine this year and he was the cutest one to have ever walked this earth.

Oliver put his hands on my cheeks. "Mommy, who's your Balentine?"

"You are, of course. You're so sweet, I could eat you up." I sprang up and enveloped him in a monster-sized hug, lifting him clean off the bed and pretending to chomp at his neck. My heart squeezed at his giggles.

He flopped down on the bed next to me, all rosy cheeks and sparkling eyes. "Gotta get dressed and make sure all my Balentines are in my backpack."

I saluted him. "Get to it. Be extra quiet so we don't wake up Mr. Dalton though, okay?"

Gil moving into the house hadn't been the big adjustment I was worried it might be. It had been two weeks and we rarely saw him. Oliver and I were up and out of the house before he woke up, and in bed early. Gil, for his part, spent the evenings in his room.

Grinning, Oliver hopped off the bed and scurried to the door but just before he made it, he turned. "Mommy, I love you."

"I love you, too, Ollie-Bear. You're my favorite."

I dressed quickly in some leggings, a t-shirt, and a University of Texas hoodie, threw my hair up into a ponytail and slapped on some moisturizer with SPF. I shook my head, thinking of me at sixteen with a vanity full of eye shadows and lip glosses. And the hour it took me to get ready to go anywhere.

I liked that those days were gone. It was nice not to feel like I had to look perfect every second of the day. Maybe that was the biggest blessing of moving to Two Harts. No one knew me here, or my past, or the stupid decisions I'd made. I could be a new Ellie, a better Ellie. Or at least one who'd grown up.

After checking on Oliver's progress (and helping him fix the shirt he'd put on backwards), I made my way to the kitchen to pack lunch for the kid and check on the overnight oats.

The oats were not for me—I preferred food with flavor—but I'd been mulling Sunny's advice. Gil and I did need to work together to figure out our next steps. Plus, perhaps Gil would see my effort, realize what a kind, generous person I was and listen to reason when it came to not selling the house. Thus, an olive branch in the form of overnight oats. Although to be honest, an olive branch might be tastier. I'd offered muffins and donuts and cookies and brownies, but he wasn't interested. My love language was baking but it was clear Gil didn't have much of a sweet tooth.

That felt a little personal.

I rounded the corner into the kitchen, feeling pretty good about this plan of mine, and caught the image of a shadowy figure sitting at the kitchen table. I screamed.

"Holy fork!" Fumbling around, I found the light and flipped it on.

Gil squinted at the sudden brightness. "Good morning to you, too."

Breathing hard, I pressed a hand to my chest. "You scared me half to death."

"I see that," he said dryly.

"You can't go sneaking up on people like that."

"Technically, you snuck up on me." He dropped his forehead into his hand.

Even in the pre-dawn of the day, he had a certain smug "I'm in charge here" quality in his voice which grated on me. "I didn't expect a man to be sitting in the dark in the kitchen at four thirty in the morning. So, excuse me."

He looked a little rough around the edges, his hair mussed from sleeping. A pillow line bisected one of his cheeks. More than that, his eyes looked red and irritated as though he'd been rubbing them. He looked horrible, if I were honest.

"You okay?" I asked.

Wincing, he held up a hand to block out the brightness. "Would you mind turning off the light?"

"Oh, um, sure." I snapped it off. The bit of moonlight streamed in through the window in front of the table, surrounding him with an otherworldly glow. "What's wrong?"

"Just a headache." His voice was low and gravelly.

"Sounds like a bad one."

"Migraine," he muttered. "I took something for it. Just waiting for it to kick in."

"Oh." I shuffled over to the counter and pulled the bread from the top of the refrigerator. "Will the light above the stove bother you? I need to make Oliver's lunch."

"It's fine."

The silence overwhelmed me as I worked on Oliver's PB&J. I was not good at silence. I worried about what other people were thinking about me. It was best not to let them think about that too much.

I turned. "Is there anything I can do?"

He looked up and a corner of his mouth lifted. "You can put that knife down, for one."

Knife? But there it was in the hand I was waving in the air—a butter knife loaded with peanut butter. "Oh."

"Yeah. Oh." He squinted at me with one eye. "I'm worried you'll actually use it on me."

I sniffed and put the knife down. "Please. If I were going to use a weapon on you, it would not be a puny butter knife. I watch a lot of true crime documentaries. I keep a list of tips. In case I need to make someone disappear. I've always thought those shows were part 'how-to' videos. I mean, if I were a budding murderer, I could get great practical tips for not getting caught. Like this one guy in Alaska would—"

He held up a hand and I shut my mouth. "Can we talk about murder training on another day, please?"

"Right. Sure."

"Thanks," he muttered, wincing as he turned his head.

I had a sudden desire to rub his back or smooth his hair down or give him a hug or... do something to make him feel better. So, I filled up a glass with water and set it next to him. "You should stay hydrated."

He stared at the glass for a long moment before looking up at me, his expression unreadable. "Thanks."

"No problem." I turned back to the counter.

Oliver practically flew into the kitchen, such was his Valentine's Day high. "Mommy, I made this for you."

He held up a bright-pink piece of construction paper that looked like someone had gone to town on it with scissors and enthusiasm.

"It's a heart. Mrs. Sullivan let me cut it out all byed myself and see what I wrote?" He pointed in the center where he'd carefully written *I love you, Mommy* in his oversized scrawl.

"I love it." I snagged him under his arms and picked him up to place kisses all over his face. He giggled and pretended to be "grossed out" but his arms and legs wrapped around me like a baby koala.

"Mommy, put me down," he managed to get out between bouts of laughter. "I gots to give Mr. Dalton his Balentine, too."

I pulled back enough to look down at him. "You made one for Mr. Dalton?"

"He needed a card too, silly. It's Balentine Day." After peeking at Gil over my shoulder, he whisper-yelled, "Do you think he'll like it?"

"He better or I'll beat him up."

His eyes grew about fourteen sizes. "You could beat him up?"

"Are you kidding? For you, kid, I'd beat up a whole army." After placing a last kiss on his cheek, I set him down. "Go on and give it to him, sweets. We have to get going."

When Oliver turned his back, I held up the knife and shot Gil a look—mostly in jest. Mostly. With a tiny nod, he acknowledged my threat. I turned around to finish making Oliver's lunch. And to hide my grin.

I couldn't quite make out their conversation, but Oliver's giggles made me like Gil Dalton a tiny bit more. Maybe Sunny was right. Gil and I could be friends, and I'd win him over and he'd stop mentioning anything about selling and the—

"Did you get Mommy a Balentine's?" Oliver asked.

I whipped around. "Oh, no, Oliver. That's fine. I don't need a—"

"She got you one," he said, talking over me.

"I did not."

His face scrunched up in a frown. "But you made him breakfast for today. It's Balentine's Day."

Biting back a groan, I dropped my head forward. I had made Gil breakfast, but I hadn't even put two and two together. Leave it to Oliver to connect the dots. Even if they did not form a picture.

"I made you overnight oats." I waved a hand at the crockpot. "That's all."

"What?" Gil said, clearly confused.

"I, um, made overnight oats."

"Okay." He still looked confused.

"My therapist—her name's Sunny—she suggested I try to get to know you better... since we're in this together. But then I wasn't too sure how to do that because I get along with most people, and those I don't, I win them over with baked goods. But you don't like my baked goods. Not even my muffins." I frowned. "Are you allergic to sugar, or something?"

He stared at the crockpot for such a long moment, I thought the conversation might be over. "I try to avoid a lot of sugar. And chocolate. It's a trigger for the migraines."

"No sugar? No *chocolate*?" I stared at him in horror. "How do you live like that?"

"It's my cross to bear," he said solemnly. "But somehow I manage."

I sat down across from him at the table, my eyes touching on the oddly shaped red heart with "Happy Valentine Day, Mr. Dalton" sprawled across it.

Oliver looked back and forth between us with interest. "Mr. Dalton doesn't have a girlfriend. I asked him."

"Oliver! Why don't you go find your shoes and backpack, bud?" Surprisingly, he didn't argue. "They've been talking about love at school. His teacher's a newlywed. I didn't even think about it being Valentine's Day. Do not want you to get the wrong idea."

One dark eyebrow raised. "Wow. I'm that bad, huh?"

"I didn't mean it like that." I sighed and tried to organize my thoughts. "Look, can we start over here? We have a lot of decisions to make together, and we didn't seem to get off on the best foot. I know you might not like me exactly, but we are living in this house together and I was hoping we could be friendly."

"So, you made me oatmeal?"

"Yes."

He stood slowly and tightened the belt of the red flannel robe he was wearing.

"Thanks." He avoided eye contact, looking uncomfortable. "I'm looking forward to it."

Maybe this plan would work.

Step One: Get him to like me.

Step Two: Get him to like the house.

Step Three: Get him to agree to not selling.

Step Four (only used in case the other three don't work): Refer to those notes from the true crime docs.

I hopped up from the table. "If you decide to get wild, there's some fruit in the fridge."

He hesitated. Cleared his throat. Raked his fingers through his hair. He seemed rattled. "I'm going to lay back down and sleep off the rest of this headache."

"Hope you feel better."

He shuffled past me, leaving behind that warm, laundry soap smell in his wake.

"Hey," Gil said, his voice soft. I turned and found him leaning on the door jamb, one foot draped over the other.

"Yep?"

His chest expanded. "I'm sorry if I made you feel like I didn't like you."

"I get it. We're in a bizarre situation." My heart thumped against my ribs as I turned back to the counter. But I knew he hadn't left; I could feel him watching me.

For a moment, and for the first time in a long, long time, I didn't feel so alone.

NINETEEN

Love is my mom taking me to get my favorite food or drink when I've had a bad day.

—CALEB R., AGE 13

By the time February slid into March, we'd developed a routine of sorts. Mainly avoidance but, hey, it worked.

The first Friday in March, Oliver had a half day of school and stayed at the café with me until it closed. Oliver was basically the café mascot at this point. The old men who hung out in the back corner had already taught him to play chess. When we got busy, he knew how to wipe down tables or hand out menus. He enjoyed helping. He made good tips, too. Already had a pretty hefty college fund started.

I was continuing a time-honored tradition of unpaid child labor. My dad had been a contractor my whole life. When I was a kid, it wasn't unusual to find us loading up his truck with supplies. Mom often took calls for him and did his books. Chris was wrangled into working in the summers when he wasn't in one football camp or another. We'd all complain about having to give up a Saturday afternoon to help with something but, secretly, I'd loved it.

Using my hands, moving my body, creating things, those things had always come more naturally to me than sitting at a desk studying. That was reflected in my subpar grades unless I was excited about the topic. If that were the case, I'd read everything I could get my hands on. I'd enjoyed chemistry and creative writing. I hated geometry.

It had taken me three tries to pass that class. Pythagoras' Theorem had *haunted* my dreams. Despite what every math teacher told me, no, I had not used that theorem once in my adult life. Figuring out the least amount of money the electric company would take to keep the lights on? Calculating how many tips I needed to make in one night to get all the rent money? Now those were useful equations.

Mom and Dad tried to help. They got me tutors and spent hours upon hours with me doing homework, encouraging me, and sometimes bribing me to get through one more test. For my brother and sisters, school had been easy, but for me, it mostly felt like torture. Looking back, I could see how having undiagnosed ADHD made school a challenge.

How many phone calls home had my parents received about my daydreaming in class?

Answer: A lot.

How many times had I gotten a ding on my report card for my messy, disorganized desk in elementary school?

Answer: A lot.

How many times had I felt a bit different from everyone else?

Answer: A lot.

But the first time I took a theater class in middle school, something clicked. I loved everything about it. The silly warmups, the improv lessons, the scenes we'd perform. Costume and makeup. The audience and the lights. I'd found my people too.

The drama kids were different, like me, creative but not in the way our teachers wanted us to be. Because it was the first place I'd found where I fit, I knew in my soul I was meant to be an actress.

But sometimes your first love isn't your forever love. Sometimes, there are things you can't possibly imagine, better things, that are meant for you. Going to LA had been a teenager's dream; coming here to Two Harts and working at the Sit-n-Eat, this was my grown-up dream. To think, I never would have known that without going through all the hard times.

It was half an hour before close and only a few straggling customers remained. Oliver had escaped into the office to play. Gil sat at the counter, texting and eating his lunch. Bits of food and grease stains were splattered on his green polo which made him look like he'd been on the losing end of a monster food fight.

He'd been on dish duty today. Despite the apron he'd worn, he still managed to get more water on himself and the floor than the dishes. Mentally, I crossed that job off the list of things he could do around here.

Next, we'd try refilling the napkin holders. That seemed less damaging to his wardrobe. I grinned. It was terrible of me, I know, but he seemed like a capable guy, someone who could take care of business. Unless the business was doing dishes. Or making pancakes (Jorge said never again). Or remembering who needed a drink refill. Those things were second nature to me; I was good at this. Gil wasn't.

"Oliver, you want a cookie?" I yelled. That was another bonus he'd discovered about hanging out with me at the café. Extra cookies.

He ran into the room, carting his dinosaur encyclopedia. "Mommy, guess what?"

"What?"

"I found a new dinosaur." He held up the enormous book we'd checked out from the library and pointed at a shape on a page. "It had feathers on it and eated plants and look how big the claws are. How do you say the name?"

Confession: I have no idea how to pronounce dinosaur names. They were at least twenty letters long and the letters were not in any order that made sense. It was like trying to read a different language. The day Oliver realized I was basically making up the names as we went along was going to be a sad day for us all.

"That's a T and then a H." His tongue stuck out as he studied the word.

I took a deep breath and took the book from his hands, acutely aware Gil was sitting across the counter listening to all of this and not bothering to hide it. "That's good, kiddo. T and H together say thhh. And the e and the r say er so ther..."

Look at that. Only fifteen more letters to go.

"Therizinosaurus," Gilbert said in a clear voice.

Oliver's head whipped around to stare at Gil. "Say it again." Gil repeated it. Oliver bounced on the balls of his feet in excitement. "Do you like dinosaurs?"

Gil nodded solemnly. "I sure do."

"Wow," Oliver said in a voice he reserved only for my brother, dinosaurs, and the reptile hut at the zoo.

Gil leaned a little closer and pointed at another dinosaur on the page. "The deinocheirus is cool, too. They had a duck bill instead of big teeth and it was even bigger than a T-rex."

"Whoa." Oliver stared at Gil in pure, unadulterated hero worship. It was inevitable. Oliver had already asked a million questions about Gil when he lived in a tent in the backyard. Now that he'd moved into the house, his curiosity was unending.

Oliver set the book in front of Gil. He ran around the counter and climbed up on the stool next to him. Now that he'd discovered Gil knew dinosaurs, it would be impossible to keep the kid away.

Oliver pointed at a dinosaur in the book. "What's that one called?"

"Okay, Oliver, how about we let Mr. Dalton get back to his lunch." I tried to slide the book from the counter, but Gil stopped me.

"It's okay. I don't mind." And then Gil Dalton, the same guy who had a resting frown face, smiled. At me. It was an adorable smile, a little crooked and unsure. My heart thumped hard, just once.

"If you're sure." I hesitated, watching the two of them together, before I took myself into the kitchen to work on a couple of batches of magic cookie bars for tomorrow.

Gil's low murmur and Oliver's giggles were my background music. Occasionally, I'd peek through into the dining area to see the two of them side by side, two dark heads bent over that encyclopedia.

They stayed like that until I closed for the day. "Time to go. Go get your backpack."

"Mom," he said, making the word about fifteen seconds long.

I gently pushed him. "Backpack. Now. Let's go."

Oliver trudged back to the office while Gil went back to eating his (cold) soup.

"What was that?" I asked.

"What was what?"

"That." I waved a hand in Oliver's general direction. "You were so... so... sweet to him."

"He's a kid."

"But he's not your kid. You weren't just nice, you were... likable."

His spoon clinked when he dropped it in the bowl. "I can be likable."

I pressed my lips together in response.

"I am."

"You're kind of... stern. Like a principal on lunch duty. Just waiting to give detention to someone."

Leaning back, he crossed his arms, a fierce frown marring his face. "That's not true."

"Sure." I grabbed my purse from under the counter.

"It's not."

Oliver ran back into the room, his dinosaur backpack thudding with each step. "Ready." He waved at Gil. "Bye, Mr. Dalton."

"You can call me Gilbert."

"Okay, Mr. Gilbert. Can we talk about dinosaurs later?"

"You got it." Then he smiled and made sure to look right at me when he did it.

TWENTY

[Love is...] when people make a personal sacrifice or give personal time.

—SADIE S., AGE 14

Later that night as I was headed to bed, I discovered Gil's bedroom door wide open. His door was never opened. Whether he was in it or not, he kept it closed up tight. Probably stuck a piece of hair across it to make sure I wasn't sneaking in. Light from his room spilled into the hallway. I crept closer and peeked in. I'd just say hello and goodnight and scurry off to my room. Like a polite roommate.

Gil was lying on his bed, fully clothed, still wearing the spattered t-shirt and jeans from his work at the café earlier in the day. Even his shoes were on, although untied as though he'd started to take them off and then gave up. One arm was slung over his eyes and even from my place by the door, I could see the steady rise and fall of his chest. So, he wasn't dead, at least.

I bit back a grin. Poor guy. We must have exhausted him.

I cleared my throat. He didn't budge.

Hmm. In the name of making sure he was okay, I tiptoed into the room. Fine. I wanted to check out his space. I hadn't been in his room at all since he moved in, and I was curious.

The dress mannequins were still in place against the wall. The clowns were still smiling maniacally, although some had been turned to face the wall. But new things had been added. There was a guitar case leaning in the corner. Did he play? He didn't seem like a musician exactly.

The accordion doors on the closet were open and hanging there was a selection of button-downs in basic colors and khakis the likes of which any accountant would be proud of. After a quick peek at Gil—still hadn't moved at all—I slunk a little closer to the dresser to inspect the things on the top.

A worn brown leather wallet sat in the middle. Next to it, a handful of loose change. There was a small shower caddy that held personal items: shampoo, body wash, a blue loofa sponge, toothpaste and toothbrush, floss—because of course he flossed daily, probably twice a day—and a small bottle of cologne. After a peek at Gil's still sleeping body, I carefully picked it up and popped the top. Hmm, a touch of citrus, maybe some sandalwood, something spicy that lingered. Nice. I set the bottle back in place and reached for the wallet.

This was bad. I should not be snooping. But the guy was a bit of an enigma. I knew he had a brother, weird taste buds, migraines, and resting frown face.

I froze when I heard a sound coming from the bed. Slowly I turned on my heel, expecting to be caught and already working on an excuse for entering his room and invading his personal space.

But Gil hadn't moved a muscle, his arm was still draped over his eyes. The part of his face I could see was soft, his lips puckered gently in sleep. I hadn't noticed before, but he had a nice mouth, with a full bottom lip and the sweetest cupid's bow on the top.

That was purely a scientific observation, of course.

After abandoning the wallet, I strolled over to the night-stand and picked up the framed photo next to his glasses. There was Gil standing between two men, arms looped around each other's shoulders. One looked to be in his late sixties, early seventies, and another that looked a little older than Gil. He was slightly balding with ears that stuck out a bit and a huge grin. Actually, all three of them were smiling.

Was this the stepdad he mentioned? Who was the other man? A cousin, maybe?

Gil groaned and lifted the arm from his eyes. I bit back a gasp. As quickly as I could, I set the frame down and backed away. He rubbed his hand over his face and reached blindly for his glasses on the nightstand.

If I could just make it to the door...

"What the hell are you doing in here?" he asked.

With a squeak, I jumped and turned. He sat up, and for once his hair was not neatly parted and combed. The messy bits stood up like a cat with its hackles raised. He slid his glasses on.

I should have told the truth—I'm a creepy creeper who crept into your room. But that smug voice of his annoyed me. I straightened and crossed my arms. "I believe half this room is mine. I needed to get this."

Blindly, I grabbed the first thing my hand connected with off one of the wall shelves.

Gil's eyes narrowed. "You came into my room because you couldn't go another minute without a statue of a sad clown riding a bicycle."

I glanced down at the abomination in my hand and shud-dered. "Obviously. Couldn't dream of sleeping without it right by my bedside another night."

"I guess I'll have to duck in your room and see that..." he pointed at the figurine "...in its new space. Seeing as how half your room is mine, too."

Damn it. Throwing my words back at me was a devilishly good move.

I looked down my nose at him. "Fred the Clown will be pedaling his heart out right next to my bed."

"You named him Fred?"

"Of course he looks like a Fred." I headed to the door. "I'll just be going to bed now."

"You do that."

"I will."

"Fine."

"Goodnight." And to show what a considerate person I was, I closed his door behind me.

TWENTY-ONE

Love is my puppy running to me first when we get home.

—LAUREN C., AGE 17

From the sticky note correspondence of Gilbert Dalton and Ellie Sterns:

> *Eleanor—*
>
> *Would it be possible for you to close the kitchen cabinets after you open them?*
>
> *Thank you.*
>
> *—Gilbert*
>
> *P.S. Can you pick a day and time for us to go through Ollie's room?*

Gil—

That seems kind of nit-picky, doesn't it? I haven't said
a word about the toilet seat.

—Ellie

P.S. Sure. I'll check my calendar and get back to you.

Eleanor—

That's because I am always considerate enough to put
the toilet seat down. You even left the microwave door
open. I banged my head on it this morning.

—Gilbert

P.S. Right. Your calendar. Is it the same place you keep
your keys?

"So, every Friday, he leaves?" Mae asked as she refilled her roller with a pale-green paint with the fanciful name of Sage Wisdom. But like every time she'd reloaded, she got more paint on herself and the plastic protecting the floors than on the roller. Mae was good at a lot of things. Turns out painting was not one of them.

"And comes back Sunday afternoon." I reached up from my spot on the stepladder to cut in the paint on the top edge of the ceiling. Because I am good at painting.

"Where do you think he goes?"

"Austin. Or at least that's what his notes say."

"Notes?" Ali asked, peeking out from the closet where she was painting. "He leaves you notes?"

I shrugged. "We leave each other notes."

"That's kind of sweet," Mae said.

"It's not sweet," I said. "It's a form of communication. Like smoke signals or telegraph."

Mae hummed.

I half turned to face her. "There will be no humming. It's not a big deal."

"What could be in Austin?" Ali jumped out of the closet that she'd been giving a fresh coat of paint. "Oooh. We could follow him one of these Fridays and see where he's going. It could be a stakeout. I already have a stakeout outfit."

"No," Mae and I said at the exact same time.

"Mayors do not spy on people. It's impolite," Mae said.

"And probably illegal," I added.

"You all suck the fun out of everything."

"Someone has to keep you reined in," Mae muttered. "Lord knows Theo would let you get away with almost anything."

Ali's grin was practically wicked. "I have no idea what you're talking about."

Mae snorted. "Yeah."

Ali hopped over to the stepladder and looked up at me. "But how are things with him there? How is Oliver with the new roommate situation?"

"Oliver loves him. In fact, I think Gil may be his favorite person right now. They talk dinosaurs." Which was fine. It wasn't like I *wanted* to talk about dinosaurs, but also, I at least wanted to be *asked* to talk about dinosaurs.

Sunny and I were going to have a talk about these feelings of jealousy.

"Oliver follows Gil around, too. Reminds me a little of how he was with Ollie."

"They were so cute together," Mae said. "Remember that Halloween Oliver insisted Ollie dress up with him?"

Ali giggled. "Ollie in that chicken costume will forever live rent-free in my mind."

"Oliver was so excited. He has a picture of the two of them in those chicken get-ups in his room." I grinned. "Ollie as Santa Claus was the best. I appreciated Chris dressing up this year, but I don't think Oliver bought it when I said Santa must have eaten all his vegetables to grow a whole foot in a year."

Mae sniffled. "I miss Ollie."

"Please don't start crying," I said. "Then I'll start."

"I'm sorry. These stupid hormones. I am all over the place."

"She cried yesterday when I told her the library budget has been approved," Ali said. "Bawled her eyes out right there in her office."

"Shut up," Mae grumbled, swiping at her cheeks.

Time to change the subject or we'd all be in a puddle. "Gil has a motorcycle," I blurted out.

"A motorcycle?" Ali pursed her lips. "Wasn't that on your list of no-no's when it comes to men?"

I scoffed. "I'm not interested in him like that."

Mae shot Ali a look that said, *who's lying now?*

Whatever. I *wasn't* interested in him that way.

"I heard he's going to start subbing at the elementary school," Mae said.

I hadn't heard that. Not once was it mentioned in a single sticky note conversation. In fact, the more I thought about it, the more I realized our relationship was very one-sided. "He knows a lot more about me than I know about him. That doesn't seem fair."

"Have you asked him about him?"

I froze mid-paint stroke. "Yes. Sort of. Maybe?"

"You should," Ali said. "When you get home, go right up to his bedroom door and demand some answers."

"Or maybe just casually bring it up next time you see him," Mae said dryly.

"Fine," Ali muttered. "Do that."

"Maybe I will," I said. I set my roller down and hopped off the ladder. "Is it time to eat yet? You bribed me with pizza and cheesecake."

"God, yes. Let's go eat," Mae said.

TWENTY-TWO

Love is hugging.

—HYRUM, AGE 3

I glided into the living room and spun in a circle to show off my yellow polka-dot skirt. I'd paired it with a wide-collared white sweater that hung off one shoulder, and the wedges that added an extra two inches to my height. I wanted to look like I cared, especially since this was the first of the three blind dates Ali and Mae had arranged for me.

Honestly though, my heart wasn't in it. I hadn't been joking when I said I was ready to give up dating. After a nice, long break, maybe my man picker would recalibrate.

"Okay, O, what do you think? On a scale of one to ten, how's this for a first date outfit?" Yes, I was asking my six-year-old for fashion advice. He's been my right-hand man his entire life. Who else would I ask?

But Oliver wasn't sitting on the couch where I'd left him with his encyclopedia of dinosaurs. Nope, he was over by the window next to Gil who was on his knees trying to pry the window open. It was one of many in this house that had been painted shut. Since moving in, Gil had been on a mission to fix them. Something about a fire hazard, but I'd been too busy staring to listen.

Gil and Oliver had developed a bit of a relationship over the last couple of weeks. If Gil made an appearance, Oliver was sure to be following him around. For his part, Gil was good with him, patient and soft-spoken. It was sweet to see the two of them with their heads bent over a dinosaur book or Oliver standing by while Gil calmly explained how he fixed the toilet. No, no, that wasn't the problem.

The problem was that Gil was wearing his toolbelt.

That's not some weird euphemism. It was a real toolbelt. Bright yellow and slung low on his hips and full of tools. Hammers and wrenches and screwdrivers, oh my.

That man knew how to use all of them.

Oliver was enamored. He'd even asked for his own toolbelt for his birthday. Not that I blamed him. I might have followed Gil around a time or two. Secretly watching him fix things had become a weird new hobby of mine.

The other day he used a wireless drill and... phew. I wanted to fan myself just thinking about it. I may have discovered a latent obsession with handymen.

Both swung their heads in my direction.

"Oh, um, Gil, I didn't know you were here." Did my voice sound a little breathless?

He stood slowly. "Thought I'd work on a few things tonight."

"I, ah, have a date with..." What had Ali said his name was? I couldn't remember a single detail about him suddenly. "Oliver, we need to go in a few minutes so I can drop you off."

"Mommy, you look very pretty," Oliver said, after inspecting me from head to toe. "Mr. Gil, doesn't Mommy look pretty?"

I laughed, twisting my hands at my waist. "Buddy, Mr. Gil doesn't need—"

Gil settled his hands on his hips, right above that toolbelt. His eyes traveled down the length of me, leaving a tingling trail in their wake. "Very pretty."

"You don't have to sa—"

Gil's head tilted. He wasn't exactly smiling, a facial expression that, I was learning, was not common for him. "I never say anything I don't mean. A man's word is his promise. Right, Oliver?" He held a fist out.

"Right." Oliver fist-bumped him. "We say what we meaned and we meaned what we say. We learned that in our Man Club."

"Your what?"

"It's a club for us guys to talk about guy stuff. Like when you go and see the aunts and talk about girl stuff." Oliver puffed his chest out. "I need a club for being a man. I'm the president. Mr. Gil is the vice president."

"Oh, really?"

I wasn't sure how I felt about all this. Oliver had never seemed all that interested in knowing about his dad. I knew one day he would be, of course. At the very least, there would be questions. Chris and my dad had done a great job stepping up as role models and Oliver loved his Uncle Chris and his Papa. But I'd never seen him become attached to a man unrelated to us, except for Ollie. Oliver had adored Ollie, and the feeling had been mutual.

My phone rang. I scooped it off the coffee table and answered. "Hey, you're on speakerphone."

"Can't. Watch. Oliver," my brother said.

"Why do you sound like you're running a marathon? Is everything okay? Is it the baby?"

"Yes. I mean, no, but yes."

I heard someone shouting in the background. "Is that Mae? Where are you?"

"We're at the hospital and—" His voice became muffled, but I could clearly hear him say, "Yes, I'll put it on speakerphone. Calm down."

Mae's voice was loud and clear when he did just that. "...did not tell me to calm down."

"It was an accident."

"An accident? Like the one that will happen to you when you disappear?"

"I panicked, okay? I've never had a pregnant wife. I promise I won't say it next time."

"Next time? Nope. We're going to be a one-and-done family. We're getting separate beds after this. In separate bedrooms. Maybe in separate houses."

"Aw, Sprinkles. It's not so bad, is it?"

There was a loud clatter and, if I were a betting woman, I would say Chris had just had a projectile of some kind thrown at him.

"Hey, hello," I said. "What's going on?"

"She thought she was having those fake contractions," Chris said.

"Braxton Hicks," Mae said. "That's what they're called."

"Yeah, those. But then they didn't go away like they usually do and so we called and the doctor told us to head to the hospital," Chris said. "Since she's still four weeks from her due date, the doctor gave her something to stop the contractions. They're keeping her overnight just in case."

"Oh, bummer," I said.

Mae groaned. "I cannot wait for this kid to get out of me."

"I wanted to call and let you know we can't watch the O-Man tonight."

"Oh, right." I glanced at the time. "It's not too late to cancel. No big deal."

"No!" Mae shouted. "You are not allowed to cancel."

"I can't take Oliver with me on a date," I said. Although judging by my previous dating experience, Oliver would be a much better companion.

"Someone in town can watch him. Call Iris."

"The last time your sister watched him, she put red streaks in his hair, let him stay up too late and eat as much ice cream as he wanted. Which he puked up at two in the morning. Hard pass."

I turned and smiled at Oliver, but he was deep in conversation with Gil, their two heads pressed together as they whispered.

"I'm sure someone's around. What about Susie next door?"

Susie Alcorn was in her late seventies and blinder than a bat wearing noise-canceling headphones. Also, she hated kids. Even Oliver, who was the best kid in the world. "Not happening."

Gil nodded at something Oliver said and straightened, his toolbelt jangling merrily. Had he grown several inches since I met him? I was sure he'd been shorter. But even with my wedges on, he was taller than me. Maybe that toolbelt had secret powers.

"Let me think," Mae said.

"It's fine. I can reschedule. Oliver and I will have a movie night, or something." And to be honest, an evening of secretly watching Gil fix things wasn't the worst thing that could happen.

"I'll watch him," Gil said.

I shook my head and waved him off.

"It's no problem. I'll keep him busy."

"Who said that?" Mae asked. "Is it Gilbert? Say yes, you dummy. Then run out the door."

"That's nice of you to offer but it's Friday," I said. "You always leave for the weekend on Fridays."

He shrugged. His hand settled on the handle of the hammer

in his toolbelt. I forced myself not to look. "I'll leave early tomorrow. It's not that big of a deal."

"No. You clearly have plans. I don't want to inconvenience you."

It only took him three long strides to reach me. Gently, he pulled the phone from my hand, his fingers brushing mine, and spoke into it. All the while his gaze never left mine. "I'll watch Oliver tonight."

"Hey, Gilbert," my brother said. "That would be great."

"It's no problem."

"I'll owe you one," Chris said.

Gil's eyes crinkled in the corners—a not-smile smile.

No, I thought, I think I'd be the one to owe him something. I just wondered what it was he'd want.

TWENTY-THREE

Love is like you can love a person. Love is a heart.

—JACK, AGE 7

"Is he here? What do you think?" I asked.

Liliana looked up over the top of her glasses. "He is... punctual."

I waited to see if she'd add anything else. "That's it?"

She glanced over the half-wall that divided the front counter from the seating area at the Texican. "He's polite."

"Polite?"

"*Si*. He said please and thank you. That's... polite."

"Liliana."

"*Mija*, I do not know what to say about him. Sometimes there is nothing to put a finger on, you know? He's not right for you." She shrugged. "But maybe I am wrong."

She was never wrong.

With slightly less enthusiasm than I'd had five minutes before (and I hadn't had much to begin with), I let her lead me to a dark-haired man. He stood when he saw me, smiled, gave me a hug. He smelled good. Not fancy laundry soap good, but still good.

"So, you own a café? I think that's what Ali told me, eh?" he asked when we'd settled in and placed our orders.

When Ali had told me Tony Olson had an accent, she hadn't mentioned it was Canadian. Not French-Canadian. All the other non-French Canadians with their ehs and constant apologies. *That* was his accent.

Paired with my desperate need to be liked, we'd actually gotten into a vicious apology cycle the first ten minutes we met. We just kept apologizing for... well, who knew? But I'd asked Mae and Ali for a non-jerk blind date candidate and Tony fit the bill. He'd pulled out my chair for me. Seemed interested in my answers to questions.

Was that where I'd set the bar these days? If he pulled the chair out and made conversation, then he was a keeper?

I smiled. "I do."

"I'll have to come try it out." He had friendly brown eyes and a nice, easy smile. Unlike other men I knew.

Why was I thinking about Gil? Who I had left forty-five minutes ago with Oliver, the two of them sitting on the couch engaged in a serious discussion about dinosaurs in the Cretaceous period. I'd had the sudden, strange urge to cry at the sight of it.

Sunny would have something annoying to say about that, I was sure.

"You should. I have great muffins."

He laughed. "Is that right?"

I blushed. "I meant actual muffins. That was not a euphemism or anything. Just, you know, muffins."

"I like muffins." He grinned. He had a soothing sort of way about him. He wasn't mysterious or closed off. He probably doesn't own a toolbelt though.

"So, what do you do?" I said, desperate to get my mind firmly in the present. "I think Ali said you're in sales?"

"I am. Regional manager for a carpet company. I cover Texas, Louisiana, and Oklahoma."

"With carpet."

"What?"

"You cover Texas, Louisiana, and Oklahoma... with carpet... Sorry. Silly joke."

"Oh, I get it. Sorry." He sort of chuckled.

Focus on his nice face and... and his hands. He had long, elegant fingers that probably hadn't touched a hammer or a wrench or a drill. It was getting a little warm in here. It really wasn't fair of Gil to prance around in that toolbelt in front of me. Especially right before a date. It was almost indecent.

I should leave him a sticky note about it.

"So, Ali said you have a son?" he asked.

Ah, a topic I could talk about for hours. "I do. He's six and his name is Oliver. He's amazing."

"I love kids," Tony said. "I have fourteen nieces and nephews."

"Whoa. You must come from a big family."

"No, just my brother and me."

"Wait. Your brother has fourteen kids? That's... a lot."

"Two sets of twins, too. Do you want a big family?"

My palms were itchy; I rubbed them on my skirt. "I would love another one or two, sure."

"I've always wanted a huge family."

The server picked that moment to bring us our meals, thankfully. That line of conversation was getting weird. We chatted a bit about other things—our favorite movies and TV shows, hobbies, the weather. He was easy to talk to and he didn't once bring up an ex-girlfriend he was still in love with.

"So, tell me about Oliver."

"He's amazing. So smart for his age. He likes to read and

draw. Oh, and he's really into dinosaurs. He's determined to learn the names of all of them." I smiled and picked up my glass of water. "I'm sure he'll do it, too."

"I don't believe in dinosaurs," he said, taking a bite of his dinner as if he'd just announced the sky was blue.

I choked on my water, which turned into wracking coughs. When I could finally catch my breath, I stared at him. "I'm sorry? Did you say you didn't believe in dinosaurs?"

"Yep. They're all made up."

"But what about..."

"Space, too. I don't think it actually exists. It doesn't make any sense. People didn't walk on the moon. All staged." He pointed with his fork at my plate. "How is your enchilada?"

"It's fine," I whispered. Except it suddenly tasted like cardboard. It was times like this I wished I hadn't given up alcohol. People didn't just not believe in dinosaurs. And space. Right? "Let me guess... you think the earth is flat, too."

"Oh, definitely. There's proof even."

I swiveled around in my chair. "Am I being punked? Is this one of Ali's pranks? Where are they hiding? Y'all come out. Ha-ha. Very funny."

"What are you talking about? What prank?" Tony looked genuinely confused.

What planet was I on? I'd ask him but he didn't believe in *space*. My mouth opened and closed. I chugged the rest of my water.

"You going to eat your rice?" he asked, seemingly oblivious of my plight. Cool. Cool. Cool.

"Ah, no. Go ahead, you can have it. I think I'm going to run to the restroom. I'll be right back."

I ducked my head as I passed Liliana, hoping she wouldn't notice me. It felt a bit like a walk of shame.

"I was right, wasn't I?" she asked.

"I don't want to talk about it," I muttered.

The bathroom was thankfully empty. Still, I locked myself in a stall and hastily texted Mae and Ali.

ME: Where did you find this guy? Conspiracy-Theories-R-Us?

MAE: Uh-oh.

ALI: But how's it going? He's nice, right?

TWENTY-FOUR

*[Love is...] random because you never really expect it from the
other person.*

    It is unpredictable.

—MERCY, AGE 14

It was almost nine by the time I made it home. The house was
quiet and clean. Everything was put in its place. I poked my
head in the kitchen to see the counters wiped down and the sink
cleared of dishes. Gil might be a little anal-retentive, but he was
sure nice to have around at times.

I plopped myself down on the couch, kicked off the wedges
pinching my toes, and spread out like a starfish. With a groan, I
closed my eyes and tried not to think of Tony's outraged expression when I told him no, we were not going out again.

My phone vibrated more than once from its spot on the
coffee table before I sat up enough to see texts flying in from Ali
and my sister group chat. I'd deal with it tomorrow. I'd explain
this was what happened when you send a woman with a broken
man picker out on a blind date.

The date gets weird.

I dropped my head on the back of the couch and stared up at the ceiling with its plyboard patch job and suspicious water stains and felt a whole new level of loneliness. Before I moved to Two Harts, I would have rummaged around and found some wine or something stronger. I'd drink until the loneliness disappeared.

It had not been a good look for me.

A few months before I moved here, I vowed to give up alcohol. Sometimes I missed it. Like tonight. But I knew it was a slippery slope, and I didn't want it or the bad decisions it inevitably led me to.

I didn't even have it in me to bake anything. Finally, I dragged myself down the hall to my bedroom. Saturday brunch came early and waited for no one, especially single moms who needed their jobs.

Quietly, I opened Oliver's bedroom door. Through the sliver of light from the hallway, I could make out his small form, curled on his side under the covers, his hands tucked under his chin. The sight made me smile and pushed away a bit of loneliness.

I wasn't alone. Not really. I had Oliver; he would always be enough.

Gil's door was cracked open an inch or two, so I paused, my hand ready to knock and thank him for watching Oliver, when I heard him. It sounded like he was on the phone.

"I know. I know. But you know what?" he asked, his voice gentle.

There was a beat of silence.

"Tomorrow. I'll be there by lunchtime. I promise. And we can go to the park afterward."

I froze, shamelessly eavesdropping as I had on that night I heard him on the phone in the tent. He must be talking to his brother again. Sometimes it felt like he had so many secrets.

He'd moved into our home, and by that reason alone, he knew practically everything there was to know about me. But him? I had lots of questions.

"Yes, I'll push you on the swings as long as you want."

Definitely a child. I wondered how old he was? Around Oliver's age, maybe. Who did he live with?

Gil laughed softly. "A million years is a long time. I think my arms would fall off. Now, you need to get a good night's sleep though. Are you in bed?"

A beat of silence.

"Do you have Lamby? Good."

Another beat.

"Close your eyes and I'll sing it for you."

Holding my breath, I pressed my forehead on the door jamb. My mom used to sing to me when I was little. Snuggled up next to her, she'd sing "Baby Mine" from *Dumbo* until I fell asleep. I couldn't hear that song without having a visceral reaction, taking me right back to those sweet moments.

Softly strummed guitar music started. The singing came next, the words to "Amazing Grace." Gil's voice was clear and straightforward, beautiful in its simplicity. I listened to him sing all four verses before I tiptoed to my room, swiping at the tears on my cheeks.

TWENTY-FIVE

Love is when you care.

—LILIANA H., AGE 6

From the sticky note correspondence of Gilbert Dalton and Ellie Sterns:

Gil—

Have you seen my car keys? I can't find them anywhere. I had to use my spare set.

—Ellie

P.S. Do you think the earth is flat?

Eleanor—

That's because you don't put them on the key rack I hung on the wall FOR THE KEYS YOU KEEP LOSING.

—Gilbert

P.S. What kind of question is that?

Gil—

I did hang them up on the rack. Or at least I'm pretty sure I did...

—Ellie

P.S. Apparently one I have to ask my dates now.

Eleanor—

Not to sound like your mother but... if you had hung them there, they'd be there.

—Gilbert

P.S. What kind of men are you dating?

It was nice having Gil around the café. We weren't braiding each other's hair or anything, but it felt like we'd reached an unspoken agreement to get along. I thought I might be starting to figure him out, at least a little. He wasn't so much stern as he was reserved, maybe even a little shy. He thought before he spoke. He was deliberate before he acted. He was not impulsive.

Basically, he was the opposite of me in most every way.

One Tuesday about a week after my date, the café was bustling along with a steady stream of customers. My coffee cake muffins had sold out. The old men were gossiping, Ali and Theo were sharing a plate of pancakes and making each other laugh at the counter. Iris was in rare Iris form. I'd given Gil the necessary (if totally boring) job of wiping down the laminate menus.

The doorbell chimed and Peter Stone waltzed in. Iris groaned. Loudly. Peter shot her a dirty look. He spotted me behind the counter and strolled over, hands tucked in his pockets. He smiled. With a lot of teeth.

"Ellie Sterns," he said. "How are you this fine Tuesday?"

I bit back my own groan. I didn't want to see Peter for all the normal reasons. To name a few: he was annoying, arrogant, and awful. But also, for one big, abnormal reason: Gil. Because Peter was desperate to get his hands on Ollie's land and Gil was eager to sell it. While the two of us had avoided the topic of selling the property, it still loomed large in the background. But I thought, maybe, my plan to win him over was working. Kind of.

The people of Two Harts, perhaps nudged into action by a certain mayor, seemed to be warming to Gil. Mrs. Katz, one of the town's most vocal citizens, always made a point to chat with him when she came in. The old men got him to play chess with them. Gil and Malcolm Lightfoot seemed to have become friends. They chatted often over coffee and Malcolm's daughter, Annie, already had her heart set on Gil as her new boyfriend. Gil had even gone to some kind of game night with my brother and Theo. Heck, he had more of a town social life than I did.

I wanted to keep things just as they were. Peter Stone and his stupid real estate development could mess everything up. My eyes shot over to Gil, tucked in the back corner booth. I needed to get rid of Peter ASAP.

"What can I do for you?" I did not return Peter's smile.

"You having a bad day?" Despite leaning closer, his voice carried. "There someone I can beat up for you?"

Iris moseyed by. "Pu-leaze. As if."

"You need to get better help around here." Peter glared at Iris's back.

"That's funny," Iris said, her voice mild. "I was going to suggest a 'no sleazeball' policy."

I sighed. "Okay, you two. Peter, are you ordering something or are you here to harass my staff?"

Someone grunted behind me. I knew it was Gil before I even looked. I'd developed a weird sort of Gil Radar... Gil-dar? Every day it seemed to get a little stronger, my pulse seemed to race a little bit more when I discovered him nearby. He didn't even have to be wearing his toolbelt, either.

A disturbing realization, that.

I didn't want to notice Gil any more than I already did. He was in my home, at work half the time, in all the other cracks in my life I never expected to find him—hanging out with my brother, helping a neighbor move a couch, reading dinosaur books with my kid. I didn't know what to make of that.

He leaned in and whispered, "This guy bothering you?"

"He's harmless," I whispered back. "An idiot, but harmless."

"Hmm." I wanted so badly to turn around and see if he was giving Peter the full Principal Gil treatment.

"Who's this?" Peter asked, all wide-eyed and innocent. He held his hand out. "Don't know if we've met."

"Gilbert Dalton." Gil did not hold his hand out.

I stifled a giggle at Peter's hand dangling over the counter. "Peter Stone, former mayor of Two Harts."

As one of the oldest families in Two Harts, the Stones had a very high opinion of themselves. Especially Peter. He'd been mayor here like his father had been before him and his grandfather before him. And they never let anyone forget it.

Dropping his hand, Peter smiled in a used-car salesman sort of way. "Nice to meet you. I hear you're Ollie's long-lost grandson."

"I wasn't lost."

"No, no, of course not." Chuckling, Peter rocked back on his heels. "I've actually wanted to talk with you for a while now."

He pulled out his wallet and removed a business card. "If you have some time, give me a call and we can meet."

Gil took the card and read it. "Real estate developer."

"Yep. Ellie knows how much I'd love to make an offer on Ollie's property." He leaned in. "A very nice offer."

"The house?"

"Sure, and the café, but especially the land the house is on." He tucked his hands in his pockets. "I have some business partners who are interested in developing an outlet mall. Could bring a lot of business to town."

"I've already told you, Peter," I said, cutting a look to Gil that dared him to argue. "We aren't selling."

"You have mentioned that. But there are two owners, and you aren't the only one who can say yes." Peter nodded at Gil. "Give me a call. We'll talk."

As he strolled out of the café, Gil watched him, a thoughtful expression on his face I didn't like at all.

TWENTY-SIX

Love is disgusting.

—PEYTON W., AGE 14

MOM: Hi, honey. How are you? How is my grandson? I just love that photo you sent. He's so handsome.

ME: Doing great!

ME: How are you and Dad?

MOM: We're missing you and I had a thought.

ME: Can't wait to hear it!!

MOM: I was thinking we could come down for Easter weekend. It's the last Sunday in April this year.

ME: What a great idea!!!

MOM: *And all your sisters can come too. The high school has a four-day weekend so Millie has it off. Betsy might have to leave a day early for a teacher workday. Aggie said it was the perfect time to take a couple of days off from work.*

ME: *Oh, awesome! I can't wait to see you all!*

MOM: *We can have a big Easter lunch together. Won't that be fun?*

ME: *The funnest!!!!*

MOM: *One more thing, sweetie.*

ME: *Yes?!*

MOM: *How is that slipper going? You think it will be done by Easter?*

ME: *I'm on it!!!!*

I always used entirely too many exclamation points when I texted with my mother.

Everything's great! No, no, you should all come for Easter! The house is absolutely falling apart but definitely come! I don't have a strange man I secretly think is kind of hot living in my house! Can't wait to see you!

There may have been a few things I'd kept from my parents. Honestly, I tried to tell Chris as little as possible, too. It was easier that way.

There was a part of me that would always feel guilty over how much grief I put my mom and dad through. It was always me not quite toeing the line in a family full of line-toe-ers. I was the one who got the phone calls home from teachers, the afterschool detentions for being tardy, or the barely passing grades.

My mom was a teacher herself and worked at the same elementary school that all us kids went to. She'd never admit to this, but I think there was an expectation that teacher's kids had to be a little bit better than everyone else. The thing was... I wasn't. I was fine. I wasn't a bad kid. I didn't purposely seek out trouble although sometimes it did find me.

I was just okay, middling, fine.

But in a family with a sport star brother, a talented artist-turned-teacher, and a braniac sister, being okay never felt good enough.

I was eleven when my youngest sister Millie came along, born with a congenital heart defect called HLHS. Mom quit teaching and spent her days in hospital rooms, doctors' offices, and surgery waiting rooms, especially those first couple of years after Millie's birth. She lived on prayer and caffeine and kind of disappeared from our lives, when she'd always been the most present mom.

When I moved away at eighteen, it was to seek fame and fortune (major fail), and maybe a small part was to get away from my family, to prove I could do great things and that I didn't need them. Only to find out I did need them. But I was stubborn and couldn't admit that back then. It was hard to admit even now.

At this rate, I was going to be seeing Sunny for the next thirty years.

Now that I was a mother, I can see how that must have hurt my mom more than she ever let on. When I called to tell her I was pregnant she'd been so calm, so understanding, so comforting. Three years later when I'd been drinking too much, spiraling out of control, and so utterly lost, she'd flown to LA and kept Oliver for a month while I checked into a sort of treatment center.

And still she loved me, comforted me, never let me know she was disappointed.

Which was probably for the best. I was disappointed enough in myself for both of us.

I guess that was why I tried my hardest to make sure she only knew of the good things in my life. For once, I didn't want her to worry about me.

Hence all the exclamation points.

Hence the churning pool of panic when I even thought of my entire family coming to visit.

'Cause they were about to find out things were not quite so picture-perfect as I'd been telling them.

TWENTY-SEVEN

*[Love is...] when two people like each other and it gets stronger
and stronger.*

—EMMIE, AGE 8

From the sticky note correspondence of Gilbert Dalton and
Ellie Sterns:

Eleanor—

We need to talk.

—Gilbert

Dearest Gil,

*No person in the history of the world likes to see the
words "We need to talk" directed at them.*

—Ellie

> P.S. Sorry about leaving my, ahem, unmentionables hanging in the bathroom to dry.

Eleanor—

How else should I say it? Let's chat? Is that better.

Let's chat ASAP.

—Gilbert

P.S. No comment.

> Gil, Gil, Gil—
>
> Let's chat is better. I guess. Or, and I know this is crazy, how about just start talking instead of telling me you need to talk and then I can skip the anxiety of waiting for us to talk.
>
> —Ellie
>
> P.S. I did think hanging everything from my bedroom doorknob was a bit much.

After that text from my mom, the day had only seemed to pile more on me. Work had gone sideways almost immediately with one wrong order after another. Iris had a party of five who'd dined-and-dashed, which had her seeing red. A big order of produce came in without a potato in sight.

By the time I dragged myself home, got caught up on all the first grade drama from Oliver, made dinner, and cleaned up from dinner, I was done. I stumbled into the living room and kicked off my shoes. The groan I let out was embarrassingly loud, but my feet felt like I'd gone to town on them with a meat tenderizer.

I splayed out on the couch and stared up at nothing. It wasn't just the physical exhaustion getting to me today. That kind of tired I could handle. It meant I'd put in a good day's work. It was a bone-deep exhaustion and loneliness. I felt that kind of exhaustion all the time as though I was a computer with a program always running in the background. I was one keystroke away from giving up and crawling into bed and never getting out of it.

Sometimes, life could get a girl down. And sometimes, I couldn't put my finger on any one thing that brought the feeling on. It just... was.

Oliver perched on his knees at the edge of the couch. I smiled at him. "Buddy, why don't you go play in your room for a little bit?"

He put his little hand on my cheek and stared right into my eyes. "You look sad. It's okay to be sad, is what you tell me. Do you need me to kiss you and make you feel better?"

I brushed his hair off his forehead. "You know what? I think that would help a lot." I turned my head and tapped my cheek. A grin escaped at the loud smacking kiss he gave me.

Oliver pulled back. "Is that better?"

"Yes. My turn." I threw my arms around him and squeezed. He broke into giggles as I rained kisses on his face.

Finally, I let him wriggle free and he ran off down the hallway toward his room. A little Oliver Therapy was always good to brighten my mood. But still, the sadness lingered. More so than usual lately.

Sunny said we needed to allow ourselves to "feel the feelings." My natural inclination was to push those feelings down deep and keep on smiling. And for the most part, that's what I did. But Sunny was right. Sometimes I just needed to feel the feelings.

So, I did.

I set the timer on my phone to three minutes to attend a pity party of my own making. I closed my eyes and let the worry and doubt and fear of all the things—being a single mother, being alone, the café, this house, the disappointment I've been to a lot of people, that weird noise the toilet kept making—I let all those things crash down on me.

But just for three minutes. Because the same things that exhausted me also needed me to be okay. And I would be okay. I'd proven that to myself the last three years I'd lived in Two Harts. I could come back from my mistakes. I could be a person I was proud of. I could be strong for my son and a good friend to Ali and Mae. I could be a good business owner and muffin maker. I could do all those things.

It's just that sometimes I needed those three little minutes to remind me how far I'd come.

At around two minutes, forty-two seconds, someone cleared their throat. I cracked open an eye to find Gil hovering near the couch, staring down at me with something that might have been concern. "Are you okay?"

"I'm feeling my feelings." The timer beeped on my phone. "I'm done now."

"Feeling your feelings?" He took a step back as I sat up.

"You should try it sometime. Might make you smile more."

He frowned and I bit back my amusement. "I smile."

"Sure."

"I do."

I yawned. "Okay."

He muttered something under his breath as he sat down on the couch as far away from me as he could. In case my feelings rubbed off on him, I guess.

"I thought you were sleeping," he said after an awkward moment of silence.

My head flopped back, and I rolled it in his direction. "I

hear there are people who take naps whenever the heck they want." I jabbed a finger on my chest. "I am not one of those people. But enough about me, how was the park?"

A co-op soccer team had started up in Two Harts last year. They met every Tuesday night at Legacy Park and Theo had invited Gil to give it a try. Which explained the gym shorts. His legs were stretched out in front of him, crossed at the ankles. Long, long legs, the muscles lean and defined. Sweat stains marred his t-shirt. His cheeks were ruddy and eyes bright. He looked... good.

"It was nice. I saw the Legacy Tree, too. Bigger than I thought it would be."

"The tree is one of my favorite things in Two Harts. All those people who've carved their initials in it over the years. You know the biggest heart with the E and J in it? That's from one of the Hart brothers, who founded the town. The rumor is that the two brothers were in love with the same woman. One married her; one pined for her his whole life."

"That's depressing."

"Maybe. Or maybe it's enough to love someone from afar as long as you got to be around them."

"Bet it made for some awkward Christmas dinners."

"That too."

Then he did this *thing*. He slid his glasses off and used the hem of his t-shirt to wipe his face, revealing a strip of pale stomach with a dusting of dark hair. Right there on the couch where I could see. Like his legs, his ab muscles were lean and defined. Not like he spent four hours a day in a gym. More like he'd earned them playing driveway basketball or using this tool-belt to make things that required toolbelts. Obviously, he played soccer. I wondered if he played anything else. Maybe he was a runner.

The room had become very quiet in the last minute. Maybe because I was staring at Gil's exposed stomach and Gil was staring at me staring at his naked stomach. Was it hot in here?

"Are you a runner?" I blurted.

"What?" he asked as his shirt slipped back into place.

"Nothing." I tore my eyes away, praying he would let it go.

"Did you ask me if I was a runner?"

Of course he wasn't going to let it go. "Just making conversation, you know. Just two people doing people things."

The corner of his mouth tipped up. "Yes, I run. About four times a week."

"Cool. I used to run. Especially when I lived in LA. Hated every single second. But anything to keep the weight off. Had to keep it tight and trim to fit in that kangaroo pouch."

He laughed, sounded a bit rusty but it was nice. With twinkling eyes, he gave me a once-over that had me fighting a blush. "I think you'd fit just fine in it right now."

"Oh, no thank you. Do you know how hot it was in that thing?" I shrugged. "I went to some auditions after Ollie was born but I never lost the baby weight, and I kept getting comments from casting directors about it. The dream lost its luster, you could say. Now I can eat muffins, and I don't have to run." I pointed out the window at the blue, cloudless March sky. "Although now that the weather is nicer, Oliver and I like to go on walks out behind the house."

"I haven't been back there."

"You should come with us. It's so pretty. One day, I'd love to have a gazebo, maybe put in a trail or two. It would be fun to have some chickens and a goat."

"You're a real farm girl, huh?"

"Me?" I laughed. "Oh, no. Raised in Oklahoma City in the 'burbs. My parents do live in the country now, though they moved after I left. But I love it out here with all the land. Gives Oliver lots of space to run and explore. What about you? City or country?"

"Mostly the city but my stepdad loved camping and fishing, so we were always outdoors doing something." He leaned back and stared out the window across the room. "I loved it. Not necessarily because we were doing things outdoors but that we were doing things together."

"Sounds like you miss him."

"I do. He was the best," he said softly. "He was a janitor at the elementary school around the corner from our house. He could have done other things, but after my mom died, he didn't have anyone to watch us, especially my brother. The principal didn't mind him bringing us with him in the evenings when he worked." He blinked as though pulling himself out of whatever place his mind had gone. "Sorry. I didn't mean to say all that."

I nudged him with a foot. "That's what friends are for."

"Yeah." He gave me a long, unreadable look. "Friends."

I twisted and pulled open the drawer to the little end table. Inside was my bottle of heavy-duty, maximum-strength foot cream. This was not one of those bottles of floral-scented stuff. Nope.

"Udder Butter?" Gil asked, eyeing the bottle. "I'm scared to even ask what that's for."

"My feet." I peeled a sock off. "They hurt after being on them all day. This stuff is industrial-strength. If it's good enough for cows, it's good enough for me."

"Right." He watched me squirt lotion on my hand, looking mildly uncomfortable. I liked making him a little uncomfortable. He cleared his throat. "We need to talk."

I groaned. "This again?"

"Forget I said that."

"Too late. I'm already on high alert." I moved onto my second foot.

"Let's start over." He rubbed his forehead. I noticed he did that a lot around me. I also noticed something looked different about him.

"I can't just forget. I'm not a machine."

"Why am I always exhausted after talking to you?" he asked.

He wasn't wearing his glasses. That's what was different. Without them, his face was more striking, more handsome in the classical sense; it even made him seem less stern and more youthful. I sort of liked stern Gil. "Put your glasses back on. I like them."

Surprisingly, he did it without argument. "I am going to have whiplash after this conversation."

"It's never calm up here." I tapped my head and set my feet on the coffee table.

"I'm sure your brain is a scary thing," he said and even though his face hadn't changed expression, his eyes warmed. They were very nice eyes—all navy blue with inky-black eyelashes surrounding them.

I swallowed and dropped my gaze to the lotion bottle I had clutched in my hand. "It's like fifty squirrels all running around shouting, 'I have an idea,' 'No, I have a better idea' and they're all good ideas, but then I don't know which one to pick."

"Why squirrels?"

"What?"

"In your head. Why squirrels and not cats or octopuses?"

With a shrug, I tossed the lotion on the coffee table. "I don't know. They've always been squirrels. Cute, non-threatening woodland creatures with a lot of energy."

"Who like nuts."

"Don't squirrels seem like such anxious animals? Always in a hurry but never quite sure why? So, yeah, squirrels."

"This has definitely become one of the weirdest conversations I have ever had in my life."

"But not the weirdest?" I nodded. "Challenge accepted."

"I have been warned." He took a deep breath. Probably trying to reach a level of Zen he would never accomplish with me around. It was cute, though. "I wanted to *not* talk to you about something."

"Oh, smart. Reverse psychology." I gave him my full attention. "Do go on."

"Ollie's room."

I groaned.

"We need to start going through it. We haven't even opened the door. Who knows what we'll find in there? I'm not subbing tomorrow. I can start."

My hands balled into fists. "Why are you in such a rush?"

"Why are you so set on waiting?"

"Because... because it seems like a real goodbye, okay?" I threw my hands up. "That room is basically one of the last things we have left of Ollie and once we go in there and go through his things, that's it."

Gil tilted his head. "That's not true, you know."

"I know," I snapped. "But that's how it feels."

The thundering of tiny feet came from the hallway, jolting both of us.

"No running in the house, Oliver," I yelled.

The thundering screeched to a halt and then started back again, with only slightly less enthusiasm. Oliver raced around the couch and threw himself on my stomach. "Mommy. Come play dinosaurs with me. Please. Please. Please."

Yawning, I nodded and set my feet on the ground. "You got it, bud."

"How about we let your mom rest, and I'll play?" Gil asked.

Oliver bounced on his feet. "Yes! Come on." Without waiting, he took off at full steam to his room.

"You don't have to do that." I scrambled to my feet and suddenly I was standing mere inches from him. He did not take a step back.

"It's not a big deal," he said.

"But..." My voice trailed off. His eyes drifted down my face and stopped on my mouth. My heartbeat ratcheted up.

"You have some lotion on your face," he said.

"Oh, where?" I rubbed my cheeks, hoping they didn't look as red as they felt. "Did I get it?"

"No." He pointed at a spot above his own mouth. "Right there."

"Here?" I swiped my hand across my mouth. "Still there?"

"No, just, um... here." He hesitated before reaching out a hand slowly. His thumb landed on a spot above my lip. I held perfectly still as he moved his finger, softly, carefully, brushing against my top lip in the process, and then his hand was gone.

It was such a small touch—safe, innocent—and yet, there was a funny little hitch in my breath. My eyes locked with his for one breath, then two. Neither of us moved. I swallowed and told myself to laugh this off immediately. It meant nothing.

"Thanks. I'm such a mess." To prove my point, I pointed to the large red spot on my t-shirt. "Spaghetti accident."

His head tilted to the side, eyes roaming my face in a way that made me want to squirm.

"Mr. Gil, are you coming?" Oliver shouted from his bedroom, breaking whatever strange moment we were having.

"You're sure about this?" I asked.

"It's fine." He took a couple of steps backwards. "We both know I can pronounce the dinosaur names better than you, anyway."

After he left, I reset the timer on my phone and then I closed my eyes and thought about that small innocent touch and for three more minutes, I let myself feel all the feelings.

TWENTY-EIGHT

Love is when you spread kindness to another.

—ANA E., AGE 7

From the sticky note correspondence of Gilbert Dalton and Ellie Sterns:

Gil—

You are hereby formally invited to Easter dinner next month.

It will be at Chris's house. You should come.

—Ellie

P.S. I should probably mention my entire family will be there. So, I understand if you'd rather do pretty much anything other than come to dinner. In fact, can I come with you instead?

Eleanor—

What time is the blessed event?

—Gilbert

P.S. Just admit it. You don't want me to meet your family because then I'll find out you come from a family of traveling circus performers.

Gil—

Around 3 p.m.

—Ellie

P.S. You aren't that far off.

The living room has been put back together. It was the first thing I noticed when Oliver and I got home that night one warm evening at the end of March. It had been a mess when I'd left this morning after I'd torn it apart looking for my car keys.

Spoiler: they were in the bottom of my purse.

But now, all the couch cushions had been straightened. The throw pillows neatly lined up across the back of the couch. The basket of mail I'd overturned in my haste had been righted. Even our shoes had been neatly lined up against the wall by the door.

This whole neatness thing had been happening a lot. Part of me struggled with the embarrassment of knowing that Gil was cleaning up after me; another part of me was just grateful there was someone else around who helped with this stuff.

Messiness seemed to be a way of life for me. Not dirty. I didn't like dirt. But piles? Piles were my jam. I always knew what was in each pile, too. Maybe Gil knew that on some level because while the piles were straightened, they were never sorted through or moved. I'd never lived with someone who noticed little things like that about me.

"Do you want a bath or a shower tonight?" I asked Oliver.

"Do I have to?"

"Yes, you have to. You gotta get the funk off you before bed."

"A shower, then." He bowed his head and slowly, slowly shuffled across the kitchen and down the hall.

"Trust me, when you're older, you'll thank me for instilling the importance of good hygiene," I said as I walked over to the chores board.

I turned to the SOON section and shook my head. Someone, obviously Gil, had decided to organize my sticky notes into categories—household chores, errands, etc. Not only that, but I was positive the number of notes had been slowly and surely dwindling. This coincided with things getting done around the house.

Gil never said a word. For that matter, I hadn't either. I wasn't sure what to make of it exactly. Sure, some things were for the house—like mowing the lawn or replacing the air conditioner filter. With every item that was fixed around the house, it gave me a tiny bit of hope that maybe he was starting to think about the possibility of not selling, a subject I was avoiding as much as possible. Why would he spend time fixing up a house he'd said needed to be bulldozed if he wasn't considering keeping it?

But other things had nothing to do with the house—like buying the book of stamps I'd been meaning to get. I'd found them on the kitchen counter along with a sticky note that just had my name on it. Or the little rack for the keys he'd hung next to the door. It was confusing. Because I liked it. I liked it a lot.

"Mom," Oliver yelled, startling me. "Come here."

"Coming." I hustled down the hallway. "Where are you?"

"Mr. Gil's room."

"Why are you..." My voice faded as I rounded the doorway and into Gil's room and stopped short at the sight in front of me. Gil and Oliver were on the floor along with two tiny black balls of fur.

"Kittens?" I gasped. "How?"

"Look, Mommy." Oliver scooped up one of the kittens and held it close to his face. The kitten rubbed against his nose. He giggled. "Can we keep them, pretty please?"

I dropped to my knees and reached out a hand. Of course I wanted to touch it. I'd always wanted a cat when I was a kid but most of my family were dog people. Once, I found a cat in our backyard and begged to keep it. But its owner showed up at our front door three days later and I had to give it back.

The cat distribution system had never graced me again.

I gave the top of its head a scratch and glanced at Gil. He had the second kitten cuddled up next to his chest. It looked especially tiny in his big hands and, not gonna lie, everything about me wanted to melt at the sight. Handsome man holding kittens. Excuse me? Sign me up.

"Why do you have kittens?" I arranged myself so I was sitting next to him, both of our backs against the side of his bed.

"I found them in the backyard a couple of days ago." The kitten let out a tiny mew and Gil smiled down at it. "They were in those bushes under my window. I could hear them meowing. I waited around for hours, kept checking on them to see if the mama cat returned, but..."

I narrowed my eyes. "And you didn't say anything?"

He had the grace to look sheepish. "I wasn't sure how you felt about cats, and I couldn't just leave them there."

"What exactly was the plan here?" I waved a hand in front of me. Oliver was now laying on the ground. The kitten crawled across his chest and settled under his chin.

Gil shifted uncomfortably. "There wasn't a plan exactly. I thought I'd make sure they were healthy, then find them homes."

I crossed my arms, hoping I looked serious and stern. "And I was never going to find out?"

"No." He glanced down at the squirmy furball in his hand. "I mean, possibly."

"Gilbert Dalton, did you just try to dupe me?"

"Maybe?" He smiled crookedly as he held the kitten toward me. "They're so little and fluffy. Could you resist that face?"

The kitten blinked, then stretched out a tiny paw toward my nose. I held onto a glare for as long as I could before bursting into laughter. I held out my hands. "Can I hold it?"

He slid the kitten into my hands. My skin tingled where our hands touched. The kitten mewed and plopped down. "How old are they, do you think?"

"I guess five weeks, maybe? They've been eating the dry food I got and doing a good job of using the litter box. They do seem to have their days and nights mixed up, though."

I grinned and held up my hands to eye level. The kitten lifted its head and seemed to stare right into my soul. "Just like human babies."

He yawned. "They are all over the place at night."

"Been there, done that." I cuddled the kitten to my chest. "Oliver was the cutest baby. He was born with this scrunched-up, old man face and had these huge eyes."

"I looked like Ollie, didn't I?" Oliver asked even though I'd explained Ollie wasn't an actual relative.

"Exactly like him. Being cute was probably the only reason you survived." I nudged him with my foot.

He giggled. "'Cause I liked to cry all the time."

"All the time. He was perfect during the day but once evening hit, a switch went on and he was inconsolable unless he was being held or attached to my boob." I smiled, remembering those long, long nights. "It's weird, though. It was hard when I was in the middle of it, but I'd give one of my kidneys to hold him one more time when he was that little."

I glanced Gil's way to find him staring at me with a soft expression. I swallowed and looked away.

Gil scooted closer and gently scratched the kitten's head. "I bet you handled it like a champ."

I snorted and glanced at Oliver, who was holding a fully one-sided conversation with the kitten and seemed oblivious to us. Still, I lowered my voice and leaned in, my shoulder brushing his arm. "I was terrified. I was a new mom, single. My mother had stayed with me a whole month before she had to get back. I had no idea what I was doing. Still don't most days."

He dipped his head closer, his voice low and quiet. "You're a great mom. Anyone can see that."

Warmth bloomed in my chest, but I kept my eyes on the kitten, almost embarrassed to look at him.

Slowly, he raised his hand and brushed my cheek with a featherlight touch. His fingers left a trail of warmth behind. I wanted him to do it again. "You had something on your cheek."

I swallowed and looked at him. "Thanks."

His eyes moved between my eyes before dropping to my mouth. My heart flipped over in my chest. If either of us moved a couple of inches, what would happen? Would he kis—

"Do they have names?" Oliver asked. Both of us sprang apart.

I'd completely forgotten about my own child for a minute there. What had I been thinking? Was I so starved of affection that I took a compliment and an innocent touch and blew it out of proportion?

Gil cleared his throat. "No, I haven't. Everyone knows if you name a stray, they're yours forever."

Oliver sat up and set the kitten in his lap. "Mom. Mom.

Mom. *Please* can we keep them? I'll help take care of them and everything."

I sighed. Did I really need more things to keep alive and fed and happy? No. But how could I deny the kid? "Well, I guess we should start thinking about names."

TWENTY-NINE

[Love is...] Mommy playing with me and giving me hugs.

—NATHAN, AGE 6

From the group text chat of the Sterns sisters:

MILLIE: *Why did you send us a photo of kittens?*

ELLIE: *We found them in the backyard.*

AGGIE: *They're so cute.*

BETSY: *Are you keeping them?*

ELLIE: *Yep. Oliver is very attached already.*

MILLIE: *Yay! Do they have names?*

ELLIE: *I'm letting Oliver name them. Right now, his top choices are Peach Love and Apple Heart.*

BETSY: *Is it me or do those sound like stripper names?*

March rolled into April and brought gorgeous weather, topping out in the eighties but not quite humid enough to feel like I was melting when I stepped outside. After dinner, I'd hoped to bribe Oliver with ice cream if he'd drag himself to the outlet mall with me so I could pick up a birthday present for one of my sisters.

There was just one teeny-tiny problem. My purse was missing. I'd spent the last fifteen minutes opening every cabinet in the kitchen, looking under the kitchen table and in the tub of shoes in the living room, even the bathroom. (It had happened once; don't judge.)

I did find one sock (under the coffee table), one of the four pairs of spare car keys I kept hidden (in the kitchen junk drawer), a forgotten bag of Halloween candy (chocolate was still good after five months, right?).

"Where are they?" I muttered then yelled, "Oliver? Gil? Anyone seen my purse?"

No one answered. As I passed through the living room to find them, I caught motion in the front driveway. Looking out the window, I could see Oliver standing next to my car, which had been moved out from under the carport. Obviously not by him... I hoped. The hood stood open, but Oliver was looking down at the pair of jean-clad legs sticking out from under the car.

I pulled open the front door and stepped out. "Um, what's going on here?"

"Mommy!" Oliver ran to me and pushed me back toward the house. "You aren't supposed to see yet. It's a surprise."

"For me?"

Oliver stamped his foot. "Yes. You have to go back inside."

"But—"

"Right now, Mommy."

"Alright." I held up my hands in defeat. "I get it. I'm going."

Once I was back inside, I peeked through the curtains and watched the scene before me. Oliver hovered near Gil who was still under the car. Although I couldn't hear what he was saying, I knew he was jabbering a hundred miles a minute. Knowing that kid, he had probably already asked seven thousand questions.

After a few minutes, Gil slid out from under the car and stood up.

My mouth dropped.

Mr. Gilbert "Buttoned-Up, Hair Always Combed, Pants with Creases" Dalton was none of those things at the moment. He had on worn blue jeans—there was even a hole in one of the knees—and I watched while he grabbed the back of his black t-shirt and whipped it over his head.

I sucked in a breath. "Oh. Mama."

This Gilbert Dalton was dirty and messy, his hair all over the place. His back was facing me. I now understood why the hero in a Regency romance novel is overcome with desperate attraction when some saucy woman flashes her ankle at him. In this case, those ankles were Gil's back and, oh my stars, his arms!

Big, strong arms attached to wide shoulders that tapered down to his waist. I'd only seen a flash of this a couple of weeks ago. But now, he had no idea I was watching, and I could look my fill. He wasn't overly muscled or a rippling mass or made of two percent body fat and protein shakes, nor did he resemble a marble statue. But that made it even better because he looked real and... and touchable.

And then there were the tattoos. Principal Gil had tattoos, or rather one large one. I could see it clearly from my vantage point hiding behind the living room curtain. It looked to be a bundle of colored bluebonnets and Indian paintbrushes off-center of his back and reaching up to touch his neck. A butterfly frozen in flight fluttered above the flowers as though it was about to land. I wanted to see it up close and discover what it meant, and could I touch them, please and thank you.

This was not good. Men with tattoos that took up half their back were nothing but trouble. Been there, done that. No, thank you. But tattoos on Gil… that was next-level temptation. That's what it was.

"Oh, no," I whispered. I might need an emergency session with Sunny.

Oliver began walking toward the house. I raced to the couch and threw myself down, trying to look like I hadn't been drooling at the window mere seconds ago.

Oliver burst in. "Mommy!"

"Where is your shirt?" I asked.

He puffed out his skinny chest. "I tooked it off. So did Mr. Gil. 'Cause it got hot after all our hard work."

"I see." I stood up. "We should get you some sunscreen."

"Later." He grabbed one of my hands and tugged me toward the door. "Come see what we did."

"Coming." I fussed with my hair, trying to calm the flyaway bits, as I made my way outside. Oliver skipped ahead, his steps light with excitement.

Gil was leaning against the door of my car, still shirtless. My crappy, twenty-something-year-old car with more than a few dents and dings, one taillight that needed replacing every six months or so because there was an electrical short somewhere, and at least one tire that needed to be replaced soon, had never looked so good.

Don't stare. Don't stare. Do not stare. I pulled my t-shirt away from my chest to let a little air in. It was *super* hot out here.

Oliver ran ahead and mimicked Gil's stance. "Guess what? Guess what? We did a…" He turned to Gil. "What did we do?"

"An oil change."

"An oil change," I repeated.

Gil crossed his arms. Don't look. Don't look. Don't—I looked. I looked and I looked. There was another tattoo on his chest, the simple outline of a heart. Just above it was what appeared to be stylized birds in flight, two of them. Each was a different color. Gil didn't have the frat boy, drunken night of debauchery and blurry trips to a tattoo shop feel about him. He was methodical about his *laundry*. Surely, he'd put even more thought into what was put permanently on his skin.

"It was on one of your sticky notes."

"Hmm?" Pay attention. I dragged my gaze back up to his face. One corner of his mouth inched up a tiny bit. But his cheeks were pink and something about the tension in his body screamed nervous energy.

"One of your sticky notes said you needed an oil change. So..." he rubbed at the back of his neck which, in turn, made the muscles in that arm bulge which, in turn, distracted me "...it's been up there the whole time I've been here. I thought I could take care of it."

"Oh," I whispered, his words sinking in. He'd seen my sticky note and he'd taken care of it. I had a sudden urge to cry. "I don't know what to say."

"It wasn't a big deal," Gil said, pushing off from the car, and I had a feeling he wanted to get out of the spotlight, and fast. "You needed it."

This time I blushed, my toes curling in my shoes. "I know. It's one of those things I don't think about and then I let it go too long."

Aside from my dad when I lived at home, I'd never had anyone who did things like this for me. It was so... practical. Apparently that was a big turn-on for me. I mean, yes, I wanted the flowers, and the chocolates, and the love notes but, wow oh wow, changing my oil might be the way to my heart.

"I got to be his assistant." Oliver puffed his chest out.

"I bet you did a great job, too." I kissed the top of his head. "Thank you very much."

Without thinking about it too hard, I stepped closer to Gil. Stretching on my tippy-toes, I pressed a kiss to his cheek. "Thank you, too."

"You're welcome," he said gruffly.

Our eyes met. He smiled slowly. A real, full-on smile that made my insides melt.

I swallowed. "I should go make dinner."

On autopilot, I turned and started back to the house. Eternally happy he didn't say a word about how we'd eaten dinner an hour ago so there was none for me to make.

Right as I ducked into the house, I heard Oliver ask, "Does this mean you're Mommy's boyfriend now?"

THIRTY

[Love] means having joy with your friends and family.

—BRENDAN M., AGE 7

From the sticky note correspondence of Gilbert Dalton and Ellie Sterns:

Gil—

There's leftover meatloaf in the fridge. Feel free to have some.

—Ellie

Eleanor—

The meatloaf was good.

—Gilbert

P.S. Pick a day to go through Ollie's room. Please.

Gil—

There's leftover chili in there too. Have at it.

—Ellie

P.S. Maybe next week.

Eleanor—

Do you ever make pork chops?

—Gilbert

P.S. Maybe I could start without you.

Gil—

You should just eat dinner with Oliver and me tomorrow. 5:30 p.m.

Don't be late or all the pork chops will be gone.

—Ellie

P.S. Do not go through his room without me!

I set the serving plate piled high with breaded pork chops in the center of the table. It joined the mashed potatoes and roasted Brussels sprouts. I gestured to Gil and Oliver who were already seated. "Let's eat."

I typically brought home leftovers from the café for us to eat. Saved me from having to cook a full dinner, especially just for Oliver and me. But I'd wanted to make Gil pork chops as a thank you for changing my oil and the other little things he'd done around the house. That was it, I swear. A home-cooked meal was an excellent way to endear him to me and this house. It was part of my plan. That's all.

Oh, fine, maybe a teeny-tiny part of me wanted to impress him, to make something special just for him. Why? I don't know. My brain was making weird decisions where Gil was involved lately. To say my feelings toward Gil were confusing would be an understatement.

Sunny tried to tell me that maybe I should see where these feelings led. Then we'd had a whole different discussion involving the other times in my life I let my feelings lead me. For example:

Impulsively running off to Los Angeles the day after high school graduation because it sounded exciting? CHECK.

Dating that one guy because I loved that he called me "Babe" for almost three months only to realize he called me that because he didn't know my name? CHECK.

Letting my drummer boyfriend move in after the first date because I was pretty sure it was love at first sight only to watch him move out after he knocked me up? DOUBLE CHECK.

My feelings were not to be trusted. Period.

I slid in my seat and helped Oliver load his plate. He happily took a pork chop and the potatoes but wrinkled his nose at the Brussels sprouts. "Do I have to eat those?"

"Yes, sir. What's the rule?"

He sighed with all the fervor of a six-year-old. "We have to eat one green thing for dinner."

Yes, I did take that parenting tip from *Sleepless in Seattle.* Why reinvent the wheel?

"Bingo." I spooned two on his plate.

Gil reached for the bowl of Brussels sprouts. "You made baby lettuce."

Oliver giggled. "Those aren't baby lettuces, silly."

"They aren't?" Frowning, Gil speared a sprout and held it

up to eye level. "Nope, that's a baby lettuce. We had these all the time when I was a kid. These, and baby trees."

"Baby trees? We don't eat baby trees."

"Some people call it broccoli but that's because they don't know they're secretly baby trees." He nodded to the bowl of Brussels sprouts. "Just like those are baby lettuce in disguise. They're like the Superman of vegetables."

I covered my mouth to hide my smile.

Oliver's eyes darted between the vegetable in question and Gil, looking more curious than suspicious.

Gil reached for Oliver's plate. "If you aren't going to eat yours..."

"No. Wait. I'll eat them. See?" He picked one up (with his fingers, no less) and shoved the whole thing in his mouth. He chewed slowly, his face going through a myriad of expressions— disgust, resignation, victory. After swallowing, he grinned.

"Pretty good, huh?" Gil said.

To answer, Oliver shoved another one in his mouth.

The Superman of vegetables? I mouthed after catching Gil's eye.

It worked, right? He shrugged and took his first bite of pork chop. It was a family recipe and one I'd grown up eating. His eyes slid shut and he almost, almost smiled.

At first the conversation was stilted and awkward, but Oliver quickly took the reins. He shared about his day and silly new jokes he learned and a new dinosaur he'd discovered and about his "girlfriend," Darla.

"Don't you think you're a little young to settle down?" I asked.

"I love Darla," Oliver said with rock-solid conviction that was impressive.

I set my fork down and made a mental note to figure out which little girl Darla was, and fast. "Love? That's a big word."

"'I love her," Oliver said with a firm nod of his head.

"'Cause she always gives me her chocolate pudding at lunch and she liked dinosaurs too and she's pretty and that's why I love her and I'm gonna grow up and get married to her."

Gil coughed to cover a laugh. "That seems like a big commitment."

Oliver's expression turned thoughtful. "I have to get big first and save up lots of money to buy us a house. It's going to have a slide in the backyard because Darla likes slides the best. Teacher says when you love someone, you do all their favorite things with them even if you don't like them. But first Mom has to find a boyfriend and get married and give me a baby brother."

I groaned. "Oliver."

"What?" he said, all innocent big eyes.

"I'll get a boyfriend when I'm good and ready. And you're too young to talk about marriage. You need to be at least ten before you start doing that."

"Your mom has a point. I'm thirty-one and I haven't given marriage much thought at all," Gil said.

Oliver gasped. "You're old."

"Oliver!" I jumped in. "You don't tell people they're old. It's not polite."

"Sorry. You aren't old." Oliver patted Gil's arm. "Have you never had a girlfriend afore? My mom needs a boyfriend. I think you should be it. Then you can get married."

My mouth dropped open, my face burning. Gil's eyes met mine over the pork chops. One side of his mouth quirked, and his eyes twinkled in amusement. I liked when he smiled. I liked seeing those little lines in the corners of his eyes crinkle. I liked how easy he was with Oliver, too. I liked how my stomach swooshed and my pulse jumped when I saw any of those things.

That was an awful lot to like about the man in so little time. Especially when I'd been so concerned with *not* liking him not so long ago.

For one awful, terrible, wonderful moment, my mind imagined another life where we three were a family, huddled around our dinner table as we told each other about our day and laughed at silly things Oliver said.

"Ollie told me all about you, Mr. Gil. He said you would be a good boyfriend for my mom. He said you two should meet one day and he was going to make it happen come hell or high water." Oliver paused and gave me a sheepish look. "Don't get mad at me 'cause I said hell. I'm just saying what Ollie said."

There were very few times in my life where I could say I was speechless. But this was one of them. After several beats of silence, I touched his arm, keeping my voice gentle. "Oliver, what do you mean, Ollie said all that? You know Ollie's in Heaven now."

"Of course I know that." He shrugged and stuffed a bit of potato in his mouth. "He tolded me before he went to Heaven. He said I shouldn't be sad about him going because he wasn't sad about it. He made me promise."

I flopped back in my seat, overwhelmed by this piece of news. What did a person say to this? Especially to a six-year-old. Ollie had told Oliver about Gil? How had my kid kept such a secret? And the very idea of Ollie as a matchmaker? I almost wanted to laugh.

He couldn't have cared less about my love life. There'd been just once, when I'd broken it off with someone I'd dated a whole month, a nice guy, a guy I'd thought might have potential. But on our fifth date, he gave me the "it's not you, it's me" speech. Yeah, right. I'd gone into the café after. Oliver played with his building blocks; I rage-baked.

I'd only been there twenty minutes when Ollie slipped in. He didn't say anything, just went about helping me roll out the dough for pie crust. We worked like that for almost an hour, side by side. Ollie's silence could drive a person crazy most days but sometimes it was nice to have someone who understood that there wasn't much to be said.

When someone's sad or upset, others feel like they need to make them feel better by saying things like, "It will all be okay," or "This was for the best," or "God has a plan." And then in response, I felt like I had to reassure them. "Thank you, I know it will get better."

But you know what? In the moment, it never felt like it would get better. It was an open wound, and all their comments felt more like they were pouring alcohol on it. Sometimes I just wanted someone to sit beside me and let me be angry or sad or lonely or confused.

And gruff, standoffish Ollie? He'd been that person for me. It was only after I announced I needed to get Oliver home to bed that he turned to me and said six words: "He's an idiot. It's his loss."

I'd been three seconds away from reaching out and hugging the man. But I stopped myself in time. This was Ollie; he'd probably never speak to me again if I did that.

I really missed him.

And I had no idea what to make of what Oliver's announcement or these *feelings* about Gil. Time to avoid, and deal with it later.

"I think it's time for dessert." Without waiting for a response, I stood up and took up my plate and Oliver's and practically sprinted to the kitchen.

I took the lid off the container of brownies I'd made last night. That was after searching for a low-sugar, chocolate-but-not-real-chocolate recipe. I cut it into squares and piled them on a plate. With a flourish, I set it in the middle of the table.

"I made banana walnut brownies. No added sugar and made with carob instead of chocolate."

Oliver's nose scrunched. "Why didn't you make the fudge brownies? Those are my favorite."

"Just eat it, okay?" I set one on his napkin and took a seat, nervous to look over at Gil. Nervous he'd read into these brownies more than he should. They were just brownies. That's it. They didn't mean anything significant. I was being kind. That's all. Because he had changed my oil.

"No sugar, no chocolate," Gil said quietly. He took one for himself.

I shrugged. "I know you said sugar and chocolate give you migraines. No promises though. It could taste terrible."

Judging by the expression on his face after the first bite, they didn't taste terrible at all. His eyes slid shut as he chewed slowly like he was savoring every bit.

Then his eyes opened. His gaze met mine, his eyes soft but no less intense. He didn't say a word, but my mouth went dry. Hastily, I chugged down the rest of my water.

"Can I have another one?" Oliver asked, brown crumbs marching down his chin to his shirt.

"One is enough for now." I stood and picked up the plate to take back into the kitchen. As I moved away, Gil's hand wrapped around my wrist.

"Wait," he said. His thumb stroked gently on the inside of my wrist where the skin was delicate and extra sensitive. I wasn't even sure he knew he was doing it. But I knew. A zing of longing hit me in the chest, and it was hard to breathe for one beat, then two. "Thank you."

With a nod, I tugged my arm from his grip, feeling like I'd been bowled over by a tornado in the last fifteen seconds. Because I'd just made a discovery.

I liked Gilbert Dalton.

Not just liked, but *liked*.

Panic prickled the back of my neck. In the kitchen, I set down the dishes and pinched myself. That was easier than pounding my head into the nearest hard surface. I could do that later in the privacy of my own room. My mind raced at breakneck speed toward the worst possible scenario.

Catastrophizing Level: Expert.

We all *knew* my feelings could not be trusted when it came to men. Just look at my record. I was guilty of attracting every red flag man in continental USA and probably Canada, too. Europe most likely lived in fear I'd come for a visit.

If I were feeling any sort of soft, fuzzy feelings toward Gil, I needed to get my head on straight.

No, I should not be making meaningful glances at Gil over the dinner table. I should definitely not admire his toolbelt. I should not be a little turned on by the school principal energy he gave off when he was annoyed. I should not be replaying a simple, innocent touch. I should not be recalling the sound of his voice singing "Amazing Grace" when I laid down to sleep at night.

Lest we all forget, my man picker had picked wrong so many times before. And the one fact I couldn't escape... the two of us had very different ideas about what would happen to Ollie's property in a couple of months. If he got his way, I'd lose everything I'd worked for during the last three years. And he'd made no qualms about the fact he was leaving as soon as his six months were over.

Gil Dalton could break my heart in so many ways.

Nope. For once in my life, I would not be relying on my man picker.

And that was that.

THIRTY-ONE

I don't know, it means you love them.

—LAUREN S., AGE 4

"I'm going to see the kittens," Oliver said the second we stepped in the house. We'd gone for a long walk after dinner. It had been an especially beautiful day with lower-than-average humidity for the beginning of April.

Oliver shot out of the kitchen without waiting for me to reply. We'd moved them to our laundry room when no one was home and let them out when we were. Oliver still hadn't decided on names although he was workshopping Cinnamon and Sugar.

"Not for too long. It's past bedtime," I called. But I wasn't too worried. Oliver had all week off for spring break, so staying up a little later wouldn't hurt too much.

I headed to my bedroom to gather some clothes for the wash. But then I saw it. There at the end of the hallway, the door to Ollie's room was open.

I froze, my stomach flipped. Gil wouldn't have, would he?

But there was the evidence as clear as day. Hands curled into fists, I stormed down the hallway and burst into the room. "What are you doing in here?"

Gil sat on the bed, staring down at a picture frame. He glanced up at me and back down without saying anything.

I stomped over to him. "Excuse me. I thought we were going to do this together."

"I got tired of waiting," he mumbled, his eyes never leaving the picture.

"I cannot believe you. You knew how I felt about this." I waved an arm around the room. Ollie's room.

Slowly, I turned in a circle to take everything in. The first thing of note: this room was clean, neat, organized. Not at all like the rest of the house had been when we moved in. Soft blue paint covered the walls and a wallpaper border with alternating ships and whales wrapped around the room. A long chest of drawers, a dresser, two nightstands, a small file cabinet next to a desk, wood floors that looked worn but cared for. Overall, a very normal room. Except for the picture frames resting on every available surface and wall space. I'd never seen so many photographs displayed in one place at a time.

"Whoa. This is not what I expected." When he didn't reply, I whirled back to him. He looked pale, his expression almost sad. "Hey, are you okay? I'm trying to yell at you, and you look like someone stole your lunch."

Slowly, he turned the picture frame around to reveal a skinny, dark-haired boy standing on a boat dock wearing a pair of blue swim trunks and a huge smile and holding a fish dangling from his hand with a line.

"This is me. I was eight here," Gil said. "It was taken when my stepdad took me fishing for the first time."

"Oh." I sat next to him on the bed and took the frame from him and studied it. Little Boy Gil had gangly arms, knobby, skinned-up knees, and eyeglasses a touch too big for his face.

Gil picked up another photo from a small pile on the other side of him. "This was when I won the school spelling bee in seventh grade. That's my mom." His fingers traced the boy in the photo holding up a ribbon that said first place. Standing next to him was a pretty dark-haired woman with smiling blue eyes. Gil had her eyes. "I remember the exact moment this photo was taken."

"What was the winning word?"

"Silhouette." He huffed a laugh. "It wasn't even a word I'd studied. But my mom loved to read those Harlequin Silhouette books and that's how I knew it." The amusement drained from his face. "She died two days later in a car accident."

My heart screeched to a halt. "Oh, Gil. I'm so sorry."

"It was a long time ago."

"I don't think that's something you ever get over."

He set the photo aside. "I was lucky. I had my stepdad. He never made me feel unwanted, even though I wasn't related to him by blood. And I was a little shit for a while there. I pushed every button he had. He was a good man."

"Sounds like it."

"He would have liked you." Before I even had a moment to process this, he picked up another photo. "My mom and stepdad's wedding." And another. "My mom's high school graduation." And yet another. "My high school graduation."

I grabbed that last picture from him and studied it. The teenage boy in the photo was still growing into his body, but the bones were there. Tall, lanky, with wide shoulders. A cocky expression. He wasn't smiling; he was smirking.

I grinned. "You had long hair?"

He snatched the frame back. "It was a phase."

"That is a *look*. Please tell me you were in a garage band."

His cheeks pinked up. "No."

"No, you weren't?"

"No, I'm not telling you."

I bounced on the bed. "Tell me your band name. Please tell me."

"No."

"Please?" I wrapped my hands around his arm and leaned into him, batting my eyes playfully. "Pretty please."

Shaking his head, he closed his eyes and muttered something.

"What was that?"

"Jungle Cat Dropouts."

"No," I breathed. "This is amazing."

"Whatever." He laid the photo down on the bed, picture side down. "All these photos. All of them are of me or my mom. Years and years of photos. How? I didn't even know Ollie's name until last year when the letters from the attorney came. My mom didn't even know until her mother passed away and, even then, she never told me. Maybe she would have but she died when I was young."

I stood and took my time inspecting the other photos in the room. Aside from a few photos of Ollie's Two Harts family, almost all the photos were of Gil or his mom. There were even a few of Oliver. I picked one photo that made me smile.

Somehow, I'd managed to talk Ollie into going on a little outing to Legacy Park. Oliver was about four at the time, his cheeks round and pinchable. Oliver was clutching Ollie's hand and the two of them were ahead of me. I'd snapped a photo at just the right moment with the sunshine peeking through the trees and casting a ray of light on them. It was one of my favorite pictures. I'd printed it out, framed it, and given it to Ollie that Christmas. He'd stared at it for a long time, muttered a thank you, and we never spoke of it again. And to think, all this time, it had been sitting right here in his room.

"I had no idea Ollie was so sentimental." I set the photo back on the dresser.

"All of these photos. He... he knew about us? How do you think he got these?" Gil stood and moved to stand next to me.

"I don't know." I moved around the room, Gil following me. There were more photos than I'd noticed at first. Every available inch of space held some memory, it seemed.

"Oh, my goodness, look at these." I paused in front of four or five sepia-colored photos on the wall.

"Wait," Gil said, peering at one photo of Ollie and two other people. One was a tall guy about Ollie's age with wild hair and a huge smile. Something about him seemed familiar but I couldn't put my finger on why. The other person was a slender, dark-haired woman. Ollie had his arm around her shoulders. "I think that's my grandma."

"Really?" I moved closer, my shoulder brushing against his arm. At first the photo seemed it was nothing more than two friends laughing but the more I stared at the photo, the more I realized these two were more than friends. It was in the subtle tilt of her head toward him, in how they stood a little closer than was necessary. "What was her name?"

"Amelia."

"Amelia." I rolled the name around. "I like that. Did you spend a lot of time with her?"

"Every summer. They lived in Louisiana so we'd go and visit, and my mom would leave me there for a good month in the summertime."

"Sounds fun."

"Oh, it was. Grandpa Joe, her husband, the man my mother knew as her father, was Cajun and wild on top of it." He smiled slowly. "He was always getting into something or another and I got to follow along."

I wanted to keep asking him questions. I'd already learned more about him in the last ten minutes than I'd learned in the last six weeks.

"I don't know what this all means." Gil moved to the middle

of the room and stood, hands on hips. His eyes landed near the desk. "I wonder what that filing cabinet has in it."

"We could check."

"We could."

Neither of us moved.

"Or not," I said. "We don't have to look right now."

Gil took a deep breath and marched across the room. He tugged on the top drawer. "It's locked."

"There's probably a key somewhere." I began opening drawers and searching the tops of the dressers.

"Mommy?" Oliver asked from the doorway. "Why are you in here?"

"Mr. Gil wanted to see what Ollie's room looked like."

"Oh." His expression bordering on reverent, he turned in a circle, taking in the room.

"Found it," Gil said. The top drawer of the file cabinet was opened to reveal... files.

"Why's there a key in the door?" Oliver fingered the doorknob.

Gil glanced over his shoulder. "That's how I got in. You know that bowl of random keys in the kitchen? One of them worked." He pulled out a file and began to flip through it.

"Oh." Oliver stared at the key.

Even from the other side of the room, I could practically hear the gears in his head moving. "What's going on over there?"

Oliver jolted. His gaze swung between Gil and me. "I love you, Mommy."

"Love you, too, kiddo. Why don't you go get your pajamas on? We'll skip bathtime for tonight. I'll be in there to read in five minutes."

"Okay." He backed out of the room, pulling the door closed behind him.

"Sometimes I wish I knew what was going on in that kid's

head." I crossed the room and stood next to Gil, trying to peek at the folder. "Did you find something?"

"Maybe," he said, his eyes never leaving the pages.

I waited for more information and did not get any. "You gonna give me a little more than that?"

"It's all about my mom." He shut the file and held it out to me. "There's everything. A copy of her birth certificate, a list of places she worked, the address for the house where we lived."

I peered over his shoulder. "That doesn't seem like information a man who abandoned his kid would have."

The file snapped shut. "If that's the case, why didn't he ever contact her?"

"Maybe he did, and you don't know about it."

With a frown, he set the file on top of the cabinet and went back to thumbing through the files. "I don't get it."

"I need to go put Oliver to bed," I said.

"Sure." He didn't even glance my way.

"Okay, then." I pulled at the bedroom door and... it didn't budge. I tried it again. Huh. I put a little more oomph into it but still, nothing. "Ah, Gil?"

"Yeah?"

I laughed nervously. "Any reason this door wouldn't open?"

"Not that I can think of," he said absently.

I gave the door another jerk. Nothing. "And yet, it's not opening."

"Don't be ridiculous. It opens." He walked over and brushed my hand off the doorknob. With all the confidence of a grown man getting weighed at the doctor's office, he yanked on the knob and still nothing happened. He glared at it like it had personally offended his mother, his grandmother, and his virility. "It won't open."

"I told you that." I knocked on the door. "Oliver? Oliver!"

I waited several long seconds before I heard him stampeding down the hallway. "Yes, Mommy?"

"Can you open the door?"

"You probably have to turn the key in the lock," Gil said.

"There isn't a key in the lock."

"Honey, yes, there is. It was right there a minute ago."

Silence. A long, long silence. Eerie silence. The sort of silence I knew did not bode well.

"Oliver?" I put a little growl in my voice.

"I took the key out," he said and quickly added, "but I have it safe. I didn't lose it or nothing. And don't worry, I brushed my teef and I locked all the doors in the house and made sure the kittens had food and water, and I'll go right to sleep so you don't have to worry about me and you'll see, in the morning, you'll come out and be in love and be boyfriend and girlfriend. Ollie tolded me that was the plan."

I laid my hand on the door. "Oliver Lucas Sterns, we talked about this. Ollie is in Heaven. He couldn't have told you that."

"But he did," Oliver insisted.

"It is not okay to make up stories."

"I'm not making it up. Ollie tolded me about Mr. Gil."

"Oliver, you need to open this door immediately," Gil said. The grumpiness in his voice needed its own zip code.

"I can't, Mr. Gil. I promised Ollie. And a man's word is his promise, right? That's what the Man Club motto is."

I glared at Gil. "You had to start a stupid club with him, didn't you?"

"I'm going to bed now. Love you, Mommy. Night."

"Open this door. Now. Do you hear me?" I pressed my forehead against the door.

"I cannot believe this," Gil said.

I turned and held out my hand. "Give me your phone."

"I don't have my phone."

"Of course you do."

"I don't. It's in my room. Use your phone."

I could picture it right now sitting on the kitchen counter with my purse. "I don't have it on me."

"We're phoneless?" He gave the door one more yank. "And we're stuck."

I took a deep breath, determined I would not panic. It wasn't that big of a deal. It could be worse. I could be locked in a room with Gilbert Dalton while he was wearing his toolbelt and cuddling kittens and have to talk myself out of mauling him.

That wouldn't be bad either, a voice said in my head. Not bad at all.

Neither of us spoke. I felt his eyes on my face but when I turned, he looked away. This was awkward. We were two grown adult humans who could weather the course for a few hours locked up in a room together. It would be a breeze, all things considered.

"So, Jungle Cat Dropouts," I said. "Please tell me they did a cover of 'The Lion Sleeps Tonight.' Maybe 'Eye of the Tiger.' Oh, I know, I know. 'Welcome to the Jungle.'"

With a groan, Gil threw himself on the bed and pulled a pillow over his head.

THIRTY-TWO

Love is a feeling of deep affection.

—MICHAEL D., AGE 13

"Good news," I said as I walked out of the attached master bathroom. It wasn't especially master-like but it was functional and clean. Well, clean enough after months of disuse. "There's plenty of toilet paper."

"What are we going to do?" Gil stalked back and forth across the room.

Yawning, I flopped down on the bed and stared up at the ceiling. "I'm going to take away every dinosaur toy and book that kid owns for the rest of his life."

Or a week. Probably just a week.

"What time is it?" I asked, feeling that 4 a.m. wake-up coming back to haunt me.

"A little after nine."

I groaned and buried my face in a pillow. "I'm so tired. Can you stop pacing?"

"No."

I sat up. "Why not?"

"Because."

"Would it kill you to say more than one word at a time?"

"Yes."

I sat up and hiked a throw pillow at his head. It hit the target; I was impressed. Gil wasn't. But he did sit on the other side of the bed, all silent and brooding and grumpy and annoyed.

"Your anxiety is going to make my anxiety start and then we'll just be two anxious people trapped in a room together and we might get desperate. We might, I don't know, seek comfort in each other's arms."

"What?" he said, his voice strangled.

"See? It could be worse."

"This is because you read those romance novels."

"Excuse me?"

"They're all over the house. Found one in the bathroom, on the couch. Even found one next to the milk in the refrigerator. I don't want to see a half-naked man mauling a woman when I'm trying to make breakfast."

I laid back down and crossed my arms. "Whatever."

"Although the pirate thing surprised me."

"Okay. Okay. I got it."

"Actually, the romance novels in general. You really into that?" The bed dipped and groaned as he stretched out on it.

"Mae and Ali are making me read them."

"Why?"

I nibbled my bottom lip before I flipped on my side to face him. He was lying on his back, hands folded behind his head at the very edge of the bed, as though he wanted to be as far away from me as humanly possible. I almost laughed out loud. Sometimes I wondered if he was afraid of me.

"I have a broken man picker."

Slowly he turned his head. "A broken what?"

"Man picker. I can't pick out the good ones. They're always deadbeats, losers, bums, weirdos, emotionally unavailable, jerks or a combination of any and all of the above. My therapist Sunny says I attract them because I need to love myself first before I find a partner who will love me like I deserve. I'm working on that."

He was quiet for a moment before asking, "So then Oliver's dad..."

"Ah, yes. Oliver's dad has seen him exactly twice his whole life. Sometimes he sends a birthday card. Occasionally a present that's completely inappropriate. Last Christmas, he sent him a pocketknife."

"Sounds like a nice guy."

"If there's a jerk anywhere in a ten-mile radius, he will find me. I will fall for him, and it will end badly for me." I stared at the stitching on the blue floral quilt covering Ollie's bed. "I'm oversharing. Sorry."

"I asked." He paused and then, "So, the pirates are supposed to teach you about romance?"

"To remind me romance exists. I don't believe in all that stuff. Or maybe I did once upon a time but not anymore. Sometimes I wish it were true. I'd love the grand gesture and the flowers and chocolates and hand-holding and asking my dad to marry me, a meet-cute."

Gil's brow wrinkled. "What is a meet-cute?"

"It's the first time you meet The One. Like you're both hailing the same cab or she bumps into you and spills her coffee all over you and you're on your way to the biggest meeting of your life. The story you'll tell your grandkids one day."

"Ah." He turned on his side. We were facing each other, which felt strangely intimate despite the three feet between us. This was an absurdly large bed for a guy who'd been as compact as Ollie has been.

"I've always thought maybe one day I'd be in a bookstore, looking at—"

"Pirate romances." His grin was quick and lethal. Boy, oh, boy, when he smiled, it made my stomach flutter in the most delicious way.

I laughed. "A good book about a serial killer."

"How romantic."

"Yeah, well. Maybe if I ever get a happily ever after, I'll become a romantic." I shook my head. "You did it again."

"Did what?"

"You got information out of me, and I still know so little about you."

He shifted onto his back. "Not much about me to tell."

"Really?" I tapped my chin with a finger as though I was thinking about what to ask him when, in fact, I had a list of questions so long, it riveled a CVS receipt. "Because I have a huge list of questions. Do you iron your underwear? Why did you break up with your last girlfriend? Have you ever been arrested? What are your hopes and dreams? What's your brother like?"

He didn't answer right away, and I thought maybe he wouldn't at all. I could all but see the gears working overtime in his head.

"No, I do not iron my underwear. Who does that?"

"Not even one time?"

"No."

I hummed in disbelief.

He closed his eyes. "Once, but I recognized the final product was not worth the effort."

"I knew it."

"Okay, and what about you? Do you ever fold your clothes?"

"Hey, now, Oliver's clothes are always folded and put away."

Principal Gil raised a brow in reply. A piece of dark hair fell across his forehead in rebellion. I itched to push it back in place, so I shoved my hands under my cheek to stop myself.

"I have a very advanced clothing system," I said. "A clean pile, a dirty pile, and a I-wore-this-once-and-I-can-wear-it-again pile. It works out pretty well for me."

He laughed softly. "Question number two. My last girl-friend and I broke up because I moved back home with my stepdad and brother. It was a very mature, adult break-up. We discussed it over coffee and then parted ways."

"Whoa. I can feel the passion. Did you break up or change phone carriers?"

"She was great, really." He paused, searching for his words. His glasses were a little crooked from laying on his side. It was adorable. "I think I was the problem. Life got complicated. What about you? Last break-up?"

"Oophf." I sat up and curled my legs under me. Better to put distance between us. "That would have been back in LA. Oliver was about two? He broke up with me because he thought the universe was telling him it was time. Turns out the universe was also telling him to get back with his ex-girlfriend."

"Ouch." He sat up and scooted a little closer. "Sounds like an idiot."

"Broken man picker, remember?"

"No other relationships since?"

I shrugged and hugged a pillow to my chest. "Lots of first dates, a few lasted for a month or so but no one serious and no one I wanted to introduce to Oliver. That kid only gets the best of the best and that hasn't happened yet."

He looked at me from the corner of his eye for a long moment. "Yes to the arrest question. The first time, I was thir-teen. It was the year my mom died, and I started to act out a lot. Some neighborhood kids found a bunch of spray paint in their garage, and we started daring each other to tag things. I was the one who got caught."

"You rebel."

"The police officer didn't really arrest me. He did put hand-cuffs on me, put me in the back of the patrol car, and drove me home to make an example out of me. I got a lecture the whole drive, too. It didn't help. I was determined to ruin my life." He shook his head.

"Sounds like you were a handful."

"More like a kid who couldn't deal with his feelings. I can see that now but being that age is hard and losing my mom... I didn't know how to cope. Unfortunately, it lasted for a few years. I'm not sure how my stepdad didn't kick me out. I skipped school constantly, got into fights, snuck out of the house. When I was seventeen, I got caught driving around in a stolen car with friends."

"What happened?"

"I got lucky. The judge decided to give me one last chance. I had to do a lot of community service and pay restitution. I ended up volunteering at an afterschool program for kids and something sort of clicked."

"What do you mean?"

"I like helping—kids, animals, people with special needs. It made me feel good and stopped me from thinking of my own problems. No, that's not right. It made me feel like I was making a difference, even if it was something small."

"So, you became a teacher."

"So, I became a special education teacher. I taught elemen-tary school for a few years while I got my master's in social work, then I moved on to the community center. I worked with a lot of at-risk kids until my program was cut at the beginning of the school year."

I was a little giddy he was answering all my questions. "What are you going to do now?"

"I don't know exactly. I've been offered a teaching position for the fall in Austin."

For reasons I would examine later (or never), a wave of sadness washed over me. He had plans in place already. I knew he'd be leaving at the end of the six months. Of course I knew that. It shouldn't hit me quite so hard. Shake it off, Ellie.

I smiled. "That's great."

"But if we're talking about my hopes and dreams..." He shifted a little closer, not on purpose but I noticed. Boy, did I notice. "I'd want to open a day program or group home, maybe both, for kids and adults with special needs. I'd love to have a place where I could create a little community. I visited a place like that once. It was residential with a café and a shop. The clients who lived there made the items they sold, worked in the café, led productive, happy lives. They went on field trips and were out in the community but surrounded by so much support, you know?"

"That's a big dream," I said quietly. "You know, you could always move to a small town like, oh, I don't know, Two Harts, where you already own part of a house and a business and twenty acres of land."

With a grunt, he laid back and stared at the ceiling, his mouth pressed in a thin line. A mouth I was having a hard time not looking at. Absently I wondered what it would be like to kiss it—would his lips be firm and demanding, soft and coaxing, somewhere in between? Would—

"All of that is just a dream, one I have no way of accomplishing any time soon." He gave me a hard look. "Besides, I can't just move to Two Harts, especially since I won't own any property or business once it gets sold."

Or he could open his mouth and say something like that, and all thoughts of kissing would go right down the toilet.

I shot off of the bed. "Why are you so set on selling? Is it money? You can see this is the only home Oliver has ever known. You can see how much this means to me." I paused in front of the bed, my hands on my hips. "Tell me what it is that's this important to you. Make me understand why."

"Do you know how selfish you sound? You aren't the only one who has responsibilities." Selfish? Was I? I opened my mouth to argue but he kept going. "I get that all of it is important to you. Find a way to buy me out, then."

"I can't afford that."

He sat up and removed his glasses. When he spoke, his voice was quiet but no less intense. "I need the money."

I sat on the edge of the bed. "Why? If I knew, maybe we could figure out a way to make this all work."

He hesitated, avoided eye contact.

"Okay, then. How about something else? For example, why do you go to Austin every weekend?"

After sliding his glasses on, he crossed his arms. Stern, Principal Gil expression clicked into place. Except for a second, his gaze hit my eyes, and it wasn't anger or annoyance there; it was confusion, a sadness that was unexpected. Then he looked away.

But it was enough. Enough to make me wonder if stern Gil was just a cover for the real Gil. That Gil was a little uncertain, the one who didn't have all the answers.

"You aren't going to tell me, are you?"

Maybe it was unreasonable to expect that from him. Just like it was unreasonable to think my problems, my dreams, were bigger than his. It seemed an impossible decision. In the end, one of us would win. And that meant the other person would lose.

"I'm going to try to get some sleep," I said, suddenly very tired. My head on the pillow, I curled up and closed my eyes. I was asleep within minutes. Gil never said a word.

THIRTY-THREE

Love is a complex emotion that involves affection, care, and commitment to someone or something.

—BRILEY J., AGE 16

ME: *What does it mean if you get locked in a bedroom overnight with a guy and you wake up wrapped around each other like pretzels?*

ALI: 👀

MAE: *Would this man happen to be a certain roommate of yours?*

ME: *Asking for a FRIEND, of course. FOR A FRIEND.*

ALI: *Are you the friend? IS THE FRIEND YOU?*

My eyes popped open at 1:47 a.m. I knew this because the only light in the room came from the glow of a digital clock two feet from my face. I still had two hours and thirteen more minutes to sleep. I closed my eyes, hoping to return to the dream I'd been in the middle of—the one where Gil is fixing a broken pipe under the kitchen sink, if you know what I mean.

Again, not a euphemism. He was there with his toolbelt, laying on the ground, partially tucked under the sink, looking all handyman hot, and he was—

My eyes snapped back open. I didn't own a digital clock.

I tried to sit up, but an arm was wrapped around my waist, big and solid, warm. I swallowed a gasp as the where and why clicked into place.

I forced myself to breathe normally, though my heart felt like it was ready to burst out of my chest. Last night came back in pieces. Oliver locking us in here. Talking to Gil. Getting annoyed with Gil. Falling asleep. Waking up at some point to see Gil sitting on the floor surrounded by folders from the file cabinet. Yelling at him to turn the light off and go to sleep.

Obviously, I was missing a few pieces. I did not remember the part where Gilbert Dalton and I started cuddling. I felt like I should remember that.

"Gil," I whispered.

His fingers flexed into the strip of exposed skin between my shorts and t-shirt. Every part of my body felt as tense as a bowstring.

I cleared my throat. The leg slung over mine shifted, tucking me closer to him. I hadn't been this close to a man in so long. That the man was Gil made it feel strangely safe. A shiver raced through me.

"Gil," I said a little louder.

"Go to sleep," he mumbled.

"Gilbert Dalton!" I wiggled and squirmed until I'd turned around to face him.

"Stop moving." With a frustrated groan, he pulled me closer

until my face was pressed against his t-shirt. He smelled warm and sleepy.

This was bad, so, so bad. Our conversation earlier was a reminder; Gil and I had very different plans, plans that were in such opposition to each other, it wouldn't end nicely. Like every other time I let myself fall for a man. But that didn't change the fact that I wanted to stay right there where I was surrounded by warm, strong arms and pretend it meant something it didn't. It took epic amounts of superhuman self-restraint not to do that. I deserved a medal or something.

"You asked for it." I pinched him like my mother did to me when I couldn't sit still in church on Sunday mornings.

He shot up, his head knocking into mine in the process. "What the..."

"Ouch!" Glaring, I sat up slowly and rubbed my head. "That hurt."

"Was I...? Were we...?" He swallowed audibly. "Did we...?"

I leaned over and snapped on a lamp. "Would never have thought you'd be a cuddler."

Gil's head swiveled around the room, looking everywhere and anywhere that wasn't me. He shoved a hand through his hair. "Look. I'm sorry. I didn't mean to do whatever we were doing... together... just now... and, um, well..."

Huffing a laugh, I laid back down. "Seriously. Your face right now. We were sleeping; it doesn't count."

"Right. Yeah." He got up and went to the bathroom, staying there at least ten minutes, and I swore I could hear him talking to himself. When he finally came out, he'd brushed his hair (somehow) and looked much more composed. He paused by my side of the bed. "I apologize. That should not have happened."

I reached out and touched the back of his hand. He flinched but didn't pull away. "It's okay. I didn't mean to invade your personal space." I was half joking. We'd been in the middle of the bed. That sure seemed like we'd both invaded each other's personal space. Together. Joint effort.

"Personal bubble," he muttered as he climbed back into bed, staying as far on his side as humanly possible.

"Oh, right. Personal bubble. Although let the record show when we bumped into each other in the hallway last week, I'm pretty sure you smelled my hair."

He flipped on his side, giving me his back. "I'm going back to sleep."

"I bet you are." I clicked off the lamp and the room was shrouded in darkness again. In silence, too.

I sat up and pounded my pillow and threw myself down again, wriggled around until I found a comfortable sleeping position. Tried to forget how nice it had felt to be held like that. Tried not to think about how much I wished it would happen again.

"Your hair smelled like peaches," Gil said quietly.

"It's my shampoo. Peaches and Cream. I can change it if it bothers you."

"No," he said quickly. "Don't change it."

"Okay," I said, my voice much breathier than I intended. I wanted to ask him, to see if he could feel this thing growing between us. Somehow this feeling had started, one I refused to name. But each day, it seemed to grow a little stronger. It was terrifying.

"We'll pretend that didn't happen, okay?" I said. "It never happened."

"Right. Never happened."

"Because nothing can happen," I said quickly. "I mean, it wouldn't be right for a lot of reasons. Oliver doesn't need to get the wrong idea and... and you and me, we want different things, you know, and only one of us is going to get what we want. You're going back to your life in three months and I'm getting on with mine. So, nothing happened. Or will happen. Not that anything was going to happen." My face was on fire, and I'd never been happier for darkness.

"I get it," he said quietly. "We should sleep."

"Yes. Sleep is good." I closed my eyes and willed myself to sleep. My brain was not listening. I tossed and turned. Went to the bathroom. Stubbed my toe in the process. Laid back down. And still, my brain kept braining. Finally, I gave up. "I can't sleep."

He didn't answer. In fact, after several minutes of silence, I was sure he was so sound asleep he didn't hear me, so I almost fell out of the bed when he did speak such was my surprise.

"I go to Austin every weekend to see my brother. He's all alone with Dad gone, and I need to check on him." His voice was low, practically a whisper, all gravelly and serious.

"What's his name?"

"Mikey." He paused and I heard him swallow. I held my breath, part of me hoping he'd continue while another part wished he hadn't told me, that he wouldn't give me another reason to like him just a little bit more.

"Mikey." I should let it go but I turned toward him. "How old is he?"

"Thirty-five."

I couldn't stop my gasp. "But I've heard you on the phone with him. I thought he was Oliver's age."

"He suffered a traumatic brain injury in a car accident, the same accident my mom..." His voice trailed off.

"Oh, Gil," I breathed and reached out a hand. It brushed against his shoulder, and I kept it there. "I'm so sorry."

He placed his hand over mine and wrapped his fingers around it, squeezed gently. "It's been my brother and my dad and me for a long time. Mikey has always lived at home. When my stepdad passed, he wanted me to put Mikey in a group home, said he didn't want me to feel obligated. 'He'll be just fine,' he told me."

"Has it been?" Had I shuffled closer to him somehow? Stupid girl.

He huffed. "Not really. He's having a hard time. I go and check him out on the weekends and spend the time with him at home where he's comfortable. He likes home. It's familiar. There's been so many changes. His dad dies, his brother moves him into this group home and then leaves. He doesn't understand a lot of it, so I try to keep it as simple and easy as possible."

I turned the hand he was gripping until we were palm to palm. His fingers tangled with mine. "That's a lot for you, too."

"I want to bring him back to the house where he's happiest. But I can't be there all day once I go back to work, and paying for a full-time caregiver is—"

"—expensive."

"Dad didn't have a lot of money. It's expensive to have a child with special needs. He had a life insurance policy, which covered his funeral and has paid the bills since he passed. All I have left is the house... and Mikey. I have to do right by him."

I sucked in a breath as an ache took up residence in my chest. It wasn't all he had left. Maybe... maybe... he had more people than he realized. Maybe I could be one of those people? But was that me being impulsive and letting my feelings take over? What would he say if I said this out loud? I couldn't. I just couldn't. Could I?

"I expected more talking. Have I broken you?"

"Maybe?"

He laughed softly. "For what it's worth, you're the first person in a long time I've wanted to share things with."

My heart flopped over in surrender. How was I supposed to resist him? "That's worth a lot, actually."

"Good. Now go to sleep."

And even though I knew better, I went to sleep still holding his hand.

THIRTY-FOUR

Love is hugs and kisses.

—ZOE L., AGE 6

"Mommy?" A finger poked my shoulder. "Mom. Mommy."

I groaned and pried open an eye. The pale light from the hallway streamed into the bedroom and shone directly on Oliver. He was standing in front of me wearing his favorite pair of cargo shorts and one of the new button-down shirts he'd insisted on using some of his birthday money to buy. He said he wanted to match Mr. Gil.

"Little man, the alarm hasn't gone off yet. You know the rule."

"It's four forty-two." He pointed at the digital clock next to the bed.

"What? No! It can't be." I needed to get dressed, obsess about what happened last night, make Oliver's lunch, get to the café, and do it all in eighteen minutes. I tried to sit up but somehow, I was trapped. *Again.*

"Hi, Mr. Gil." Oliver waved.

I froze and took stock of my surroundings. Oliver's little stunt. Ollie's room. Bed. Arm around my waist. My back pressed against a warm wall. That wall belonged to the one person I should not be cuddling with, especially in front of Oliver. Talk about giving him ideas. He's going to think that Gil is my—

"Mommy, is Mr. Gil your boyfriend now?" he asked, practically levitating in his excitement.

Exactly that.

With a grunt, I shoved Gil's arm off me and scrambled out of the bed. My hair had been in a messy bun but now it flopped forward to cover my eyes. I shoved it back.

"Young man, you are in deep, deep trouble for locking us in here." I set my fists on my hips. His precious little face fell, and my heart squeezed. Punishing him was the worst. I had to be firm here. "It was not cool at all."

His eyes darted from me to Gil and whatever he was doing behind me and then back to me. "I'm sorry. I just wanted you and Mr. Gil to spend time together. Teacher says that's what dating is. She says that's how you fall in love and be boyfriend and girlfriend."

"Oliver—"

"And then you can be married, and I can get a baby brother."

"Oliver," I groaned. "That's not how these things happen."

His little forehead scrunched in confusion. "How does it happen then?"

"How does what happen?"

"Getting a baby brother?"

"No, sir, we are not talking about where baby brothers come from." I pointed at the clock. "We have twelve minutes to get ready now. That conversation will require a lot more time and visual aids and... and... Just not now. Go get your shoes on and wait for me."

Shoulders slumped, he hung his head and nodded. "Okay."

I hated to see him so sad even though there was a dang good reason for it. With a sigh, I looped my arms around him and gave him a squeeze. "I love you, you know that. But there will be consequences for this."

He buried his face in my stomach. "I know."

After kissing the top of his head, I shooed him out of the room.

"A baby brother?" Gil asked.

He was all rumpled and messy and unshaven and he looked good that way, too. I glared at him.

"That was not supposed to happen again, remember? We are not people who cuddle. Especially in front Oliver. Oliver's already gotten too close to you. He'll be devastated when he finds out his new favorite person wants to sell the only home he's known and walk on out of his life, on top of it." My hand curled into a fist. I was getting real worked up now. "Do you get it, Gilbert? That kid does not deserve to have his heart broken."

Me neither, I thought but I didn't say that out loud. Because with a sudden clarity that bordered on painful, I realized Gil could break my heart. I was so tired of my heart getting broken.

He stood, still looking far too rumpled and sleepy. With a groan, he gripped his hair and gave it a tug. "Can we just sit for a second and talk?"

"No," I snapped. "I have eight minutes to get to work."

I stomped out of the room without a backwards glance.

THIRTY-FIVE

*[Love is...] everything. Without love there would be no goodness
inside you.*

Love is the strongest thing you have.

—DOTTIE R., AGE 6

I stewed in my feelings all day. And not the healthy stewing that
Sunny would have approved of.

Jorge noticed.

Iris noticed.

Several customers noticed.

Ali and Mae definitely noticed because, of course, they'd
picked today to come for lunch.

"What do you think peed in Ellie's coffee today?" Ali whisper-yelled to Mae, the two of them at a table in the middle of the
café. Kind of rude, if you ask me. Especially since I was standing
right in front of her.

We'd just closed for the day, and they'd decided to make
themselves comfortable despite that.

"Or who," Mae said, taking a break from inhaling her bowl of chili.

"Good point." Ali tapped her chin. "Whoever could it be?"

I scowled. "Do you want anything else?"

"Iris's customer service skills are rubbing off on you," Mae said.

"Only for my favorite customers," I said in a sugar-sweet voice before turning around and marching back behind the counter.

Ali grinned. "Touchy-touchy."

"Did you know someone volunteered to run preschool story hour for me until my replacement starts?" Mae asked.

"I did not. Who could it be?" Ali snatched a piece of corn-bread from Mae's plate and took a bite. She almost lost a finger when Mae tried to stab her with a fork.

"Why, it's Gilbert Dalton. He plays guitar and he has such a nice voice. He's great with the kids."

"Is he? He seems so reserved." Ali pointed with the knife she was using to cut up her meatloaf. "It's always the quiet ones, though. Hidden depths beneath still waters. Or something like that."

I slammed a bottle of ketchup on their table. Neither of them asked for it. But they got it anyway. "Don't get any ideas."

Ali leaned in, her eyes twinkling with mischief. "I like ideas. What are the ideas?"

I glared. "None you need to worry about. And stop teasing me. I barely slept last night because Oliver locked Gil and me in Ollie's bedroom together with some silly notion about me getting a boyfriend and then a baby brother for him. And then we cuddled—*only* cuddled, so get your minds out of the gutter—in Ollie's bed and then I told him that couldn't happen again."

"Sounds horrible," Ali said.

"That's the thing. It was nice." Mae waved a hand at me. I ignored it. "I haven't cuddled in so long and it was Gil and he waltzes around the house all the time in a toolbelt and he fixes things with the tools and he rescues kittens and cleans up after himself and, if I'm honest, he cleans up after me and he's so sweet with Oliver. But he also wants to sell the house and Oliver is already attached to him and that's scary because there is nothing at all permanent about our situation and Oliver can't be some kind of collateral damage in all this. And... and... I shouldn't have all these... these feeli—"

Ali suddenly jumped up and threw her arms around me in a bone-crushing hug.

After a good twenty seconds of being unable to move my arms or breathe properly, I choked out, "Why are you hugging me?"

"Because Gil is right behind you," she whispered, "and I didn't think you wanted to finish that sentence."

"No," I said in horror.

"Looks pretty frowny. He must be in a mood, too."

I winced. "Please pick up that butter knife and run it right through my heart. Tell Oliver I loved him."

"I'll do no such thing." She pulled away and grinned. "Just play along."

"What?"

"I'm so excited you said yes. Abe will be in town for a long weekend in May and I said to Mae, 'Those two have so much in common.' You're both single parents, you both love me. It's perfect, right? Mae agreed. No trying to get out of it either. We still have two more matchmaking dates. You promised." Her eyes screamed at me to agree.

Abe was Ali's youngest brother and her husband's lifelong best friend. He lived out of state and had a little girl. We'd met a handful of times. While he was a nice guy, fun to hang out with and we did have a lot in common, there were zero sparks.

"Okay. Sure. Right. That sounds great. Thanks," I said.

Ali's eyes shifted to the right. "Oh, hey, Gil. I didn't see you there."

"Morning," he said, his voice deep and gravelly and, because I knew his moods, a little pissed off. He stalked past the table, accidentally (on purpose), brushing my shoulder. "I'll be in the office."

A few seconds later, there was the distinct sound of the office door slamming shut. I winced. "How much do you think he heard?"

"All of it," Mae said.

I sighed. "Oh, goody."

THIRTY-SIX

Love is something where someone really cares about someone else, like a family member or also marriage.

—DART L., AGE 9

Gil did not come out once from the office, just shut himself in there like he was in a zombie movie and any wrong move could be his demise. I'd been standing in front of the door for five minutes, trying to talk myself into knocking. Jorge had just left so the place was quiet, except for the dulcet sounds of Spanish pop music coming from the radio Jorge had forgotten to shut off.

Sunny would tell me I was procrastinating. "Just pull the band-aid off," she'd surely say. "You'll feel better after."

Sometimes I wondered if Sunny ever made a mess of her life and had to clean it up. She always seemed like she had it all figured out.

"Just do it," I muttered and lifted my hand to knock.

The door swung open before I had the chance. Gil filled the doorway.

"What do you want?" he asked, wariness and annoyance fighting for position on his face.

I frowned. It's not like I expected an enthusiastic greeting but at least something a little less... caustic. "We need to talk."

He leaned a shoulder against the doorframe. "I thought you didn't believe in announcing your intentions when it came to talking."

"Fine, then." I wished I wasn't standing quite so close to him. But taking a step back felt like I was showing weakness, or something. "We need to be adults and talk about what happened. Oliver saw us. He likes you a lot." *I like you a lot.* "I'm worried he'll get the wrong idea." *I'm worried I'll get the wrong idea.*

"What idea would that be?" he asked.

"You know exactly what I mean. Oliver's got it in his head that we're going to fall in love or some such nonsense." I fisted my hands at my sides. "I've made a lot of mistakes as a mom, trust me, but I've always been careful to keep my dating life separate from Oliver. He deserves better than watching a bunch of jerks parade in and out of his mom's life. Or worse, he get attached to one of them. And like we both agreed last night, we have different life plans here. If you get what you want, I have to pick up my entire life and figure things out all over again."

He stared at me intensely. The would-be silence punctuated by the polka beat of the song on the radio. I swayed a touch closer without meaning to. His arm brushed my shoulder. He didn't give an inch, just kept watching me. His gaze traveled my face, stopping at my mouth long enough for my breath to become unsteady, then back to my eyes.

I had to put space between us, or I'd be begging him to kiss me.

"I saved you a taco plate. Come eat and we can talk." With that, I twisted on my heels and all but sprinted into the dining room. A few moments later, he followed.

I didn't look at him as I pulled his plate from under the heating lamp and placed it at the counter. He sat while I poured him a glass of iced tea.

"We made things weird," I said when I couldn't take all his silence.

"I get it," he said without looking up.

There was one piece of lemon meringue left so I plated it and took a seat next to him. This felt a little less intimidating. We weren't looking at each other.

"I don't think you do." I loaded up my fork with pie. "I left for LA at eighteen. My high school boyfriend went with me. After he broke up with me, I did what I wanted to do. I didn't have my parents watching over everything I did. I was single. I didn't even care if the guys I saw wanted anything more. I just wanted fun."

I could feel his eyes on me, but I stared down at my pie.

"Then I hooked up with Oliver's father. When he left, everything changed. For a while, I was trying my hardest to do the right things. It was so, so hard being a single mom. I was working and taking care of Oliver, and that postpartum depression is a real kick in the ass, let me tell you."

Those days had been so hard. I had no idea what I was doing. My mom lived halfway across the country. And I didn't want anyone to know how much I was struggling.

"I thought if I tried to be the old Ellie, the girl who liked to have fun, maybe that would fix me. But all it did was make things worse. I drank too much. Way too much. I made a lot of mistakes, and I was miserable. Then I got my brother in the middle of my mess."

I swallowed, feeling tears pressing against the backs of my eyes. My fork clinked against the plate because my hand was shaking.

Gil gently reached out and took it from me. He laced our

fingers together and I held on like it was my one connection to reality. "What happened?"

"It was so dumb. He was in Vegas for his birthday party. He's not really that kind of guy but his friends on the team organized it so he went. I drove over from LA to see him. We talked at least once a week, and he'd come and visit. We're close. But I didn't even tell him how much I was struggling."

I turned on the stool toward Gil, staring at where his hand wrapped around mine, his skin tanned and rough with calluses, but oh-so gentle. "I showed up at the party and started drinking and I made a mess of everything. I don't even remember most of it. Chris tells me I deemed myself the entertainment—dancing on tables, stripping down to my underwear, singing the National Anthem while doing a headstand, real classy stuff."

"Sounds like you came close to having to forfeit your Miss Tomato Harvest title," Gil said.

"Imagine the disgrace." I snorted. "Chris has always had a reputation as a real standup guy. He's an actual Eagle Scout, you know? He got concerned about how I was acting at the party, so he threw a towel around me and walked me to his hotel room next door. Got me cleaned up and in bed. Called our mom because he was so worried about me." I propped my elbow on the table and my chin in my palm. "But someone took a video of him helping me and sold it to a gossip site and one thing led to another. It was plastered everywhere that my brother was involved with a Vegas stripper, and it ballooned from there."

"I think I remember hearing about that," Gil said. "So... you were the stripper. From Miss Tomato Harvest to Vegas stripper. How the mighty fall."

"I know it sounds dumb, funny even, but it could have ruined a lot of things for him. It was a whole big thing. Anyway, my mom flew out to Vegas, drove me back to LA, and we had a long, long talk. I think I was on the verge of some kind of breakdown. Chris found this place on the coast where I could go and rest and work with a therapist. I was there for a little over a month."

I chipped off a tiny piece of my pie crust. "It was good for me. For the first time in maybe ever, I had this clarity about life. I stopped drinking, admitted that the whole acting thing wasn't working out."

"After *Kangaroo'd Three*, it was only down from there." He squeezed my hand, his thumb making circles on the back.

I huffed a laugh. "Exactly. Then one day, I woke up and realized I didn't want Oliver to grow up in LA. I wanted him to have more than that. I didn't want my screw-ups to affect his life."

"So, you packed up and came here to Two Harts."

I nodded. "The plan was to go to Oklahoma and stay with my parents for a while. At the last minute, I took a detour. I wanted to meet Mae. But it had been a long drive, so I decided to rest for a couple of days. The next day, I took Oliver to find some lunch and stumbled across the Sit-n-Eat. That's when I met Ollie."

"And you never left."

"Nope, Two Harts is more than just a town to me. I was raised in Oklahoma, grew up fast in Los Angeles, but here in Two Harts is where I've become an adult, you know? I'm becoming a person I like, one who makes good decisions and doesn't beat herself up if she makes a mistake."

He made a low sound of encouragement.

"This town, the people here, Ollie? They've all been part of helping." I took a deep breath, fighting back an overwhelming urge to cry. "I know it's just a house and a business and some land for you in some podunk town but not to sound too dramatic here, it kind of saved my life."

"No one sees you that way, you know."

"How?"

"They don't see a woman mostly made of her bad decisions.

They see a woman made of joy and laughter and hard work and fierce love. I'm glad I know her."

A tear slid down my cheek. He caught it with his thumb. Somehow, we'd turned toward each other, my legs trapped between his. The tension, this primitive pull between us ratcheted up to a level ten, and the desire to lean forward and kiss him was part survival. Like maybe I couldn't survive without it. I licked my bottom lip. He pulled me a fraction of an inch closer.

Someone knocked on the back door, loud and persistent. I jerked away and stood, leaving my half-eaten pie, and possibly my heart, on the counter. "I need to get that."

It was Teddy. He waltzed into the kitchen, wearing the suspenders I'd given him last month. "Hiya, Ellie." His brow crinkled. "You okay? You look like you've been crying."

I pressed my hands to my cheeks. "Oh, no. I'm fine. You caught me in the middle of cutting onions."

Teddy scanned the kitchen where zero evidence of onions or of me cutting them could be found. Eyes narrowed, he straightened to his full height. He was well over six feet but thin as a rail. Maybe once upon a time he'd been big and tall and weighty enough to cause some real concern. Nowadays, he hardly looked strong enough to walk more than a mile. "Someone made you cry. Who is it? I can take care of them for you, if you want."

"Now who's lying," I said.

He pressed a hand to his heart, looking terribly put out. "It's not about the size." He tapped a finger to his head. "It's about the brains."

I shook my head and smiled. "You hungry?"

"Always."

"Let's get you something to eat." I linked my arm through his. "Ollie's grandson is here."

Teddy's eyes lit up. "Is that so?"

I brought him into the dining area and stopped at the counter. "Teddy, this is Gilbert Dalton, Ollie's grandson. And Gil, this is Teddy Cane."

Teddy rounded the counter and shook Gil's hand like he was getting paid for his enthusiasm. When he stopped, he gazed at Gil carefully. "I've been wanting to meet you for a long time."

Gil's head tilted to the side. "Did she say your last name is Cane?'

Teddy smiled slowly and looked at Gil expectantly. "It is, indeed. Since the day I was born."

"Sit on down," I said. "Tell Gil some of your Ollie stories. Let me go get you something to eat."

The second I disappeared into the other room, I rushed into the bathroom and studied myself in the mirror, seeing the slightly puffy eyes and flushed cheeks. What had just happened? I was supposed to be setting boundaries. I splashed water on my face and dried it as best I could. Back in the kitchen, the murmur of voices drifted in. I quickly warmed up the taco plate I'd set aside for Teddy and brought it to him.

He and Gil had moved to a table. Gil was listening intently as Teddy rambled on, in the middle of one of his stories. I slid his plate on the table and pulled a chair over to sit, not next to Gil—that way seemed dangerous.

"We used to get in all kinds of trouble. Stealing laundry off the line, went cow tipping once." Teddy's blue eyes sparkled. "My younger sister was always on our tail. If we wanted to do something, so did she. We blamed a lot of things on her when we got caught. You'd think she'd learn but she always came back."

"Poor girl," I said.

"Nah," Teddy said. "We weren't mean or nothing. Just making mischief. Wasn't much else to do. Mom kicked us out when the sun came up to do the chores. After lunch, we weren't expected back before it got dark." Teddy smiled softly, watching the memories in his head. "Long, hot summer days. Good times, I miss that."

"What happened to your sister?" I asked. I hadn't heard much talk of Teddy or his family. "Is she still in Two Harts?"

"Oh, no." His smile wilted a bit. "She left a long time ago. Never did come back to Two Harts. She met a nice man in Houston and married real quick. Didn't even have a wedding really, just went down to the Justice of the Peace. He was from Louisiana, so she moved there."

"She came back to visit, I bet," I said.

"I wish she had. Would have loved to meet my niece." His eyes moved to Gil, watching his face intently. "She didn't think it was a good idea to come back."

"Why?"

"It's complicated, I guess. Easier to stay away." He frowned. "Sometimes it's hard being the only one who remembers from back then. Ollie's gone now. Amelia passed on years ago."

My heart stopped. Gil's grandmother's name was Amelia. He'd said he spent the summers with her in Louisiana. "Amelia?"

I looked to Gil whose gaze had sharpened on the older man.

"My sister," Teddy replied as he picked up a taco. He gestured toward Gil. "She was your grandma. I guess that makes me your grand-uncle."

THIRTY-SEVEN

Love is something when you fall in love with someone, and you want them to marry you and stuff. That's what love means, basically.

—CHRISTIAN L., AGE 9

From the sticky note correspondence of Gilbert Dalton and Ellie Sterns:

Eleanor—

Leaving for Austin. I'll be back in time for Easter dinner on Sunday. Should I bring anything?

—Gilbert

P.S. I found a bunch of stuff in Ollie's file cabinet I wanted to show you. When you have time.

Gil—

You don't need to bring a thing. Just yourself and your smile. (Okay, the smile is a stretch, I know.) Dinner is at 3. Do you know where my brother's place is?

—Ellie

P.S. Next week some time.

Eleanor—

I've been to Chris's house a few times.

—Gilbert

P.S. Fine.

Gil—

You've been to Chris's house? When?

—Ellie

P.S. Great.

Eleanor—

I get around.

—Gilbert

P.S. Sure.

"Which one is Aggie again?" Gil leaned close and whispered. He'd arrived just before three and after a quick round of introductions, we'd gone straight into dinner.

"Keep up, Dalton. She's the tall one at the end."

"The one who has olives on all her fingers and is making Oliver laugh?"

"Yep, that's her. She's number four out of five and just graduated from University of Texas. On the other side of her is Betsy."

"Pink hair?"

"Classic middle child. Always looking for attention. She's an art teacher in Oklahoma City."

"Which leaves Millie. The blonde one across from us."

"The baby. She's a senior in high school this year. And an evil mastermind." I leaned in a bit closer and lowered my voice. "If she asks to get you alone, just smile and nod at whatever she says."

Gil's eyes flashed with concern. "What does that mean?"

I shrugged and began cutting up the slice of ham on my plate. "She *might* try and threaten your life if you hurt me. I've already told her it's not like that between us but... she gets ideas."

"What?"

"It's just a thing she does. She's a sweetheart." I took a bite and chewed slowly. After swallowing, I smiled. "Mostly. I'm pretty sure they're empty threats, at least."

"She's not really joking," Mae said from Gil's other side. "I got the talk when Chris brought me home for the first time. That girl could make a mafia boss shake in their boots."

I shrugged. "I told you. My family's... a bit extra, shall we say?"

Like she'd been summoned, my mom caught Gil's eye. "Gilbert, it's so nice you could join us. Ellie's told us so much about you."

"That's a big whopping lie," Aggie said, nearly flinging an olive across the table when she pointed at me. "She's told us almost nothing."

"Agnes, take those off your fingers," my mom glared at her. "You are not a child."

"Debatable," Betsy murmured.

"We have company here. Can we try to be normal for once?" Mom set her glass down with a bit too much force.

"Okay, Margot. Chill." Aggie bit an olive off a finger.

"Luke," my mom stared down the long table in Mae and Chris's formal dining room at my father, "tell your daughters to be normal, please. And remind them I spent hours upon hours in excruciating pain that it felt like my body was being torn in half and burned at the stake to give them life, so they should be referring to me as Mom, not Margot."

Mae made a choking sound and scrambled to guzzle her water.

"Nice one, Mom." Chris patted his wife's back. "Good thing she's not about to have a baby any day now."

"Mae, you'll be fine," Margot said, gentling her voice. "And it's all worth it. Every second of it so you can meet your child. At least until they start to have opinions. Things go downhill from there."

"Girls, listen to your mother," Dad said, sounding almost bored. Mostly because this was a regular occurrence at any Sterns family meal, not just special for the holidays.

Mom turned back to Gil. "Now, Gilbert, where are you from originally?"

"Fort Worth, but I live in Austin now."

"Oh, I love Austin. It has flavor," Mom said, her dark eyes sparkling. "And what do you do?"

"I taught elementary school for a few years and then worked as a youth counselor at a community center."

"Oh, you like kids." Mom sent a pointed look in my direction. I smiled uneasily. I'd told her before they'd even arrived that Gil was more of a business partner than anything else.

Don't get any ideas, I'd told her. That look was filled with ideas though.

"Mr. Gil knows everything about dinosaurs," Oliver said. "And he teaches me how to fix stuff. We're in the Man Club together."

"The Man Club?" Millie shot Gil an assessing look.

Gil's cheeks pinked. "It's nothing. Just a... a..."

"It's the best. We fixed all the windows in the house and the leak under the sink and made the door on the dryer stay shut without tape, and next week, Mr. Gil said we're going to figure out why the floor in the living room is soft when you step on it." Oliver stuffed half a roll in his mouth.

"You didn't tell me you had all that work needed to be done," my dad said quietly. "You know I can come help you any time."

"It wasn't a big deal," I said quickly. "We're doing fine."

"You've never even let us come and see the house." My father was a patient man—five kids and my mother would do that—and it took a lot to get him worked up. But I could see he wasn't happy with me at all. "You said Ollie didn't like visitors."

"That's true, he didn't." He hadn't. I mean, if I'd asked, he probably wouldn't have had a problem with my parents stopping by.

"Did you know about this?" Dad directed this question to Chris.

Chris shifted uncomfortably. "A little. I helped whenever she'd let me. You know how she is."

"I'm sitting right here," I snapped. "I just don't want to bother anyone and besides, I can figure it out on my own."

With a scowl, Dad crossed his arms. I imagined my brother would look like him in twenty-five years' time with his salt-and-pepper hair and deep laugh lines. "We're going to talk about this later, young lady."

"We'll see," I said. "And I'm not such a young lady anymore.

I'm an adult and I've been one for a long time now." I set my fork down, my eyes bouncing between my parents at either end of the table. A hand landed on my knee and squeezed gently. I side-eyed Gil, but he was looking my father square in the face.

"I've been helping where I can," he said. "She's done a good job with the place. Put a lot of work into it."

"Thanks," I whispered.

"It's true," he said. "I know what that place means to you."

I turned my head sharply and stared at him. He'd been quieter than usual since our night in Ollie's room. Everything seemed so complicated at the moment. Worse, my heart was involved, although I'd only admit that to myself. And Sunny.

Why couldn't I meet a nice, emotionally available guy who wasn't trying to sell everything I'd worked for and fall in love with him, get married, and live happily ever after?

"You two are so sweet together. Luke, aren't they sweet?" Mom smiled widely and I could already see her planning a wedding in her mind.

"Thank you for helping out," my dad said to Gil. "I appreciate it."

"No problem, sir."

Sir, I mouthed. Gil looked down at his plate but not before I saw a smile curve his mouth. He was enjoying this.

"I'm so glad we could all be together," Mom said in her outside voice (even if we were inside). "Look at how our family is growing. We have Mae, and the baby any day. Now Ellie introduces us to Gilbert. It's making my mama heart so happy."

"Mom." I groaned. "I've already told you we're business partners, not, you know..."

Mom didn't look like she believed it. In fact, no one looked like they believed that. Me included. My mother opened her mouth to argue when a miracle happened right there at Easter dinner.

"Oh," Mae said, her eyes huge. "I think my water broke."

THIRTY-EIGHT

[*Love is...*] *dedication.*

—BETHANY, AGE 17

The entirety of the hospital waiting room was composed of Sterns family members and Sterns family-adjacent members. Lucy, Mae's mother, and Iris were here, too. In true fashion, they'd made themselves at home, sprawled across the room like we were paying rent. Someone must have cleaned out every vending machine in the hospital judging by the mound of candy bars and bags of chips.

"You know, you can go home," I said. I was sitting in one of the pale-pink waiting room chairs; Oliver was cuddled up next to me, sound asleep. Gil was in the next seat. "This is probably not how you expected to spend your Sunday evening."

Gil looked up from the *Women's Health* magazine (circa two thousand and three) he was reading and shook his head. "I'm right in the middle of this article about perimenopause and weight gain. I need to finish it."

"Oh, I bet. Sounds like the kind of practical information you need."

He snapped the magazine. "Exactly."

After he'd hidden behind the magazine for another few minutes, I used a finger to pull the top down. "I'm serious. Don't feel like you have to stay. I know this might be a lot for you."

He leaned closer. "It is a lot, but in a good way. It was just my dad and brother and me growing up. You have a whole family."

"Oh, I know it, trust me." I loved my family with every fiber of my being, but I wasn't sad about not living closer to them. Absence makes the heart grow fonder?

Sure, we'll go with that.

He studied the people in the room, his expression thoughtful. "You're lucky, you know. They really love you."

"They do. I love them, too. But I always feel like I'm the one kid who didn't fall in line. Like I'm a disappointment."

"I'm a third-party observer, but it seems to me they're pretty proud of you."

"You think?" I felt dumb for asking, embarrassed even. But I hoped that was true. I wanted so badly for that to be true.

"Yeah, I think." Gil caught my eye and smiled. My heart rolled over and begged for more. "More than that, I think they like you, too, and they want the best for you whatever that looks like." He nodded toward my mom who was fussing at one of my sisters. "That's not a mom who sees you as a disappointment; that's a mom who sees all the best things about you and doesn't want you to settle."

"Thanks," I whispered, pulling Oliver a little closer to my side.

"It's the truth."

I fiddled with a tiny bit of pleather peeling from the waiting room chair. "Um, the whole weird thing about my mom thinking we're together... don't worry, I'll set her straight again."

"Okay." He picked the magazine back up and held it in front of his face.

"That's it? Okay. Didn't it weird you out?"

Without moving the magazine, he said, "That your family thinks a smart, driven, funny, beautiful woman would want to date me? Nope, not weirded out at all."

Had he just said that about me? I looked away, trying to hide how flushed my face was.

"Of course, after that talk your dad had with me, we might be engaged now."

I whipped my head around. "Excuse me? What?"

A pair of dark-blue eyes behind dark-framed glasses peeked over the top of the magazine. "He asked me what my intentions were. I panicked."

"You didn't."

His eyebrows rose and a twinkle settled in his eyes.

"You're making that up, you jerk."

"What's a business partner to do?" Then he did the most unlikely Gil thing ever; he winked. Before I could respond, he hid behind the magazine again.

Chris burst through the doors in the waiting room. We all froze. "She wants to see her mom."

"Coming." Lucy disappeared behind the door.

The rest of us stared at my brother. Mr. Cool was looking anything but. His hair was standing straight on end from running his fingers through it so much. He was in khakis and a light-purple polo shirt, which was now untucked, parts of it looking like it had been pulled and twisted. Probably by Mae.

He slumped in the nearest chair next to me and pressed his palms into his eyes. "It never ends. I just want her to stop hurting. She's refusing an epidural."

I whistled. "That's brave." And really painful.

"You know once she gets something in her head, she's not changing her mind. I begged. I pleaded. I tried to bribe her, but she won't do it." He blew out his breath. "I don't like seeing her like this."

I patted him on the knee. "She's going to be okay. You'll see. Mae is tough."

"Not as tough as everyone thinks," he muttered.

Mom plopped down in the chair next to Chris and rubbed his back. "You were almost twelve pounds, and I popped you right out."

"You did some screaming if I remember correctly," Dad said across the room.

Mom smiled grimly. "I didn't say it was easy, just that I did it. I got the epidural for the rest of my deliveries. Once you prove you can do something, no sense in having to prove it again."

"Mom, you are not helping." Chris leaned his head against the wall.

"Sweetie, it will be fine."

Ten minutes later, Lucy pushed through the doors. "They want her to start pushing. Go meet your child, Chris."

Chris jumped up from his seat, his eyes wild, and dashed through the doors.

"Oh, I can't wait to hold that grandbaby," Mom said. She moved over a seat, so she was right next to me and lowered her voice. "It's been too long since I've had a tiny little baby to snuggle with."

"Oliver's a little big for that now, I guess."

"I'm hoping it won't be too long before Oliver gets a baby brother or sister." She looked around me at Gil who was still reading. That article must be a whopper. Mom smiled.

"Mom. I already told you—"

She patted my knee and leaned in, keeping her voice quiet. "Honey, I know what you said. But I also know you. That boy doesn't stand a chance."

"It's... complicated."

She tsked. "Love is always complicated because people are complicated. Love is ten percent hearts and rainbows and instant attraction. The other ninety percent is the hard work, the choosing every day to love someone. Heck, if it were easy, we'd fall in and out of love every time there was a stiff wind. No, ma'am, love is in the details... how we treat each other on our worst days or find a way to put the other person first every day. Love is a choice. The feelings are awful nice, but they change just like we do."

"I've never thought of it that way," I murmured. Wasn't that how I'd always thought love was meant to be, though? Passion and fire. Had I expected love to be easy? Like stumbling upon the right man and knowing in an instant we were meant to be?

My eyes drifted to Gil. He'd tipped his head back against the wall. His eyes were closed and the soft lighting in the waiting room played with the ridges and edges of his face, creating shadows. My chest grew tight the longer I looked at him, thinking of him changing my oil or making that key rack I still forgot to use, picking up stamps for me, and fixing the bathtub faucet.

If love was in the details, I was in big, big trouble.

He must have felt my eyes on him because one of his cracked open. "You okay?"

No, I was not okay. I was having a freakout of the epic variety. But I smiled and pretended otherwise. "Just tired."

"It's late. You should try to sleep a little."

"Yeah," I said, weakly. "I'll try."

Two hours later, we met my niece, Louisa Madeline Sterns. And yes, Mae made it through just fine. Chris did have a black eye, but no one was talking about how that happened.

THIRTY-NINE

What love is depends on the scenario. Is it chocolate cake or a person?

Love is when you really like something.

—CAERA, AGE 16

"Thanks for letting me stay here tonight," Aggie said as she pulled her hair up into a messy bun. "I know you like your privacy."

"Oh, right. And that stopped you when you were younger?" I gave her a pointed look as I climbed into bed next to her. "You were so careful not to invade my privacy. Unless it was to borrow my clothes, get into my makeup, and read my diary."

"You were so bad at hiding things," she said primly. "It was just my way of teaching you a lesson."

I hit her with a pillow. "Such a humanitarian."

She grinned and flipped on her side to face me. It was fun to share a bed with her and bicker and argue and gossip. Since there were seven years between us, we hadn't had much of that growing up.

Aggie had an early morning flight back to Oklahoma City for work. At the auction house she worked at, they were preparing for one of their biggest events of the year. Besides, Aggie was never good at staying still for too long and that's what would happen over the next few days. A whole lot of, "let me sit quietly and hold the baby," or "let me stand here and stare at the baby."

"I like Gil," she said. "He's cute in a... well, a..."

"Accountant slash principal slash knows how to knock down a wall kind of way?"

She laughed. "Yes, actually. Exactly that. You would make cute babies."

I sighed. "We aren't going to have cute babies. It isn't like that."

"Okay, if you say so."

"It's true."

"El, I watched him all dinner. He does that thing where he leans close to you even when you're not talking. And he kept glancing at you like he wanted to make sure you were real. It's adorable."

"He did not," I said. Had he? A flutter of excitement twisted in my stomach.

"Yes, he did," she said in the sing-song voice that only little sisters use to irritate their older sisters. "He likes you."

"Even if he did, it's... complicated. You know how Ollie left half of everything to me and the other half to Gil?" I couldn't believe I was about to tell her this; even my parents didn't know. "The other part of that is that we have to live on the property for six months for our claim to be valid. That's why he moved in. At the end of the six months, he's determined to sell everything and leave."

"And you don't want to?"

"Of course not. I love it here."

Aggie propped her head up on her hand. "You're happy here. It suits you."

"That was nice of you to say." Aggie was not known for her sentimentality. I put a hand on her forehead. "No fever. Are you dying?"

With a laugh, she flopped over on her side facing away from me. "Excuse me. I'll never say anything nice about you again."

"There's the sister I know and love." I pulled the project I'd been working on each night before bed. Well, most nights. Okay, some nights. "Will the light bother you if I keep it on for a little while?"

"Nah. I was going to read a little anyway." She looked over her shoulder. "Oh, you're crocheting again. Yay. I need another scarf. To add to the four others you've given me."

I scowled. "I'll have you know those scarves were made with love. And I'm just crocheting until I finish this." I held up an unidentifiable shape made of bright-pink yarn. "It's a slipper for Mom for Mother's Day."

"Let me guess. It'll match the one you gave her for Mother's Day, what, two years ago? You know most people think slippers should come in pairs."

I looked down my nose at her. "This kind of quality takes time. It will be worth the wait." Having an attention span only slightly longer than a gnat, I could only get one finished before Mother's Day that year. But I wrapped it up with a note that said the second one would be coming soon. Two years was soon, right?

Aggie cackled. "I love you."

"Same."

"Question." Aggie sat up and plunked Fred the Sad Bicycle Clown from the nightstand. "Can we talk about this?"

"That's Fred. Keeps me company at night." He still gave me the creeps, but I was getting used to him.

"Boy, do we need to get you a man."

"Ha. Ha. Someone in Ollie's family was really into them. There's a lot of these in Gil's room. Fred isn't the creepiest. By far."

Aggie studied the figurine for a while, even flipped it over like she was looking for a maker's mark. She pulled her phone out and began to scroll around on it. "You're not going to believe this."

"What?"

She held up the phone to my face. "Fred had some aging on him, and if you look at it closely, it's really well done. Definitely hand-painted. It reminded me of something I'd seen at work. It turns out Fred is by a famous artist."

"No way." I took the phone from her. An online auction site was pulled up to a page of figurines similar in style to Fred, all by the same artist.

"Every one of his figures are one-offs." She leaned over to look at the phone with me. "Look how much his other ones are worth."

"Holy crap," I breathed. "Does that say three thousand dollars?" I scrolled further. "That one sold for fifty-five hundred."

Aggie held Fred up. "This dude is a gold mine."

"No way." I stared into Fred's soulless eyes. "But he's so... creepy."

"You said there's a whole room of them."

I nodded.

She bumped me with her shoulder. "Not so creepy now, huh?"

FORTY

Love is caring for someone. It means that you really like someone.

—BOONE K., AGE 5

Since he'd introduced himself to Gil, Teddy had been showing up more frequently, now during business hours and always when he spotted Gil through the window. He'd sidle up to a stool at the counter and, over a glass of iced tea, he would chatter away. I'd heard most of his stories already—about Ollie and the antics they got into. Occasionally, he'd bring up Gil's grandmother, hoping, I think, to engage Gil in some way. But Gil kept his distance, always polite but never anything more.

"You know, he doesn't mean you any harm," I said one day as we were closing. It was a hot day in late April but Iris had volunteered to walk to the bus stop and pick up Oliver anyway. Probably to get out of cleaning up. "He was Ollie's best friend and your grandmother's brother. Maybe give him a chance?"

Gil grunted in reply.

"I was thinking if anyone knew the story of what happened

between your grandmother and Ollie, he'd be the one. But I guess you'd have to actually sit down and talk to him."

He scowled as he scrubbed down a table in the dining room.

I put a hand on my hip. "I don't get it. Why are you avoiding him? He's a harmless old man who just wants to get to know you."

He stomped across the room to a table further away.

"Now you're avoiding me, too? That's going to be tough since we live in the same house. Do you know how annoying I can be when I put my mind to it?"

Still nothing, just continued to wipe down tables aggressively.

I sighed. "This isn't at all like you."

"You don't know that." He glared at me. "You hardly know me."

"Ha! He talks." I waltzed over to him. "Bet I know you better than you think."

He straightened. "Prove it."

"Okay." I shuffled closer until I was two or three inches away. "This makes you uncomfortable when I stand this close to you."

He crossed his arms, brushing against me in the process. "No, it doesn't."

"You're dying to take a step back."

"I'm not." To prove me wrong, he took a small step closer and glowered at me. "See?"

"So brave," I murmured. "Another thing I know about you: you buy expensive laundry detergent."

"What?"

I leaned in and pressed my nose to his shoulder. "Yup. That's the smell."

He froze, his whole body going solid, and then his hands wrapped around my waist. "That's not a good idea."

"You're right." But I didn't move.

Gently, he pushed me away. His hands on my waist flexed before he dropped them. He took two big steps backwards before returning to wiping down tables.

"Sorry," I mumbled and plopped down at the nearest table. "I was just teasing you."

"It's fine."

I huffed a laugh. "Sure. I still think you should consider talking with Teddy."

He threw down the dishtowel and ripped off his apron. "I don't understand why my one living relative has to be... has to be..." He shoved his hand in his hair. "His hands shake and... and he smells like alcohol. He's too thin and frail, and I can't. I can't be responsible for another person. I already have Mikey and I have Dad's place in Austin and this place and the house and you and—"

I interrupted him. "You aren't responsible for me."

"I know I'm not responsible for you. That doesn't mean I don't want to take care of you." His gaze caught mine; something in my chest cracked at the look in his eye. I didn't want to think about what it was.

I opened my mouth, but I couldn't think of anything rational to say to that. Instead, I walked behind the counter and pulled out an envelope. I set it down and tapped it with my fingertip. "Teddy was here earlier. He left those for you. They're photos of Ollie and your grandma. He thought you might want to see them."

His look was unreadable as he stared at the spot on the counter.

After removing my apron, I grabbed my purse and headed to the back door. "I'm going to go meet Iris and Oliver. I'll come back later and finish cleaning."

FORTY-ONE

Love is like you can love a person. Love is a heart.

—JACK, AGE 7

From the group text messages of Ellie, Mae, and Ali:

MAE: *Anyone up?*

ALI: *You know it's after midnight. Some of us are trying to sleep.*

MAE: *Whoops.*

ALI: *Whoops?*

MAE: *Iris came over tonight with a little gossip. But I'll let you get back to sleep.*

ALI: *Do not even think about it. Spill it.*

MAE: *I was hoping Ellie would spill it.*

ALI: *Ooo. TELL ME.*

MAE: *It involves Gil, Ellie, and a mouse.*

ELLIE: *Can you two STOP TEXTING RIGHT NOW? I have to get up at 4.*

ELLIE: *Also, Iris has a big mouth.*

ALI: *Well, you're up now. You might as well tell us.*

ALI: *Ellie?*

ALI: *You don't think she blocked us, do you?*

April slid into May and Gil didn't bring up Teddy again. In fact, we never talked much about the things we should talk about—the tension between us or selling the property. Both of us, it seemed, were very good at pretending everything was just fine.

As Gil spent more time in the café, I made him try every job in the place, hoping something would pique his interest. Jorge taught him to make decent waffles. Iris trained him on serving. Which didn't mean much since Iris's version of serving was a little suspect. He rotated through bathroom duty, mopping the floors, clearing tables. His strongest showing was running the cash register until Mr. Grueber complained Gil shortchanged him.

What Gil didn't know was that Mr. Grueber always complained about being shortchanged. Mr. Grueber was eighty-seven, hard of hearing, and mean as an angry goat. Plus, I think he was a little lonely since his wife had passed on and he enjoyed the whole ritual of the arguing. I always gave him back the fifty-seven cents (or whatever minute amount he was grumbling about) so he would leave, but Gil was not me and he and Mr. Grueber got into a loud "discussion" about it before I could intervene.

After that, we all thought it wise Gil should not have a customer-facing position.

So, it seemed I'd found something Gilbert Dalton wasn't good at. I was probably an awful person for feeling almost gleeful about this piece of information. Finally, something Mr. Competent couldn't do.

It was when I'd mentioned I needed to pay bills one day that he volunteered to take over the accounting, a job I gladly handed off. I had been managing it, but all that time at a computer double-checking numbers and accounts was mind-numbing.

"Here are all the receipts." I placed a banker's box on the desk in the office.

Gil looked at it with horror. "That is a box."

"Of receipts." After pulling the lid off, I reached in and held up a handful of receipts and invoices. "It's every single one, I swear."

"Eleanor," he said in his principal voice. A shiver raced up my back. I really liked that voice. "This is not how you keep books."

"I know this looks bad." I crossed my arms. "But I swear it's because I've just gotten a tiny bit behind. I'll show you."

I stomped around the desk and nudged him to move over so I could log onto the dinosaur of a computer. It took forever to boot up, enough time for me to realize how close I was to Gil. Very close. So close that when he took a deep breath and exhaled, the bits of frizzy hair on the back of my neck moved. So close that if I moved two inches to the side, I'd be touching him.

Here was the wild thing: I sort of wanted to see what would

happen if I did it. I laughed under my breath at the thought. We'd been through this already. Nothing was happening between us.

"What's so funny?" Gil asked, his voice so close I almost jumped.

I ignored the question. Using the wireless mouse, I clicked around on the computer until I pulled up the accounting program. "See, I'm only four months behind for the year."

His fingers brushed my hand as he shooed it aside to get to the mouse. "It's the beginning of May."

"Yes, I know that."

"Before April is March and February and January," he said.

I glared at him over my shoulder. "Are we going to learn all the months of the year today, Teacher?"

"None of the accounting has been done for the entire year?" He sounded incredulous, scandalized even.

"Okay, you know what? Never mind." I moved the mouse to close the program. "I can do this myself, thank you very much."

"No." He plucked the mouse from me.

"Yes." I smacked his hand to get him to release it.

He held on tighter, his knuckles turning white. "No."

"Yes." I gave his hand a good, strong yank; it didn't move. "Give me the mouse."

"Make me."

"Are you serious? How old are you?" I didn't give him time to answer. I was one of five kids. *Make me* was basically a war cry.

I lunged.

I used both hands to move his one. He used his shoulder to nudge me away. I planted my feet and grabbed onto his forearm for better leverage. He locked himself in place like a freaking statue.

As the younger sister of a very big dude—Chris was six five and solid muscle and he'd been that way for a long time—I'd learned a thing or two about getting one over on him. In my younger years, if I had reached an impasse such as this, I would have licked his face. Worked every time. And while the thought had some merit, I didn't think it was the best course of action with Gil.

The office chair was on wheels, so my next brilliant idea was to pull him away from the desk. Which almost worked except...

"Holy fork, how much do you weigh?" I blew at the hair that had fallen out of my ponytail and into my face and gave the chair another yank. "Just give me the mouse."

"No." To punctate his point, he picked the mouse up and shoved it down his t-shirt.

"You cheat," I yelled, letting go of the chair and almost falling from the momentum.

With a smirk, he crossed his arms. "I didn't think there were rules."

I don't know if it was the smirk or the tension that had been building for days, weeks, months, but I launched myself at him. With an *oomph*, he unfurled his arms and latched onto my waist. I landed on his lap, my legs to one side. Without hesitation (or thought), I shoved my hand up his shirt.

Both of us froze.

My hand skimmed over his skin; the spray of hair tickled my palm. I made a small sound in the back of my throat. His skin rippled under my fingers in response. I moved my hand higher, resting it on his chest. It was warm there, soft and hard all at once. I could feel the rapid tattoo of his heart. My own heartbeat matched it.

"What are you doing?" he whispered, his mouth so close to my ear. I shivered.

I swallowed. What was I doing? There was a reason for this, right? I definitely wasn't feeling the guy up. That could not be it.

"I... don't remember." I met his eyes. They were darker than usual, the pupils blown wide and his breathing was a little funny. So was mine. "I should definitely get my hand out of your shirt."

"Probably."

Neither of us moved. Our faces were close, maybe two inches apart. I could feel his breath on my lips.

"I'll do that right now," I murmured.

He nodded. But still, I didn't move my hand, and he didn't move it for me. In fact, both of us drifted closer to each other. Closer and closer. The pull was so strong, and I wanted so badly to see how far we would go.

"Oh, no. Am I interrupting?" said a voice from the doorway. A very amused voice. "Do you want me to close the door? Give you both a little privacy?"

With a gasp, I snatched my hand from his shirt and scrambled to my feet, Gil's hands on my waist to steady me. I brushed them off and crossed my arms, hoping to appear calm and collected. Judging by Iris's grin, I looked anything but.

"Nope," I said. "We were discussing some accounting stuff. Gil is taking it over for now."

"Exactly, right." Gil stood. A loud clank filled the room when the mouse fell from under his shirt. We ignored it but Iris rolled her lips together, clearly holding in laughter. "Thank you for your help, Eleanor."

"No problem, Gil." I gave my t-shirt a yank. "I'll get back to work then. Let me know if you have any questions."

Then I got the heck out of that room.

FORTY-TWO

—NATHAN B., AGE 11

"Outfit check," I said, doing a spin in the living room. Oliver and Gil were sitting side by side on the couch wearing identical serious expressions.

Oliver tilted his head, a finger on his chin like a mini fashion critic. "I like it."

"Excellent." I smoothed a hand down the soft blue sundress with tiny white and yellow flowers on it. I'd paired it with white flats and simple hoop earrings. I hadn't wanted to get too dressed up for this date arranged by my two matchmakers, Ali and Mae. In fact, I'd tried to weasel out of the whole thing. Mainly because of the other guy on the couch, the one frowning at me.

"It's showing a lot of skin, don't you think?" Gil asked, his voice deeper than usual.

I looked down at my dress. It was tea-length with a cinched-in waist and a bell-like skirt. "No."

Narrowing his eyes, he waved his hand around his shoulders. "This area is very exposed. Maybe you should wear a sweater."

"It has spaghetti straps. They're fine. And it's almost ninety degrees out there. I'm not wearing a sweater."

Gil pressed his lips together until the edges turned white, but he didn't say anything else. I grabbed my purse and double-checked I had everything I needed before taking a seat in the living room.

"What time will he be here?" Gil asked.

"Any minute now." I tucked my phone in my purse. "Thank you for hanging out with Oliver tonight."

"No problem." His face said otherwise.

I ducked my head to hide a smile. I had agreed to this date with Ali's brother, Abe, over a month ago. In my head, I didn't even think of it as a date. It was Abe. We'd talk about our kids all night and joke around. I'd tried to explain this to Gil, but he'd only gotten grumpier the closer we got to the date.

Almost like he was jealous.

I didn't think a man had ever shown jealousy on my account. I liked it. I was probably a terrible person for liking it but I did.

"Oliver, come give me a hug." He scrambled onto my lap. "Remember it's a school night so bed by seven and nothing to drink after six."

He rolled his eyes. "I know, Mom."

Abe arrived right on time, looking sharp in a pair of khakis and a white button-down that had the sleeves rolled up to show off his tattoos. Then again, he had a lot of tattoos. His shoulder-length hair was pulled back in a low ponytail I normally wouldn't find attractive but on him, it worked. It also showed off the nickel-sized gauges in his ears. His smile was pure mischief and reminded me of Ali. Above all, he was a genuinely nice guy.

I brought him into the living room to introduce him. "You

know Oliver, and this is Gilbert Dalton. He's my... business partner."

Gil stood, back ramrod straight. No smile to speak of. He held his hand out.

"Nice to meet you," he said in a way that made it clear there was nothing nice about this experience.

Abe took his hand and shook it, wincing ever so slightly. "Nice to meet you, too."

Oliver stared at Abe in wonder. "Why do you have holes in your ears?"

Abe chuckled. "I liked them."

"I like them, too. Can I touch one?" Oliver asked.

"And on that note, we should get going." I grabbed my purse.

"When will you be home?" Gil asked. I knew the question was directed at me, but his eyes never left Abe.

"Early-ish. I have to work in the morning," I said.

He nodded. "Can you be back by eight? I have stuff to do after that."

"You never leave the house after dinner. What? You have a date, too?" I joked. But as soon as the words left my mouth, I started to wonder. Did he? Who would he even go out with?

"I have something to do tonight."

My eyes narrowed. I turned to Abe. "Give me a minute. I need to show Gil something." Turning, I snagged Gil's arm and half dragged him deep enough into the hallway we couldn't be overheard easily. "Do you really have something tonight? Is it a date? It's Cammie, isn't it? She's had her eye on you since you broke into my house."

"I did not break into your house. It's our house."

"Where are you taking her?" I asked.

"Who?" Now he looked confused. What was his problem?

"Cammie. The dispatcher at the sheriff's office." I shook my head. "She's all wrong for you, you know?"

He smiled slowly. "I don't have a date."

"You don't?"

"No. You do."

I blinked. "Oh, right."

"Have fun." He dropped a kiss on my forehead and strolled back into the living room. Frowning, I followed.

"Let's go," I said to Abe. "Be good for Gil, Oliver."

"I will." Oliver nodded. "Be good for my mom, Mr. Abe."

FORTY-THREE

[Love is...] when two people have a strong connection to each other.

—MAGGIE, AGE 10

That night when I got home, Oliver was already in bed and Gil was in his room. I knocked on his door. "I'm home."

"Good."

"Thanks for watching Oliver. Everything go okay?"

"Yeah. It was fine," he said, his voice muffled through the door.

"Good. I'm home now so... if you were going out, you're free."

"It was canceled."

I raised an eyebrow but didn't call him out on his obviously fake plans. "Oh. Got it."

I waited to see if he'd say anything else, maybe ask me about my date, or possibly snap, throw me over his shoulder like a tool-wielding caveman, and have his way with me. But he did none of those things. "Well, goodnight then."

I tossed and turned, tried to read, refused to think about accounting programs and toolbelts and computer mice and jealous roommates at all. The minutes felt like hours as they ticked by. I tried counting sheep but started to wonder if sheep came in mini sizes like horses. They do, I googled it. After it led me down a rabbit hole into the world of miniature animals, which led me to the world of competitive chicken showing, I forced myself to put the phone down and go to sleep.

It did not work.

"Ugh." I threw the covers off and shuffled to the bathroom. After I peeked in on Oliver who was sound asleep, two black balls of fluff curled up next to him. One kitten lifted its head but not sensing much in the way of danger, it fell back to sleep. I thought that was the one Oliver was calling Duck. The other one was Goose. At least for now.

Since sleeping was impossible, I crept quietly to the living room. Maybe I could work on Mom's slipper. Mother's Day was in a couple of days, and I wasn't even half done. The curse of the unfinished project haunted me on the daily. The evidence was that hall closet I pretended to ignore.

Sunny and I had worked on the concept of finishing something fully. "If you did fewer things in a day, but finished them all, how would life be different?" she'd asked. She was eating one of my muffins at the time.

But my plans were waylaid when I realized someone was already in the living room. Gil was stretched out on the couch in a t-shirt and gym shorts, ankles crossed and an arm covering his eyes.

I stared down at him, enjoying the way the moonlight seeped through the edges of the curtains and highlighted tantalizing strips of Gil—the hand spread over his stomach, the slice of skin where his t-shirt had ridden up. Even his feet caught my attention.

There was something truly wrong with me when I realized I found his feet attractive.

"Should I turn over so you can get another view?" he asked, even though his eyes were still covered.

"Excuse me, I was getting a drink of water and couldn't help noticing you."

His arm slipped down to reveal his face. "It's okay. If I came upon you laid out on the couch, I'd stop and take in the view, too."

I flushed. "Couldn't sleep?"

He shook his head, winced, and closed his eyes. "Migraine."

"Oh." I rounded the couch. "You eat something sugary?"

"I may have caved and eaten a muffin." He cracked one eye open. "Strawberry cream cheese muffins? Who does that? Who makes those and leaves them laying around in the open?"

"So, it's my fault?"

"Lately? Yes," he muttered but I wasn't sure I was supposed to hear it.

"Can I get you anything?"

"Nah. I'm fine." He covered his face again. "Just waiting for the meds to kick in."

"Okay then, I'll get that water and get out of your way."

He mumbled something that sounded like goodnight.

I bit the inside of my cheek as I made my way to the kitchen but halfway there, an idea hit me. "You know, when I was younger and any of us had a headache, my grandma swore by this little trick she did. I'm not sure if it actually works, but... I could try it." I paused. "On you, I mean."

"What does it involve?"

"Pressure points on your hands." I shuffled back to the couch. "Like I said, I don't know if it actually works, but I always felt better after."

He sighed deeply. "Fine."

A giddy feeling rushed through me for some reason. "Are you okay to sit up? That'll make it easier."

He pulled himself up slowly and settled on one half of the couch. I hesitated before sitting next to him. With a leg tucked under me, I faced him. "Come on then. Get a little closer."

He did as I asked, until his leg pressed against mine. My eyes darted to his, and then away, afraid he might see how one small touch was affecting me.

I took a slow breath. What a stupid idea this was. Let's get closer to the fire. Just put myself right here next to it. Let the flames make you feel all warm and soft and pliable. Playing with fire was always the smart move.

"Hold your hands out," I said, my voice lower.

Again, he did as asked, stretching out his hands, palms down.

I slowly slid my hands under his, like I was waiting for him to be the voice of reason and tell me to stop. He didn't. Warm, dry skin coasted over mine, rough, calloused hands. Hands that knew what a toolbelt was and how to use it.

Stop thinking about his toolbelt.

I wondered what he'd do if my hands kept going. What would the skin on his wrists feel like? Would his arms be just as warm? Suddenly, I wanted to know more than I wanted my next breath.

With a frown, I snatched my hands back. Get your act together. He's in pain. Focus.

"Is everything okay?" Gil asked, his voice sleepy and low.

I cleared my throat. "Uh, yeah. C-can you turn your hands over?" When he did, I rubbed my hands together quickly. "Grandy said this was important. To gather all the energy."

He scoffed. "Seriously?"

"Yes, seriously." I did not bring up the fact that Grandy was also convinced a little bourbon in a baby's bottle was good for them. "Now be quiet. You don't want the energy I'm gathering to be angry and annoyed, do you?"

"Am I really supposed to answer that?"

"Quiet. I'm working here." After rubbing my hands together for another twenty seconds, I found the spot at the base of his thumb and forefinger on each hand and squeezed. Not painfully, but firmly. I counted to twenty under my breath and then loosened my hold enough to make small circles with my fingers.

His eyes were on my face, I could feel them. I repeated the process two times. The quiet of the room surrounded us. The slide of his breath tickled the shell of my ear. My heartbeat fluttered when he exhaled.

I released his hands. "All done."

His hands hovered before falling to his lap. He moved his head back and forth slowly. "That might have helped a little."

"Good." I smiled.

"Thanks."

Something brushed the tips of my fingers. When I looked down, Gil's hands had inched closer to mine. Probably not on purpose. I should move away, get up, and leave.

Except I didn't.

He didn't either. His fingers traced the backs of my hands with a featherlight touch that sent a shiver through me.

With a shaky breath, I looked up. Our eyes met and held. We were so close now. My heart pounded. I couldn't move. I could barely think.

"Kiss me," I whispered.

"I want to," he said just as quietly. "But I won't. It's not a good idea."

I snatched my hands back and shot to my feet, mortified. "I-I'm sorry. I don't know why I said that. Of course it's not a good idea. You and me, we need to keep our eye on the prize. Except my prize is different from your prize and that's the problem, isn't it?" I shook my head, words spilling out of my mouth at lightning speed. "I lost my mind there for a minute. Lack of sleep. I tried counting mini sheep and it didn't help so... Well, anyway, did you know there are competitive chicken shows?"

He stood up slowly. "You should go back to bed."

"Good idea. Yes, that would be good." I could crawl under my covers and pray a sinkhole opened under my bed in the next two hours. I tried to squeeze between him and the couch, but he stopped me with a hand on my arm, sending a shot of pure heat through me.

"I'm sorry," he said quietly.

Without looking at him, I scurried by and scrambled to my room.

FORTY-FOUR

When you find a person attractive, that's what love is.

—ELLA F., AGE 10

From the group text chats of Ellie, Ali, and Mae:

ALI: *Abe says he is not in love with you.*

ELLIE: *That's good news since I'm not in love with him. We had a good time though. Talked about our kids the whole time.*

ALI: *Ugh. You people with kids never shut up about it. Yes, yes. You have kids. I GET IT.*

ELLIE: *Wait until you get one.*

MAE: *Look at this photo of Louisa. Look what she can do now!!! Isn't she the cutest, sweetest, most precious thing you've ever seen?*

ALI: She's laying on a blanket. I expected more from the three exclamation points. What exactly is it she's doing?

MAE: She's smiling and it's not from gas.

ELLIE: She's adorable! I remember the day Oliver did that. I should find those photos. I think I took a hundred of them.

ALI: I need new friends.

"How you doing, Ellie?" Teddy asked as he traipsed into the café a couple of weeks later, wearing a worn t-shirt and a pair of shorts. He still looked too thin, but he was lighter these days. Spring had melted into an early summer and now, in late May, we were already getting scorchers in the nineties.

Gil was finally, cautiously, speaking to Teddy. I liked to think it was because of our talk a few weeks ago but whatever had spurred him on, it was nice to see the two of them looking through photos together or talking about Teddy and Ollie's childhood. Gil was always kind and polite and they never seemed to veer into more serious topics.

"Let's get you something to eat, shall we?" I ushered him into the dining area. Gil was already there with a stack of file folders.

"Gilbert," Teddy said, giving him a hearty pat on the back. "What do you have here?"

"Lots of stuff. I found it all in Ollie's room." He opened one of the folders and removed a stack of photos. "Have a seat. I bet you know the people in these photos."

I left to get Teddy's place and returned as he was saying, "...and we snuck out of the house to do it."

"What happened after?" Gill asked.

Teddy chuckled. "Amelia ratted us out 'cause we wouldn't let her come, too. Whoo-ee, I got a whupping for that. I haven't thought about that in a long time." He smiled wistfully before setting the photos aside and pulling the plate of meatloaf and mashed potatoes toward him. "Glad you found those."

"I made copies so those are all yours."

"That's awfully nice of you." He pointed with his fork at me. "Isn't he a nice guy?"

Gil picked up another file folder. "I was hoping I could go over this stuff with you."

With a flourish, Teddy unfolded a paper napkin and laid it across his lap. "I suppose it's time to answer your questions. Ollie said you'd have some."

"I'll let you two talk." I rose from my seat, but Gil stopped me.

"I think you should stay."

"Okay." I folded myself back in the seat.

"So, what's the story, Teddy?" Gil asked. "What happened with Ollie and my grandmother?"

"It's a long, sad one." He took a bite, his expression thoughtful. "I don't look so good in this, I guess. But here goes..."

As Teddy explained, Ollie and Amelia had been sweethearts for as long as the both of them seemed old enough to understand what it meant. "Joined at the hip, those two. Heck, I was Ollie's best friend, and she was my sister, and I was the one who usually felt like the third wheel."

Ollie graduated high school two years before Amelia and settled in to work at the café. "Amelia had her heart set on college and Ollie was planning on joining her, not for school— he was a terrible student—but there was talk of a marriage."

But two weeks before Amelia was to head off to college, Ollie's father had a stroke. "It was real sad. He couldn't hardly talk after, let alone walk. He needed care around the clock."

"And Ollie didn't have any siblings," Gil said. "There wasn't anyone else to take over the café, was there?"

"Indeed. Ollie's mother had her hands full taking care of her husband." Teddy finished off his meatloaf and pushed his plate aside. "Is there any more of that apple pie?"

"I'll get you a piece." I stood. "Keep talking."

"So, Amelia went off to school on her own."

I brought the pie back to the table. "When did she figure out she was pregnant?"

"I'm not exactly sure." He shoved a forkful of pie into his mouth. Chewing slowly, his eyes drifted shut. "Ellie, I don't know how you make it so good."

Gil and I watched him eat for a good three minutes before Gil cleared his throat. "And then what?"

"Oh, right." Teddy straightened in his seat. If I didn't know better, I would say he was enjoying having an audience hang on his every word. "Amelia started classes, and she loved it. She would call home once a week to tell us all about it. There were letters, too. There was a boy she met who took a liking to her, I remember her telling us about him. She let him down easy, but they remained friends."

Gil held up a stack of envelopes, yellowed with age. "She wrote to Ollie, too. Found a whole stack of them."

"Did they have a plan?" I asked. "Were they still planning on being together?"

"Oh, yes. Ollie planned to move as soon as his father was better and could take over again but..." Teddy shrugged.

"He never got better, did he?"

"'Fraid not. Back then, the Holder family owned most of Main Street. Kept Ollie busy from sunup to sundown. I rarely saw him, and I lived here."

"I didn't know they owned more property," I said.

"Oh, sure. It's all been sold off now." Teddy fiddled with his glass of iced tea, his eyes downcast. "About three months after she left for school, we got a phone call. She'd married that boy who had a crush on her. It was right out of the blue and none of us knew what to think. We hadn't even been invited to the wedding. She told us it was all so sudden because he was shipping out to Vietnam, and they wanted to do it before he left. That was true. Now I know she was also about four months pregnant."

"That's it?" A wave of anger rolled through me on Ollie's account. "Did Ollie have any say at all in this?"

"You gotta understand, this was the mid-sixties. Being pregnant and unwed was not the done thing. Not like now, anyway." He smiled sheepishly at me. "Years later, I found out she'd written to Ollie and begged him to come to see her. She didn't want to tell him in a letter, and she was afraid to come home for fear someone would figure it out."

"But Ollie didn't go," Gil said.

"He was underwater here, trying to keep everything going. He couldn't just leave for a week."

"If he'd known..." I whispered.

"If he'd known." Teddy nodded.

Gil leaned back. "And she didn't tell anyone about the baby?"

"Not at first, but when your mother was born, I figured it out." He tapped his head. "Always was good at math. I wrote to her and asked. She made me promise I wouldn't tell anyone, even Ollie."

"Why didn't she ever tell him?" Gil asked, his voice low.

"She knew Ollie was under enough pressure and she didn't want to pile it on. By then, she was married. Her new husband knew of the baby and agreed to raise her as his own. I told her to tell him, but she was stubborn. Felt like she was protecting Ollie and all and doing right by the baby."

Gil crossed his arms. "How did Ollie find out?"

His cheeks reddened. "I had a bit too much to drink one night, and I let it slip."

"What did he do?" I asked.

"Only fight we ever had." He pointed at a faded half-inch

white line on his forehead near his hairline. "Left me with this scar, he did. Your grandma was in her twenties by then. Ollie made me tell him everything I knew about his daughter. Then he hired a private detective to find out the rest."

"That's what all this is." Gil opened the file folder. "There are yearly reports from the PI going back years. He knew everything about us."

Teddy nodded. "Ollie wanted to go introduce himself and have a place in your mother's life. He went so far as to drive over to where she was living up in north Texas somewhere. Parked in front of her house and watched for a long time. He said she looked so happy. He got to thinking what would happen if he just showed up in her life and decided he'd rather her be happy. He didn't want to mess up her life. So, he turned around and drove back to Two Harts. Never tried to reach out again. But he always kept track of you all. Knew everything about you. I think he understood Amelia's thinking, deep down—she thought she was doing this in his best interest."

Gil pulled out yet another folder.

"How many of those do you have?" I asked.

"A lot." He opened it. "These are all receipts for college tuition. To my college. I was told I had a scholarship."

Teddy snorted. "Wasn't no scholarship. It was Ollie. He was real proud of you." He pointed to me. "You, too. Used to go on and on about how much you reminded him of Amelia."

"Really?"

He squinted. "Oh, sure. You with your big smile and always being so nice to everyone. And that boy of yours. He loved that boy."

I blinked back tears.

With a chuckle, Teddy waved a hand between Gil and me. "He had this big idea if the two of you met, you'd get along real good." He leaned closer like he was telling us a secret. "Personally, I think his whole plan was to play matchmaker."

I made the mistake of turning my head. My gaze caught on Gil's and held. The look in his eye made the rhythm of my heartbeat change, become slow and languid. I wondered what he was thinking behind those dark-blue eyes, and was it of me... of an us that didn't exist.

Teddy chuckled, pulling my attention away. "I'm serious. Ollie was a romantic. He used to write poetry to Amelia. You were his favorite people. He liked to say you two needed each other. Too bad he had to die to make it happen."

"Teddy, we aren't a..." I took a deep breath. "We're business partners. That's all."

Teddy snorted and stuffed a large forkful of mashed potatoes in his mouth. "Sure thing."

"Why do you think he never gave me a chance to meet him?" Gil asked.

"I think mostly he didn't want to interrupt your life. He just wanted to know you were happy and healthy. I guess that was enough for him."

"Maybe that is enough," Gil murmured.

Teddy leaned over and patted Gil's shoulder. "Don't be too hard on Ollie. Always made me sad but I guess I understood. Ollie loved you enough to let you go."

FORTY-FIVE

"I'll do the cutting in," Gil said, hands on his hips.

It was a Sunday afternoon at the end of May, although the weather was overcast and humid and thunderclouds loomed in the distance. Gil had come home early from his weekend trip to beat the storms and right as I was dragging everything out of the bathroom to paint.

I mimicked his stance. "I said I would do it. I like doing it."

"Nobody likes cutting in. It's tedious."

I picked up a paintbrush and climbed up the ladder. "Then I guess I like tedious. You're my friend and you might be the most tedious thing in my life right now."

His eyes narrowed. "Fine. You do it."

Shaking my head, I watched him stomp off, probably to work on taking wallpaper off some wall in this house. Lately, he'd spent a lot of time removing wallpaper. It was like an obsession with him—aggressive wallpaper removal. I had no idea what that wallpaper had ever done to him, but he was taking no prisoners, that was for sure.

The tension between us had ratcheted up considerably since my date with Abe. It was like a secret switch had been thrown. If I were in a room, Gil left it. I brushed passed him in the hallway, he practically climbed the wall to get away from me. He'd stopped eating dinner with us, although he had no problem eating the leftovers. When he was at the café, he hid in the office, but he always made time to talk with Teddy or Malcolm when they were around. He hung out with Oliver.

But he stayed far away from me.

Maybe it was better this way. Getting closer would only make these jumbled-up feelings inside me grow. I kept reminding myself we had different goals. Opposing goals. One of us would win and one of us would lose. We only had a little over nine weeks left of our six months. After that, who knew what would happen. A wave of anxiety tore through me, and I pushed it down.

My arm started to get sore after finishing the second wall, so I climbed down and took a break, sitting on the closed toilet and texting my mother. My stomach rumbled, reminding me I hadn't eaten lunch yet. In the kitchen, I got out the ingredients for a turkey and cheese sandwich.

"Mommy," Oliver called from somewhere in the house.

"What?" I yelled.

"I need you."

"Coming." With one last look of longing at my half-made sandwich, I went to search for him. He was in his bedroom, which resembled a disaster zone.

"I'm trying to build a fort," he said. "I need help."

I huffed. "I need this room clean."

"Now?"

"How about get your dirty clothes together so I can wash them. Then I'll help you." After we got the dirty clothes settled,

I spent the next twenty minutes rigging up a fort with every bed sheet we owned.

"This is awesome," Oliver said, diving under the sheet canopy. "Thanks, Mom."

With his dirty clothes basket in hand, I headed to the laundry room, briefly deterred by a kitten—we were calling them Salt and Pepper for now—who felt personally offended by my shoelaces. After getting the washer going, I discovered the towels I'd washed the day before in the dryer and carried the pile of them into the living room where I started to fold them.

I'd gotten through half of them when I saw the mailman pull into the driveway. I grabbed the birthday card I'd meant to mail to a cousin and ran out to meet him. We chatted for a bit about the weather—all Texans, I've learned, complained about the weather—and he mentioned something about the grass looking a bit thirsty.

After he left, I got the hose out and gave the yard a good soak. I needed to add GET A SPRINKLER to my notes. By the time I was through, I was sticky with sweat and dying for ice water.

Also, I was kind of hungry.

In the kitchen, I found a turkey sandwich, made just the way I liked it, with mayo on both sides, cheese and tomato, on a plate on the counter. Huh. Had I made this? I did remember starting to make it, at least.

In the living room, all the towels were folded and neatly stacked.

In the laundry room, Oliver's clothes had been moved to the dryer.

In the bathroom, I found Gil balanced on the ladder doing all the tedious work I'd said I would do.

"I'm sorry." I hovered in the doorway. "I don't know what happened."

"I know what happened," he said. "You got distracted."

I winced, shame bubbling up. Sunny would be disappointed that was my first reaction. "I'm sorry. Some days, I can't seem to focus on one thing no matter how hard I try."

Up on the ladder, he'd put down the paintbrush and hopped down. A smudge of the off-white paint was on his cheekbone. My fingers itched to wipe it off. "It's fine."

I pointed at the wall. "I really am sorry for not being done yet."

"I give up," he muttered as he wrapped a hand around my arm. "Your brain has been built to see the world differently. It's not your fault. It wasn't your fault as a kid. It's not your fault now."

"Even if it isn't my fault, it usually leads to other people cleaning up my mess. Look at what happened just now. You made the sandwich. You folded the towels. You're finishing the painting when I said I would do it. I meant to do it. I'll still do it." I pulled my arm from his hand and stared at the wall over his shoulder. My eyes stung and that only frustrated me more. "It creates a whole lot of extra work for everyone else."

"Do you think I'm annoyed at you?" he asked.

"Yes!" I shouted. "Why wouldn't you be?"

"I'll tell you why." He took a step toward me, and I shuffled back. "My brain likes the way your brain thinks."

My eyes widened.

"I don't mind cleaning up after you, or closing a cabinet you left open, or putting your clothes in the dryer after you've washed them three times because you keep forgetting to put them in the dryer. What does that say about my brain?" Another step forward, "My brain likes the way you take care of Oliver, how you seem to know my moods and don't mind them, how you put others before yourself every time. It really likes your pork chops, too."

"They're really good pork chops," I whispered.

"Yes, they are and they aren't even close to the best thing about you."

The back of my thighs bumped against the edge of the sink. "I don't know what to say."

"Mostly... mostly my brain likes you. Even the things I don't understand—I like those things, too. I like you. A lot. And it's about to drive me crazy pretending I don't."

He slid a hand around to the back of my neck, leaving a trail of heat wherever he touched me. He pressed his forehead to mine. "My brain wants to kiss you."

"You said it was a bad idea," I whispered.

"It probably still is." The tip of his nose skated down the side of my face in a featherlight touch. I shivered. "It definitely still is."

"I want you to kiss me." I licked my bottom lip. "But I'm worried about what happens after."

He pulled back to look at me, his expression steady, patient, as though waiting for me to make the next move. This is going to hurt later, I thought, right before I fisted his t-shirt and kissed him.

To be honest, I'd been dreaming about kissing him for weeks now. My imagination was pretty good but nothing like the real thing.

And he wasn't even wearing the toolbelt.

Gil took over the kiss almost immediately, hauling me against him, one hand sliding into my hair and the other settling low on my back. I was surrounded by him, and it felt so good. The tension I'd been holding onto for weeks melted as his kiss became more insistent, deeper. My heart thrummed against my ribs. Fire heated my blood, warming me from the inside out.

My hands tangled in his hair and tugged. He broke the kiss long enough for me to take a breath before he was kissing me again; I returned it with an edge of desperation, the knowing that this wasn't a new beginning. It was a beginning to an end.

All my bad decisions came down to this one moment, this one kiss, this one man.

Because the other thing about this kiss, it was the first time I'd been kissed by someone who wanted all the parts of me, good and bad.

He wanted me. Just me. *Only me.*

And I know it sounds clichéd and so romance-novel-y but looking back, it was the exact moment I made the best worst decision of my life: I fell in love with Gilbert Dalton.

FORTY-SIX

[Love is...] when you care deeply about someone.

—CARTER A., AGE 10

What do you do when you finally get the thing you wanted more than anything? You protect it, you keep it somewhere safe, and you don't tell a soul. I guess that's what was happening right now between Gil and me. For the last week, we'd been in a bubble that protected us from everyone else's opinions.

We didn't even tell Oliver. Then again, I wasn't sure what we would tell him. But at night after he went to bed, Gil and I didn't avoid each other anymore. In fact, we did the opposite of that. It was kind of fun sneaking around like teenagers.

School got out the first week in June and Oliver stayed home with Gil most days. They were working on some secret project together. Oliver was practically salivating to tell me what it was, even came close a time or two, but he'd sworn an oath of fealty, or something. Every day, I came home and there was Gil asking me how my day was or insisting I sit down while he did the dishes.

Who was this man and how could I keep him?

That was the million-dollar question. While we talked about all kinds of things, what we didn't do was bring up the subject of selling the house. It was an unspoken dark cloud that neither of us was willing to deal with.

"Mommy," Oliver yelled the second I walked in the door from work one Tuesday in early June. "Something happened."

I dumped my stuff on the kitchen counter. "What?"

He patted my arm. Like he was consoling me. "I don't want you to be mad at Mr. Gil."

"Why?"

"He forgot and he opened..." he leaned in and whispered "... the hallway closet we aren't supposed to open."

"No," I breathed and rushed from the kitchen. "Please, please, please."

But no amount of pleading could reverse the damage. Because there was Gil, standing in front of that closet. The door was open. Skeins of brightly colored yarn—at least thirty of them—lay on the floor at his feet. Oreo and Cookie (the most recent names of the kittens) were in the middle of it. One of them leapt in the air and attacked a large ball of red yarn.

I groaned. "What did you do?"

"I was looking for extra towels." A bemused Gil clutched a pile of said towels against his chest.

"No, don't look at those." I dashed over to him and tried to grab them out of his hands, but he was faster.

He held one up. It was a hand towel with the words POTTY LIKE A ROCK STAR embroidered in red. And another one that read: YOU'RE A POOP STAR. He pressed his lips together, holding back amusement, before choking out, "Why?"

"Don't laugh." I smacked his shoulder. "I was into embroidering at the time and thought I could make some extra money and Oliver had just finished potty training and, well..." I waved at them weakly. "I sold them at craft fairs and online until I kind of got over dealing with it and just stopped."

"You made these?" He'd pulled another towel out: HOPE EVERYTHING COMES OUT OKAY.

"That was my biggest seller." I stuck my hands in my pockets and hoped I would be abducted by aliens any second.

Gil pressed his lips together and nodded. He looked up at the ceiling, then the floor, then back to the ceiling. I thought he might be counting to himself. Finally, he took a deep breath. "The yarn?"

"Crocheting. I was pretty good at it but after a while..." I shrugged. "I tried knitting, too, but I got frustrated with it."

"Is this a whole closet of craft supplies?"

This is what happened with all my crafty ideas. The excitement was overwhelming and lasted just long enough for me to buy all the things I needed (and didn't need). In fact, shopping for crafty items was most of the fun of starting a new hobby. I'd organize everything, spend hours online looking at tutorials and patterns and ideas. I'd attempt to make a few things. I might even enjoy it. I might even be good at it. Until I lost interest, or another brighter, shinier craft came along.

"Yeah," I said. "I know it's kind of nuts. I'll admit the six months I decided I was going to make all of Oliver's clothes was a dark time and I have no talent for watercolors or oil painting. Needlepoint is, wow, yeah, not for me. There's stuff to make soap and candles, too."

He reached in and pulled out a huge bag of balloons. "Why would one person need this many balloons?"

I closed my eyes. "For balloon animals."

"Wow," he said in a strangled voice.

"I got pretty good at it," I said defensively. "It's my secret shame, okay?"

"I can see why." He coughed.

"No laughing."

"Me? No. Of course not." He snickered.

"Okay, fine. Ha. Ha." I snatched the bag of balloons out of his hand and tossed it in the closet. After trying and failing to wrestle a ball of yarn from a kitten, I pushed the rest of it into the closet and tried to shove the door closed. It popped back open like it was taunting me.

"You weren't supposed to see this. It makes me feel like such a... loser."

He grinned. "Hey, you've never seen my craft closet."

I shoved the door closed again and leaned my body against it, putting me squarely in the middle of the door and Gil. "I bet there's a lot of lot of drills and hammers and screwdrivers. I don't know. I think I'd like your craft closet."

Gil looked left and right. "No Oliver. I could steal a kiss."

I walked my fingers up his chest. "You sure you want to kiss a woman who makes balloon animals?"

The right side of his mouth ticked up. "Literally nothing in the world I want more."

And then, he did.

FORTY-SEVEN

Love is when they smooch each other when they're getting married.

—ANDREW, AGE 7

The next week, I arrived home to a sticky note on the door.

Go in the backyard.
Follow the signs.
—G and O

I smiled as I wandered around to the backyard. There were signs, arrows drawn in crayon. They led me past where Gil had set up his tent compound way back in February and toward the old, faded red barn. The grass should have been wildly out of control, but it had been cut back so that there was a clear path. The humid, still June heat pressed down and created an instant sheen of sweat.

ALMOST THERE, a sign read, dangling from a tree. I

paused to look at the picture Oliver had drawn hanging next to it. It was of the house with flowers blooming and a tire swing on the tree out front. Three people stood in front of the house. Oliver, me with a yellow ponytail, and on the other side of Oliver, there was a man with dark hair and carefully drawn glasses. We were all holding hands and smiling.

But it was the fourth person in the drawing that made me tear up. In one of the puffy white clouds sat an old man with bushy eyebrows. He might have had the biggest smile of all of us.

"Mommy, hurry up." Oliver appeared about twenty yards ahead, waving his arms and yelling, "Hurry."

"I'm coming." Thirty seconds later, the path turned and I saw it. A gazebo. A big pink bow had been tied on a post.

Oliver ran to me and grabbed my hand. As he pulled me closer, he talked at warp speed. "Come see what Mr. Gil and I builted for you. Uncle Chris helped some and Mr. Theo, too. And then Mr. Malcolm came, and all these people came and helped a little at a time while you were at work. I had to keep it a secret for a long time but every week I kept it a secret, Mr. Gil gave me one whole dollar and now I have four of them but I'm going to save them 'cause I want to get a guitar like Mr. Gil has."

Gil stood on the top step of the gazebo, one shoulder leaned again the post, his hands tucked into his jean pockets, his gray t-shirt molded to his chest with sweat. And the toolbelt. He had that on.

I couldn't take my eyes off him; he'd never looked hotter. My pulse rocketed the closer I got. "How did this happen?"

He lifted a shoulder and came down a step. "You had GAZEBO written on one of your sticky notes. I figured that meant you wanted one."

"It's beautiful." I ran my hand along the railing and looked up at him. "You built this?"

"I had a lot of help from this guy." He ruffled Oliver's hair.

Oliver grinned and took off at a dead run into the expanse behind the gazebo. Acres and acres to run. "And some other friends. Regulars from the café. Even Teddy. It was a group effort."

"But how did you do this without me knowing?"

He came down another step. "It wasn't too hard. You're gone all day. You never take a day off. You never even take a lunch as far as I know."

"Am I really that oblivious?" A scary thought for when Oliver was a teenager.

Gently, he tucked a piece of flyaway hair behind one of my ears and stared down at me, his eyes liquid and intense and completely unreadable. "I guess so."

I peeked around his shoulder and caught a glimpse of Oliver chasing a butterfly. "No one's ever done something like this for me."

"You deserve it." He leaned closer and gave me a small, chaste kiss on the mouth.

When he made to move away, I slid a hand around his neck. "That's it."

"Oliver might see."

"I'll risk it."

Carefully, like I was precious, he cupped my cheeks. He rubbed his nose against mine. He smelled like sweat and sawdust and a hint of varnish and hard work. I loved it.

The kiss was slow and sweet, lazy and thorough. It made my chest ache with how easy it was to stand here with this man and make up dreams in my head. Like how one day, maybe the two of us could stand in this very spot on the steps of the gazebo he built and say I do.

He pulled back and I kept my eyes closed for just a bit longer. Long enough to keep that made-up dream in my head. Because the truth was, I didn't know what the future held. I knew, for now, Gil and I were on a timer that was close to reaching the end. This gazebo he's spent all this time on? If we sold this place, I'd never see it again. Maybe I'd never see Gil either.

Stay in the present, Sunny liked to tell me. Don't let your anxiety steal the joy of what's right in front of you.

So, I opened my eyes and smiled.

"Oliver," Gil yelled. "Come on. Let's go to dinner."

"I can make something here," I said.

He gave me a stern look. "No. We're going out to eat. It's your birthday. Looks like I'm not the only one who can keep secrets."

I was pleasantly surprised when Gil drove us to the Texican for dinner. A server seated us at a table much too large for us. "Are we expecting company?"

Gil smiled. "Maybe."

Oliver giggled before slapping a hand over his mouth.

"Not suspicious at all," I said with a laugh.

"It's a birthday party, Mommy," Oliver said. "We even got a cake."

My chest tightened, too many feelings to even name. I met Gil's eyes and smiled. "Thank you."

"Don't thank me yet. I made the cake."

"I helped," Oliver added, his face beaming.

I choked back a laugh. "I can't wait to see it. I'm going to run to the bathroom before everyone gets here."

Liliana stopped me as I passed her at the front counter. "Who is this one?"

"That's Gil."

"A date?" She gave a long look over the half-wall. "He is very handsome. And Oliver likes him, no?"

"Not a date. He's..." Something. "We're business partners." Who kiss.

"You do not blush like he's your business partner." She turned her speculative gaze on me. "I like this one."

My mouth dropped open. Never, ever, in the two years I'd been bringing dates to the Texican, had Liliana given her stamp of approval. Some of them had gotten a maybe, lots of immediate nos. And she was never wrong. Ever.

"*Si*, this one I like." She peeked at Gil and then back to me. "Yes, this is a good one for you."

"You haven't met him. How do you even know?"

Liliana pffts. "I do not get to be this old being stupid. You can tell by the way he looks at you. I watched. I saw."

I ran a fingernail along the edge of the counter between us. "How would you say he looked at me?"

She put a hand over mine. "Like you are precious. Not perfect, but precious. That is how a man should look at a woman."

"I'm not sure it's going to work out between us," I said quietly.

"Another thing I have learned is things have a way of working out the way they are supposed to." She gave my hand a final pat. "Now, go back to your table. You are going to have a busy night, no? A table for fifteen." She frowned. "It's your birthday. Why did you not tell me this?"

"I didn't know I was supposed to tell the owner of my favorite restaurant when my birthday was."

She harrumphed. "Just for that, we're singing 'Happy Birthday' in English *and* Spanish, and you have to wear the sombrero all night."

FORTY-EIGHT

[Love is...] *sharing things, loving people, giving people things, making people things, doing things for people.*

—LAUREN MARIE S., AGE 5

"When you get a moment, can you come into the office?" Gil asked. "I had a quick question."

"Sure thing." I nodded and went right back to clearing off a table, humming softly.

Iris slid up next to me. "Hey, boss, it seems to me that man has an awful lot of questions lately."

"We are business partners. It's logical we'd have things to discuss."

"I hear you. It's just that most business partners don't come out of their meeting with their hair looking like someone has shoved their hands in it."

I blushed. "I don't look like that."

"Hey, no judgement here." Iris grinned. "I will absolutely make fun of you, though."

"Go away."

After I finished cleaning up a second table, I made myself wait an appropriate amount of time so as not to seem eager—five minutes seemed long enough—before I dashed back to the office. Gil had left the door cracked open. He was at the desk, frowning at whatever he was looking at on the computer.

I knocked softly. "You had a question."

"Ah, yes." Good grief, those glasses of his had to be illegal in forty-seven countries. "Come over here."

After shutting the door, I rounded the desk. "I'm here to serve."

He snickered and pulled me onto his lap. I landed with a squeal and looped my arms around his neck.

"Hi." He buried his face in my neck.

I giggled as he kissed me there. "Iris is on to us."

He was busy; he didn't answer.

"You should come up with a good question to throw her off the trail. Something about overhead or this month's P&I." I gasped when he moved up my neck and nibbled my ear.

"Was that a good gasp or a bad gasp?" he whispered.

"It was a 'do that again later but kiss me right now' gasp."

"Kiss you here?" He kissed my forehead. It was fascinating, this... thing... with Gil. It surprised me how playful he was.

"Not close enough."

"What about here?" He kissed the tip of my nose.

"You're getting warmer."

"Here?" He brushed the corner of my mouth.

"So, so close. Maybe we should get your eyes checked." I smiled; he smiled back. We stared at each other with silly, sloppy smiles. His eyes shone with an emotion neither of us was willing to name.

Instead of words, he answered me with a kiss exactly where it belonged.

"Nailed it," I said when we came up for air.

He trailed a hand down my hair. Here was another

surprising thing about Gilbert Dalton: He liked to touch. Small, sweet touches—a soft caress to my cheek in passing, the brush his fingers on the small of my back, nuzzling that spot where my neck met my shoulder when Oliver wasn't looking.

"I'll probably have another question in forty-five minutes or so," he said, a serious expression on his face.

"Of course you will."

I looked over at the computer. "What are you working on?"

"The budget."

"Sounds fun." My eyes skipped over the desk and landed on a glossy folder half hidden under a stack of receipts I knew hadn't been in here yesterday. I eased it out and read the cover: Forsham Development Group. "What's this?"

Gil gave me a wary look. "It's from a real estate development group. Peter Stone dropped it off."

I stood, my eyes darting between the folder and the man. "Oh."

I took a deep breath, my heart sinking as I realized my mistake. I laid the folder down slowly and walked to the door. No matter how many stolen kisses we shared, nothing had changed.

"I'm looking at options," he said. "Putting feelers out to see who might be interested in buying."

"I don't want to sell," I said. "That hasn't changed."

"And I have my brother to take care of. That hasn't changed," he said, his voice gentle.

"I have responsibilities, too." I took a step closer. "Maybe we could figure this out... together?"

He rubbed his forehead. "We've been living in a bubble, haven't we?"

It had been such a nice bubble, where I could forget about the future. "What are we going to do?"

FORTY-NINE

[Love is...] um...I don't know.

—ELEANOR P., AGE 4

"My turn." I stretched my hands out to take the baby from Ali. "She's my niece, I want to hold her."

"You're working." Ali held up Lulu, the nickname given to Louisa almost immediately. "That mean old aunty is trying to steal you from me. Boo!"

"I know the boss, she's fine with me holding her. Gimme." Reluctantly, Ali handed her over. I cuddled her close and smelled the top of her head. "She still has that new baby smell. Best smell in the world."

"Smell it all you want." Mae pushed her plate aside. "I'll just curl up under the table and take a nap."

"Are you keeping your mama up all night?" I asked. Lulu puckered her lips and blinked up at me with fuzzy eyes that couldn't quite pick a color. Her hair, on the other hand, was a vibrant red, brighter than Mae's.

"She likes her meals on time, that's for sure," Mae muttered.

"I hope Chris is helping you out. I can go beat some sense into him if he isn't."

"He's been a little *too* helpful. She's two months old and it's the first time he's let me out of the house without insisting he come with us. He's there for every cry, every feeding, every diaper." Mae smiled and rattled the ice in her glass.

The bell over the door tinkled. Oliver raced over, Gil behind him. He slung an arm around my neck and stared down at his cousin in awe. "She's so little."

He said that every time he saw her, like he couldn't believe people came this small. The birth of Lulu had also brought up a lot of questions: how did the baby get in Aunt Mae's tummy? How did the baby get out? When was he going to get a baby brother already? I was ready to go steal a baby just to make the questions stop. But at night when I was in bed, sometimes I let myself wonder what our child would look like if Gil and I had a baby.

I knew it was dangerous. I knew we were on borrowed time. I knew since our talk in the office last week, things had been strained. But I also knew I couldn't stop my feelings. Which was annoying. Next session, I planned to ask Sunny about this whole focus on "feelings." Feelings were dumb and they hurt like hell.

"Isn't she so little?" Oliver asked, craning his head to look up at Gil.

Gil smiled down at the baby. "So little."

"You should hold her," I said to Gil. "Sit down."

A look of pure horror crossed his face. "I don't think that's a good idea. I've never... held a baby."

"Never?"

"Never ever."

"Well, you're doing it today." I nodded at a chair. "Sit."

Warily, he sat. I carried her over. "Cross your arms. Make

sure you support her head." I transferred Lulu over. After adjusting his hold, I stood back and smiled.

"I don't want to drop her," he said.

"You aren't going to drop her. You're doing great."

Slowly he loosened up. Soon, the terror was replaced by wonder. "She's so little."

Oliver nodded. "That's what I said."

I'd been wrong about Gil wearing a toolbelt and cuddling a kitten because this scene in front of me was really doing things for me. I suddenly wanted to give Oliver that baby brother real fast. I picked up one of the menus and fanned my face. Ali caught my eye and smirked, like she knew exactly what I was thinking.

Mae pulled her phone out and took a photo. *I'll send it to you*, she mouthed to me.

I flushed.

"While I have you here, I wanted to double-check you'll be selling pie at the Fourth of July Festival?" Ali picked up the clipboard she had permanently attached to her these days.

The festival was one of Ali's pet projects, a hometown celebration, and this would be the second year for it. The whole of downtown was closed off to cars, and vendors came in from as far as the Dallas/Fort Worth area. There was a co-ed baseball game and a fireworks show at night. Legacy Park would house the food trucks and petting zoo and games. To make extra sure we weren't competing with the bigger events in Houston, we held it on the Saturday before the Fourth.

"Yes, ma'am," I said. "Apple, blueberry, and strawberry rhubarb."

Ali checked something off on the clipboard. "Perfect." She turned a blinding smile in Gil's direction. "Since you're here, I was wondering if you'd be willing to volunteer to work security. Just for an hour shift, that's all."

Lulu started to fuss. Instead of panicking, Gil stood and

began to sway back and forth. The baby quieted. He was a natural. "When is it?"

Ali told him the date and time slot she hoped he'd fill.

He shook his head. "I can't. Sorry."

"That's right, you leave on the weekends." Ali tapped her fingertips on the table.

"I visit my brother on the weekends."

Ali snapped her fingers. "I've got it. Bring him with you."

Gil stopped mid-sway. "It's not so easy."

"He's not in prison, right." Ali started to laugh and then slid Gil a look. "He isn't, is he?"

"No."

"Is he okay to travel?"

"I mean, sure." Gil looked a little panicked.

"Then, it's settled." Ali stood and tucked the clipboard under her arm. "You'll bring him. I love it when a plan comes together, don't you?"

"He's asleep?" Gil asked.

"Finally." I sat down next to him on the bench we'd uncovered in the backyard. After a good cleaning and fixing a few loose screws, it had become a favorite place for Gil and me to sit after Oliver went to bed. "He wanted me to explain how Lulu got in Aunt Mae's tummy."

"What did you tell him?"

"The truth, obviously." I leaned back and waved a hand at the inky-black sky. "Aliens."

Laughing, he patted my leg. "You're a good mom."

I rested my head on his shoulder. "I don't feel like it most of the time."

"You are all the time. That's the first thing I liked about you."

"That I was a mom?"

"That you were a good mom. I could tell from that meeting with the lawyer when you wouldn't let me stay in the house because you didn't want strangers around Oliver."

I lifted my head and looked at him coyly. "What's the second thing you liked about me?"

Absently, his hand on my knee wandered up to my thigh. My heart skittered at the delicious weight of it resting there. "Everything."

"I like you, too," I said. "Even when you wear your toolbelt."

"I think especially when I wear my toolbelt. I feel faintly objectified when I wear it around you."

I gasped. "I do not objectify you."

"Good thing I like it." He kissed the side of my head. "Why do you think I keep wearing it?"

Jokingly, I elbowed him in the ribs only to snuggle into his side right after. "About the Fourth of the July Festival, listen, I can get you out of that. When Ali goes into high gear, she steamrolls people into agreeing."

"I can see how she's good at her job," he said dryly.

I picked at the frayed edge of my jean shorts. "But also, if you wanted to bring Mikey here for the weekend, I think it would be nice to meet him."

"I don't know. He likes his routine and being in familiar places. It might be way too much for him."

"Or you could try it and see what happens."

"I don't know if I want to experiment on him."

"Not an experiment. How are you going to know how he'll do in a new situation if you don't let him try? When's the last time you took him somewhere new?"

Gil frowned. "I guess it's been a while. I've been a little busy the past few months."

"Exactly. Bring him here. Maybe just for the day. You can take him back home after. But I want to meet him." I turned and tucked a leg under me. "He's important to you. You've met all my important people."

Tilting his head to the side, he looked at me for a long moment. "I just figured something out."

"What?"

"You can talk me into things, too."

"Does this mean you'll bring him?" When he nodded, I clapped my hands. "What does he like to eat? Is he a dessert guy? Please tell me he likes dessert? Cookies or cake? Pie, maybe? Brownies? Oooh, muffins?"

He grinned. "Mikey is gonna love you."

"You think?"

"How could he not?" His smile slipped. With the back of his hand, he touched my cheek.

I swallowed and turned back in the seat, the metal from the back of the bench pressed against my spine. The overwhelming need to cry hit me hard. My heart physically ached. "What happens? Next month when the six months are up?"

He slid an arm around my shoulders. "I don't know."

We sat like that for a long time. The cicadas serenaded us, a toad or two added in their two cents. Beyond the lights of the house, there would be snakes and armadillos, coyotes and possums. Beyond that, the rest of the world waited and with it, the responsibilities and pressures we each carried.

But right now, here on this bench, it was just Gil and me, the steady beat of his heart, the quiet rising and falling of his chest with each breath. A feeling wrapped around me, kept me right there pretending nothing else existed, that my happily ever after was within reach.

It was a nice illusion. One that I knew wouldn't last.

FIFTY

Love is when my parents help me practice my ballet.

—MAKENLEY G., AGE 10

The day before the Fourth of July celebration was hectic, and that was after a busy week of baking pies non-stop. Just when I thought I was caught up, Ali would show up with an updated estimate for the number of attendees.

"This is going to be huge," she said, doing a little dance in the middle of the café. "Last year's was pretty good. But this one... it's going to blow it away. What town has the hardest-working mayor around?"

"She's sure not the quietest," someone muttered.

"Whoops, sorry," she said, not looking even a tiny bit apologetic. "Gil still bringing his brother?"

I beckoned her to take a seat at the counter, so I wasn't talking across the room. "I think he's nervous. His brother was in a car accident when he was a teenager, and he sustained a brain injury."

Ali nodded. "He told me a little."

"He did? When?" He sure was getting around the town. Here I thought he stayed home all day and stared at paint drying.

"He had lunch with Theo and me last week. I was picking his brain about Two Harts getting its own community center. He had a lot of great ideas. I like him, Ellie. Are you sure the two of you aren't..." she made an awkward gesture with the pointer fingers of both hands "...together?"

I covered her hands. "Never do that again, okay?"

She laughed. "Seriously, El. He's a great guy."

"Yeah, I know." Boy, did I know it. "It's complicated."

"People say that all the time and you know what? It usually isn't. It's usually something a real long talk over a piece of pie could make much easier."

"Thanks for the tip."

"You're welcome." She grinned. "I asked him about what his future plans were. Thought maybe I could lure him to Two Harts for the community center—"

"That we don't have yet."

"Details. Details. He didn't say much else to that and then he and Theo started talking about baseball." She pulled a sheet of paper from her magic clipboard and cleared her throat. "I did come in here on official business. You are hereby notified you have been nominated for Small Business Owner of the Year."

On the table, she placed a flyer with my photo and two other smiling business owners I recognized. "Me?"

"Yep. We decided to give out three awards. One for volunteer of the year, one for city employee of the year, and one to a small business owner. Show a little pride in our people, you know? At the last city council meeting, we took nominations, then people voted online. The winners are announced tomorrow." She pushed the flyer toward me. "You should hang it up in the window."

"Thank you," I whispered. "I'm not sure what to say."

"You say, 'Hell yeah, I'm winning this thing.' You deserve it, Ellie. Two Harts loves you. You're one of us. Now, I have about seven million things to do before tomorrow, including the finishing touches on the City Hall float for the parade. We went with a gnome theme this year."

"You did a gnome theme last year."

"I know. It makes Peter Stone see red. I have no idea what he has against gnomes," she said with wide, innocent eyes. There was a story there. It involved gnomes in inappropriate positions left on his lawn. The culprit had never been caught; she *had* been elected mayor though.

Long after she left, I stared down at the flyer. It seemed so silly, this huge lump in my throat. I loved this town. How could I leave? But how could I stay? It was almost a foregone conclusion that Peter and his real estate developers would snap it up and he'd happily bulldoze everything to the ground—Ollie's house, the café, and anything else that stood in his way.

When that happened, the climate of Two Harts would change. People from the city would crawl their way out here to buy McMansions in "planned communities." The mom-and-pop shops would slowly disappear, replaced by chains and big box stores.

Two Harts as we knew it would disappear.

"He's here. He's here." Oliver's shriek startled the kittens—Charlotte and Avery this week after his teacher began reading *Charlotte's Web* to the class. Oliver had had his face pressed to the front window for over an hour, the kittens taking a seat on the sill next to him. Before I could say a word, he'd dashed out the door to meet Gil and his brother, Mikey.

I bit my lip and followed slowly. All week, Gil and I had been explaining to Oliver how Mikey would be different from other adults he knew. How Mikey didn't like a lot of loud noise and sometimes wore headphones to protect his ears, or how he might need a break if he were overwhelmed. How sweet Mikey was but sometimes got mad when he didn't understand what was going on.

"We treat him like any other person," I said. "But we help him when he needs it, okay?"

Oliver had listened carefully, and I swear if he were capable, he would have taken notes and reviewed them later. "I hope he likes me."

"Of course he'll like you," Gil said. "You're awesome."

Still, Oliver had picked out his outfit carefully, donning his favorite dinosaur shirt. He'd been sitting at the window since seven thirty in the morning.

With Main Street blocked off for the parade and festivities, the café was opening late and only serving selected items. It had been strange waking up after five. I'd laid in bed because I could, read a little more of *The Pirate's Booty*. It wasn't half bad, but did have me questioning if all the characters in romance novels were able to defy the limitations of physics and body movement.

Gil waved as he rounded the car. But Mikey hadn't waited for his brother. He was already out of the car and grinning widely, revealing a snaggletooth. He was a little shorter than Gil. His hair was more gray than brown, and he was beginning to bald. His eyes were blue behind glasses that were almost identical to Gil's. A long white scar started atop his right eyebrow and went above his hairline, making it impossible for the hair to grow there.

Oliver screeched to a halt in front of him. He tipped his head back to look up at him. Next to Mikey, he looked so small.

"Hello," Mikey said in a loud voice. He grinned down at Oliver. "My name is Mikey. I'm thirty five. Can I be your friend? What's your name?"

"I'm Oliver. I'm six. We can be friends."

Mikey punched a fist in the air with excitement. "Yay. I like your shirt. It has a dinosaur on it. I like dinosaurs." He pointed to his own t-shirt. It was blue with a couple of smiling sheep and the words, HOW EWE DOING? above them. "Sheep are my favorite, and this is my favorite shirt because it's funny. Did you know a lady sheep is called a ewe?"

Oliver giggled. "Do you want to go see my room and I can show you all my dinosaurs?"

"Yes." Oliver grabbed Mikey's hand and started to pull him toward the front door.

"Hold on a second. Mikey, I want you to meet someone else." Gil put his arm around my shoulders. "This is Eleanor."

Mikey froze, his blue eyes behind his glasses wide. He looked me up and down. He didn't say a word.

I held my hand out. "You can call me Ellie. It's nice to meet you. Your brother has told me all about you."

"You're a princess. Gilly said you were a princess because you have long yellow hair and you're so pretty," Mikey said, excitement making his voice shake.

Gilly? I mouthed at Gil. I grinned; he shook his head.

Then Mikey did the most unexpected thing. He turned over the hand I'd offered and placed a kiss on the back of it. "Your Majesty."

I giggled. "Oh, my, goodness. If I'm a princess, the whole kingdom will probably burn down when I forget to turn off the oven."

"Are you flirting again?" Gil asked his brother.

Mikey straightened, his grin wide. "Who, me?"

I got the feeling this was schtick the two of them played before. I looked at Gil with narrowed eyes. "Gilbert Dalton, do you use Mikey to pick up women?"

Gil grinned slowly. "Who, me?"

FIFTY-ONE

Love is kindness to someone.

—TOBY K., AGE 8

"Whoever decided the Fourth of July should be in the summer was not from Texas," Iris grumbled. She guzzled down the rest of her bottle of water before tossing it into the recycle bin.

The café's air conditioning was usually effective for cooling the place on a normal day. But today, the door had been opened and closed so many times, it was its own kind of hellish sauna.

"I'm pretty sure Texas wasn't even a twinkle in America's eye when that was decided." I hip-checked her. "It's almost over. Only an hour more."

For the first time in five hours, there was a lull long enough to catch a breath. The number of people who showed up was far more than expected. The line had seemed endless at one point. We were down to two pies, but Jorge was still grilling up our limited menu of hamburgers and hot dogs.

Iris fanned herself with a menu. "If I melt into a puddle, flush my phone down the toilet. Or something."

"Why?"

"No reason."

I exaggerated a shiver. "You're right. I don't want to know."

My phone vibrated in my back pocket. I pulled it out to find a text from Gil. I'd been getting updates all day. This one was a photo of Oliver and Mikey at the petting zoo. A goat was trying to eat Mikey's shirt while he sat on the ground, holding a baby sheep. Next to him, Oliver was doubled over with laughter.

Iris leaned over to look. "They sure are having fun."

"I know. Gil was worried it would be too much for Mikey but so far, so good." With a sigh, I tucked my phone back in my pocket.

"You know, it's slowed down a lot. If you want to find them, go ahead. I got it here."

I bit the inside of my cheek. "Are you sure?"

"Um, yeah. I'm not trying to be nice. I'm buttering you up for a raise." Iris put a hand on her hip. "Can I have a raise?"

I tossed her my apron and hustled to the door before she changed her mind. "Maybe."

"Just be back by closing. I am not shutting down and cleaning up by myself."

I saluted her and got the heck out of there.

I found the guys across the street and four stores up at the ice cream parlor. The place was packed but they were seated at a little round table in the corner.

Oliver and Mikey were wearing identical chocolate mustaches from the ice cream cones they were working on. Gil sat next to them, smiling at something Oliver was saying. I paused to watch them, drinking in all that happiness at one little table. A little niggling of what if began. What if life could be like this right here? Before they noticed, I snapped a photo.

I moseyed over to their table. "Can I join you?"

"Mommy!" Oliver threw his arms around my waist, transferring chocolate from his face to the front of my t-shirt. "Mr.

Gil got me a chocolate ice cream. And we had cotton candy, too. It was so good." His body was practically vibrating with sugar.

"You are never going to sleep tonight, are you?"

He didn't seem unhappy about that.

Gil stood up. "Here, you can have my seat."

I frowned, realizing there were only three. "I'm not taking your chair."

He frowned back. "I'm not sitting in that chair."

I crossed my arms. "Then we are at an impasse, I guess."

"Oh, I know," Mikey said. "You can sit on Gilly's lap."

"I don't think that's a great idea," I said. "Oliver can sit on my lap. How about that?"

"Okay." Oliver took a bite out of the middle of his cone. Chocolate ice cream dripped down onto his hand and landed on his red shorts. He seemed totally oblivious to it.

I cringed and handed a napkin to Oliver. "On second thought, I'll stand."

Gil's eyes swung between the chair and me. Before I knew it, he had his hands around my waist and the next second, I was sitting on his lap.

"Someone might see us," I whispered. But by looking around the parlor, I didn't recognize anyone except for the two teenagers behind the counter and they weren't paying us any attention.

"It's only for a few minutes, right?" He had his arms wrapped around my waist, not too tight but in a way that made me feel like he wouldn't ever drop me.

"I guess." After a minute or two, I relaxed and leaned back into him. I could feel every breath he took, steady and true. "Thanks for sending me updates."

"We've had a great time. I was worried this would be too much for him." I knew he meant Mikey. "But it seems to help that Oliver is around. Makes him a little braver."

I watched the two of them as they raced to see who could

finish their ice cream first. To no one's surprise (except Oliver), Mikey won. He pumped a fist in victory.

"They're pretty cute together," I said. This could be what our life was like if Gil and Mikey lived in Two Harts. They were a package deal; just like Oliver and I were. I shoved the thought away before it took hold. "I have thirty minutes before I need to be back for clean-up, so what are we doing next?"

Oliver and Mikey looked at each other. "Balloon animals!"

FIFTY-TWO

—MARSHALL, AGE 6

That night, we found a piece of grass on the high school soccer field and spread out a blanket. All four of us piled on with bottles of water and a tub of kettle corn Mikey had begged for. After much debate, Mikey and Oliver had agreed to get matching balloon swords and were, at this very moment, off to the side, engaged in a battle. Whenever he was "injured," Mikey would drop to the ground with theatrical abandon making Oliver laugh so hard, he'd end up on the ground, too. I snapped a photo of that.

At one end of the field, a portable platform had been erected where a local rockabilly band played. It was almost nine. I was exhausted and had never been gladder that tomorrow was Sunday, and I could sleep in. I slipped off my shoes and socks and groaned. Reclining on my elbows, I stretched my feet out, twisting and turning them. Gil moved down the blanket and before I realized what he was doing, he had one of my feet in his lap and was pressing firmly into the bottom of my foot with his thumbs. I gasped and my eyes rolled back.

"Too hard?" he asked, watching my face closely.

I shook my head and dropped my head back. It did border on painful but the best kind of pain. "Never, ever stop."

He chuckled, low and deep, and I felt it in my stomach.

"Why are you so nice to me?" I asked jokingly. But I realized I was genuinely curious.

His magic fingers paused. "Because you deserve it. I don't think you've had enough of it in your life, and it makes me sad."

My breath caught. I glanced at Mikey and then back at Gil. "You deserve that, too. Looks like both of us take care of someone."

He made a noncommittal noise and switched feet. For the rest of my impromptu foot massage, he was quiet, and I wondered if I'd upset him somehow. But there wasn't much time to think of that once the band wrapped up and Ali stepped up to the microphone. Her speech was short, thank goodness. Oliver was hopped up on sugar and over exhausted. I expected the biggest meltdown ever, or for him to fall dead asleep any time in the next ten minutes.

I started cleaning up the blanket of empty water bottles and wrappers so we could lay down to watch the fireworks, which were up next. So, I wasn't quite paying attention when Ali got to the part of her speech where she announced the Small Business Owner of the Year. One second, I was crawling around on my hands and knees cleaning up popcorn kernels and the next, the crowd burst into applause.

"Mommy, you won!" Oliver danced over to our blanket, clapping his hands.

"Woo-hoo. Ellie," someone yelled.

"Ellie! Ellie!" said another.

I sat back on my heels. "What?"

Gil stood and held out a hand. "You won."

"I... what?" I let him pull me up and realized everyone's attention was on me. I heard someone behind me yell my name and realized it was Teddy, sitting in a lawn chair with a beer and a smile.

"Come on, Mommy. We gotta go get the award." Oliver tugged my hand, and I followed him to the front of the field and up the makeshift platform. Somehow, I ended up clutching a shiny plaque with my name etched into it.

Ali hugged me. "You weren't paying attention, were you?"

"Not so much."

She handed me a microphone. "Tell everyone thank you."

"Oh." I took it and Ali shoved me forward. I wasn't a shy person. In fact, I'd spent several years of my life trying my damnedest to get in front of large crowds of people. But staring out at that field, my eyes catching on people I knew, who came into the Sit-n-Eat once a day or once a month, I found myself speaking into the microphone with a trembling voice.

"Um, thank you? I didn't expect this at all. I, well... It's been a rough year with Ollie passing. I have tried to make him proud even though he's not with us anymore. Could you all imagine if he'd won this award?"

Those who could, laughed.

"He loved this town. I do, too. Three years ago, I came here exhausted and without a plan. And you all, you've made me feel like I've always been here. Thank you for that." I took a deep breath. "I don't know what the next few months will hold. There might be changes. I don't know if I'll still be here, but I want you to know there's something special about Two Harts."

Oliver tugged on my shirt. "Can I say something?"

"Sure." I lowered it to his face.

"Thank you for making my mommy win," he said, getting another laugh from the crowd.

When we got back to our spot, Gil stood there smiling. He

seemed to hesitate for a half second before he caught me up in a hug. "Who cares what they think?" he whispered.

Fifteen minutes later, the four of us were lying on the blanket on our backs so we could watch the fireworks. First me, then Oliver, then Mikey with his headphones on, then Gil. As the bursts of light pulled out oohs and ahhs from us, I had a moment of such happiness, it made my chest ache.

A man I loved and his brother who I was already half in love with. A kid I'd move mountains for. A town I loved. I had to wonder why we got glimpses like this—of what life could be—only for it all to be taken away from us.

I knew it couldn't last but for this minute in time, it was perfect.

It was everything.

FIFTY-THREE

"Do you think Mikey will come back and visit?" Oliver asked as he knelt on a stool at the counter, a bit of sticky maple syrup on his chin from his waffles. Since it was summer break, he'd be hanging out here until lunch. After, he had a standing playdate with a friend from school like he did every Thursday this summer. "It was almost like having a brother. 'Cept he's real tall."

I ruffled his hair. "You'll have to ask Gil, buddy."

"I'm guessing the visit went well." Iris leaned a hip against the counter.

It wasn't quite eight and the first morning rush had come and gone. A couple of the regulars were tucked in at a booth. Malcolm had brought his laptop to work on what he called his Great American Novel.

"It did." Mikey had ended up staying the night. He and Oliver had a "sleepover" in the living room, falling asleep to a movie within minutes of the lights turning off. When Gil said it was time to leave, Mikey sulked and dragged his feet and tried to talk Gil into letting him stay just one more day. In the end, they'd both left Sunday morning and only Gil returned Sunday evening.

"Mikey is my friend," Oliver said like he'd been awarded first place in a spelling bee. "I'm gonna write letters to him and Gil will mail them in the mailbox."

"That's pretty sweet, dude." Iris held up a fist and Oliver bumped it.

"I'm gonna go write him one right now." He hopped off the stool and raced back to the office where he kept all his art supplies.

Iris eyed me over the rim of her coffee cup. "So..."

"So what?"

"How are things with you and Mr. Dalton?" She waggled her eyebrows. "If you know what I mean."

I ducked my head to hide a smile. "I have no idea what you mean."

Iris snorted. "Suuure, boss."

"Look, right now—"

Gil burst into the café. Water dripped down from his hair and it looked like it might still have shampoo in it. He wore a t-shirt, a ratty pair of shorts, flip-flops, and a frantic expression.

"What's wrong?" I asked.

"I was in the shower and my phone kept ringing and ringing and ringing..." He waved his phone around. "The group home called, and... and the police."

I went to him, pulse racing. "Why? What's happened?"

"Mikey is gone."

"Gone? What do you mean?"

Gil stared at his phone. "He escaped... ran away. They had some surveillance footage of him leaving but it was the middle of the night. It's been hours. Hours."

"He can't just be gone." My heart lurched at the thought of Mikey out in the world somewhere all alone. He looked like an adult but acted like a child, and we lived in an "act first, ask questions later" kind of world.

He shoved a shaky hand through his hair. "I need to go find him."

"Of course you do." I wanted to wrap my arms around him and tell him it would be okay, to calm some of the panic in his eyes. But I was aware of the other people watching us, and maybe it wasn't my job to soothe him. We weren't a couple exactly; we weren't anything permanent. "Take a deep breath. Get yourself together. You'll go to Austin, and you will find him."

"Yes, I will. I'll find him." His chest expanded. He closed his eyes and when they opened, they were a little less frantic, a little calmer.

He shot to the door but hesitated with his hand on the handle. With a suddenness I didn't expect, he turned and strode back with purpose. Without hesitation, he pulled me into his arms and kissed me with an emotion that bordered on desperation.

"Would you look at that," someone said.

"Told you," another replied. The gossip train was about to pick up a lot of speed and I didn't even care.

He pulled back and rested his forehead on mine. "Thank you."

"You're going to find him and he's going to be fine. I know it," I said fiercely. I put a hand on his cheek. He turned his head and kissed my palm.

And then he was gone.

Iris walked by me. "I guess that answers my question."

. . .

Oliver was beside himself when he understood what had happened. At bedtime that night, he asked five hundred questions I couldn't answer. "Nothing can happen to Mikey. He's my new friend."

"Mr. Gil is going to find him," I said. I thought if I kept saying it, it would be true. "He's going to be fine."

Still Oliver asked me to lie with him until he fell asleep. There was no real sleep for me that night, so after he fell asleep I did what I usually did in times of stress; I baked—brownies, cookies, and a huge mound of waffles to freeze.

I checked my phone constantly for updates from Gil so when he called at 4 a.m., I answered immediately.

"We found him," he said, the relief in his voice a tangible thing.

"Is he okay?"

"He's okay. Actually, he's great. If you ask him, he went on a big adventure."

"Do you know what happened?'

"Yeah. He thought he could remember how to get to Two Harts all on his own, so he started walking. Then he came across a twenty-four-hour McDonald's and decided he was hungry. I always keep twenty dollars in his wallet as spending money. He ordered an ice cream cone and while he was sitting at a table eating it, he noticed a bus at a stop on the corner."

"And then?" I asked.

"He got on the bus, insisting he needed to go to Two Harts. The bus driver realized something was off right away and she tried to explain this wasn't that kind of bus. She was able to contact the police, and they recognized him immediately."

"That does sound like an adventure."

"Yes," he said. "He asked when he could ride the bus again."

I laughed softly. "Are you with him now?"

"We're at home. He's sleeping. Adventuring is exhausting, apparently." He let out a heavy breath. "There's more. I found out that he attempted to run away twice in the last couple of weeks. He never actually succeeded so no one notified me."

"What?" I said in outrage. "Well, he is not going back to that place. I hope you know that."

Gil was silent for a moment. "No, he's not going back there."

"You're bringing him here." It was a fact, not a question.

"Is that okay?" he asked quietly. "We still have two weeks until—"

I refused to hear the end of that sentence. Not yet, anyway. "Of course, you dummy. Come home already."

FIFTY-FOUR

Love is something two people do that means there's a connection, and it's very important.

—GABRIELLA G., AGE 9

"It's Tuesday. That's meatloaf day." Mikey grinned as he sat at the kitchen counter watching me heat up dinner. "I love meatloaf. Gilly doesn't make me meatloaf."

"What does he make?" I asked.

Mikey made a show of looking around for Gil before he whisper-yelled, "Oatmeal. A lot of oatmeal."

"Hey." Gil appeared in the doorway. "That's not the only thing I make."

"Yes, it is 'cause Gilly's not allowed to cook at home." Mikey grinned and pointed at himself. "But Dad taught me how to make grilled cheese sandwiches and mac and cheese and spaghetti."

"Really?" I leaned a hip on the counter. "I guess that makes you a better cook than your brother, huh?"

He nodded with enthusiasm. "One time, Gilly set the stove on fire."

Gil's cheeks turned pink. "It was a small grease fire. Over before it started, really."

"And another time, we all got real sick after he made tacos and I was stuck in the bathroom for a whole day 'cause of it."

"Bad meat," Gil said weakly.

I pressed my lips together to keep from laughing. "That's no fun."

Mikey shook his head. "So, Gilly isn't allowed to cook. Dad said and that's that."

My eyes met Gil's. "We will absolutely not let him cook."

"When you and me get home, you don't have to cook. I'll cook us grilled cheese for every meal, Gilly, okay?"

Although Mikey had seemed happy the last week, I noticed he brought up home at least once a day. And every time, I told myself to calm down. It didn't mean anything. Mikey was doing so well here that, just maybe, Gil was starting to come around to my way of thinking.

Gil shook his head. "No cooking when we get home, dude."

"Mikey, why don't you go find Oliver and let him know it's almost dinnertime?"

Mikey hopped up. "Okay."

When he was out of the room, Gil cleared his throat. "I, ah, won't be here for dinner. I was wondering if Mikey could hang out with you and Oliver?"

Now that he said something, I noticed he was in his pressed khakis and dress shirt, clothes he didn't wear as often these days. He looked freshly showered and shaved, hair parted and slicked back. Those little bits of gray around his hairline were more noticeable when he wore his hair that way. I liked it.

Then again, what didn't I like about him? My hand curled around the glass of water.

"Oh." Don't ask. It's not really your business, right? I asked anyway. "Where are you going?"

He hesitated, his eyes darting to the cabinet above my head. "Just a meeting. I should be back before eight."

"Okay. No problem." But something inside me, a swirling in my stomach, said otherwise.

I watched the door close behind him as he left.

It was well after eight and Gil wasn't yet back, Oliver was asleep, and Mikey was sitting with his nightly bowl of popcorn watching his favorite television show. Occasionally, his loud, joyous laughter would filter through the house, and I smiled in response at the sound.

I was working on my mother's one slipper. Um, no, it had not been completed for Mother's Day, but I was hoping for Christmas now. My phone dinged with a notification. When I read the message, my stomach dropped like a stone.

ALI: *Why is Gilbert having dinner with Peter Stone?*

ME: *I don't know. Are you sure it's him?*

ALI: *Oh, it's him and Peter and a couple of other guys in suits. I recognize them, too. They're with that development group that's been sniffing around.*

ME: *Oh.*

ALI: *I thought Gil had changed his mind about selling.*

ME: *I was HOPING he would change his mind.*

The way my heart was tangled up in a knot at the moment,

I'd put a lot more hope in that than I'd realized. There was only one real reason for him to meet with them.

And he hadn't even told me he was.

ALI: *I should go over there and break that meeting up. Maybe I could accidentally spill something on Peter. For funsies.*

ME: *Don't do that.*

ME: *Please.*

ME: *Ali?*

An hour later, Gil found me lying in the middle of the gazebo, arms and legs spread out like a starfish. I couldn't see the night sky through the wooden roof, but it pressed in all around me. Since that text from Ali, my brain had been in panic mode, zipping around at breakneck speed, one thought after another until I wasn't sure anything made sense.

But if I thought hard enough, I would have realized nothing had made sense for a while. We had been living in a dream and everyone had to wake up from those at some point.

"Hi." Gil stood above me, staring down at me. "Why are you on the ground?"

"I'm thinking."

"Ah. How's that going for you?"

"Horribly." I sat up.

Gil stuffed his hands in his pockets and kicked at an invisible rock. "I guess you heard. Nothing really is a secret in this town."

"Not unless you're Ollie, it seems." I folded my knees to my chest, wrapping my arms around them.

After a long moment, Gil sat down next to me. "We've been avoiding this."

"Yeah."

"The six months end next week."

"I know," I snapped. I took a deep breath. "Sorry."

He said nothing in response.

Finally, I couldn't stand it anymore. "Just say it. Whatever it is you need to say. I won't break." Liar, liar, pants on fire. I was going to bake so many muffins in the coming week.

"Maybe *I* will," he said under his breath. His gaze landed on me finally. "Peter made a really good offer. Like seven figures."

That was an incredible amount of money, even split in half. I could make a lot of muffins with that. I could move to another small town, find a café or diner for sale, maybe even build my own. But staying in Two Harts and watching my whole life get partitioned out for a strip mall? That, I didn't think I could do.

"I thought maybe you'd changed your mind. You were worried about Mikey leaving Austin, but he's been here for a week now. He's doing great. We're doing great."

Gil stood and paced, his shoes clacking on the wooden floor of the gazebo. "For now, he is. But I have to work. What happens then? Are you going to take him with you to the café every day?"

I climbed to my feet. "I don't know exactly. Maybe... maybe you could get a teaching job here in Two Harts and... but we could figure it out together."

He slammed a hand down on a wooden post, the sound surprisingly loud. I jumped in response. "It's not that easy. Mikey is all I have."

"No, he's not." I took a step closer, my voice growing louder. "You have me. You have Oliver. You have Teddy and the whole damn town of Two Harts. You are not some island. You have people right here."

"Do I?" he asked, his voice just as loud. "This has been a nice vacation, but you've never seen Mikey have a meltdown. You've never seen what it's like when he gets angry. You don't know what it's like when I'm exhausted or when I'm not so patient." He yanked at his hair. "You see all the good things. Why do you think you ended up with such losers before? You only saw the good things."

It felt like he'd slapped me. Tears stung the backs of my eyes, but I refused to cry. Not now. "Maybe you're right. Maybe I was that person, but I'm not now. Trust me, I have my faults. And you have yours, too. But you're not even trying. Everything's been decided in that dumb head of yours. At least I'm willing to compromise." I stepped close, so close that my chest brushed his when I took a breath. "Well, fine. You know what? Go home then. We'll sell everything. You win."

Our eyes locked. My anger simmered at the surface. Both of our heads jerked to the side at the sound of a cry. But nothing was there. Or whatever it was had left already. Probably just an animal.

"I don't know what the hell I'm supposed to do," he said in a low voice. A thread of despair laced his words.

I shook my head. "Let me know when you figure it out."

FIFTY-FIVE

Love is Mommy and Daddy.

—ALLIE, AGE 7

A pounding on my bedroom door ripped me from sleep. "Eleanor, wake up."

Gil burst through the door before I even had a chance to get out of bed. He flipped the light on, his eyes wild. "Is he in here?"

I stumbled out of bed, tripping on my sheet in the process, and righted myself before falling headfirst into my nightstand. "Is who here?"

"Mikey. He's gone again."

"What?"

He shoved a piece of paper at me. It was a note written in large, oversized child-like script. Some of the words were misspelled:

I am not staeing hear withowt Gilly.

I turned the paper over. "What is this?"

"I found the note on his bed. His backpack is gone, too."

"He can't have gotten far, right?"

"Mommy, why is Mr. Gil in your room?" Oliver's sleep-rumpled form appeared in the doorway. "Why is everyone yelling?"

"Everything's fine. Mikey seems to have gone on another adventure."

Oliver nodded. "He came and tolded me goodbye."

"What?" Gil rushed to him and cupped his shoulders. "When?"

"I don't know. I'm six. Telling time is hard."

"I have to go look for him." Gil rushed to the door.

"We'll help." With a grimace, I took in the short cotton nightgown with the words, Do You Know the Muffin Lady? on the front. "Just let me put clothes on."

After getting dressed in the first pair of shorts and t-shirt I could find, I dragged a sleepy Oliver with me and settled him into the backseat of my car. Gil ordered me to go in one direction while he went in the other.

"We'll cover more ground. You have your phone?"

I held it up. "I'll call if we find him."

"Don't yell at him. He doesn't like loud voices."

"I know. I got it."

I crept down Main Street at a snail's pace. I saw a figure sitting on a bench in front of one of the antique stores. It wasn't yet five in the morning and the sun was a couple of hours from rising. Everything looked like a person-sized shape in these conditions. But there he sat, clutching a sheep plushie he slept with every night. I parked and marched over to him.

"Mikey, what are you doing?" The tension in my shoulders eased.

"I'm going home."

"You can't leave without telling anyone." I sat next to him on the bench.

He moved as far away as he could. "You yelled at Gilly and told him to go home."

"You heard that?"

"I wanted to see if I could watch another episode, and you were yelling at Gilly and you told him to go home. Where Gilly goes, I go." He nodded once, his jaw tight, as he stared into the distance.

"Why didn't you wait and go with Gil?"

He opened his mouth and then snapped it shut, frustration stamped on his face. "I don't know. Sometimes he doesn't listen to me when I want him to listen."

"What do you want to tell him?"

He shrugged. "I want to be with Gil and be home. That's what I want."

I wanted to ask him more—what did he mean by that? Gil was convinced Mikey wanted to be back in their house in Austin. But sometimes I wondered if that wasn't what Mikey wanted at all. Maybe home to him wasn't a place; it was a person. Except Gil knew his brother better than anyone. He knew what Mikey needed.

"How about I take you back to Gil? You can tell him that, okay? He's worried about you."

Mikey frowned. "I didn't mean to make him worry."

I stood and held out a hand. "Come on, I'll take you to him."

FIFTY-SIX

[Love is...] when you care for them and are there for them when you need them.

—LEOR K., AGE 13

A grim-faced Gil met us at the house. He took Mikey into Ollie's old room, where he'd been sleeping, and closed the door. I had to get to work, so I didn't have time to see what happened and no amount of putting my ear to the door was getting me any information.

All through breakfast, I replayed Mikey explaining that he wanted to go home. "Where Gilly goes, I go."

Maybe it was time for me to let this all go. Who was I to say my dreams were bigger than Gil's reality? It was selfish—selfish and cruel of me to keep fighting this. Gil needed the money. I'd get a lot of money, too. Oliver and I would be fine. Maybe we'd move up to Oklahoma where my parents were. Not with them, but near them.

The award for Small Business Owner of the Year glinted from its place of honor where I'd hung it. I'd started over once before here in Two Harts. I could leave my brother and Mae and Ali and the café and that gazebo and it would be okay. Maybe my time here was done. Maybe there was a new dream somewhere else. It would be hard, but as Sunny liked to say, nothing good ever comes easy.

I hoped I could convince Sunny to do video sessions with me.

Of course, there was Gil. Even now, tears welled up thinking about him and what could have been. But he'd never said the words or made promises, even if I'd foolishly hoped for more. I wasn't going to be another person who he had to take care of. I refused to put that on him.

Chris picked up Oliver at lunchtime to spend some time with his cousin. The rest of the day went by quickly and it being a Tuesday, Teddy stopped by after closing to get a meal and chat. But Gil also showed up. He had bags under his eyes and the lines around his mouth seemed deeper somehow. I wanted to smooth out the worry lines on his forehead with my fingers. He seemed a decade older than he had yesterday. Mikey trailed behind him with his tablet and tucked himself into a booth in the far corner.

"Hey there, Gilbert," Teddy said, raising a fork in the air. "How are you?"

"Been better." Gil's smile was lukewarm at best, but he slid into a seat across from his great-uncle. "How about you?"

Teddy grinned. "Better now that I get to eat this."

I brought over a piece of lemon cream pie and set it in front of him. Before I could move away, Teddy's hand wrapped around my wrist. "What's up with you two? You look as sad as those clown figures Ollie's mother collected. Those things always gave me the creeps, to be honest."

I pulled out a chair and sat next to him. "Just tired."

And hurt and sad and wishing life worked out the way I wanted it to. Just once.

Teddy dug into his pie. "I was worried about you two at first, but I do think Ollie was right. You look real good together."

"We aren't together," I said, but I was looking at Gil. "Gil is leaving next week to go back to Austin. It looks like we'll be selling."

Teddy's fork clanked on the table. "You're what?"

"Selling. It's the best decision," I said firmly, directing my words to Gil. The words didn't hurt to say out loud as much as I thought they would. In fact, it felt like a weight had been lifted from my chest. A decision had been made. Plans could be made. I could get on with figuring out life without Gil's presence.

"We need to talk about this," he said; there was a look in his eyes I couldn't read.

Teddy slumped in his seat. "That's not what's supposed to happen."

"A lot of things weren't supposed to happen," Gil said, still watching me. "Seems like we don't have any control of those things most of the time."

Teddy's head swiveled as he looked between the two of us.

"There's been so much this year," Gil said. "My stepdad, Mikey, Ollie, and... other things."

"Am I the other things?" I asked.

"Yeah." He shook his head and turned away. "Mikey hasn't had time to process everything that's happened."

"Neither have you," I said gently.

"What happens now?" he asked.

"Let's not make a hasty decision," Teddy said. We both ignored him.

"You wait five more days and you go back to Austin and your life with Mikey. We'll take that offer from Peter and live our lives." Not together though. That had never been on the table, had it?

Gil looked at me, something like longing in his expression. "What will you do?"

I tried to smile. "Don't worry about Oliver and me. We'll be okay. We always are."

And that was the truth. We would be okay.

A shroud of silence seemed to cover the house over the next five days. Oliver and Mikey were, at first, oblivious to it. But when Gil began to pack up his room, sadness joined the party.

"Mommy," Oliver said one night at bedtime, "why is that day circled on the calendar?"

I remembered circling that date—exactly six months from the day Gil moved into the backyard. It was a countdown, the prize at the end of this was Gil leaving. Or at least, that's what past me was sure of way back then. But six months could change a lot of things.

"Remember how Gil and Mikey have a home in Austin?" I crawled into his bed and laid down next to him.

He nodded and fought back a yawn.

"That's the day they're moving back to their house."

"But that's in two days." He slow-blinked. "I don't want them to go."

"I know, honey," I said. "But that's just the way it is."

I was thankful he fell asleep before he could reply.

———

The last day, Gil didn't say much. His room was cleaned out, his toolbelt packed. He even sold the motorcycle. He'd been quietly saying goodbye to the friends he'd made over the last week, but he hadn't said it to me. Not yet. I was dreading it.

He knocked on my bedroom door a little after midnight.

I flipped on the light and answered, knowing I looked like a hot mess in mismatched pajamas. If he looked closely enough, he'd see I'd cried myself to sleep. To be honest, he wasn't winning any beauty contests either. I'd never seen him quite so disheveled.

"I can't sleep," he said. He looked so pitiful. "I'm so tired."

With a sigh, I pulled him into my room. If he was shocked, he didn't show it. He walked slowly around my room and I realized he'd never been in here before. I imagined him taking note of my clothes piles or how my shoes were thrown in the closet and not matched. He picked up a few of the photos I had on my dresser. Smiled at one with Oliver in it.

My heart sank as I realized we didn't have a photo of us together. Another thing to lament later, when he was gone, and I was living with Oliver in a van by the river because we no longer had a home. But a very nice van and a very safe river with all of our money in the bank.

Yes, I was being dramatic. I used to be an actress. They don't let just anyone play the love interest in *Kangaroo'd Three*.

Finally, he made his way back to me. Carefully, he wrapped his arms around me and pulled me in for a hug. I didn't resist. I'd thought I'd cried all the tears already, but I planted my face on his chest, and they came again. He let me stay there for a while, until, for the second time, all the tears were gone, before leading me to the bed and tucking me in.

When he was done, he kissed my forehead. "Night."

"Stay with me." I grabbed his hand before he could leave and tugged.

He hesitated.

"Please?" *I love you.*

"Okay." *I pretended he said I love you back.*

So, he did. He turned off the lights and crawled in next to me. He let me curl around him. We laid there for a long time before my eyes grew heavy and I fell asleep to the steady beat of his heart.

FIFTY-SEVEN

[Love is...] when people they like each other and like stuff.

—SOREN S., AGE 10

Gil must have slipped out of my room before my alarm went off. His side of the bed was still warm and I'm a little embarrassed to admit how long I may have laid there and smelled the pillow he'd slept on like a sad, sad... clown.

Now I was identifying with those creepy clown figures. This is what my life was now.

I dragged Oliver with me to work. Gil and I hadn't discussed what the plan was. Was he leaving today? When? Would we get one more meal together? One more time for Oliver and Mikey to explore the field in the backyard together? One more stolen kiss?

But in the end, I think I already knew what I would find when I got home. Gil wasn't there. Mikey wasn't there. Gil's car wasn't there. Gil's guitar and toolbelt and container of oatmeal weren't there, either. But an envelope with my name was sitting on his bed. The clowns smiled at me sadly as I opened it and two pieces of paper fell out.

The first letter was in Gil's straight, sure handwriting:

Eleanor—

I know you might think this is the coward's way out, leaving before saying goodbye. Maybe it is. There's a lot left unsaid between us, and I think it's better that way. Saying it would make this harder than it already is.

I don't know where my life is going right now, and I have to figure it out. There are decisions to make. Big ones. About Mikey, the future. For the first time in my life, I don't have a plan and that's terrifying.

I've already called the attorney this morning to let him know how to contact me from now on and that I have no interest in selling Ollie's property. I guess I'm not quite ready to give up on Ollie and Teddy. That surprises me probably as much as it surprises you, I bet.

I gasped and reread that last part again and again and still once more. He didn't mean that, did he? I'd already told him I was willing to sell. My chest tightened with something... confusion, longing, love. Maybe all three at once.

Gilbert Dalton, what are you doing? My hands shook as I read the rest of the letter.

But more importantly, I didn't want to be just another jackass who got what he wanted from you and left.

You deserve so much better. You deserve everything. You'll have to settle for a dilapidated old house and a café in need of a makeover, though. And no, I'm not changing my mind so don't even try it. I'm doing this for you, yes, but I'm doing it for me, too.

I never had the courage to say this out loud to you but

*Be happy, you and Oliver both. Know that somewhere not
too far away, someone is thinking about you,*

Gilbert

P.S. I found this going through Ollie's papers.

I clutched the paper to my chest, my vision going blurry with tears. This wasn't one of those delicate, tasteful cries where each tear fell slowly down my cheeks.

No, I was in the midst of a full-on, snotty-nosed, red-faced, soul-deep sobbing session. I smoothed a hand over the letter. My finger traced the letters of his signature.

What was I supposed to do with this? Aside from rereading it over and over until it was full of tearstains, then memorizing it and placing the original in my underwear drawer to keep it safe but close by so I could look at it when I felt sad.

I let out a wet laugh. I finally got a grand gesture. A whole twenty acres' worth.

With shaky hands, I unfolded the second letter. I recognized this handwriting too. Strangely, Ollie had had lovely, loopy cursive lettering, and I smiled to see it.

Dear Ellie—

I suppose if you're reading this, I've kicked the bucket. I'm not good with all these feelings and whatnot but this attorney thought it might be a good idea for me to write a letter and let you know what I was thinking with this will. I'm paying him an awful lot for his ideas, so I figured I should get my money's worth.

I guess I'll tell you a story:

Once upon a time, I fell in love with a girl, loved her practi-

cally my whole life. We had plans but sometimes in life, the more plans we make, the less chance they'll come true. I suppose that's what happened with Amelia and me. That, and pure stubbornness.

But I made my choice to live in Two Harts, though I knew I'd never love another like I'd loved Amelia. Years later, I discovered I had a daughter who had a son. I hired me a private detective to find them. My daughter, she was real pretty, and her son, Gilbert, he's a fine, upstanding man.

Unless he's one of them men who does weird stuff on the internet. I tried to get the detective to check on that but he never did.

I tried to see them once. I was scared out of my mind to knock on their door. Then I saw them, out in the front yard, and they looked so happy, smiling, and carefree. Well, I chickened out. They had a good life all on their own. They didn't need some old man busting in and making all kind of claims. But I kept track of them. Every year, like clockwork, I got a report from the detective.

I'm not a fanciful man, you know that. But when you and Oliver showed up at the Sit-n-Eat that day, something about you reminded me of my Amelia. You looked terrible, if I'm being honest, tired and stressed. Made me think of Amelia going off into the world all alone.

A funny thing happened, too. It turned out I was wrong. I could love again. Not the kind of love I'd had with Amelia. It was the kind of love that made my heart swell with pride when I watched you start a new life. Like what it felt like to be a father, I imagine.

I'm real proud I got to watch you these years. You made this old man real happy.

—Ollie

P.S. You've probably met that grandson of mine by now too. He seems like a good sort, real smart and educated and tall, too. Nothing like me, but maybe that's exactly how it should be. Maybe he won't be afraid to follow his heart.

"Hey, kiddo, got a minute to talk to me?"

Oliver looked up from the building block set he was working on. It was a dinosaur, of course. "Sure. Have a seat."

I smiled. Sometimes he sounded so grown up. But he was just a little boy, and I was going to make him very sad about now.

"I need to tell you something." I picked up a long orange building block and spun it around.

Oliver plucked it out of my hands. "I need that one. See?" He held up the instruction book and I nodded even though I had no idea what I was looking at.

"Mr. Gil and Mikey left."

He stilled and turned his head to look at me. "Without even saying goodbye?"

"They needed to get back to their house," I said in a gentle voice. "Remember we talked about this?"

His face fell. "But I thought they liked it here. I-I thought Mr. Gil was your boyfriend now. I saw you kissing him and Teacher says that's what boyfriend and girlfriends do."

"Kiddo, it's complicated."

Oliver put down the building blocks. "Grown-ups say that only 'cause they don't want to tell kids the real reason."

I laughed softly. "You're kind of smart, you know that?"

"I know." He sighed like it was some great burden, this information.

"Look, Mr. Gil needs to be with Mikey and Mikey feels most comfortable at his home."

"I wish they could stay here with us forever." He leaned against my leg.

I wrapped an arm around his shoulder. "I know, sweetie. But sometimes people come into our lives for only a little bit. They teach you something and they go off to teach someone else something. What do you think Mr. Gil taught you?"

"How to be a man," he said without hesitation. "He said a man sometimes has to do stuff he doesn't want to do because it's the right thing to do, and we should always think of other people first." He knelt and put his cheek on my knee. I rubbed his back. "I don't know if I can do all that without his help."

"I think you'll do just fine." The love I felt for this kid was endless. And while it was sad Gil and I weren't going to work out, I did have Oliver. I would always have him. A different kind of love, like Ollie had said in his letter.

"What did Mr. Gil teach you?" he asked.

That good men existed, that someone could see past all my mistakes, that you could fall in love without ever saying the words and know in your heart it's true. That maybe, just maybe I'm stronger than I think I am. "He did teach me to fold a fitted sheet. That's a pretty big deal."

Oliver stood up. "Mommy, you're crying."

I put a hand to my face and felt the moisture there. "I guess I am."

He darted away and came back with a tissue. "You should help me build this dinosaur. Dinosaurs always make me feel better."

So, we built a dinosaur and Oliver chattered about the latest creature he'd learned about and, even though my heart hurt, it also beat just as strong for the life I did have. For the happy ending I did get with this new life I'd built for Oliver and for me.

It wasn't the kind of happy ending I expected, but it was the one I was getting just the same.

FIFTY-EIGHT

Love is caring deeply about someone that you would sacrifice your life for them.

—KATHERINE P., AGE 11

From the text conversation of Ellie Sterns and her mother:

MOM: *Good morning.*

ELLIE: *Morning.*

MOM: *Honey, your brother mentioned Gilbert moved back to Austin.*

ELLIE: *I'll have to thank him for that.*

MOM: *Be nice to Chris. He's delicate.*

ELLIE: *And I'm not?*

MOM: *You, Eleanor Sterns, are made of strong stuff.*

ELLIE: *Really?*

MOM: *Of course. Don't you ever forget it.*

ELLIE: *Thanks. That means a lot.*

MOM: *Now tell me what happened.*

I waffled back and forth about reaching out to Gil. The first couple of days after he left, I had almost convinced myself he'd return. Of course he wouldn't just leave. Would he? But there were no phone calls or texts from him, no surprise knocks at the front door. With each day that passed that first week, my heart grew heavier and heavier until I felt like I was dragging it around on a chain everywhere I went.

People asked where he was even though they knew the answer. Nothing happened here without someone finding out, after all.

The first week after he left, the café was busier than ever—mostly full of Nosy Nellies and I was a recipient of many long looks of pity.

"How are you holding up?" they'd ask.

"Doing fine," I'd say with a reassuring smile, and got about my business.

What I'd wanted to say, as my heart clanged around on that chain, was, "Careful there, don't step on it. I only have the one and it's fragile."

The next couple of weeks, I kept as busy as I could. There were muffins, of course, as well as an assortment of baked goods. So many baked goods, I dropped off some to the fire station, the sheriff's office, and the one nursing home in town.

I not only finished the slipper for Mom, but I crocheted an entire sweater. Well, almost. I needed to finish one of the sleeves.

I spent a lot of time at Chris and Mae's house in a shameless campaign to hold my niece as much as humanly possible. I took Oliver shopping for school supplies and in mid-August he started the second grade. He made me promise not to cry when I dropped him off on the first day. One I kept until I got back in the car, so I think that's a win.

By week three, my sadness had begun to take a decidedly angry edge after I began to find sticky notes Gil had left behind that said things like, *Check the washing machine. You have clothes in there.* And dammit all, I did. I found another one in the office at work: *Don't forget to add in the receipts every day.* So, I found myself sitting at the computer doing just that.

It wasn't fair he knew me so well. What right did he have? I decided I was done dragging my heart around. It was too messy, and I just needed to forget about him and move on.

The next day, Iris came into work with red-rimmed eyes and a promise ring missing from her finger.

"Love sucks," she said.

"Yeah, it does," I said. "You wanna talk about it?"

So, we did. Over muffins and pie, we talked.

"Men suck," Iris said.

"Yeah, they do."

I didn't say it was a deep conversation, but we understood each other on an elemental level, the element being rage.

That weekend, I filled up a box of things that reminded me of Gil. He'd not left much behind, so I improvised—an old screwdriver, what was left of his expensive laundry soap, an iron (it wasn't like I planned on using it ever), and a few other odds and ends. I donated it all to the church thrift store.

But that night I lay in bed, worrying I'd been too hasty. The bargaining stage came quickly thereafter. I reasoned with God, asked if there was anything I could do to bring Gil for a visit. Just one time so I could thank him properly. I promised to never miss a Sunday school class. (Except when I overslept.) I promised to do more volunteer work. I promised to never speak badly of Peter Stone again. (I was desperate, okay?)

"Mommy, come see," Oliver called from his room one day.

"What is this? You cleaned your room." Everything was put away with the precision and care of a six-year-old boy. "It looks awesome. I didn't even ask you to do it."

"I'm the Man Club president, I gotta follow the rules," he said. Before I could answer, he grabbed my hand and pulled me over to his dresser. "I found something."

"What's that?" I asked, trying to not step on the loose building blocks that were still hidden in the carpet.

He pulled a black sweatshirt from one of his drawers. "I found it when I was cleaning. It's Mr. Gil's. We should send it back to him."

I took the sweatshirt from him, remembering how Gil liked to wear it in the mornings. Heart racing, I promised to make sure he got it back but then I realized it smelled just like him and I couldn't part with it. Even though just holding it made me feel like crying.

When I made it in to see Sunny, I'd been in a constant state of near tears. I hated it. I wanted to get over Gil the way I got over all the other guys I'd dated: pick up the pieces of my broken heart and move on.

"Ellie, how has that worked out for you before?" Sunny asked.

"I don't want to talk about it." I crossed my arms and stared at her.

"Okay." She crossed her arms and stared right back.

It was like a game of therapy chicken. Who would speak first? Me. It was me. I lost.

"I want to stop feeling all these... these..."

"Feelings?"

"Yes. Those."

"Sorry. Feelings are part of being human. Be gentle with yourself now. It's okay to cry or not cry, to laugh or not laugh, to be angry or sad. Feelings aren't the bad thing." She said it like it was the easiest thing in the world.

"Sure," I said, slumping against the couch.

"How do you think Gil is feeling right now?"

I shrugged. "I don't know."

"Have you reached out to him?"

"It didn't seem like a good idea, especially with how he left."

Sunny nodded. "What about a letter?"

"Maybe," I said.

It turns out I did have a reason to send him a letter, about a month after he left.

Dear Gil—

Hi. I've debated whether I should contact you, and Sunny (my therapist) said a letter was least confrontational. Not that I'm confrontational. At least not right now. Two weeks ago? Definitely.

I hope Mikey is doing well. Oliver misses him a lot. He talks about both of you all the time. Some days I think he'd happily trade me out for you two. He's hoping Mikey will answer the letter he sent soon.

You never gave me the chance to thank you, so... thank you. It's the most remarkable thing anyone has ever done for me. But sometimes, especially at night, I think about how unfair it all seems, and I get angry. At you, at me. But I guess that's how life is. Ollie taught me a lot of things but especially that life doesn't just stop when things don't work out. Otherwise, you end up old and grumpy and alone.

You've probably already noticed the big cashier's check in this envelope, and you might be wondering if I robbed a bank. I did not.

Remember at Easter when my sister Aggie stayed the night? She happened to admire Fred the Sad Clown on a Bike. If you don't know, Aggie works for a big auction house in Oklahoma City. She thought Fred looked familiar, so I let her take it back with her to get it checked out. It took her a while, but it turns out he was created by some fancy Italian artist. Hand-painted, one of a kind, and all that. He sold at auction for over two thousand dollars.

When I sent in photos of all the other clowns, Aggie was over the moon. There were a lot more valuable clowns in the bunch. A lot more. Who knew? Aggie put feelers out for someone who might want to buy the whole lot of them, and someone paid big money. This is your half. I hope you can use it to help with Mikey or to buy yourself a fancy iron for your clothes. I guess you could buy a whole lot of irons now if you wanted.

So, raise a glass to creepy clowns and the people who love them.

I hope you're happy too, Gil.

Ellie

P.S. You'll be happy to know after many weeks of consideration, Oliver finally settled on names for the kittens—Gilly and Mikey. Wonder where he got those?

P.P.S. I miss you.

P.P.P.S. I probably shouldn't have told you that, but it's the truth.

I waited an entire week before I mailed the letter to Gil. First, I had to track down his home address from the attorney who gave it to me after extorting a dozen muffins. After that, I put a stamp on it and took it to the Sit-n-Eat and set it on the desk in the office where it had been for the last four days.

For some reason, mailing that letter felt like a momentous step, like a final farewell to Gil. We'd always be connected. We were joint owners in the property, but that could all be done through the attorney. I didn't have any other reason to reach out to him. Mailing that letter felt like the end.

Teddy showed up right as I was closing, in his usual happy-go-lucky mood. "How you doing, Ellie?"

"I think I'm doing okay," I said as I set a plate of chicken fried steak in front of him. I wasn't even lying either. Maybe for the first time in weeks, I did feel okay. I wasn't sad or angry or depressed.

"That's real good," he said around a forkful of mashed potatoes.

"It is, isn't it?" I grinned.

"Oh, shoot, I got something for you," he said. He frantically patted at his shirt before he pulled out two photos from the front pocket. "Now this one is an old one I found."

The photo showed three teenagers spread out on a blanket. I recognized them immediately. "This is you"—I pointed to the lanky guy at the end—"and that's Amelia." She smiled back at me with eyes that sparkled with intelligence. Finally, I tapped the boy in the middle, smaller than Teddy and with wildly thick eyebrows that worked on him. His smile was there but smaller, quiet, even shy. "That would be Ollie."

"Yup. That was the last Fourth of July we spent together."

He traced the faces in the photo, smiling wistfully. "It was a real good day. We were young and happy to be together. Didn't know what was coming next and we didn't mind that so much back then. It was nice to be happy right then, together."

I swallowed back the lump in my throat. "I guess a lot changed after that."

"It sure did. Lately, I've been wondering what life would have been like if things had happened differently. But I'm an old man now and I'm allowed to get all sentimental, I suppose. I'm here on borrowed time and stubbornness." With a sigh, he gently pushed the photo away. "But you young people... You have so much life left to live and maybe learn a thing or two from the mistakes that have gone before you."

Before I could think of a way to respond, he flipped over the second photo. I gasped and snatched it up from the table. It was also of another Fourth of July but it had been taken only two months ago. "Where did you get this?"

"Saw someone with a camera and asked them. Not a one of you was paying any attention."

There in the photo were Oliver and Mikey, Gil and me, all laid out on that blanket, staring up at the sky. Although it was dark, the fireworks cast enough light to pick out our smiles. "I don't have a photo of all of us together."

"And now you do," Teddy said.

I threw my arms around him. "Thank you."

"It's not a big deal, I swear," he said.

"Yes, it is."

"You all looked so happy there." He shrugged. "Maybe that means something."

"Maybe it does," I said. It meant that, for a little while, I'd been loved and had loved. It hadn't been like the romance novels. Not a pirate in sight. But it had been real and messy, and I would treasure every second of it.

"Don't start crying," Teddy said with more than a little trepidation. "I ain't so good with crying women."

I smiled at him. "Would you do me a favor?"

"Of course."

"I have a letter that needs mailing. Would you drop it off for me?"

FIFTY-NINE

Love is YOU!

—EVERETT, AGE 5

"Do I have to do this?" I whined.

"Yes," Ali and Mae said at the same time. And because they were worried I might make a getaway, they flanked me as we walked down the street toward Bookmarks, the bookstore in town.

"You promised us three blind dates. We have one more shot," Mae said, Lulu strapped to her chest. My niece was almost six months old and cuter than ever. She faced forward in Mae's carrier, her arms and legs kicking in excitement. I guess it was worth it to see Lulu even if it meant I had to go on yet another blind date.

"I sort of figured there was an expiration date on those dates."

"Wrong. Honey and blind dates. The only two things in the world that don't expire." Ali stopped in front of the bookstore.

I sighed. "It's only been six weeks and I'm not sure I want to get back up on that horse for a good long while. Plus I'm going to have to pretend to be interested in everything he says."

"That's the spirit," Ali said.

"Who am I meeting again?" I asked in resignation.

Mae and Ali shared a look.

"I need to tell you a couple of things," Mae said. "He has a few… areas of concern."

"What does that mean?"

"He does have tattoos," Ali said. "And he knows how to ride a motorcycle, and he plays the guitar."

I threw my hands up. "Why even bother? You're just wasting my time now. I could be home with Oliver."

"Just try to go into it with an open mind," Mae said. "You never know."

I held a finger out to Lulu who grabbed it and stuffed it in her mouth. "Lulu, I like you more than your mama, you know that?"

"He knows you'll be wearing a red dress." Ali pulled a piece of lint, or maybe a crumb from the cookie I ate before we left, from my dress. "He'll find you."

"Fine."

"Smile," Ali demanded. "And stand up straight. And don't make that face."

"What face?"

"The one you're making right now."

Ali and Mae stood back, inspecting me with a critical eye. Lulu smiled, a string of drool dangling from her mouth. "You're both acting weird."

"Just go in," Mae said, waving a hand at me.

"And call us later," Ali said.

I pulled open the door and stepped inside. Bookmarks was a cute little shop with both used and new books. A teenage girl behind the counter said hello. On a table right at the front was a huge display of pirate romances by Alicia Night. Front and center, *The Pirate's Booty*. I still hadn't finished that book. Maybe one day. I made a beeline for the true crime section. Nothing like serial killers to keep a girl warm at night.

Keeping my eye open for tall, dark, and handsome. Or maybe short, blond, and okay-ish? Ali and Mae had given me very little information about this guy. I had no idea what his name was or what he looked like. Blind date was right.

In the true crime section, I browsed the books before pulling one out to look at it more closely.

"I've heard that one's pretty good," a man's voice said right next to me. "Although I also heard he had a thing for clowns."

I gasped and fumbled the book. It landed with a thud on the floor between us.

"Sorry, didn't mean to startle you." He bent down and picked up the book. His fingers brushed my hand when he passed it back to me. I stared at the spot, fascinated by the zap of electricity that one small touch seemed to produce.

"Are you my blind date?" I asked breathlessly.

"You're the woman in the red dress." He leaned down and whispered, "You look beautiful, Eleanor."

"Thank you." He was in a gray suit, his dark hair combed into submission. Navy-blue eyes stared back at me through dark-rimmed glasses. He looked good in that suit. I wondered if he'd wear a toolbelt with it if I asked nicely.

"Thanks for agreeing to go out with me," he said. "I'm new to town."

"You are?" My voice was barely above a whisper. But I hardly had the strength to talk; all that energy was needed to keep me standing upright. I placed a hand on a bookshelf to steady myself.

"Yes, my brother and I just moved here. I lived here for a few months not long ago. In fact, I think we've even met."

"I think so, too."

"My brother loves it here. Asked every single day if we were coming back. I thought he wanted to live back at our house in Austin. But it turns out, he just wanted to be wherever I was."

I smiled slowly. "He sounds like a great brother."

"He definitely is. So, we sold our house and moved to Two Harts. We found a little house to rent for the time being. We're looking for a fresh start."

I cleared my throat. "I did that a few years ago. Came to Two Harts for a fresh start."

"How'd that work out for you?" he asked, his voice low and calm, the exact opposite of what was happening inside me right now.

"It worked out pretty well, actually. But why Two Harts?"

"Did you know it was number two hundred and eighty-seven on the list of three hundred best places to live in nineteen eighty-seven?"

I grinned. "I have seen the plaque, even."

"Well, there you go. Your mayor is persistent, too."

"Ali?" What had she done?

"See, I have a plan. I'm hoping to open a group home for adults with disabilities and she thinks that would be a great addition to Two Harts, so she wooed me. It will take some time, though."

I smiled. "That sounds like an amazing idea."

"Actually, I'm looking for some land. I've heard someone around here has twenty acres of land lying around. You know anything about that?"

"I just might." My heart beat wildly as hope raced through me. "But why did you decide to jump into the dating pool so quickly?"

"Oh, that's easy. There's a woman who stole my heart here in Two Harts. I'm not sure if she'll have me, but I'm planning on making sure she knows exactly how I feel about her every single day."

"Something tells me you'll win her over." I straightened and held out my hand, my pulse fluttering. "I'm at a disadvantage here. You know my name. What did you say yours was?"

He smiled slowly and I felt it in my toes. "Gilbert Dalton." He tilted his head to the side, his eyes warm and soft. "But you? You can call me Gil."

A LETTER FROM SHARON

Dearest Reader,

I cannot say thank you enough for choosing to read *The Fix-Up*. If you'd like to keep up to date with all my book news, just sign up at the following link. Never fear, your email address will never be shared, and you can unsubscribe at any time.

www.bookouture.com/sharon-m-peterson

Even though this is my fourth novel, I'm still wrapping my head around the idea that you—yes, you, dear reader—chose my book out of so many other choices. I know time is precious; thank you for using it to get to know Ellie and Gil and the rest of the gang. I'd love to hear what you think. Reviews are a great way to share that, and they make such a difference helping new readers to discover one of my books for the first time.

If you ever have questions, want to chat, or need a random picture of a baby animal to brighten your day, please feel free to find me online. You can find me on my Facebook page, over-sharing on Instagram, posting nonsense on Threads, adding too many books to my TBR list on Goodreads, making awkward videos on TikTok, or my website.

Happy reading,

Sharon

KEEP IN TOUCH WITH SHARON

www.sharonmpeterson.com

facebook.com/SharonMPetersonAuthor
instagram.com/stone4031
tiktok.com/@stone4031
threads.net/@stone4031

ACKNOWLEDGMENTS

This was a hard book to write. No, I mean it. Every single word was almost painful. Why? I'm not sure. I love Ellie and Gil. I love their story. And yet... their story made me want to pull my hair out.

I'm really selling it here, aren't I? I hope the literal blood, sweat, and tears I've put into this book have made it a book you fell in love with. If not, feel free to lie to me. (Kidding. Kind of.)

You'll have noticed the chapter epigraphs this go-around were all quotes from kids. I reached out to readers on social media and asked them to ask the kids in their lives what love is. They're answers were sweet, heartwarming, silly, and all-around perfect. Thank you, once again, dear readers, for your willingness to help. And for having such adorable kids in your lives.

Ellie is a character close to my heart. Like her, I was diagnosed with ADHD as an adult, although I was forty-four. I used my own experiences when shaping Ellie. Does she represent every woman with ADHD? No. But I hope you'll see her struggles and her gifts. If you'd like to learn more about ADHD, I've learned so much from Jessica McCabe and her How to ADHD YouTube Channel. You can find it here: www.youtube.com/@HowtoADHD

About a year ago, I saw a TikTok video that affected me so much, it shaped how I saw Gil and Ellie's relationship. The creator (@ryans_truth_) shares his experience of being married to a wife with ADHD. His patience, understanding, and love shine through. He sees his wife so clearly and it's a beautiful thing. This is the link to TikTok. (Please note there is some language. But watch it anyway, especially if you or someone you know has ADHD.) www.tiktok.com/@ryans_truth_/video/7348071511258942762

Another character that is dear to me is Mikey. If you don't know, I have two sons with autism. One of them is profoundly autistic and also has an intellectual disability. He's fifteen and a big bear of a kid who loves squeezes, giggling, and stealing Dad's Diet Dr. Pepper. Because of his disabilities, he functions as a four-year-old in most areas. He requires 24/7 supervision and will for the rest of his life. In the book, Mikey suffers a traumatic brain injury in a car accident, so his disability came about differently than my son's. But some of their struggles are very similar and I wanted to show a taste of that in this story.

I also wanted to shine a little light on the challenges of being a caregiver via Gil, who is under a tremendous amount of stress as he works through what life will look like now for him and Mikey. Again, I am not speaking for all people with an intellectual disability or who are full-time caregivers. Everyone's experience is different. I relied on my own experiences and the experiences of the many, many friends who are also in similar situations.

And now on to the people who've helped me get this book in your hands.

Many, many thanks to my agent, Nalini Akolekar, who has been a constant support and who works tirelessly to get my books into the world. I'm forever grateful that you believed in me, sometimes when I did not believe in myself. Thank you for seeing I am an anxiety monster and never letting me feel bad about it. Thanks also to the rest of the gang at Spencerhill Associates.

To my editor Lucy Frederick. I cannot thank you enough for your endless patience and reassurances. I promise I won't always be this needy. (Probably.) This book in particular has been a grueling process, but you've encouraged me every single step of the way. Thank you!

To the rest of the Bookouture team, to Jess Readett, Kim Nash, the marketing and publicity teams, Saidah Graham, Richard King, and so many others who have worked to get my books in readers' hands, thank you! Thank you to Clare Stacey for your gorgeous, inspired covers and to Donna Hillyer, copy editor extraordinaire, who manages to make my timelines make sense—a true superpower.

To Christie, for telling everyone you know about your friend who writes books and for being a friend who has always been like family. To Noydena and Mat, for always being willing to answer my weird, random tech questions. To the rest of the gang—Andrea, Stephanie, and Shawn—thank you for letting me vent (a lot), for your encouragement, and for funny memes just when I need them. And Brian, sorry... no FDR this go-around, but he's here in spirit.

To Google for always answering my weird questions.

To Panera Bread, you know what you did. Thank you.

To Melissa Weisner. Thank you for being a listening ear, for answering countless questions, for letting me vent, and for encouraging me. I'm really glad you're my friend. I honestly don't think I could have written this book without you.

To the ladies at the Eleventh Chapter—Kerry, Colleen, Caitlin, Jen, Jenn, Tanya, Maggie, and Sayward. I'm so grateful to be part of a group of women writers who support each other in so many ways. HOWARD!

To Courtney Lott, who has been cheering me on since the very first word of my first book, read countless drafts, and is the queen of encouragement. I could never, ever have finished writing my very first chapter without you.

To Maria Gonzalez-Gorosito, who, along with a group of moms who barely knew me, surprised me with a new laptop when mine broke. It remains one of the most remarkable gifts I've ever been given. It wasn't just a laptop you gave me; you gave me the courage to write. You're going to be thanked in every book, so just get used to it.

To the ladies of the Ink Tank. Your constant support and the safe place you've provided for me to vent/scream/cry/lament/laugh/celebrate is such an important part of my writing life. You are all amazing.

To Tracey Christensen. Thank you for always telling me the truth even when I might not want to hear it. Your wisdom and friendship have truly been a gift from God. I'm so very glad I know you, my friend. HONEYMOON BABY, forever!

Thank you to the members of the Women's Fiction Writers Association and the League of Romance Writers, for giving writers support and opportunities to grow.

To my mom and Aunt CC, thank you for being my cheerleaders and believing that I could make a dream like this a reality. Love you bunches.

To my sister Gabbie, who will never get to hold one of my books in her hands. I miss you always; love you forever. And I fully expect you to sell a copy of this book to every single angel in Heaven.

To Daniel, Benjamin, Gideon, and Katherine. I am incredibly blessed to be your mother. Thank you for putting up with a mom who makes you repeat everything you say at least twice because my mind was somewhere else the first time you said it. You are in my heart always. I hope you only need a regular amount of therapy when you grow up.

To Carl. You've put up with my exhaustion, my tears, my anger, my disappointment, my excitement, my crazy ideas, my ramblings about made-up people in made-up worlds, and way too many pizza dinners. You've never wavered in your support of me. Ever. I love you.

To the many, many others I can't even begin to list here, but you know who you are. Your endless support, encouragement, and prayers have kept and continue to keep me going daily. Thank you for always believing in me.

Lastly, thank you to the readers. Aside from having really good reading taste, you all have been incredibly welcoming and kind to me over these three years. I'm humbled each time someone takes the time to send me a message or email, writes a review, or spends time reading one of my books. You are literally the reason I get to have this job and I can't thank you enough. I'll try though. I'll try to thank you all the time. I'll probably make it real awkward, too.

PUBLISHING TEAM

Turning a manuscript into a book requires the efforts of many people. The publishing team at Bookouture would like to acknowledge everyone who contributed to this publication.

Commercial
Lauren Morrissette
Hannah Richmond
Imogen Allport

Cover design
Head Design Ltd

Data and analysis
Mark Alder
Mohamed Bussuri

Editorial
Lucy Frederick
Melissa Tran

Copyeditor
Donna Hillyer

Proofreader
Jenny Page

Marketing
Alex Crow
Melanie Price
Occy Carr
Cíara Rosney
Martyna Młynarska

Operations and distribution
Marina Valles
Stephanie Straub
Joe Morris

Production
Hannah Snetsinger
Mandy Kullar
Ria Clare
Nadia Michael

Publicity
Kim Nash
Noelle Holten
Jess Readett
Sarah Hardy

Rights and contracts
Peta Nightingale
Richard King
Saidah Graham

www.ingramcontent.com/pod-product-compliance
Lightning Source LLC
Chambersburg PA
CBHW030520190726

48283CB00006B/1702